World's Greatest Christmas Stories

ZIFF  DAVIS
PUBLISHING COMPANY
Chicago · New York · Los Angeles

World's Greatest

Christmas Stories

Edited by

ERIC POSSELT

ZIFF-DAVIS PUBLISHING COMPANY

CHICAGO · NEW YORK

30310

PN
6071
C6
P6

FOR

ERA

Introduction

No EVENT in the history of mankind has had a deeper and more lasting effect than the Nativity. It has influenced people in every walk of life, but its impact on the creative geniuses of the world has been particularly profound. The world's greatest paintings, the world's most famous music, and certainly a great number of masterpieces of prose have been directly inspired by it.

The national atmosphere and the intellectual climate in which the individual artists live cause them to react in different ways. In some the story of the advent of Christ on earth has inspired deep spirituality and devotion, in others pensiveness and brooding, and in yet others gaiety and joy even though, in essence, all of them are merely retelling in their own way and in their own fashion the one eternal story of peace on earth, good will toward men, and glory to God in the highest.

There have been, over a period of years, quite a few anthologies of Christmas stories, some of them excellent; but all of them were limited almost exclusively to stories by American and English authors. Here, then, for the first time, the masterpieces of twenty-three different nations are brought together, justifying the proud title, "World's Greatest Christmas Stories."

It is, of course, impossible to avoid the inclusion of a number of stories that are already the common property of the world. Thus, Charles Dickens' immortal "A Christmas Carol" had to be included, irrespective of how well it is known and how often it has been reprinted. By the same token it was inevitable that O. Henry's "Gift of the Magi" should be found in the present volume. Most of the European stories, however, either are completely unknown to the English-speaking world, or have been printed only in some long since forgotten magazine. The great majority certainly have never found their way into an American or British anthology of Christmas tales. By actual count fourteen of the thirty-nine stories were, indeed, translated especially for this volume.

I shall make no attempt to categorize the contents, and assign each individual story to its proper pigeonhole, just as I would consider any attempt to summarize them nothing less than presumptuous. Should I, then, speak about the individual authors? The genius of, let us say, Aquilino Ribeiro and his influence on Portuguese letters? Or about the classical stature of Božena Němcová, the grand old lady of Czech literature? Of Felix Timmermans, the great Flemish artist, or of Borisav Stankovich, the outstanding Croat writer of the past century? I think not. They speak infinitely better for themselves.

However, a few sentences would seem to be in order about certain stories *not* to be found in this volume. A number of meritorious ones, particularly from the American field, had to be left out, in fact, because the United States can boast of more Christmas stories than all other nations combined. Honoré de Balzac's famous "Christ in Flanders" was eliminated for the reason that, while it is a story about Christ, it is essentially not a Christmas story. Adalbert Stifter's lovely Austrian tale, "Rock Crystal," was not included because it is practically book length, and even the most judicious cutting would mar its beauty. None of the three Christmas stories by one of Germany's early Nobel Prize winners, Paul Heyse, appears because I felt that they are hopelessly old fashioned. And neither Norway nor Greece are represented because Asbjoernson's "Troll Feast"— one of the very few Christmas stories from Norway I have been able to find—seemed as lacking in appeal as Marie Hamsun's "Christmas Star" and Papadiamantis' tales were lacking in quality.

The Christmas songs with which each country is introduced are, with the exception of the English ones and a few gems like "Silent Night," completely unknown in America. Quite outside of the fact that they, too, open windows into a beautiful though sometimes strange world, they may well become, in English translations, a valuable addition to our catalogue of sacred music.

I consider myself singularly fortunate to have been able to walk for a span with the great of the world's literature. The task of finding in so many different lands and languages at least one fine story for each has frequently been difficult; but the joy of discovery is the explorer's own reward.

And may all your holidays be merry ones.

ERIC POSSELT

Acknowledgments

THE EDITOR herewith expresses his gratitude to the following individuals for their invaluable help in selecting and securing stories and songs:

N. P. Todoroff, Department Chief of the Ministry of Information, Sofia, Bulgaria, for the Bulgarian material; *Professor Václav Polák* of the University of Prague, Czechoslovakia, for the Czech story; *C. H. W. Hasselried* of the Danish Information Office in New York for the material from Denmark; *V. Niskanen*, Consul General, and *Olli Kaila*, Vice Consul of Finland, for the Finnish story and the song used; *Dr. Knud C. Knudsen* of the Christian Verlag, Berlin, Germany, for the stories by Gerhart Hauptmann and Theodor Storm; *H. Landheer*, Chief of the Research Department of the Netherland Information Bureau in New York, and *Louise M. Boerlage*, Director of the Inlichtingbureau voor Jeugdlektuur an Kinderleeszalen, Amsterdam, Holland, for the Dutch material; *Andrew Szik*, Cultural Attaché of the Hungarian Legation in Washington, D. C., for the story by Maurus Jókai, and the *Reverend Ladislaus Harsany* of the First Magyar Presbyterian Church in New York for the Hungarian song; *R. J. Hayes*, Director of the National Library of Ireland, Dublin, Eire, for the Irish story, and *Father Stephen S. Brown, S.J.*, of the Central Catholic Library Association, Dublin, Eire, for the Gaelic song; *Salvatore Viola* of the Book Center in New York for the Italian story; the *Reverend S. T. Thele* of the Danish and Norwegian Central Methodist Church in New York for the Danish song and Ivan A. Jacobsen of the Royal Norwegian Information Service for its translation. *A. Tavares de Almeida*, Chief of the

Secretario Nacional da Informação, Lisbon, Portugal, for the story by Aquilino Ribeiro; the *Reverend Vasile Hartegan* of the Romanian Orthodox Church St. Dumitru in New York for the Romanian material; H. Heide, Literary Editor of the New Yorker Staats Zeitung & Herold, for Anton Chekhov's Vanyka; *Allan Kastrup* of the American-Swedish News Exchange in New York for the story by Selma Lagerlöf; *Manuel Aznar,* Minister Plenipotentiary of Spain in Washington, D. C., for the Spanish story, and the *Reverend Father N. Otaño, S.J.,* Director of the National Conservatory, Madrid, Spain, for the Spanish Christmas song; *Alex N. Dragnich,* Cultural Officer, American Embassy, Belgrade, Yugoslavia, for the Croatian story.

Thanks are due to Jonas Singer for autographing the music for the songs.

Contents

U. S. A.

O Little Town of Bethlehem

PHILLIPS BROOKS   LEWIS H. REDNER

O lit-tle town of Beth-le-hem, How still we see thee lie, A-bove thy deep and dream-less sleep The si-lent stars go by; Yet in thy dark streets shin-eth The ev-er-last-ing light, The hopes and fears of all the years, Are met in thee to-night.

For Christ is born of Mary
And gathered all above,
While mortals sleep, the angels keep
Their watch of wond'ring love.
O morning stars, together
Proclaim the holy birth,
And praises sing to God the King,
And peace to men on earth.

A Shepherd

HEYWOOD BROUN

THE HOST of heaven and the angel of the Lord had filled the sky with radiance. Now the glory of God was gone and the shepherds and the sheep stood under dim starlight. The men were shaken by the wonders they had seen and heard and, like the animals, they huddled close.

"Let us now," said the eldest of the shepherds, "go even unto Bethlehem, and see this thing which has come to pass, which the Lord hath made known unto us."

The City of David lay beyond a far, high hill, upon the crest of which there danced a star. The men made haste to be away, but as they broke out of the circle there was one called Amos who remained. He dug his crook into the turf and clung to it.

"Come," cried the eldest of the shepherds, but Amos shook his head. They marveled, and one called out, "It is true. It was an angel. You heard the tidings. A Savior is born!"

"I heard," said Amos. "I will abide."

The eldest walked back from the road to the little knoll on which Amos stood.

"You do not understand," the old man told him. "We have a sign from God. An angel commanded us. We go to worship the Savior, who is even now born in Bethlehem. God has made His will manifest."

"It is not in my heart," replied Amos.

From *Collected Edition of Heywood Broun*, copyright 1941, by Heywood Hale Broun. Reprinted by permission of Harcourt, Brace and Company, Inc.

And now the eldest of the shepherds was angry.

"With your own eyes," he cried out, "you have seen the host of heaven in these dark hills. And you heard, for it was like the thunder when 'Glory to God in the highest' came ringing to us out of the night."

And again Amos said, "It is not in my heart."

Another shepherd then broke in. "Because the hills still stand and the sky has not fallen, it is not enough for Amos. He must have something louder than the voice of God."

Amos held more tightly to his crook and answered, "I have need of a whisper."

They laughed at him and said, "What should this voice say in your ear?"

He was silent and they pressed about him and shouted mockingly, "Tell us now. What says the God of Amos, the little shepherd of a hundred sheep?"

Meekness fell away from him. He took his hands from off the crook and raised them high.

"I too am a god," said Amos in a loud, strange voice, "and to my hundred sheep I am a savior."

And when the din of the angry shepherds about him slackened, Amos pointed to his hundred.

"See my flock," he said. "See the fright of them. The fear of the bright angel and of the voices is still upon them. God is busy in Bethlehem. He has no time for a hundred sheep. They are my sheep. I will abide."

This the others did not take so much amiss, for they saw that there was a terror in all the flocks and they too knew the ways of sheep. And before the shepherds departed on the road to Bethlehem toward the bright star, each talked to Amos and told him what he should do for the care of the several flocks. And yet one or two turned back a moment to taunt Amos, before they reached the dip in the road which led to the City of David. It was said, "We shall see new glories at the throne of God, and you, Amos, you will see sheep."

Amos paid no heed, for he thought to himself, "One shepherd the less will not matter at the throne of God." Nor did he have time to be troubled that he was not to see the Child who was come to save the world. There was much to be done among the flocks and Amos walked between the sheep and made under his tongue a clucking noise, which was a way he had, and to his hundred and to the others it was a sound more fine and friendly than the voice of the bright angel. Presently the animals ceased to tremble and they began to graze as the sun came up over the hill where the star had been.

"For sheep," said Amos to himself, "the angels shine too much. A shepherd is better."

With the morning the others came up the road from Bethlehem, and they told Amos of the manger and of the wise men who had mingled there with shepherds. And they described to him the gifts: gold, frankincense and myrrh. And when they were done they said, "And did you see wonders here in the fields with the sheep?"

Amos told them, "Now my hundred are one hundred and one," and he showed them a lamb which had been born just before the dawn.

"Was there for this a great voice out of heaven?" asked the eldest of the shepherds.

Amos shook his head and smiled, and there was upon his face that which seemed to the shepherds a wonder even in a night of wonders.

"To my heart," he said, "there came a whisper."

How Santa Claus Came
to Simpson's Bar

BRET HARTE

I T HAD been raining in the valley of the Sacramento. The North Fork had overflowed its banks, and Rattlesnake Creek was impassable. The few boulders that had marked the summer ford at Simpson's Crossing were obliterated by a vast sheet of water stretching to the foothills. The up-stage was stopped at Granger's; the last mail had been abandoned in the tules, the rider swimming for his life. 'An area,' remarked the *Sierra Avalanche,* with pensive local pride, 'as large as the State of Massachusetts is now under water.'

Nor was the weather any better in the foothills. The mud lay deep on the mountain road; wagons that neither physical force nor moral objurgation could move from the evil ways into which they had fallen encumbered the track, and the way to Simpson's Bar was indicated by broken-down teams and hard swearing. And further on, cut off and inaccessible, rained upon and bedraggled, smitten by high winds and threatened by high water, Simpson's Bar, on the eve of Christmas Day, 1862, clung like a swallow's nest to the rocky entablature and splintered capitals of Table Mountain, and shook in the blast.

As night shut down on the settlement, a few lights gleamed

By Bret Harte. Reprinted by permission of Houghton Mifflin Co.

through the mist from the windows of cabins on either side of the highway, now crossed and gullied by lawless streams and swept by marauding winds. Happily most of the population were gathered at Thompson's store, clustered around a red-hot stove, at which they silently spat in some accepted sense of social communion that perhaps rendered conversation unnecessary. Indeed, most methods of diversion had long since been exhausted on Simpson's Bar; high water had suspended the regular occupations on gulch and on river, and a consequent lack of money and whiskey had taken the zest from most illegitimate recreation.

Even Mr. Hamlin was fain to leave the Bar with fifty dollars in his pocket—the only amount actually realized of the large sums won by him in the successful exercise of his arduous profession. 'Ef I was asked,' he remarked somewhat later—'ef I was asked to pint out a purty little village where a retired sport as didn't care for money could exercise hisself, frequent and lively, I'd say Simpson's Bar; but for a young man with a large family depending on his exertions, it don't pay.' As Mr. Hamlin's family consisted mainly of female adults, this remark is quoted rather to show the breadth of his humor than the exact extent of his responsibilities.

Howbeit, the unconscious objects of this satire sat that evening in the listless apathy begotten of idleness and lack of excitement. Even the sudden splashing of hoofs before the door did not arouse them. Dick Bullen alone paused in the act of scraping out his pipe, and lifted his head, but no other one of the group indicated any interest in, or recognition of, the man who entered.

It was a figure familiar enough to the company, and known in Simpson's Bar as 'The Old Man.' A man of perhaps fifty years; grizzled and scant of hair, but still fresh and youthful of complexion. A face full of ready but not very powerful sympathy, with a chameleon-like aptitude for taking on the shade and color of contiguous moods and feelings. He had evidently just left some hilarious companions, and did not at first notice

the gravity of the group, but clapped the shoulder of the nearest
man jocularly, and threw himself into a vacant chair.

'Jest heard the best thing out, boys! Ye know Smiley, over
yar—Jim Smiley—funniest man in the Bar? Well, Jim was jest
telling the richest yarn about——'

'Smiley's a —— fool,' interrupted a gloomy voice.

'A particular —— skunk,' added another in sepulchral accents.

A silence followed these positive statements. The Old Man
glanced quickly around the group. Then his face slowly changed.
'That's so,' he said reflectively, after a pause, 'certainly a sort
of a skunk and suthin' of a fool. In course.' He was silent for a
moment, as in painful contemplation of the unsavoriness and
folly of the unpopular Smiley. 'Dismal weather, ain't it?' he
added, now fully embarked on the current of prevailing sentiment. 'Mighty rough papers on the boys, and no show for
money this season. And tomorrow's Christmas.'

There was a movement among the men at this announcement, but whether of satisfaction or disgust was not plain. 'Yes,'
continued the Old Man in the lugubrious tone he had, within
the last few moments, unconsciously adopted,—'yes, Christmas,
and tonight's Christmas Eve. Ye see, boys, I kinder thought—
that is, I sorter had an idee, jest passin' like, you know—that
maybe ye'd all like to come over to my house tonight and have
a sort of tear round. But I suppose, now, you wouldn't? Don't
feel like it, maybe?' he added with anxious sympathy, peering
into the faces of his companions.

'Well, I don't know,' responded Tom Flynn with some
cheerfulness. 'P'r'aps we may. But how about your wife, Old
Man? What does *she* say to it?'

The Old Man hesitated. His conjugal experience had not
been a happy one, and the fact was known to Simpson's Bar.
His first wife, a delicate, pretty little woman, had suffered keenly
and secretly from the jealous suspicions of her husband, until
one day he invited the whole Bar to his house to expose her
infidelity. On arriving, the party found the shy, petite creature
quietly engaged in her household duties, and retired abashed
and discomfited. But the sensitive woman did not easily recover

from the shock of this extraordinary outrage. It was with difficulty she regained her equanimity sufficiently to release her
lover from the closet in which he was concealed, and escape
with him. She left a boy of three years to comfort her bereaved
husband. The Old Man's present wife had been his cook. She
was large, loyal, and aggressive.

Before he could reply, Joe Dimmick suggested with great di-
rectness that it was the 'Old Man's house,' and that, invoking
the Divine Power, if the case were his own, he would invite
whom he pleased, even if in so doing he imperiled his salvation.
The Powers of Evil, he further remarked, should contend against
him vainly. All this delivered with a terseness and vigor lost in
this necessary translation.

'In course. Certainly. Thet's it,' said the Old Man with a
sympathetic frown. 'Thar's no trouble about thet. It's my own
house, built every stick on it myself. Don't you be afeard o' her,
boys. She may cut up a trifle rough—ez wimmin do—but she'll
come round.' Secretly the Old Man trusted to the exaltation of
liquor and the power of courageous example to sustain him in
such an emergency.

As yet, Dick Bullen, the oracle and leader of Simpson's Bar,
had not spoken. He now took his pipe from his lips. 'Old Man,
how's that yer Johnny gettin' on? Seems to me he didn't look
so peart last time I seed him on the bluff heavin' rocks at
Chinamen. Didn't seem to take much interest in it. Thar was
a gang of 'em by yar yesterday—drownded out up the river—
and I kinder thought o' Johnny, and how he'd miss 'em! Maybe
now, we'd be in the way ef he wus sick?'

The father, evidently touched not only by this pathetic picture of Johnny's deprivation, but by the considerate delicacy
of the speaker, hastened to assure him that Johnny was better,
and that a 'little fun might 'liven him up.' Whereupon Dick
arose, shook himself, and saying, 'I'm ready. Lead the way, Old
Man: here goes,' himself led the way with a leap, a characteristic
howl, and darted out into the night. As he passed through the
outer room he caught up a blazing brand from the hearth. The
action was repeated by the rest of the party, closely following

and elbowing each other, and before the astonished proprietor of Thompson's grocery was aware of the intention of his guests, the room was deserted.

The night was pitchy dark. In the first gust of wind their temporary torches were extinguished, and only the red brands dancing and flitting in the gloom like drunken will-o'-the-wisps indicated their whereabouts. Their way led up Pine-Tree Cañon, at the head of which a broad, low, bark-thatched cabin burrowed in the mountain-side. It was the home of the Old Man, and the entrance to the tunnel in which he worked when he worked at all. Here the crowd paused for a moment, out of delicate deference to their host, who came up panting in the rear.

'P'r'aps ye'd better hold on a second out yer, whilst I go in and see that things is all right,' said the Old Man, with an indifference he was far from feeling. The suggestion was graciously accepted, the door opened and closed on the host, and the crowd, leaning their backs against the wall and cowering under the eaves, waited and listened.

For a few moments there was no sound but the dripping of water from the eaves, and the stir and rustle of wrestling boughs above them. Then the men became uneasy, and whispered suggestion and suspicion passed from the one to the other. 'Reckon she's caved in his head the first lick!' 'Decoyed him inter the tunnel and barred him up, likely.' 'Got him down and sittin' on him.' 'Prob'ly biling suthin' to heave on us: stand clear the door, boys!' For just then the latch clicked, the door slowly opened, and a voice said, 'Come in out o' the wet.'

The voice was neither that of the Old Man nor of his wife. It was the voice of a small boy, its weak treble broken by that preternatural hoarseness which only vagabondage and the habit of premature self-assertion can give.

It was the face of a small boy that looked up at theirs—a face that might have been pretty, and even refined, but that it was darkened by evil knowledge from within, and dirt and hard experience from without. He had a blanket around his shoulders, and had evidently just risen from his bed.

'Come in,' he repeated, 'and don't make no noise. The Old Man's in there talking to mar,' he continued, pointing to an adjacent room which seemed to be a kitchen, from which the Old Man's voice came in deprecating accents. 'Let me be,' he added querulously, to Dick Bullen, who had caught him up, blanket and all, and was affecting to toss him into the fire, 'let go o' me, you d——d old fool, d' ye hear?'

Thus adjured, Dick Bullen lowered Johnny to the ground with a smothered laugh, while the men, entering quietly, ranged themselves around a long table of rough boards which occupied the centre of the room. Johnny then gravely proceeded to a cupboard and brought out several articles, which he deposited on the table. 'Thar's whiskey. And crackers. And red herons. And cheese.' He took a bite of the latter on his way to the table. 'And sugar.' He scooped up a mouthful *en route* with a small and very dirty hand. 'And terbacker. Thar's dried appils too on the shelf, but I don't admire 'em. Appils is swellin'. Thar,' he concluded, 'now wade in, and don't be afeard. I don't mind the old woman. She don't b'long to me. S'long.'

He had stepped to the threshold of a small room, scarcely larger than a closet, partitioned off from the main apartment, and holding in its dim recess a small bed. He stood there a moment looking at the company, his bare feet peeping from the blanket, and nodded.

'Hello, Johnny! You ain't goin' to turn in agin, are ye?' said Dick.

'Yes, I are,' responded Johnny decidedly.

'Why, wot's up, old fellow?'

'I'm sick.'

'How sick?'

'I've got a fevier. And childblains. And roomatiz,' returned Johnny, and vanished within. After a moment's pause, he added in the dark, apparently from under the bedclothes—'And biles!'

There was an embarrassing silence. The men looked at each other and at the fire. Even with the appetizing banquet before them, it seemed as if they might again fall into the despondency of Thompson's grocery, when the voice of the Old Man, incautiously lifted, came deprecatingly from the kitchen.

'Certainly! Thet's so. In course they is. A gang o' lazy, drunken loafers, and that ar Dick Bullen's the orneriest of all. Didn't hev no more *sabe* than to come round yar with sickness in the house and no provision. Thet's what I said: "Bullen," sez I, "it's crazy drunk you are, or a fool," sez I, "to think o' such a thing. Staples," I sez, "be you a man, Staples, and 'spect to raise h—ll under my roof and invalids lyin' round?" But they would come—they would. Thet's wot you must 'spect o' such trash as lays round the Bar.'

A burst of laughter from the men followed this unfortunate exposure. Whether it was overheard in the kitchen, or whether the Old Man's irate companion had just then exhausted all other modes of expressing her contemptuous indignation, I cannot say, but a back door was suddenly slammed with great violence. A moment later and the Old Man reappeared, haply unconscious of the cause of the late hilarious outburst, and smiled blandly.

'The old woman thought she'd jest run over to Mrs. Mac-Fadden's for a sociable call,' he explained with jaunty indifference, as he took a seat at the board.

Oddly enough it needed this untoward incident to relieve the embarrassment that was beginning to be felt by the party, and their natural audacity returned with their host. I do not propose to record the convivialities of that evening. The inquisitive reader will accept the statement that the conversation was characterized by the same intellectual exaltation, the same cautious reverence, the same fastidious delicacy, the same rhetorical precision, and the same logical and coherent discourse somewhat later in the evening, which distinguish similar gatherings of the masculine sex in more civilized localities and under more favorable auspices. No glasses were broken in the absence of any; no liquor was uselessly spilt on the floor or table in the scarcity of that article.

It was nearly midnight when the festivities were interrupted. 'Hush,' said Dick Bullen, holding up his hand. It was the querulous voice of Johnny from his adjacent closet: 'O dad!'

The Old Man arose hurriedly and disappeared in the closet. Presently he reappeared. 'His rheumatiz is coming on agin bad,' he explained, 'and he wants rubbin'.' He lifted the demijohn of whiskey from the table and shook it. It was empty. Dick Bullen put down his tin cup with an embarrassed laugh. So did the others. The Old Man examined their contents and said hopefully, 'I reckon that's enough; he don't need much. You hold on all o' you for a spell, and I'll be back'; and vanished in the closet with an old flannel shirt and the whiskey. The door closed but imperfectly, and the following dialogue was distinctly audible:

'Now, sonny, whar does she ache worst?'

'Sometimes over yar and sometimes under yer; but it's most powerful from yer to yer. Rub yer, dad.'

A silence seemed to indicate a brisk rubbing. Then Johnny:

'Hevin' a good time out yer, dad?'

'Yes, sonny.'

'To-morrer's Chrismuss—ain't it?'

'Yes, sonny. How does she feel now?'

'Better. Rub a little furder down. Wot's Chrismuss, anyway? Wot's it all about?'

'Oh, it's a day.'

This exhaustive definition was apparently satisfactory, for there was a silent interval of rubbing. Presently Johnny again:

'Mar sez that everywhere else but yer everybody gives things to everybody Chrismuss, and then she jist waded inter you. She sez thar's a man they call Sandy Claws, not a white man, you know, but a kind o' Chinemin, comes down the chimbley night afore Chrismuss and gives things to chillern—boys like me. Puts 'em in their butes! Thet's what she tried to play upon me. Easy now, pop, whar are you rubbin' to—thet's a mile from the place. She jest made that up, didn't she, jest to aggrewate me and you? Don't rub thar. . . . Why, dad?'

In the great quiet that seemed to have fallen upon the house the sigh of the near pines and the drip of leaves without was very distinct. Johnny's voice, too, was lowered as he went on,

'Don't you take on now, for I'm gettin' all right fast. Wot's the boys doin' out thar?'

The Old Man partly opened the door and peered through. His guests were sitting there sociably enough, and there were a few silver coins and a lean buckskin purse on the table. 'Bettin' on suthin'—some little game or 'nother. They're all right,' he replied to Johnny, and recommenced his rubbing.

'I'd like to take a hand and win some money,' said Johnny reflectively after a pause.

The Old Man glibly repeated what was evidently a familiar formula, that if Johnny would wait until he struck it rich in the tunnel he'd have lots of money, etc., etc.

'Yes,' said Johnny, 'but you don't. And whether you strike it or I win it, it's about the same. It's all luck. But it's mighty cur'o's about Chrismuss—ain't it? Why do they call it Chrismuss?'

Perhaps from some instinctive deference to the overhearing of his guests, or from some vague sense of incongruity, the Old Man's reply was so low as to be inaudible beyond the room.

'Yes,' said Johnny, with some slight abatement of interest, 'I've heerd o' him before. Thar, that'll do, dad. I don't ache near so bad as I did. Now wrap me tight in this yer blanket. So. Now,' he added in a muffled whisper, 'sit down yer by me till I go asleep.' To assure himself of obedience, he disengaged one hand from the blanket, and, grasping his father's sleeve, again composed himself to rest.

For some moments the Old Man waited patiently. Then the unwonted stillness of the house excited his curiosity, and without moving from the bed he cautiously opened the door with his disengaged hand, and looked into the main room. To his infinite surprise it was dark and deserted. But even then a smouldering log on the hearth broke, and by the upspringing blaze he saw the figure of Dick Bullen sitting by the dying embers.

'Hello!'

Dick started, rose, and came somewhat unsteadily toward him.

'Whar's the boys?' said the Old Man.

'Gone up the cañon on a little *pasear*. They're coming back for me in a minit. I'm waitin' round for 'em. What are you starin' at, Old Man?' he added, with a forced laugh; 'do you think I'm drunk?'

The Old Man might have been pardoned the supposition, for Dick's eyes were humid and his face flushed. He loitered and lounged back to the chimney, yawned, shook himself, buttoned up his coat and laughed. 'Liquor ain't so plenty as that, Old Man. Now don't you get up,' he continued, as the Old Man made a movement to release his sleeve from Johnny's hand. 'Don't you mind manners. Sit jest whar you be, I'm goin' in a jiffy. Thar, that's them now.'

There was a low tap at the door. Dick Bullen opened it quickly, nodded 'Good-night' to his host, and disappeared. The Old Man would have followed him but for the hand that still unconsciously grasped his sleeve. He could have easily disengaged it: it was small, weak, and emaciated. But perhaps because it was small, weak, and emaciated he changed his mind, and, drawing his chair closer to the bed, rested his head upon it. In this defenseless attitude the potency of his earlier potations surprised him. The room flickered and faded before his eyes, reappeared, faded again, went out, and left him—asleep.

Meantime Dick Bullen, closing the door, confronted his companions. 'Are you ready?' said Staples.

'Ready,' said Dick, 'What's the time?'

'Past twelve,' was the reply; 'can you make it?—it's nigh on fifty miles, the round trip hither and yon.'

'I reckon,' returned Dick shortly. 'Whar's the mare?'

'Bill and Jack's holdin' her at the crossin'.'

'Let 'em hold on a minit longer,' said Dick.

He turned and re-entered the house softly. By the light of the guttering candle and dying fire he saw that the door of the little room was open. He stepped toward it on tiptoe and looked in. The Old Man had fallen back in his chair, snoring, his helpless feet thrust out in a line with his collapsed shoulders, and his hat pulled over his eyes. Beside him, on a narrow wooden bedstead, lay Johnny, muffled tightly in a blanket that hid all save a strip of forehead and a few curls damp with perspiration.

Dick Bullen made a step forward, hesitated, and glanced over his shoulder into the deserted room. Everything was quiet. With a sudden resolution he parted his huge mustaches with both hands and stooped over the sleeping boy. But even as he did so a mischievous blast, lying in wait, swooped down the chimney, rekindled the hearth, and lit up the room with a shameless glow from which Dick fled in bashful terror.

His companions were already waiting for him at the crossing. Two of them were struggling in the darkness with some strange misshapen bulk, which as Dick came nearer took the semblance of a great yellow horse.

It was the mare. She was not a pretty picture. From her Roman nose to her rising haunches, from her arched spine hidden by the stiff *machillas* of a Mexican saddle, to her thick, straight bony legs, there was not a line of equine grace. In her half-blind but wholly vicious white eyes, in her protruding under-lip, in her monstrous color, there was nothing but ugliness and vice.

'Now then,' said Staples, 'stand cl'ar of her heels, boys, and up with you. Don't miss your first holt of her mane, and mind ye get your off stirrup quick. Ready!'

There was a leap, a scrambling struggle, a bound, a wild retreat of the crowd, a circle of flying roofs, two springless leaps that jarred the earth, a rapid play and jingle of spurs, a plunge, and then the voice of Dick somewhere in the darkness. 'All right!'

'Don't take the lower road back onless you're hard pushed for time! Don't hold her in down hill. We'll be at the ford at five. G'lang! Hoopla! Mula! GO!'

A splash, a spark struck from the ledge in the road, a clatter in the rocky cut beyond, and Dick was gone.

Sing, O Muse, the ride of Richard Bullen! Sing, O Muse, of chivalrous men! the sacred quest, the doughty deeds, the battery of low churls, the fearsome ride and gruesome perils of the

Flower of Simpson's Bar! Alack! she is dainty, this Muse! She will have none of this bucking brute and swaggering, ragged rider, and I must fain follow him in prose, afoot!

It was one o'clock, and yet he had only gained Rattlesnake Hill. For in that time Jovita had rehearsed to him all her imperfections and practiced all her vices. Thrice had she stumbled. Twice had she thrown up her Roman nose in a straight line with the reins, and, resisting bit and spur, struck out madly across country. Twice had she reared, and, rearing, fallen backward; and twice had the agile Dick, unharmed, regained his seat before she found her vicious legs again. And a mile beyond them, at the foot of a long hill, was Rattlesnake Creek.

Dick knew that here was the crucial test of his ability to perform his enterprise, set his teeth grimly, put his knees well into her flanks, and changed his defensive tactics to brisk aggression. Bullied and maddened, Jovita began the descent of the hill. Here the artful Richard pretended to hold her in with ostentatious objurgation and well-feigned cries of alarm. It is unnecessary to add that Jovita instantly ran away. Nor need I state the time made in the descent; it is written in the chronicles of Simpson's Bar. Enough that in another moment, as it seemed to Dick, she was splashing on the overflowed banks of Rattlesnake Creek.

As Dick expected, the momentum she had acquired carried her beyond the point of balking, and, holding her well together for a mighty leap, they dashed into the middle of the swiftly flowing current. A few moments of kicking, wading, and swimming, and Dick drew a long breath on the opposite bank.

The road from Rattlesnake Creek to Red Mountain was tolerably level. Either the plunge in Rattlesnake Creek had dampened her baleful fire, or the art which led to it had shown her the superior wickedness of her rider, for Jovita no longer wasted her surplus energy in wanton conceits. Once she bucked, but it was from force of habit; once she shied, but it was from a new, freshly painted meeting-house at the crossing of the country road. Hollows, ditches, gravelly deposits, patches of freshly springing grasses, flew from beneath her rattling hoofs. She began to smell unpleasantly, once or twice she coughed slightly, but there was no abatement of her strength or speed.

By two o'clock he had passed Red Mountain and begun the descent to the plain. Ten minutes later the driver of the fast Pioneer coach was overtaken and passed by a 'man on a Pinto hoss'—an event sufficiently notable for remark. At half past two Dick rose in his stirrups with a great shout. Stars were glittering through the rifted clouds, and beyond him, out of the plain, rose two spires, a flagstaff, and a straggling line of black objects. Dick jingled his spurs and swung his *riata*, Jovita bounded forward, and in another moment they swept into Tuttleville, and drew up before the wooden piazza of 'The Hotel of All Nations.'

What transpired that night at Tuttleville is not strictly a part of this record. Briefly I may state, however, that after Jovita had been handed over to a sleepy ostler, whom she at once kicked into unpleasant consciousness, Dick sallied out with the barkeeper for a tour of the sleeping town.

Lights still gleamed from a few saloons and gambling houses; but, avoiding these, they stopped before several closed shops, and by persistent tapping and judicious outcry roused the proprietors from their beds, and made them unbar the doors of their magazines and expose their wares. Sometimes they were met by curses, but oftener by interest and some concern in their needs, and the interview was invariably concluded by a drink.

It was three o'clock before this pleasantry was given over, and with a small waterproof bag of India-rubber strapped on his shoulders, Dick returned to the hotel. But here he was waylaid by Beauty—Beauty opulent in charms, affluent in dress, persuasive in speech, and Spanish in accent! In vain she repeated the invitation in 'Excelsior,' happily scorned by all Alpine-climbing youth, and rejected by this child of the Sierras—a rejection softened in this instance by a laugh and his last gold coin.

And then he sprang to the saddle and dashed down the lonely street and out into the lonelier plain, where presently the lights, the black line of houses, the spires, and the flag-staff sank into the earth behind him again and were lost in the distance.

The storm had cleared away, the air was brisk and cold, the outlines of adjacent landmarks were distinct, but it was half-past four before Dick reached the meeting-house and the crossing of the county road. To avoid the rising grade he had taken a longer and more circuitous road, in whose viscid mud Jovita sank fetlock deep at every bound. It was a poor preparation for a steady ascent of five miles more; but Jovita, gathering her legs under her, took it with her usual blind, unreasoning fury, and a half-hour later reached the long level that led to Rattlesnake Creek. Another half-hour would bring him to the creek. He threw the reins lightly upon the neck of the mare, chirruped to her, and began to sing.

Suddenly Jovita shied with a bound that would have unseated a less practiced rider. Hanging to her rein was a figure that had leaped from the bank, and at the same time from the road before her arose a shadowy horse and rider.

'Throw up your hands,' commanded the second apparition, with an oath.

Dick felt the mare tremble, quiver, and apparently sink under him. He knew what it meant and was prepared.

'Stand aside, Jack Simpson. I know you, you d——d thief! Let me pass, or——'

He did not finish the sentence. Jovita rose straight in the air with a terrific bound, throwing the figure from her bit with a single shake of her vicious head, and charged with deadly malevolence down on the impediment before her. An oath, a pistol-shot, horse and highwayman rolled over in the road, and the next moment Jovita was a hundred yards away. But the good right arm of her rider, shattered by a bullet, dropped helplessly at his side.

Without slacking his speed he shifted the reins to his left hand. But a few moments later he was obliged to halt and tighten the saddle-girths that had slipped in the onset. This in his crippled condition took some time. He had no fear of pursuit, but looking up he saw that the eastern stars were already

paling, and that the distant peaks had lost their ghostly whiteness, and now stood out blackly against a lighter sky. Day was
upon him. Then completely absorbed in a single idea, he forgot
the pain of his wound, and mounting again dashed on toward
Rattlesnake Creek. But now Jovita's breath came broken by
gasps, Dick reeled in his saddle, and brighter and brighter grew
the sky.

Ride, Richard; run, Jovita; linger, O day!

For the last few rods there was a roaring in his ears. Was it
exhaustion from loss of blood, or what? He was dazed and
giddy as he swept down the hill, and did not recognize his surroundings. Had he taken the wrong road, or was this Rattlesnake Creek?

It was. But the brawling creek he had swum a few hours before had risen, more than doubled its volume, and now rolled a
swift and resistless river between him and Rattlesnake Hill.
For the first time that night Richard's heart sank within him.
The river, the mountain, the quickening east, swam before his
eyes. He shut them to recover his self-control. In that brief interval, by some fantastic mental process, the little room at Simpson's Bar and the figures of the sleeping father and son rose
upon him.

He opened his eyes wildly, cast off his coat, pistol, boots, and
saddle, bound his precious pack tightly to his shoulders, grasped
the bare flanks of Jovita with his bared knees, and with a shout
dashed into the yellow water. A cry rose from the opposite bank
as the head of a man and horse struggled for a few moments
against the battling current, and then were swept away amidst
uprooted trees and whirling driftwood.

The Old Man started and woke. The fire on the hearth was
dead, the candle in the outer room flickering in its socket, and
somebody was rapping at the door. He opened it, but fell back
with a cry before the dripping, half-naked figure that reeled
against the doorpost.

'Dick?'

'Hush! Is he awake yet?'

'No; but, Dick——'

'Dry up, you old fool! Get me some whiskey, *quick!*' The Old Man flew and returned with—an empty bottle! Dick would have sworn, but his strength was not equal to the occasion. He staggered, caught at the handle of the door, and motioned to the Old Man.

'Thar's suthin' in my pack yer for Johnny. Take it off. I can't.'

The Old Man unstrapped the pack, and laid it before the exhausted man.

'Open it, quick.'

He did so with trembling fingers. It contained only a few poor toys—cheap and barbaric enough, goodness knows, but bright with paint and tinsel. One of them was broken; another, I fear, was irretrievably ruined by water, and on the third—ah me! there was a cruel spot.

'It don't look like much, that's a fact,' said Dick ruefully. . . . 'But it's the best we could do. . . . Take 'em, Old Man, and put 'em in his stocking, and tell him—tell him, you know—hold me, Old Man——' The Old Man caught at his sinking figure. 'Tell him,' said Dick, with a weak little laugh—'tell him Sandy Claws has come.'

And even so, bedraggled, ragged, unshaven and unshorn, with one arm hanging helplessly at his side, Santa Claus came to Simpson's Bar and fell fainting on the first threshold. The Christmas dawn came slowly after, touching the remoter peaks with the rosy warmth of ineffable love. And it looked so tenderly on Simpson's Bar that the whole mountain, as if caught in a generous action, blushed to the skies.

Dancing Dan's Christmas

DAMON RUNYON

Now one time it comes on Christmas, and in fact it is the evening before Christmas, and I am in Good Time Charley Bernstein's little speakeasy in West Forty-seventh Street, wishing Charley a Merry Christmas and having a few hot Tom and Jerrys with him.

This hot Tom and Jerry is an old-time drink that is once used by one and all in this country to celebrate Christmas with, and in fact it is once so popular that many people think Christmas is invented only to furnish an excuse for hot Tom and Jerry, although of course this is by no means true.

But anybody will tell you that there is nothing that brings out the true holiday spirit like hot Tom and Jerry, and I hear that since Tom and Jerry goes out of style in the United States, the holiday spirit is never quite the same.

Well, as Good Time Charley and I are expressing our holiday sentiments to each other over our hot Tom and Jerry, and I am trying to think up the poem about the night before Christmas and all through the house, which I know will interest Charley no little, all of a sudden there is a big knock at the front door, and when Charley opens the door, who comes in carrying a large package under one arm but a guy by the name of Dancing Dan.

This Dancing Dan is a good-looking young guy, who always seems well-dressed, and he is called by the name of Dancing Dan because he is a great hand for dancing around and about with dolls in night clubs, and other spots where there is any dancing. In fact, Dan never seems to be doing anything else, although I hear rumors that when he is not dancing he is carrying on in a most illegal manner at one thing and another. But of course you can always hear rumors in this town about anybody, and personally I am rather fond of Dancing Dan as he always seems to be getting a great belt out of life.

Anybody in town will tell you that Dancing Dan is a guy with no Barnaby whatever in him, and in fact he has about as much gizzard as anybody around, although I wish to say I always question his judgment in dancing so much with Miss Muriel O'Neill, who works in the Half Moon night club. And the reason I question his judgment in this respect is because everybody knows that Miss Muriel O'Neill is a doll who is very well thought of by Heine Schmitz, and Heine Schmitz is not such a guy as will take kindly to anybody dancing more than once and a half with a doll that he thinks well of.

Well, anyway, as Dancing Dan comes in, he weighs up the joint in one quick peek, and then he tosses the package he is carrying into a corner where it goes plunk, as if there is something very heavy in it, and then he steps up to the bar alongside of Charley and me and wishes to know what we are drinking.

Naturally we start boosting hot Tom and Jerry to Dancing Dan, and he says he will take a crack at it with us, and after one crack, Dancing Dan says he will have another crack, and Merry Christmas to us with it, and the first thing anybody knows it is a couple of hours later and we are still having cracks at the hot Tom and Jerry with Dancing Dan, and Dan says he never drinks anything so soothing in his life. In fact, Dancing Dan says he will recommend Tom and Jerry to everybody he knows, only he does not know anybody good enough for Tom and Jerry, except maybe Miss Muriel O'Neill, and she does not drink anything with drugstore rye in it.

Well, several times while we are drinking this Tom and Jerry, customers come to the door of Good Time Charley's little speakeasy and knock, but by now Charley is commencing to be afraid they will wish Tom and Jerry, too, and he does not feel we will have enough for ourselves, so he hangs out a sign which says "Closed on Account of Christmas," and the only one he will let in is a guy by the name of Ooky, who is nothing but an old rum-dum, and who is going around all week dressed like Santa Claus and carrying a sign advertising Moe Lewinsky's clothing joint around in Sixth Avenue.

This Ooky is still wearing his Santa Claus outfit when Charley lets him in, and the reason Charley permits such a character as Ooky in his joint is because Ooky does the porter work for Charley when he is not Santa Claus for Moe Lewinsky, such as sweeping out, and washing the glasses, and one thing and another.

Well, it is about nine-thirty when Ooky comes in, and his puppies are aching, and he is all petered out generally from walking up and down and here and there with his sign, for any time a guy is Santa Claus for Moe Lewinsky he must earn his dough. In fact, Ooky is so fatigued, and his puppies hurt him so much that Dancing Dan and Good Time Charley and I all feel very sorry for him, and invite him to have a few mugs of hot Tom and Jerry with us, and wish him plenty of Merry Christmas.

But old Ooky is not accustomed to Tom and Jerry and after about the fifth mug he folds up in a chair, and goes right to sleep on us. He is wearing a pretty good Santa Claus make-up, what with a nice red suit trimmed with white cotton, and a wig, and false nose, and long white whiskers, and a big sack stuffed with excelsior on his back, and if I do not know Santa Claus is not apt to be such a guy as will snore loud enough to rattle the windows, I will think Ooky is Santa Claus sure enough.

Well, we forget Ooky and let him sleep, and go on with our hot Tom and Jerry, and in the meantime we try to think up a few songs appropriate to Christmas, and Dancing Dan finally renders My Dad's Dinner Pail in a nice baritone and very loud, while I do first rate with Will You Love Me in December As You Do in May?

About midnight Dancing Dan wishes to see how he looks as Santa Claus.

So Good Time Charley and I help Dancing Dan pull off Ooky's outfit and put it on Dan, and this is easy as Ooky only has this Santa Claus outfit on over his ordinary clothes, and he does not even wake up when we are undressing him of the Santa Claus uniform.

Well, I wish to say I see many a Santa Claus in my time, but I never see a better looking Santa Claus than Dancing Dan, especially after he gets the wig and white whiskers fixed just right, and we put a sofa pillow that Good Time Charley happens to have around the joint for the cat to sleep on down his pants to give Dancing Dan a nice fat stomach such as Santa Claus is bound to have.

"Well," Charley finally says, "it is a great pity we do not know where there are some stockings hung up somewhere, because then," he says, "you can go around and stuff things in these stockings, as I always hear this is the main idea of a Santa Claus. But," Charley says, "I do not suppose anybody in this section has any stockings hung up, or if they have," he says, "the chances are they are so full of holes they will not hold anything. Anyway," Charley says, "even if there are any stockings hung up we do not have anything to stuff in them, although personally," he says, "I will gladly donate a few pints of Scotch."

Well, I am pointing out that we have no reindeer and that a Santa Claus is bound to look like a terrible sap if he goes around without any reindeer, but Charley's remarks seem to give Dancing Dan an idea, for all of a sudden he speaks as follows:

"Why," Dancing Dan says, "I know where a stocking is hung up. It is hung up at Miss Muriel O'Neill's flat over here in West Forty-ninth Street. This stocking is hung up by nobody but a party by the name of Gammer O'Neill, who is Miss Muriel O'Neill's grandmamma," Dancing Dan says. "Gammer O'Neill is going on ninety-odd," he says, "and Miss Muriel O'Neill tells me she cannot hold out much longer, what with one thing and another, including being a little childish in spots.

"Now," Dancing Dan says, "I remember Miss Muriel O'Neill is telling me just the other night how Gammer O'Neill hangs up her stocking on Christmas Eve all her life, and," he says, "I judge from what Miss Muriel O'Neill says that the old doll always believes Santa Claus will come along some Christmas and fill the stocking full of beautiful gifts. But," Dancing Dan says, "Miss Muriel O'Neill tells me Santa Claus never does this, although Miss Muriel O'Neill personally always takes a few gifts home and pops them into the stocking to make Gammer O'Neill feel better.

"But, of course," Dancing Dan says, "these gifts are nothing much because Miss Muriel O'Neill is very poor, and proud, and also good, and will not take a dime off of anybody and I can lick the guy who says she will.

"Now," Dancing Dan goes on, "it seems that while Gammer O'Neill is very happy to get whatever she finds in her stocking on Christmas morning, she does not understand why Santa Claus is not more liberal, and," he says, "Miss Muriel O'Neill is saying to me that she only wishes she can give Gammer O'-Neill one real big Christmas before the old doll puts her checks back in the rack.

"So," Dancing Dan states, "here is a job for us. Miss Muriel O'Neill and her grandmamma live all alone in this flat over in West Forty-ninth Street, and," he says, "at such an hour as this Miss Muriel O'Neill is bound to be working, and the chances are Gammer O'Neill is sound asleep, and we will just hop over there and Santa Claus will fill up her stocking with beautiful gifts."

Well, I say, I do not see where we are going to get any beautiful gifts at this time of night, what with all the stores being closed, unless we dash into an all-night drug store and buy a few bottles of perfume and a bum toilet set as guys always do when they forget about their ever-loving wives until after store hours on Christmas Eve, but Dancing Dan says never mind about this, but let us have a few more Tom and Jerrys first.

So we have a few more Tom and Jerrys, and then Dancing Dan picks up the package he heaves into the corner, and dumps most of the excelsior out of Ooky's Santa Claus sack, and puts the bundle in, and Good Time Charley turns out all the lights, but one, and leaves a bottle of Scotch on the table in front of Ooky for a Christmas gift, and away we go.

Personally, I regret very much leaving the hot Tom and Jerry, but then I am also very enthusiastic about going along to help Dancing Dan play Santa Claus, while Good Time Charley is practically overjoyed, as it is the first time in his life Charley is ever mixed up in so much holiday spirit.

As we go up Broadway, headed for Forty-ninth Street, Charley and I see many citizens we know and give them a large hello, and wish them Merry Christmas, and some of these citizens shake hands with Santa Claus, not knowing he is nobody but Dancing Dan, although later I understand there is some gossip among these citizens because they claim a Santa Claus with such a breath on him as our Santa Claus has is a little out of line.

And once we are somewhat embarrassed when a lot of little kids going home with their parents from a late Christmas party somewhere gather about Santa Claus with shouts of childish glee, and some of them wish to climb up Santa Claus' legs. Naturally, Santa Claus gets a little peevish, and calls them a few names, and one of the parents comes up and wishes to know what is the idea of Santa Claus using such language, and Santa Claus takes a punch at the parent, all of which is no doubt astonishing to the little kids who have an idea of Santa Claus as a very kindly old guy.

Well, finally we arrive in front of the place where Dancing Dan says Miss Muriel O'Neill and her grandmamma live, and it is nothing but a tenement house not far back of Madison Square Garden, and furthermore it is a walkup, and at this time there are no lights burning in the joint except a gas jet in the main hall, and by the light of this jet we look at the names on the letter boxes, such as you always find in the hall of these joints, and we see that Miss Muriel O'Neill and her grand-mamma live on the fifth floor.

This is the top floor, and personally I do not like the idea of walking up five flights of stairs, and I am willing to let Dancing Dan and Good Time Charley go, but Dancing Dan insists we must all go, and finally I agree because Charley is commencing to argue that the right way for us to do is to get on the roof and let Santa Claus go down a chimney, and is making so much noise I am afraid he will wake somebody up.

So up the stairs we climb and finally we come to a door on the top floor that has a little card in a slot that says O'Neill, so we know we reach our destination. Dancing Dan first tries the knob, and right away the door opens, and we are in a little two or three-room flat, with not much furniture in it, and what furniture there is, is very poor. One single gas jet is burning near a bed in a room just off the one the door opens into, and by this light we see a very old doll is sleeping on the bed, so we judge this is nobody but Gammer O'Neill.

On her face is a large smile, as if she is dreaming of something very pleasant. On a chair at the head of the bed is hung a long black stocking, and it seems to be such a stocking as is often patched and mended, so I can see that what Miss Muriel O'Neill tells Dancing Dan about her grandmamma hanging up her stocking is really true, although up to this time I have my doubts.

Finally Dancing Dan unslings the sack on his back, and takes out his package, and unties this package, and all of a sudden out pops a raft of big diamond bracelets, and diamond rings, and diamond brooches, and diamond necklaces, and I do not know what else in the way of diamonds, and Dancing Dan and I begin stuffing these diamonds into the stocking and Good Time Charley pitches in and helps us.

There are enough diamonds to fill the stocking to the muzzle, and it is no small stocking, at that, and I judge that Gammer O'Neill has a pretty fair set of bunting sticks when she is young. In fact, there are so many diamonds that we have enough left over to make a nice little pile on the chair after we fill the

stocking plumb up, leaving a nice diamond-studded vanity case
sticking out the top where we figure it will hit Gammer
O'Neill's eye when she wakes up.

And it is not until I get out in the fresh air again that all of
a sudden I remember seeing large headlines in the afternoon
papers about a five-hundred-G's stickup in the afternoon of one
of the biggest diamond merchants in Maiden Lane while he is
sitting in his office, and I also recall once hearing rumors that
Dancing Dan is one of the best lone-hand git-'em-up guys in
the world.

Naturally, I commence to wonder if I am in the proper com-
pany when I am with Dancing Dan, even if he is Santa Claus.
So I leave him on the next corner arguing with Good Time
Charley about whether they ought to go and find some more
presents somewhere, and look for other stockings to stuff, and
I hasten on home and go to bed.

The next day I find I have such a noggin that I do not care
to stir around, and in fact I do not stir around much for a
couple of weeks.

Then one night I drop around to Good Time Charley's little
speakeasy, and ask Charley what is doing.

"Well," Charley says, "many things are doing, and personally," he says, "I'm greatly surprised I do not see you at Gammer O'Neill's wake. You know Gammer O'Neill leaves this
wicked old world a couple of days after Christmas," Good Time
Charley says, "and," he says, "Miss Muriel O'Neill states that
Doc Moggs claims it is at least a day after she is entitled to go,
but she is sustained," Charley says, "by great happiness in finding her stocking filled with beautiful gifts on Christmas morning.

"According to Miss Muriel O'Neill," Charley says, "Gammer
O'Neill dies practically convinced that there is a Santa Claus,
although of course," he says, "Miss Muriel O'Neill does not tell
her the real owner of the gifts, an all-right guy by the name of
Shapiro leaves the gifts with her after Miss Muriel O'Neill
notifies him of the finding of same.

"It seems," Charley says, "this Shapiro is a tender-hearted

guy, who is willing to help keep Gammer O'Neill with us a little longer when Doc Moggs says leaving the gifts with her will do it.

"So," Charley says, "everything is quite all right, as the coppers cannot figure anything except that maybe the rascal who takes the gifts from Shapiro gets conscience-stricken, and leaves them the first place he can, and Miss Muriel O'Neill receives a ten-G's reward for finding the gifts and returning them. And," Charley says, "I hear Dancing Dan is in San Francisco and is figuring on reforming and becoming a dancing teacher, so he can marry Miss Muriel O'Neill, and of course," he says, "we all hope and trust she never learn any details of Dancing Dan's career."

Well, it is Christmas Eve a year later that I run into a guy by the name of Shotgun Sam, who is mobbed up with Heine Schmitz in Harlem, and who is a very, very obnoxious character indeed.

"Well, well, well," Shotgun says, "the last time I see you is another Christmas Eve like this, and you are coming out of Good Time Charley's joint, and," he says, "you certainly have your pots on."

"Well, Shotgun," I says, "I am sorry you get such a wrong impression of me, but the truth is," I say, "on the occasion you speak of, I am suffering from a dizzy feeling in my head."

"It is all right with me," Shotgun says. "I have a tip this guy Dancing Dan is in Good Time Charley's the night I see you, and Mockie Morgan, and Gunner Jack and me are casing the joint, because," he says, "Heine Schmitz is all sored up at Dan over some doll, although of course," Shotgun says, "it is all right now, as Heine has another doll.

"Anyway," he says, "we never get to see Dancing Dan. We watch the joint from six-thirty in the evening until daylight Christmas morning, and nobody goes in all night but old Ooky the Santa Claus guy in his Santa Claus makeup, and," Shotgun says, "nobody comes out except you and Good Time Charley and Ooky.

"Well," Shotgun says, "it is a great break for Dancing Dan

he never goes in or comes out of Good Time Charley's, at that, because," he says, "we are waiting for him on the second-floor front of the building across the way with some nice little sawed-offs, and are under orders from Heine not to miss."

"Well, Shotgun," I say, "Merry Christmas."

"Well, all right," Shotgun says, "Merry Christmas."

The Tree That Didn't Get Trimmed

CHRISTOPHER MORLEY

IF YOU walk through a grove of balsam trees you will notice that the young trees are silent; they are listening. But the old tall ones—especially the firs—are whispering. They are telling the story of The Tree That Didn't Get Trimmed. It sounds like a painful story, and the murmur of the old trees as they tell it is rather solemn; but it is an encouraging story for young saplings to hear. On warm autumn days when your trunk is tickled by ants and insects climbing, and the resin is hot and gummy in your knots, and the whole glade smells sweet, drowsy, and sad, and the hardwood trees are boasting of the gay colors they are beginning to show, many a young evergreen has been cheered by it.

All young fir trees, as you know by that story of Hans Ander-

Reprinted by permission of the author.

sen's—if you've forgotten it, why not read it again?—dream of being a Christmas Tree some day. They dream about it as young girls dream of being a bride, or young poets of having a volume of verse published. With the vision of that brightness and gaiety before them they patiently endure the sharp sting of the ax, the long hours pressed together on a freight car. But every December there are more trees cut down than are needed for Christmas. And that is the story that no one—not even Hans Andersen—has thought to put down.

The tree in this story should never have been cut. He wouldn't have been, but it was getting dark in the Vermont woods, and the man with the ax said to himself, "Just one more." But cutting young trees with a sharp, beautifully balanced ax is fascinating; you go on and on; there's a sort of cruel pleasure in it. The blade goes through the soft wood with one whistling stroke and the boughs sink down with a soft swish.

He was a fine, well-grown youngster, but too tall for his age; his branches were rather scraggly. If he'd been left there he would have been an unusually big tree some day; but now he was in the awkward age and didn't have the tapering shape and the thick, even foliage that people like on Christmas trees. Worse still, instead of running up to a straight, clean spire, his top was a bit lopsided, with a fork in it.

But he didn't know this as he stood with many others, leaning against the side wall of the green-grocer's shop. In those cold December days he was very happy, thinking of the pleasures to come. He had heard of the delights of Christmas Eve: the stealthy setting-up of the tree, the tinsel balls and colored toys and stars, the peppermint canes and birds with spun-glass tails. Even that old anxiety of Christmas trees—burning candles —did not worry him, for he had been told that nowadays people use strings of tiny electric bulbs which cannot set one on fire. So he looked forward to the festival with a confident heart.

"I shall be very grand," he said. "I hope there will be children to admire me. It must be a great moment when the children hang their stockings on you!" He even felt sorry for the first trees that were chosen and taken away. It would be best, he considered, not to be bought until Christmas Eve. Then, in the shining darkness someone would pick him out, put him carefully along the running board of a car, and away they would go. The tire-chains would clack and jingle merrily on the snowy road. He imagined a big house with fire glowing on a hearth; the hushed rustle of wrapping paper and parcels being unpacked. Someone would say, "Oh, what a beautiful tree!" How erect and stiff he would brace himself in his iron tripod stand.

But day after day went by, one by one the other trees were taken, and he began to grow troubled. For everyone who looked at him seemed to have an unkind word. "Too tall," said one lady. "No, this one wouldn't do, the branches are too skimpy," said another. "If I chop off the top," said the greengrocer, "it wouldn't be so bad?" The tree shuddered, but the customer had already passed on to look at others. Some of his branches ached where the grocer had bent them upward to make his shape more attractive.

Across the street was a Ten Cent Store. Its bright windows were full of scarlet odds and ends; when the doors opened he could see people crowded along the aisles, cheerfully jostling one another with bumpy packages. A buzz of talk, a shuffle of feet, a constant ringing of cash drawers came noisily out of that doorway. He could see flashes of marvelous color, ornaments for luckier trees. Every evening, as the time drew nearer, the pavements were more thronged. The handsomer trees, not so tall as he but more bushy and shapely, were ranked in front of him; as they were taken away he could see the gaiety only too well. Then he was shown to a lady who wanted a tree very cheap. "You can have this one for a dollar," said the grocer. This was only one-third of what the grocer had asked for him at first, but even so the lady refused him and went across the street to buy a little artificial tree at the toy store. The man pushed him back carelessly, and he toppled over and fell alongside the wall. No one bothered to pick him up. He was almost glad, for now his pride would be spared.

Now it was Christmas Eve. It was a foggy evening with a

drizzling rain; the alley alongside the store was thick with tram-
pled slush. As he lay there among broken boxes and fallen
scraps of holly strange thoughts came to him. In the still northern forest already his wounded stump was buried in forgetful
snow. He remembered the wintry sparkle of the woods, the big
trees with crusts and clumps of silver on their broad boughs,
the keen singing of the lonely wind. He remembered the strong,
warm feeling of his roots reaching down into the safe earth.
That is a good feeling; it means to a tree just what it means
to you to stretch your toes down toward the bottom of a well-
tucked bed. And he had given up all this to lie here, disdained
and forgotten, in a littered alley. The splash of feet, the chime
of bells, the cry of cars went past him. He trembled a little with
self-pity and vexation. "No toys and stockings for me," he
thought sadly, and shed some of his needles.

Late that night, after all the shopping was over, the grocer
came out to clear away what was left. The boxes, the broken
wreaths, the empty barrels, and our tree with one or two others
that hadn't been sold, all were thrown through the side door
into the cellar. The door was locked and he lay there in the
dark. One of his branches, doubled under him in the fall,
ached so he thought it must be broken. "So this is Christmas,"
he said to himself.

All that day it was very still in the cellar. There was an
occasional creak as one of the bruised trees tried to stretch
itself. Feet went along the pavement overhead, and there was
a booming of church bells, but everything had a slow, disappointed sound. Christmas is always a little sad, after such busy
preparations. The unwanted trees lay on the stone floor, watching the furnace light flicker on a hatchet that had been left
there.

The day after Christmas a man came in who wanted some
green boughs to decorate a cemetery. The grocer took the
hatchet, and seized the trees without ceremony. They were too
disheartened to care. Chop, chop, chop, went the blade, and
the sweet-smelling branches were carried away. The naked
trunks were thrown into a corner.

And now our tree, what was left of him, had plenty of time to think. He no longer could feel anything, for trees feel with their branches, but they think with their trunks. What did he think about as he grew dry and stiff? He thought that it had been silly of him to imagine such a fine, gay career for himself, and he was sorry for other young trees, still growing in the fresh hilly country, who were enjoying the same fantastic dreams.

Now perhaps you don't know what happens to the trunks of leftover Christmas trees. You could never guess. Farmers come in from the suburbs and buy them at five cents each for bean-poles and grape arbors. So perhaps (here begins the encouraging part of this story) they are really happier, in the end, than the trees that get trimmed for Santa Claus. They go back into the fresh, moist earth of spring, and when the sun grows hot the quick tendrils of the vines climb up them and presently they are decorated with the red blossoms of the bean or the little blue globes of the grape, just as pretty as any Christmas trinkets.

So one day the naked, dusty fir-poles were taken out of the cellar, and thrown into a truck with many others, and made a rattling journey out into the land. The farmer unloaded them in his yard and was stacking them up by the barn when his wife came out to watch him.

"There!" she said. "That's just what I want, a nice long pole with a fork in it. Jim, put that one over there to hold up the clothesline." It was the first time that anyone had praised our tree, and his dried-up heart swelled with a tingle of forgotten sap. They put him near one end of the clothesline, with his stump close to a flower bed. The fork that had been despised for a Christmas star was just the thing to hold up a clothesline. It was wash-day, and soon the farmer's wife began bringing out wet garments to swing and freshen in the clean, bright air. And the very first thing that hung near the top of the Christmas pole was a cluster of children's stockings.

That isn't quite the end of the story, as the old fir trees whisper it in the breeze. The Tree That Didn't Get Trimmed was so cheerful watching the stockings, and other gay little clothes that plumped out in the wind just as though waiting to be spanked, that he didn't notice what was going on—or going up —below him. A vine had caught hold of his trunk and was steadily twisting upward. And one morning, when the farmer's wife came out intending to shift him, she stopped and exclaimed. "Why, I mustn't move this pole," she said. "The morning glory has run right up it." So it had, and our bare pole was blue and crimson with color.

Something nice, the old firs believe, always happens to the trees that don't get trimmed. They even believe that some day one of the Christmas-tree bean-poles will be the starting-point for another Magic Beanstalk, as in the fairy tale of the boy who climbed up the bean-tree and killed the giant. When that happens, fairy tales will begin all over again.

The Gift of the Magi

O. HENRY (William Sydney Porter)

ONE DOLLAR and eighty-seven cents. That was all. And sixty cents of it was in pennies. Pennies saved one and two at a time by bulldozing the grocer and the vegetable man and the butcher until one's cheeks burned with the silent imputation of parsimony that such close dealing implied. Three times Della counted it. One dollar and eighty-seven cents. And the next day would be Christmas.

There was clearly nothing to do but flop down on the shabby

From *The Four Million* by O. Henry. Copyright 1905, by Doubleday & Co., Inc.

little couch and howl. So Della did it. Which instigates the moral reflection that life is made up of sobs, sniffles, and smiles, with sniffles predominating.

While the mistress of the home is gradually subsiding from the first stage to the second, take a look at the home. A furnished flat at $8 per week. It did not exactly beggar description, but it certainly had that word on the lookout for the mendicancy squad.

In the vestibule below was a letter-box into which no letter would go, and an electric button from which no mortal finger could coax a ring. Also appertaining thereunto was a card bearing the name "Mr. James Dillingham Young."

The "Dillingham" had been flung to the breeze during a former period of prosperity when its possessor was being paid $30 per week. Now, when the income was shrunk to $20, the letters of "Dillingham" looked blurred, as though they were thinking seriously of contracting to a modest and unassuming D. But whenever Mr. James Dillingham Young came home and reached his flat above he was called "Jim" and greatly hugged by Mrs. James Dillingham Young, already introduced to you as Della. Which is all very good.

Della finished her cry and attended to her cheeks with the powder rag. She stood by the window and looked out dully at a grey cat walking a grey fence in a grey backyard. To-morrow would be Christmas Day, and she had only $1.87 with which to buy Jim a present. She had been saving every penny she could for months, with this result. Twenty dollars a week doesn't go far. Expenses had been greater than she had calculated. They always are. Only $1.87 to buy a present for Jim. Her Jim. Many a happy hour she had spent planning for something nice for him. Something fine and rare and sterling—something just a little bit near to being worthy of the honour of being owned by Jim.

There was a pier-glass between the windows of the room. Perhaps you have seen a pier-glass in an $8 flat. A very thin and very agile person may, by observing his reflection in a rapid sequence of longitudinal strips, obtain a fairly accurate conception of his looks. Della, being slender, had mastered the art.

Suddenly she whirled from the window and stood before the glass. Her eyes were shining brilliantly, but her face had lost its colour within twenty seconds. Rapidly she pulled down her hair and let it fall to its full length.

Now, there were two possessions of the James Dillingham Youngs in which they both took a mighty pride. One was Jim's gold watch that had been his father's and his grandfather's. The other was Della's hair. Had the Queen of Sheba lived in the flat across the airshaft, Della would have let her hair hang out the window some day to dry just to depreciate Her Majesty's jewels and gifts. Had King Solomon been the janitor, with all his treasures piled up in the basement, Jim would have pulled out his watch every time he passed, just to see him pluck at his beard from envy.

So now Della's beautiful hair fell about her, rippling and shining like a cascade of brown waters. It reached below her knee and made itself almost a garment for her. And then she did it up again nervously and quickly. Once she faltered for a minute and stood still while a tear or two splashed on the worn red carpet.

On went her old brown jacket; on went her old brown hat. With a whirl of skirts and with the brilliant sparkle still in her eyes, she fluttered out the door and down the stairs to the street.

Where she stopped the sign read: "Mme. Sofronie. Hair Goods of All Kinds." One flight up Della ran, and collected herself, panting. Madame, large, too white, chilly, hardly looked the "Sofronie."

"Will you buy my hair?" asked Della.

"I buy hair," said Madame. "Take yer hat off and let's have a sight at the looks of it."

Down rippled the brown cascade.

"Twenty dollars," said Madame, lifting the mass with a practised hand.

"Give it to me quick," said Della.

Oh, and the next two hours tripped by on rosy wings. Forget the hashed metaphor. She was ransacking the stores for Jim's present.

She found it at last. It surely had been made for Jim and no one else. There was no other like it in any of the stores, and she had turned all of them inside out. It was a platinum fob chain simple and chaste in design, properly proclaiming its value by substance alone and not by meretricious ornamentation—as all good things should do. It was even worthy of The Watch. As soon as she saw it she knew that it must be Jim's. It was like him. Quietness and value—the description applied to both. Twenty-one dollars they took from her for it, and she hurried home with the 87 cents. With that chain on his watch Jim might be properly anxious about the time in any company. Grand as the watch was, he sometimes looked at it on the sly on account of the old leather strap that he used in place of a chain.

When Della reached home her intoxication gave way a little to prudence and reason. She got out her curling irons and lighted the gas and went to work repairing the ravages made by generosity added to love. Which is always a tremendous task, dear friends—a mammoth task.

Within forty minutes her head was covered with tiny, close-lying curls that made her look wonderfully like a truant schoolboy. She looked at her reflection in the mirror long, carefully, and critically.

"If Jim doesn't kill me," she said to herself, "before he takes a second look at me, he'll say I look like a Coney Island chorus girl. But what could I do—oh! what could I do with a dollar and eighty-seven cents?"

At 7 o'clock the coffee was made and the frying-pan was on the back of the stove hot and ready to cook the chops.

Jim was never late. Della doubled the fob chain in her hand and sat on the corner of the table near the door that he always entered. Then she heard his step on the stair away down on the first flight, and she turned white for just a moment. She had a habit of saying little silent prayers about the simplest every-day things, and now she whispered: "Please God, make him think I am still pretty."

The door opened and Jim stepped in and closed it. He looked thin and very serious. Poor fellow, he was only twenty-two—and to be burdened with a family! He needed a new overcoat and he was without gloves.

Jim stopped inside the door, as immovable as a setter at the scent of quail. His eyes were fixed upon Della, and there was an expression in them that she could not read, and it terrified her. It was not anger, nor surprise, nor disapproval, nor horror, nor any of the sentiments that she had been prepared for. He simply stared at her fixedly with that peculiar expression on his face.

Della wriggled off the table and went for him.

"Jim, darling," she cried, "don't look at me that way. I had my hair cut off and sold it because I couldn't have lived through Christmas without giving you a present. It'll grow out again—you won't mind, will you? I just had to do it. My hair grows awfully fast. Say 'Merry Christmas!' Jim, and let's be happy. You don't know what a nice—what a beautiful, nice gift I've got for you."

"You've cut off your hair?" asked Jim, laboriously, as if he had not arrived at that patent fact yet even after the hardest mental labour.

"Cut it off and sold it," said Della. "Don't you like me just as well, anyhow? I'm me without my hair, ain't I?"

Jim looked about the room curiously.

"You say your hair is gone?" he said, with an air almost of idiocy.

"You needn't look for it," said Della. "It's sold, I tell you—sold and gone, too. It's Christmas Eve, boy. Be good to me, for it went for you. Maybe the hairs of my head were numbered," she went on with a sudden serious sweetness, "but nobody could ever count my love for you. Shall I put the chops on, Jim?"

Out of his trance Jim seemed quickly to wake. He enfolded

his Della. For ten seconds let us regard with discreet scrutiny some inconsequential object in the other direction. Eight dollars a week or a million a year—what is the difference? A mathematician or a wit would give you the wrong answer. The magi brought valuable gifts, but that was not among them. This dark assertion will be illuminated later on.

Jim drew a package from his overcoat pocket and threw it upon the table.

"Don't make any mistake, Dell," he said, "about me. I don't think there's anything in the way of a haircut or a shave or a shampoo that could make me like my girl any less. But if you'll unwrap that package you may see why you had me going a while at first."

White fingers and nimble tore at the string and paper. And then an ecstatic scream of joy; and then, alas! a quick feminine change to hysterical tears and wails, necessitating the immediate employment of all the comforting powers of the lord of the flat.

For there lay The Combs—the set of combs, side and back, that Della had worshipped for long in a Broadway window. Beautiful combs, pure tortoise shell, with jewelled rims—just the shade to wear in the beautiful vanished hair. They were expensive combs, she knew, and her heart had simply craved and yearned over them without the least hope of possession. And now, they were hers, but the tresses that should have adorned the coveted adornments were gone.

But she hugged them to her bosom, and at length she was able to look up with dim eyes and a smile and say: "My hair grows so fast, Jim!"

And then Della leaped up like a little singed cat and cried, "Oh, oh!"

Jim had not yet seen his beautiful present. She held it out to him eagerly upon her open palm. The dull precious metal seemed to flash with a reflection of her bright and ardent spirit.

"Isn't it a dandy, Jim? I hunted all over town to find it. You'll have to look at the time a hundred times a day now. Give me your watch. I want to see how it looks on it."

Instead of obeying, Jim tumbled down on the couch and put his hands under the back of his head and smiled.

"Dell," said he, "let's put our Christmas presents away and keep 'em a while. They're too nice to use just at present. I sold the watch to get the money to buy your combs. And now suppose you put the chops on."

The magi, as you know, were wise men—wonderfully wise men—who brought gifts to the Babe in the manger. They invented the art of giving Christmas presents. Being wise, their gifts were no doubt wise ones, possibly bearing the privilege of exchange in case of duplication. And here I have lamely related to you the uneventful chronicle of two foolish children in a flat who most unwisely sacrificed for each other the greatest treasures of their house. But in a last word to the wise of these days let it be said that of all who give gifts these two were the wisest. Of all who give and receive gifts, such as they are wisest. Everywhere they are wisest. They are the magi.

AUSTRIA

Silent Night

JOSEPH MOHR   **FRANZ GRUBER**

Stil - le Nacht, hei-li-ge Nacht! Al-les schläft, ein-sam wacht nur das trau-te, hoch - hei - li - ge Paar Hol-der Kna-be im-lo-cki-gen Haar, schlaf in himm-li-scher Ruh, schlaf in himm-li-scher Ruh!

Silent night, holy night,
All is calm, all is bright
Round yon Virgin Mother and Child.
Holy Infant so tender and mild.
Sleep in heavenly peace,
Sleep in heavenly peace!

The Carpenter's Christmas

PETER K. ROSEGGER
(Translated by Eric Posselt)

AT LAST it was over, this vigorous sweeping and scrubbing and chasing of dirt, this week-long turmoil during which nothing, not a piece of furniture, not a single wall decoration, remained in its place, until every piece of wood had been cleaned, every stone whitewashed, every bit of metal polished. Now the house shone in purest cleanliness.

The calm after a storm has a solemn effect in any case, but particularly when the Christ child is about to arrive. Somewhere in the house stands the cradle in which the God child sleeps. Those who wear shoes take them off; and those in their stocking feet must walk on tiptoe, for—He sleeps.

The goodwife bustled around in her rooms purposefully; she had to see that everything was right without marking the floor; check all the chests and closets and windows without touching anything, so that everything would retain its pristine beauty. The wind rattled the windowpanes, blowing snow into every nook and cranny, and the darkness of the skies almost turned the room into night. In the living room, on a table covered with white linen, were a crucifix, a burning blessed candle, and a crock holding a branch cut from the cherry tree three weeks ago on St. Barbara's Day, which was to bloom that night. Its buds glistened and swelled and would burst into flower any moment.

The goodwife ran to the door, opened it softly, raised her forefinger and hissed, "Pssst!" into the kitchen, where the servant girl wasn't quiet enough with the dishes. "Pssst! The Christ child is asleep!"

The woman was in a deeply pious mood. Her graying hair was wound around her head in two braids; she had donned her red kerchief and her silk apron. With a rosary in her folded hands she sat in the armchair next to the table and could think of nothing except: Christmas Eve! The Christ child!

Suddenly there was a noise in the corner. Her husband, the carpenter, who was lying on the bench against the wall, turned around and bumped his elbow so hard against the back rest of the chair that it crashed to the floor.

"Pssst!" she hissed, getting up. "Man alive, but what a restless person you are!"

"I? Restless?" He brushed his hand over his face. "Can't a person sleep any more? Can't you leave me alone?"

"If you don't want to pray, you should at least be quiet, man. And you shouldn't sleep, either!"

"But, old lady, when a man sleeps he makes the least noise."

"So you think! That's when you make the most noise, when you sleep! If you're not upsetting a chair beating about with your arms you're poking a hole in the wall. Anyone would think there were at least two sawmills and a threshing machine in here."

"Yea, the sawmills and that threshing machine ought to be turned off on Christmas Eve," he answered calmly, sitting up.

"Oh, don't talk nonsense, please! Here, find yourself a nice Christmas prayer!" She reached for the prayer book on the shelf, wiped the old, worn binding with her apron—yes, it was already dusty again!—and laid it on the table.

"What's the matter with you?" he asked tranquilly. "When they ring the bell, I'll pray all right. Just now I want to sleep some more."

"Stop arguing!" she cried impatiently, kicking at a footstool below the table.

He looked at her and grinned. "Woman," he said. "Not even old age helps you—you simply won't change!"

"You're the one to talk!" she answered. "A man ought to remember at least on a day like this that he has Holy Water on him. Haven't you any piety in you at all? Don't you know that tomorrow is Christmas?"

"Am I doing anything wrong?"

"Nor are you doing anything right, either. Go on, find that Christmas prayer!"

"I've never let anyone order me to be pious. If it doesn't come by itself . . ."

"Come by itself? To you? Mary Joseph, that'd be a long wait! All week long you are so unchristian that it's a scandal. Holidays are made for piety!"

"Oh, phhhht!" the carpenter replied crossly. "If a man works hard all week and does his duty in God's name and does nobody any wrong, he's supposed to be extra-pious on Sundays, eh? Why, woman, how is a man to do that?"

"Pray, I said, and keep quiet! Holy Christ will be awakened soon enough when He comes to judge the quick and the dead. . . . Jesus Mary, what's that?!"

For a moment it was quite dark in the room, as if a black cloth had been drawn across the window; then, a heavy thud, and the wild whirling of the snow outside. The carpenter went to the window and looked out. The storm had broken off a heavy limb from the old fir tree standing in front of the house.

"Oh God, oh God, what a day!" the woman whined, wringing her hands. "That's a bad sign for a year without peace!"

"If the devil doesn't fetch you, it'll be just that," the carpenter growled amiably.

"Today I refuse to argue with you!" she answered with cold superiority. "But just you wait until the day is over. Then you'll see whom the devil will fetch!"

She took the little vessel of holy water from the door-jamb and sprinkled everything in the room, especially her husband. He stared at her grumpily and refused to stir.

"He doesn't even make the sign of the cross when he is sprinkled with holy water!"

She rushed to the kitchen, returned with a basin of glowing embers, sprinkled incense over it and carried it around, according to the old Christmas custom, close to the table, to the bed and, finally, to her husband, whose nostrils the incense attacked so vehemently that he began to curse and opened a window.

He opened the window just in time. From the road, over the whistling of the wind, came excited voices. The wind had done quite a bit of damage in the village. "Ditch-Cenzi's" roof had been torn off so that you could look from above it into the crawling children's warren.

"That's because they don't pray, those people," the carpenter's wife sneered. "Mary Joseph, that's how it is in this world. The entire Christmas Eve spoiled! And instead of saying his Christmas prayers now, he runs away! Who, I ask you, is to protect us, if not our dear Lord in heaven?"

"Ditch-Cenzi" was a widow with three small children, the oldest of which was sick in bed with scarlet fever. She wasn't much liked in the village and it was said that in the fall she sometimes harvested potatoes where she hadn't planted any. Now the roof of her hut was torn down, with the shingles lying in the road. Cenzi stumbled around with her children in the darkness and succeeded, just barely succeeded, in placing them with neighbors. Nobody wanted to harbor the child sick with scarlet fever until the teacher offered to take it in; but the teacher was ruled out because he might carry the infection into the school. The childless wife of the carpenter, too, was approached, but she didn't want her Christmas Eve spoiled by a sick child. Finally, the village priest remembered that He who was expected that very night had said that whoever takes in a child, takes in Him—even though he wasn't quite certain how the quotation really ran. And so, with kindness and the help of the quotation, he arranged with his housekeeper for the sick child to stay at the vicarage until the roof of the old home could be fixed at least temporarily.

The carpenter had gone outside. His voice was louder than

the wind as he called together his neighbors and his journeymen. They came with ladders, tools and boards. There was a hammering and sawing in the village that lasted all night under the light of the improvised torches—very much to the horror of Mrs. Carpenter, who esteemed the holy calm and heavenly peace of this night above all else.

"How can the cherry branch bloom in all this turmoil? And how is the Christ child to rest?"

When the bells in the church tower began to chime for Midnight Mass the men still shouted and hammered on Ditch-Cenzi's roof. And while the parish sang in the church, the pounding and the clanking of nails and tools still vied so with the noise of the storm that the women, thus cheated out of their Christmas humor, were positively horrified. At last, when all the bells tolled in unison and the organ jubilated at the high point of the Midnight Mass, the men who were helping to build the roof jumped down and strolled into the church, too; and the carpenter found himself alone with two of his journeymen on the skeleton of the roof. The storm seemed to blow harder now, to tear down again what the hands of men had just put up.

The carpenter had expected to have the roof ready before morning. When he saw that most of the others had deserted him and that even the boys who had held the torches had thrown them in the snow and run to church, he began to curse mightily.

"To —— with these —— hypocrites! I like that! Here they practically chew off the toes of our good Lord, and in the meantime these poor wretches can go and die with the cold. Who cares? They squat around the corners of the church until they rot. He up there in heaven can really be proud of this brood! Hear them sing, 'Praise God in the highest!' They kiss the waxen image of the Christ child and cuddle it like a doll—and let these poor little human creatures—croak, I almost said, God forgive me my sins!"

When Midnight Mass was over and the people came out of the church, the carpenter was still cursing and kicking up on his roof. One man said to the other, "Poor fellow, he'll go completely mad if we don't help him; and maybe we are a little to blame for his swearing at that! Come on, let's pitch in. We can have that roof up in less than an hour."

Then another planted himself firmly in front of the speaker and said: "Do you really think, neighbor, that I would be so unchristian as to work on Holy Christmas Morn?" But his manner was so overbearing that the effect was far from what he intended.

"Did you hear that one?" someone asked. "In the face of such hypocrisy, I prefer the carpenter and all his cussing; and I for one am going to help him finish that roof!"

Others joined him. The torches were lit again and the sawing and hammering began once more with such renewed vigor that the carpenter's wife, in desperation, covered both her ears with her hands.

"You can't sleep and you can't pray with all this noise going on. And that—that heathen husband of mine prefers this beggar woman to our Jesus Child, so that he won't even let Him rest in His cradle. . . . God forgive him!"

On Christmas day when the sun rose, the icy wind still rushed over the rooftops, and over many a gable snow clouds still danced. But the roof of the Ditch-Cenzi house was fixed and nailed down tight, a good fire crackled in her stove, and the woman with her children had returned to their home. The carpenter was lying on his bed, jacket and boots and all, snoring with a right good will. His wife stood in the doorway, staring at him in disgust.

She herself could not settle down. She was miserable. Even before the solemn High Mass she went over to the vicarage, but she could hardly say a single word between her sobs. What an unhappy woman she was, she finally managed to stammer, to have such a husband! True, he was usually quiet and industrious, but he simply had no religion! Just no religion at all! And if she were to live to be a hundred, she would never forget that night!

"Not a single Our Father did he say, nor did he welcome the Christ Child with so much as a single little prayer! What an end such a man will come to! Even this morning people are going from house to house telling each other that they have never heard anyone curse as much as this husband of mine on Holy Night! You must have heard it yourself, Your Reverence, after Midnight Mass! I was actually shivering in my soul!"

The priest sat with his hands folded in his lap and smiled benevolently at the distracted woman.

"To be sure, I heard something," he said. "But I thought it was a prayer!"

"Prayer?" the woman moaned, raising her hands and folding them high above her head, then letting them fall again as if she had had a stroke.

"My dear woman," the priest replied. "Some people have queer ways of praying. The Jews, for example. They wind their prayer-belts around their heads and arms when they pray. Others just turn the leaves of their prayer books. And still others pass the beads of their rosaries through their fingers. Well, our carpenter simply hammers nails into wooden shingles during his Our Father."

The woman again clasped her hands in despair.

"Did you say 'Our Father' Your Reverence? Some Our Father that would be! How he cursed and shouted during Holy Mass! If our dear Lord weren't so kind, the earth would have opened up and swallowed him!"

"I admit," the priest replied, "that his words may have been chosen somewhat—unfortunately. But his intentions were certainly good. And that's really what counts. All the while he was cursing and shouting, I'm sure he didn't have another thought in his head other than to provide a roof for the poor widow and her children and his conviction that other men ought to be helping him. We probably all prayed devoutly last night, but I have an idea that the carpenter's prayer with his saw and hammer pleased Our Good Lord the most."

"And now," the woman cried, "when the others are on their way to High Mass, he lies sleeping like a . . . a dormouse!"

"Let him sleep, my dear woman. Just as his work was a prayer, so is his rest."

As the carpenter's wife departed she kept shaking her head. She could make neither head nor tail of all this. What was the world coming to? If cursing was praying, what then was praying?

But she didn't get quite that far in her meditations.

BELGIUM

Song of the Three Kings

TRADITIONAL

Daer kwa-men dry ko-nin-gen met een sterr! Nu
wie-gen, nu wie-gen, nu wie-gen al wy! Uyt vrem-de lan-den, het
was zoo verr! Nu wie-gen al wy. Toen wa-ren zy bly. Al
on-zen troost en onz' toe-vlcet, 'tis Ma-ri-a zoet!

There were once three kings who followed a star—
Let us raise our voice and sing and rejoice!—
Their journey was long, for they came from afar.
Let us raise our voice and sing and rejoice,
And let us hasten on dancing feet
To Mary sweet!

The Triptych of the Three Kings

FELIX TIMMERMANS
(Translated by Helmut Ripperger)

CENTER PIECE

THE DAY before, towards dusk, a creaky little kermis wagon passed down the street. It was drawn through the falling snow by an old man and a dog. Through the window pane, one saw the pale face of a young, slender woman. Her eyes were large and troubled. They had gone by, and those who had seen them thought no more about it. The day after was Christmas and the air stood frozen crystal clear, pale blue over the wide world bedecked with white fur.

The lame shepherd Suskewiet, the eel-fisher Pitjevogel with his bald head, and the bleary-eyed beggar Schrobberbeeck went from house to house dressed as the three Holy Kings. With them they carried a cardboard star which turned on a wooden pole, a stocking to hold the money they collected and a double-sack for food. They had turned their shabby coats inside out. The shepherd had on a high hat, Schrobberbeeck wore a crown of flowers left over from the last procession, and Pitjevogel, who turned the star, had smeared his face with shoe blacking.

It had been a good year with a fat harvest. Every peasant had a pig in brine, and now they sat puffing at their pipes with their paunches before the warm stoves, and, care-free, awaited the coming of spring.

Reprinted by permission of The Morrill Press.

Suskewiet, the shepherd, knew such lovely pious songs of olden days, Pitjevogel turned the star with such regularity, and the beggar made such pitiful, convincing beggar's eyes, that when the red moon came up, the foot of the stocking was filled with money and the sack was blown up like a bellows. It was full of bread, ham bones, apples, pears, and sausage.

They were in the best of spirits and nudged each other with their elbows. They could already taste the long swigs of "vitriol" they would enjoy later in the evening in the Water Nymph. They would round out their empty bellies with the good tasty food and make them so taut that one could squash a flea on them.

It was not until the peasants had put out their lamps and had gone yawning to bed, that they stopped their singing and began to count their money in the clear moonlight. Boy, O boy! Gin for a whole week! And they could even buy some fresh meat and tobacco as well.

With the star on his shoulder, the black Pitjevogel stamped quickly ahead and the other two followed, their mouths watering. Gradually a strange feeling of oppression came over their rough souls. They were silent. Was it because of all the white snow on which the pale moon stared down so fixedly? Or was it the mighty, ghost-like shadows of the trees? Or was it because of their own shadows? Or was it this silence, the silence of moonlit snow, in which not even an owl was heard nor a dog's bark from near or far?

But these lovers and loafers of out-of-the-way streets and unfrequented river banks and fields were not easily frightened. They had seen much that was wonderful in their life. Will-o'-the-wisps, spooks, and even real ghosts. But this was something different. Something like the choking fear at the approach of some great happiness. It closed in around their hearts.

The beggar took courage and said, "I am not afraid."

"I'm not either," said each of the others at the same time. Their voices trembled.

"Today is Christmas," comforted Pitjevogel.

"And God will be born anew," added the shepherd with childlike piety.

"Is it true that the sheep will then stand with their heads turned toward the East?" asked Schrobberbeeck.

"Yes, and the bees will sing and fly."

"And you will be able to see right through the water," said Pitjevogel, "but I have never done it."

Again there was this silence, which was different from silence. It was as if one could feel a soul trembling in the moonlight.

"Do you believe that God will really come to earth again?" the beggar asked timidly, thinking of his sins.

"Yes," said the shepherd, "but where, no one knows. . . . He only comes for one night."

Their hard shadows now ran before them and increased their fear. Suddenly they noticed that they had lost their way. It was the fault of the endless snow which had covered over the frozen streams, the roads, and the entire countryside. They stood still and looked around; all about was snow and moonlight, and here and there trees, but no house, and even the familiar mill was nowhere to be seen. They had gone astray, and in the moonlight they could see the fear in each other's eyes.

"Let us pray," begged Suskewiet, the shepherd, "then no evil can happen to us."

The beggar and the shepherd mumbled a Hail Mary. Pitjevogel began to mutter, for since his First Communion he had forgotten how to pray.

They went around a clump of bushes and it was then that Pitjevogel saw a stream of friendly light in the distance. Without saying a word, but breathing more easily, they went toward it. And suddenly a miracle happened. All three saw and heard it but they did not dare to speak of it. They heard the humming of bees and under the snow, where the ditches were, it was as light as if lamps were burning there. And against a row of dreaming willows there stood a lame kermis wagon and candle-light shone from its window.

Pitjevogel climbed up the small steps and knocked. A friendly

old man with a beard opened the door. He did not seem astonished at their strange dress, the star, or the black face.

"We have come to ask you the way," Pitjevogel stammered.

"The way is here," said the man, "come in."

Amazed at this answer they followed obediently and in the
corner of the cold empty wagon they saw a young woman. She
wore a blue hooded mantle and held a very small, new-born
babe at her breast. A large, yellow dog lay at her side with his
faithful head on her lean knees. Her eyes were dreaming in sadness, but, as she saw the men, they filled with friendliness and
confidence. Even the little child, whose head was still covered
with down and whose eyes were like little slits, laughed at them
and seemed particularly pleased with the black face of Pitjevogel.

Schrobberbeeck saw the shepherd kneel down and take off
his high hat. He too knelt down and took the procession crown
from his head and suddenly began to regret the many sins that
were on his conscience. And then Pitjevogel bent his knee as
well. And as they knelt, sweet voices swelled about them and a
heavenly happiness, greater than any joy, filled them. And none
of them knew why.

In the meantime the old man tried to start a fire in the
small iron stove. Pitjevogel seeing that it would not work, asked
eagerly: "May I help you?"

"It is no use, the wood is wet," the man replied.

"But have you no coals?"

"We have no money," said the old man sadly.

"What do you eat then?" asked the shepherd.

"We have nothing to eat."

Filled with confusion and compassion, the Kings looked at
the old man and the young woman, at the child and the bony
dog. Then they looked at each other. Their thoughts were as
one and lo, the stocking with its money was emptied into the
lap of the woman, and the sack of food was turned inside out
and all that was in it was laid on the shaky little table. Eagerly
the old man reached for the bread and gave the young woman

a rosy apple. She turned it before the laughing eyes of the child
before she bit into it.

"We thank you," said the old man. "God will reward you."

Once again they were under way on the road which they now
knew so well and which led direct to the Water Nymph. But
the stocking was rolled up in Suskewiet's pocket and the sack
was empty. They hadn't a cent or a crumb.

"Do you know why we gave all of our earnings to these poor
people?" asked Pitjevogel.

"No," said the others.

"I don't either," Pitjevogel replied.

A little later the shepherd said, "I think I know why. Couldn't
the child have been God?"

"What are you thinking of?" laughed the eel-fisher. "God
wears a white mantle with borders of gold, and He has a beard
and wears a crown, as in Church."

"But formerly He was born in a stable at Christmas," asserted
the shepherd.

"Yes, formerly," said Pitjevogel, "but that was a hundred
years ago and even longer."

"But why did we give everything away then?"

"I'm breaking my head about that, too," said the beggar
whose stomach began to rumble.

Silently, with lips that thirsted for a generous swallow of gin
and longed for meat thickly spread with mustard, they passed
by the Water Nymph. It was still lighted and they heard singing and the sounds of a harmonica.

Pitjevogel gave the star to the shepherd, whose task it was to
keep it, and without saying a single word, but with content-
ment in their hearts, they parted at the crossroads, each one
going to his bed. The shepherd went to his sheep, the beggar
to his hut of straw, and Pitjevogel to his garret into which the
snow drifted.

LEFT WING

Today it was again Christmas. Suskewiet, the shepherd, who
each year with Pitjevogel and Schrobberbeeck had made the

rounds, dressed as the three Holy Kings, going from house to house with a cardboard star and singing lovely old songs, lay stretched out, sick in bed, and over him was the shadow of death. In the corner, leaning against the wall, was the pole with its colored star and there also hung a crown made of tin.

He lay, where he always lay, in the sheep stall. Through a little window next his bed he could look out far over the snow-covered country, over which the half-moon like a silver shuttle wove the lovely star dress. It was the first time that he could not accompany his comrades at Christmas. Now the two of them were under way but still they sang, "We are the three kings with their star."

Since the miracle of last year, when they had come upon a small kermis wagon on their rounds, and had found there a poor man, a young woman, and a new-born child, and for some unknown reason, and in a spirit of reverence they had never known before, they had knelt down and offered all the money and food they had collected, since that time Suskewiet had become a different person. For he had felt certain that this little child had been God Who came anew to the world each year at Christmas for one day. Oh, he remembered so well how they had lost their way in the holy hour, how they had seen light like burning lamps under the snow, and how they had heard bees singing in the air. How afraid they had been and what a heavenly sweetness had come over him and the others as well, when they saw the little child. How suddenly and with great emotion, without consulting one another, they had offered up their hard-earned food and pennies.

And had they not heard the poor man say, as Pitjevogel had asked him for the way, "The way is here"? Surely it had been the Holy Family. He had told the priest about it, but he had chased him out of doors and the sexton had said disdainfully that the shepherd was only a foundling and that his brains had frozen. Wherever he tried to tell that he had seen the Holy Family they laughed at him. His two comrades had already forgotten the impression of that hour. When they did think of it, they merely said, " 'Twas strange, 'twas strange." But beyond that they did not bother about it and they sinned more each day in order to get money and gin.

But Suskewiet had changed his life from the ground up. There had always been a faint spark of piety smoldering in his heart, but now it flamed up to a white heat which filled him with heavenly transport and lovely sweet feelings so that his body was hardly on earth. He neglected his body and forgot to tend his sheep. He knelt before the wayside shrines for hours on end, sang pious songs, and prayed childish prayers. He did penance, as well, to atone for his former sins, and allowed nothing to stop him, when it froze, from chopping open the ice and standing with his bare feet in the bitter cold water. And as he dragged his lame leg behind his herd, he constantly said his rosary. When he spoke with the peasants, he no longer talked of the weather and the potatoes, but of the Mother of God and the Christ Child, and of the blackness of sin. People who formerly had called him simple, now thought him fully mad and avoided him. His stories, they said, were good enough for the priest but not for one who ran about in ordinary clothes.

With great longing old Suskewiet awaited the new Christmas feast. It had been his duty to take care of the star and to freshen it up each year. This time, too, he had pasted it over with colored paper and chocolate tinfoil and decorated it with little golden roses that had been left over from a golden wedding. He did not wish to wear the high hat any longer, for he had found a piece of tin which the tinsmith had made into a pointed crown. He would look much better in that. He was pottering around with these when his two friends came to talk with him, for they had heard that three Kings would make the rounds and that they had a star with a little bell and for this reason they would probably earn more pennies.

But Suskewiet looked at them suspiciously, and said, "I will only go with you with the star if you agree to give all the money and food we collect to the poor."

"Are you mad?" cried Pitjevogel, the eel-fisher.

"Are we not poor enough?" asked Schrobberbeeck, the beggar with the bleary eyes.

"No," said Suskewiet, "all that you have you must give to God. And whether we give it to God or to the poor is all the same."

"Then we will stay home," said Schrobberbeeck. "Do you think that I am going to sing myself hoarse for others? One does that once and not again."

"I know something better," said the sly Pitjevogel. "We will make a star of our own. Or do you think we can't? 'Bye, mad Sus."

"Do what you want to," the shepherd called after them, "but with this star, with which we found God, you won't beg any money in order to sin."

The heavens painted the first snow over the earth and Suskewiet felt himself filled with spiritual ecstasy. He alone would now go from house to house and collect money for the poor. But Suskewiet became ill and could no longer get up from his straw sack.

Christmas approached. The shepherd received the Last Sacraments. He had seen the priest with his surplice of gold come and go. It was evening and the moon came up to look at the white world. The tears ran down Suskewiet's stubbly cheeks because he could not celebrate Christmas for the benefit of the poor. For forty-four years the star had heard him sing his songs. Now death had come to him. His heart was barely alive, but now and then his little reason flickered up. The people from the farm had sat with him for a while, but when he had fallen asleep they had gone back to the house where the yule log burned and waffles were baking. Sadly he heard their joyous noise. A clarionet was playing and songs were being sung. He had but two hours to live and he begged Heaven to allow him to see the holy hour pass.

His pale, thin face lay at an angle so that he could see the moon in the sky and the star that gleamed in the corner. His hands lay bare, large and shrivelled. The fingers were without life. Lost as he had come to earth, a foundling, now he was to die alone and forsaken. Only the good sheep remained with him and lifted their heads from time to time over the side of their stall. The moon climbed higher and higher and constantly became smaller but clear as silver. Suskewiet asked for but one thing, the grace to be allowed to go through one more Christmas hour.

He lay there for a long time. Finally he saw here and there by the mill, women in heavy hooded mantles with lanterns in their hands, going toward the village. The noise from the farm house had subsided. Later he heard the chiming of bells and the toning of an organ. At first he could not believe his ears, for the church was three-quarters of an hour away! But it was not an illusion. An organ was playing! Soft, sustained, singing tones swelled up, increasing with emotion and deep reverence. He had never heard anything so lovely in all his life. Before he could recover from his astonishment, he heard the sheep begin to bleat and, in the moonlight, he saw that they had turned their heads to the East.

"It is the holy hour," murmured Suskewiet, trembling with excitement. "God, God, my star!"

He wished to get up and fetch the star, but he could not. He exerted all his strength, pressed the cover with his feet against the foot of the bed, and then pulled himself up by means of the sheet which was stretched taut. He broke forth into a racking cough, and as it subsided, with the sweat pouring from his forehead, he made a slight headway and put his lean legs over the side of the bed. He burst into another fit of coughing but without waiting for it to cease, he stood upright, leaned against the wall, and then step by step, with bent knees, he went toward the star. At last he sat on his bed again, the tin crown on his head and the star in his arm.

When he had rested a short while, he took hold of the string and looking out into the moonlit night he sang in a monotone, accompanied by the soft tones of the mysterious organ:

> We are the three kings with their star,
> Who have come here from lands afar,
> We went and searched over hill and dale,
> Over mountains, valleys, glens and vale,
> And where the star stood still,
> We entered with good will.

The tears ran down his cheeks, his body shook with spasms and now and again the flame of his transfigured soul gleamed from his dim eyes.

But what or who was that in the distance? A stream of light came over the moonlit snow; nearer and nearer it came, straight ahead without swerving to right or left. Astonished, Suskewiet held his breath and thoughtlessly continued to pull at the string and turn the star round and round. It came nearer and nearer. Finally it seemed to be a small child in a little, white shirt, and with bare feet. He carried a terrestrial globe in his hand, and his sweet, blue-eyed face and golden hair were surrounded by a sort of rainbow-colored dawn.

"Who is that?" murmured Suskewiet. "It seems to me I have seen the little child before."

The child came straight toward him and disappeared for a moment under the window. Then the door opened. Before him stood the little child, clean and fresh as a wild rose. Suddenly the stall was filled with the scent of roses.

"Good day, Suskewiet," said the little child, smiling kindly. "Since you can no longer come to me, I have come to you. Do you remember me?"

A look of strange wonderment came over Suskewiet, and his smile revealed his two black, broken teeth. He nodded joyfully, but could not say a single word, so great was his emotion, while tears hung from the grey stubbly hairs of his cheeks.

"Do you?" said the child. "Then keep on with your song. I love to hear it."

And Suskewiet, filled with awe, took hold of the string and sang while his eyes blinked with heavenly ecstasy:

> Maria she was sore afraid,
> When she had heard the noise;
> She thought that Herod now had come,
> To seek her little child,
> She thought that Herod now had come
> To snatch her sweetest lamb.

And lo, the black apple tree which stood outside was not white with snow but white with delicate apple blossoms. And all the sheep stood there and looked over the side of the stall, and those in the rear, stood up on the backs of those in front.

"Come," said the little child, "will you come to our house?"

"O yes, yes," laughed Suskewiet. Suddenly he felt himself well again. He wanted to put on his trousers, but he did not seem to be cold, and, what is more, he was in a great hurry. He took the star and followed the child. But he turned once more to look at his sheep that were bleating sadly.

"May they not come along?" he asked. "I am a shepherd."

"The more the merrier," said the child.

"Then come along, my little ones, come."

Suskewiet opened the gate and all followed, each one pressing against the other. And they went out into the silvery, white night. In his little, warm hand the child held that of the shepherd, and led the old man through the untrodden snow. He carried the star which gleamed in the moonlight, and behind him came the sheep with heads bent in reverence.

"It is back there," said the little child, and pointed in the distance to a golden palace that reared its towers and domes high over a garden filled with spring flowers.

"O, how lovely, how lovely!" said Suskewiet, transported, and turning to his sheep. "There the grass will be much better, my little ones."

And then they entered in.

Schrobberbeeck and Pitjevogel returned from their rounds. They were drunk with the many glasses of gin they had had on their way. Their crown was crooked and the star was bent. Arm in arm they staggered along singing popular songs. Their way led them past the farm yard.

"O," shouted Pitjevogel, "let us shake our money in his ears. Not giving us his star."

But as they looked through the window, they saw Suskewiet sitting on his bed, dead. The tin crown was on his head and over it shone the lovely star. And the two men ran away in fright, leaving their broken star behind them.

The next day they found Suskewiet. All the sheep were grazing in the field. In the stall one smelled the scent of roses.

RIGHT WING

Although the moonlight flooded the snow-buried countryside, spreading a light of its own, Schrobberbeeck, the beggar, took a lighted lantern with him as he went to Midnight Mass. He did it because he was afraid of God. It was not as in former years when on this day he and his friends went from house to house dressed as the three Kings with their star. This was the day he had most fun and pocketed the most pennies.

The fear of Christmas had got into him. It had started two years ago when Pitjevogel, the fisherman, and Suskewiet, the shepherd, and he had been making their rounds as the three Kings and had seen the Holy Family in a kermis wagon. The next year he had gone the rounds with Pitjevogel. Upon their return, filled with hot gin, they had come upon Suskewiet who had turned pious since the meeting with the Holy Family, dead upon his bed, a star in his hands and surrounded by a heavenly light.

The Christmas night wanted something from him. He felt God's hand at work. Fear constantly pressed around his heart, and, because he was afraid, he now went to church every Sunday. Each time he feared that something holy would happen to him and he was more afraid of that than of the devil with whom Pitjevogel now associated. People were saying that in the past summer a terrific storm had broken out while the fisherman was bathing in the Nethe. His clothes had been carried off and, in a great fright, Pitjevogel ran through the fields until he came to the house of an unfrocked priest who had dealings with the devil. Pitjevogel was so terrible to behold that the priest thought he was the devil himself and said to him, "Welcome, Satan!"

"I am only Pitjevogel," said the fisherman shyly. But the

priest had given himself away and now he taught Pitjevogel black magic with the help of a book called "The Black Ambrosius."

Since that day, the fisherman spent as many silver dollars as one could imagine; but each evening before sundown he had to be in his house. Formerly, in the sultry summer nights when the eels were biting, Pitjevogel sat in his boat fishing; but now when the first star appeared in the sky nothing was to be seen of him. No amusement was great enough to tempt him out of doors when evening set in.

And Schrobberbeeck, who had always thought much of Pitjevogel, for the fellow could make one laugh until one's sides split, avoided him, so as not to draw God's attention to himself.

But he did not steal less than usual, for that was deep in his bones. He never succeeded in letting anything lie which he could take with him. And as was his wont, he wandered about the neighborhood, begged at each door and screwed up the blue of his inflamed eyes so that nothing more was to be seen but the yellow-white, and mumbled an "Our Father."

Now he had secured a house, a little wooden hut in which one of the peasants had formerly kept his tools. It was no longer in use but Schrobberbeeck had taken possession of it, slept and lived there, and stored in it all he could beg and steal. He even had a piece of broken mirror in which he could see his greyish-red face with its bright red stubbly beard. Though the rain came through the roof of the hut and the winds shook and rattled it as if it were a hanging sideboard, he had the proud feeling of owning a house, and he had planted a little garden as big as a table in which to grow radishes. But he, too, did not appear at night for fear of the holy thing which seemed to dog his steps.

When he begged throughout the countryside, he always took off his greasy hat before each statue and picture of Our Lady and he did it each time for the same reason, in order to be in the good graces of God. And there were many statues in the vicinity, at least twenty. They stood about in their cloaks of stone, wood, and plaster. One in a little box which hung in a tree, another on a tree stump, and others again in little stone shrines. And as he repeated his greetings day after day he came to know them all. He knew by heart what color they were, how big they were, their names, and what they were good for. He knew them all from the large Our Lady of the Seven Sorrows in the Béguine Woods, to Our Lady of Rest who was no larger than a finger and who stood in the hollow of a willow tree which had been split by lightning. He also knew the Christ on the Cross at the Big Pond where the cows drank.

Filled with fear, he had awaited Christmas, for he was afraid that something holy would happen to him. First he had thought of spending the night in the Water Nymph. In an inn, where people swear and drink gin, God will not come, he thought. But then he was afraid that if he went there, the punishment would not be lacking another night. O, where was his beggar's peace? Did he not formerly live care-free and happily from day to day?

But Christmas came nearer and nearer. He did not dare to go out with a star, much as he would have liked to do so, for he was certain that it would not be good for him to play with a star, and so he thought of going to Midnight Mass. Not for love, or faith, or piety, but merely to ward off the mysterious. And to hearten himself in the moonlit solitude, he lighted the unnecessary lantern and started off for the distant church. He would have preferred to walk with his eyes shut in order not to see anything of the strange, solemn, snowy night that seemed to stare at him like a cat's eye flecked with sulphur.

Away in the distance the bell droned and he looked about for the others who must be going to Mass but he saw no trace of anyone. He was all alone on the road. His heart began to hammer and he felt himself getting smaller and smaller as if he were drowning in the moonlit, white solitude. When he passed the black, snow-covered mill, the distance seemed again as far, and fear pressed his heart as a vise. He stepped quickly as he could but did not dare to run. Why did he not dare to run?

Suddenly he came to the tree in which Our Lady of Refuge hung, a little porcelain figure with golden lilies on her dress.

She gave him confidence and he pulled off his hat and looked up beseechingly. But Our Lady was no longer there! Only a moment ago when he had gone to fetch oil for his lantern, she had still stood in her little wooden box! "Fallen down," he thought. But the snow lay smooth and untouched though he noticed that a little mouse must have run across the snow for he could see traces of dainty steps.

"It must have been stolen," said Schrobberbeeck, as he hurried on.

He crossed the road in order to reach the church more quickly. And he thought of greeting Our Lady of Devotion who stood on the bridge on the other side of the stream. But she, too, was gone! Astonished, he stood still. The sounds of the bell died out, and the silence again pressed down over the land, this mysterious silence. He moved his lantern about and again he saw the traces of tiny steps in the snow.

Beads of perspiration appeared on his forehead. And now he began to run. O, now the miracle was to happen; now it would choke him. But despite all of his fear he was as curious as an old woman to see if Our Lady for a Holy Death was still in the stone shrine behind the grating. No, she too had disappeared! The scrolled pedestal of imitation marble was empty and the silver flowers stood useless under their glass domes, the waxen and silver votive offerings, and the smoky angels' heads.

Never in his life had Schrobberbeeck run so quickly. But no matter how quickly he ran he took heart to look up at the statues as he passed—they had all disappeared! Something had happened. Yes, something terribly holy had happened.

Once he had the pine woods with their hem of silver birches behind him, he could see the church with its inviting lighted windows. Any minute now it would strike twelve. He ran past the mysterious, silent pine trees. He did not dare to look up. Another half-minute and the church and the houses would appear and the danger would be over.

Suddenly, from the left, he heard a noise, coming nearer and nearer, and soon he saw a little figure, not two feet high, running breathlessly through the snow. It had on a red dress and a light blue swaying cape and seven tin swords were stuck in its panting breast!

"Our Lady of the Béguine Woods," stammered Schrobberbeeck. He thought he would drop dead of fright as the figure came up to him and addressed him in an anxious, every-day voice which had nothing Mother-of-God about it: "O, dear Mr. Schrobberbeeck, dearest friend, you always greet me when you pass me by, help me, help me. I have been running for an hour, my feet hurt me so, my heart is breaking, please carry me to my crucified Son at the Big Pond. Or I shall be too late for His Christmas feast."

Pleadingly she stretched out her arms, the cape fell in lovely folds from her shoulders and a scent of violets surrounded her. Schrobberbeeck stood rigid with fright, stuttered but could not utter a single word. The holy thing was again present in all of its awesomeness. Silently, distressed, he looked at her; his hair stood on end under his hat, and his eyes bulged forth from their inflamed lids.

But Our Lady continued to plead, "O, carry me, Mr. Schrobberbeeck. You can run quickly and I am light as a feather. If I must go alone it will take at least an hour and the feast will be over. O, help me, I will do anything for you. You see, I couldn't get away. A man knelt before my shrine and prayed. Someone who had sold his soul to the devil for a few dollars, someone who had run to an exiled priest during a storm and had fallen in with black magic. Dear God, how he prayed in the dead of night for my help, to save him from the devil who stood behind him like a snake on the tip of its tail. I had to help him first, didn't I, Schrobberbeeck? O, I had to battle so hard with the snake in order to save the man."

"Has Pitjevogel been saved then?" Schrobberbeeck asked suddenly with confidence.

"Yes," said Our Lady of the Seven Sorrows, "but now carry me to my Son at the Big Pond."

A lovely light transfixed Schrobberbeeck's soul. "Dearest dear Lady," he sighed, "I do not dare to carry you, for my soul is as black as my feet."

"I will shine on it till it gleams; but now carry me, carry me."

"If that's all," said Schrobberbeeck, and he picked up Our Lady and carried her as lightly as a child in his arms and ran as quickly as his long legs would let him, through the dark pine woods, across the field and toward the Big Pond. In the distance stood the Cross in a mild light.

"Now put me down, and many thanks, Schrobberbeeck."

Distraught, he put her down and she quickly ran away.

It seemed to Schrobberbeeck as if he had gone to heaven, for his heart had been so light while he was carrying the statue. Thoughtlessly he ran on, but what did he see! He knelt down in ecstasy. The Cross was all alight, the Christ seemed to be a living body, and in a semi-circle stood all of the statues of Our Lady of the vicinity each in its size, but now in real, not painted, wooden or stone dresses.

He knew them all. The porcelain one of Refuge, the one of plaster for Devotion, the one of Five Wounds, the one for a Holy Death, the one of the Red Roses, the one of Lovers, the one for our Daily Bread, the one for Purgatory, one for each the Wheat, the Potatoes, the Rain, even our Lady of Rest, large as a finger, who stood way in front because she was so small. All of them stood there and waited. They had turned their heads toward the pine woods and as they saw Our Lady of the Seven Sorrows come running up, joyous movement arose among the twenty-five living statues. When Our Lady of the Seven Sorrows had taken her place in the center, they all knelt down, they lifted their arms in praise to the Son of all of them Who opened His beautiful eyes and looked at them lovingly.

In the circle of light, Schrobberbeeck saw how the wound in the breast of the Lord Jesus burst like a grape and slowly began to bleed. And Schrobberbeeck begged that it might always remain so. For this was heaven!

The next day all of Our Ladies stood once again in their wooden and stone garments in their boxes, trees, and shrines.

But in front of the shrine of Our Lady of the Seven Sorrows in the Béguine Woods, they found Pitjevogel dead on his knees, his hands still tightly grasping the iron bars of the grating. A yellow snake, of which there are many in the Béguine Woods, lay dead next him with its belly slit open, terrible to behold.

Schrobberbeeck had now become quite a different person in his heart. He had lost all of his fears and longed for more of such solemn moments. At night he even sat awaiting them and in church, too, he looked out for them.

Outwardly he remained the same; lived in his tumbled-down hut, begged, and when he could pick up something that was not nailed down, he did not let it lie. That was in his bones and not even the strongest emotion of his soul could get that out of him.

BULGARIA

Christmas Carol

TRADITIONAL

The Virgin was in labor
Deep in the forest green,
She gave birth to the Savior
By human eyes unseen.

A golden elm was standing
Deep in the wood forlorn,
And underneath this elmtree
Is where Our Lord was born.

The Commissioner's
Christmas

DIMITR IVANOV
(Translated by Sarka B. Hrbkova)

W E'LL GET there in plenty of time, sir. Yes, we'll get there yet before daylight's gone. See — there's the village over yonder at the foot of the hill! Do you see it? As soon as we cross that low ridge we can say we're there." And the young driver, swinging his whip above the backs of his lean horses, shouted lustily to spur them on: "Vyee hey! Vyee! Sirs!"

The four wheels of the light coach splattered worse than ever through the soft mud of the country road. The rickety skeleton of the coach rattled dismally through the cheerless, dreary plain soaked by the late December rains.

The country lad shouted once more to his horses, settled himself more comfortably on the box, slapped his wet cap on his thick cape and, in a carefree voice, started up a gay tune.

"What's your name, boy?" inquired a fat man bundled up in a wolfskin coat, who sat inside the coach.

The lad continued his song.

"Ho, boy!" cried the man in a loud, harsh voice.

"What?" The boy turned around.

"Name! Your name? What's your name?"

"Ondra."

Reprinted by permission of Maxim Lieber.

"Ah, ah, Ondra. Clever lad, you are! All of you have become clever. Sly, you country bumpkins. You only know how to lie and deceive. And how you do put on! I watch 'em at court. Sheep—little lambkins—of innocence—but really regular wolves! They play with the judges!"

"We're just simple folk, sir, and they only slander us. You just think so, but we're really not bad like that. Our peasant people deceive only out of ignorance. Ignorance and poverty."

"Ah! So that's it! Because of poverty! Cursed clods! They complain of ignorance and poverty, and guzzle like fish!"

"You think it's prosperity they're suffering from, sir? From being overprosperous? No! Not from prosperity. Drink—guzzle? Yes, they all drink. To feel a bit happier, not because they're well off. That's something a man like you can set down in his note-book."

"Ah! It looks to me as if you, too, had had a drink, friend! You're still too young for that; your whiskers haven't sprouted yet. Those peasants of yours—just write it down—are a lost lot —lost, that's what!"

"You write it down, sir! We don't know how to write," said the boy and turning to his skinny horses, he called "Vyee, vyee, sirs!" and lapsed into deep thought.

The horses hesitated for a moment, as if they, too, were thinking.

The man put up the big collar of his wolf cloak, disappeared inside it and he, too, lost himself in meditation.

A crow with ruffled wings settled on a solitary tree beside the road and swinging on a dry twig croaked mournfully, while it, too, ruminated. Even the somber wintry weather seemed in a gray reflective mood, portending a gloomy Christmas on the morrow. Across the heavens thick scraggly storm-clouds crept and broke heavily beneath a cold blue sky. The earth was submerged in mud and moisture. The vistas of villages, streams, distant forests and mountains darkened, lifeless and distorted, before them. On the plains here and there glistened great pools, all cloudy, cold and glassy like the eyes of a corpse.

The small coach slowly wallowed through the deep soft mud, wading in, wading out, twisting and turning. A loose board on the side of it constantly, monotonously, dismally and senselessly rattled and banged mercilessly on the nerves of the corpulent gentleman in the fur coat. Finally, losing all patience, he opened his collar, thrust out his fat face, and shouted: "What is that horrible rattle? Devil take it!"

"It's only a loose clapboard, sir. It bangs away like a learned man: no sense to its rattle at all!"

"You're clever, Ondra, very clever! You know how to fool the young girls, I'll bet. You fellows marry young and have pretty wives."

The gentleman thrust back the tall collar of his fur coat in his attempt at jocularity.

"Say what you will, the married women are better! I know it! And you, sir, have an errand in our village, I take it?"

"I'm the court commissioner."

Ondra turned round and inspected his fare with a penetrating look.

"On official service, I suppose?"

"Service, of course. One of your fine fellows played a trick on me, but this time I'll fix him properly. I've got one official paper in my hands that'll catch him right. I got wind of the fact that this fellow was deceiving us—and I'll search him out in the evening. Believe me, he'll have cause to remember me and this Christmas! I'll confiscate all his rye—every grain of it! Not only to teach him what's what, but to set an example to all the rest of you not to try to fool the authorities. You cheat the merchants, you cheat the townspeople; you sell them spoiled eggs and rancid butter. But just wait, you peasant brood, you can't cheat the courts! We know how to punish you! What you need is the lash—a stout Russian knout—that's the only way to teach you! You've all become drunkards, low-down trash. You're failing to meet your taxes—you're destroyers of the State! Our patriotic interests are suffering! I wish I could be Czar for at least two days, and I'd fix you all *my* way! I'd make angels of all of you; yes, sir, angels! Pity I'm not the Czar!"

The court commissioner unbuttoned his fur coat, inside of which he squirmed like a chick breaking out of its shell.

"Oh, but Mr. Commissioner, God created the world and calculated that women don't need beards, so he didn't give them beards. He figured that an ass needs long ears, so he gave a pair to every donkey," answered Ondra with feigned simplicity.

"Stop your silly chatter and get along. It's getting dark, and I've got to get back to celebrate Christmas with my family. You charge too much, you imp! Three leu for twenty kilometers! You surely know how to skin us. Hurry up, will you: drive faster or those jades of yours will go to sleep!"

"Vyee, there! Vyee, sirs!" shouted Ondra, swinging his whip in the air.

"Sirs, you call them? Sirs! Better call them 'brothers,'" commented the commissioner in a rage.

"They'd resent that, Mr. Commissioner! I'd insult 'em if I didn't call 'em sirs. Why, they're regular gentlemen! *Their* service is official: they run on a regular schedule. In the morning they get up; at a certain hour we water them and give them their feed. Then we harness them up, they go, you might say, to their offices: they pull till evening. Have supper at a regular hour, drink water, 'read the news,' so to speak, and—sleep. Regular official life!"

"Where did you get your drinks, friend? Stop your jabbering and get on, or I'll be late. You've got a sly look, fellow, sly!"

"There're no wolves about, Mr. Commissioner, don't fear," the driver said in such a tone that the honorable court official looked round with apprehensive eyes.

"I'm not afraid of wolves, friend, but of the cold weather. I haven't time to nurse a cold."

They jogged on silently for a while.

"So you're on an official mission? Who's going to get scorched this time?" Ondra turned a serious face toward his passenger.

The commissioner waited for a while before answering. "Why shouldn't you know? Stanoycho they call him, little man with a thick neck."

"I know him. So you're going to take his rye, are you? He's

a poor fellow, Mr. Commissioner; let him off this time. It's Christmas, you know, and all that!"

"Poor fellow, yes, but a regular devil!" The commissioner lapsed into silence. Darkness was falling. The horses could barely crawl to the top of the hill beyond which lay the village. Ondra no longer urged them on, nor swung his long whip above them. He stopped his talk, he no longer sang, and was lost in meditation.

When they reached the summit and started down on the other side, night had come, but there was still no sign of the village. A cold penetrating wind blew over the land buried under the mire. Scattered clouds moved up toward the mountains. The blue vault of the frosty sky cleared up, widened and lifted itself to greater heights. Soon stars, cold and glistening, appeared on its surface. The air was perceptibly chillier. The horses plodded on slowly, sluggishly.

"Whip 'em up! Hurry up! You lazybones! We'll freeze to death!" shrieked the furious commissioner.

Ondra indifferently shouted to the horses and drowsily swung his whip over their heads, but as before they wearily, inertly dragged on the coach as if they had heard nothing at all.

Ondra was thinking of the miserable Stanoycho whose rye the commissioner was going to confiscate early next morning.

"It was you brought me this misfortune, Ondra," Stanoycho would say to him, and when he'd be through blaming him, he'd ask Ondra to join his family in their meal, and then he'd weep. Yes, he would surely weep. Stanoycho's heart was soft. Ondra knew that.

He must help the poor fellow, contrive to tell him to hide his rye overnight and sweep the granary clean, or else all the coming year he'd be stretching his lean ears in hunger. Yes, he must do something!

Nothing was distinguishable but mud—deep, thick mud. The road lost itself in the mire, and led nowhere except into more mud.

Ondra pulled up the lines and stopped the horses.

"I'm afraid we're in danger of losing our way, Mr. Commissioner!" And the lad peered intently into the darkness.

The commissioner looked gravely at the driver's face on which not a trace of his former mischief was visible.

"Boy, open your eyes, or I'll not answer for the consequences. You'll get a thrashing."

Ondra jerked the reins, swished his whip and cried, "Hold on tight, Mr. Commissioner!" Far off in the distance before them the lights of the village glimmered. The distant echoes of dogs' barking was carried to them. A few feet to the right of them glistened the pearly surface of a great pool of motionless water. The coach turned its course in that direction.

"What's that?" asked the commissioner.

"A swamp, Mr. Commissioner. The road leads right through it. It's shallow, don't be afraid. Only a few holes here and there. I usually miss 'em, whether I go by wagon or on foot. Vyee, there, sirs! Hold tight, Mr. Commissioner!"

The horses plunged into the cold water, which mirrored the starry sky. They proceeded more and more cautiously as they began to sink deeper and deeper into the mire. The dead surface of the pearl-green water broke into lively motion.

"Stop, you cattle!" cried the commissioner in terror, drawing his coat tightly round him. "You'll drown me, you fool! Can't you see the coach is filling with water! Stop! Stop!"

Ondra stopped. The coach sank in to the bottom, standing in the middle of a swamp whose margin was lost in the impenetrable blackness.

"Ho! Go ahead!" bawled Ondra to his horses. His powerful young voice reëchoed through the night. Near by some wild ducks fluttered excitedly and vanished in the dark.

"Guess we, too, have to turn into moor-hens and wade out," said Ondra thoughtfully, "or else—"

"Oh, you idiot! Just wait till we get out of this! I'll break every bone in your body! We'll drown here like rats! You ass!"

"No, we won't drown, Mr. Commissioner, we won't drown, don't be afraid. In this darkness anyone would miss the way. Just be calm," said Ondra, and began to examine the harness. Then he proceeded to buckle and unbuckle various straps, swearing loudly, tying, untying, cursing incessantly. Finally he resumed his place on the driver's seat, swung his whip and shouted, "Vyee, there! Go on!"

The horses pulled and went forward. Suddenly one of them slipped loose from the shaft and staggered ahead in the mire, free of the harness. The other horse stood still with the coach.

"Ho, you! What's happened now?" shrieked the commissioner.

"Stop, you! Dorcha, Dorcha!" called Ondra to the liberated horse, and began to coax it to come back.

But the animal, frightened by the water, turned round and warily made its way back in the direction of the shore, where it gradually lost itself to view, wholly oblivious of the pleadings of his master.

The commissioner stood up excitedly in the coach, terror written on every feature.

At that instant Ondra quickly leaped onto the other horse and, following in Dorcha's path, continued to call loudly, "Dorcha, Dorcha, wait! Come back—Dorcha, Dorcha!"

"Where are you going? Stop! What are you doing, you cattle? You crazy fool! Oh, you lousy peasant! I'll fix you!"

In the darkness only merry laughter was his response.

"Oh, you cattle, so you're leaving me here! To perish! For the beasts to devour me! Boy, don't do it, please, I beg you!" implored the commissioner in a trembling voice.

"Don't be afraid, don't be afraid, Mr. Commissioner," sounded Ondra's voice. "No wild beasts here in the swamp. Just wrap up, so you don't take cold. To-morrow morning— early, bright and early—I'll come. There's hay in the coach, make yourself a bed. I'll not charge you for the night's lodging!"

"Boy, don't joke," pleaded the commissioner. "Don't leave me! Come back! Pull me out of here!"

"It's dark, sir, very dark. I can't see a thing! And my horse has run away! How can I help you? I can't do it!"

The commissioner heard the mocking voice wafted back out of the darkness. Terrified at the prospect, alone there in the middle of the dismal swamp, he burst into tearful entreaty.

"Ondra, come back! Please—please! I'll pay you well—pay you anything! Help me out of this! I'll die here! I have children! They're waiting for me! It's Christmas! Have you no heart?" His voice broke in desperation. He listened, but no answer came. Then, as if bereft of his senses, he howled out into the unanswering darkness: "Ho, fellow! Cattle! You ox! You beast! Come back! Take me out of this! Have pity! My children! Christmas! You peasant cur! You dog!"

And sinking back into the coach, he drew his fur coat about him and burst out crying like a child.

But the black night gave no answer.

CANADA

Where Were You, O Sister?

TRADITIONAL

D'où viens tu ber-gèr - e, D'où viens tu?

Je viens de l'é - tabl - e, De m'y pro-me - ner;

J'ai vu un mi - ra-cle Ce soir ar-ri - vé.

Where were you, O sister,
Where were you?
I was at the stable,
Just to take the air,
And I saw a wonder
That has happened there.

One Thousand Aves

LOUIS HÉMON
(Translated by W. H. Blake)

SINCE the coming of winter they had often talked at the Chapdelaines about the holidays, and now these were drawing near.

"I am wondering whether we shall have any callers on New Year's Day," said Madame Chapdelaine one evening. She went over the list of all relatives and friends able to make the venture. "Azalma Larouche does not live so far away, but she—she is not very energetic. The people at St. Prime would not care to take the journey. Possibly Wilfrid or Ferdinand might drive from St. Gedeon if the ice on the lake were in good condition." A sigh disclosed that she still was dreaming of the coming and going in the old parishes at the time of the New Year, the family dinners, the unlooked-for visits of kindred arriving by sleigh from the next village, buried under rugs and furs, behind a horse whose coat was white with frost.

Maria's thoughts were turning in another direction. "If the roads are as bad as they were last year," said she, "we shall not be able to attend the midnight mass. And yet I should so much have liked it this time, and father promised . . ."

Through the little window they looked on the gray sky, and found little to cheer them. To go to midnight mass is the natural and strong desire of every French-Canadian peasant, even of those living farthest from the settlements. What do they not face to accomplish it! Arctic cold, the woods at night, obliterated roads, great distances do but add to the impressiveness and the mystery. This anniversary of the birth of Jesus is more to them than a mere fixture in the calendar with rites appropriate; it signifies the renewed promise of salvation, an occasion of deep rejoicing, and those gathered in the wooden church are imbued with sincerest fervour, are pervaded with a deep sense of the supernatural. This year, more than ever, Maria yearned to attend the mass after many weeks of remoteness from houses and from churches; the favors she would fain demand seemed more likely to be granted were she able to prefer them before the altar, aided in heavenward flight by the wings of music.

But toward the middle of December much snow fell, dry and fine as dust, and three days before Christmas the north-west wind arose and made an end of the roads. On the morrow of the storm Chapdelaine harnessed Charles Eugene to the heavy sleigh and departed with Tit'Bé; they took shovels to clear the way or lay out another route. The two men returned by noon, worn out, white with snow, asserting that there would be no breaking through for several days. The disappointment must be borne; Maria sighed, but the idea came to her that there might be other means of attaining the divine goodwill.

"Is it true, mother," she asked as evening was falling, "that if you repeat a thousand Aves on the day before Christmas you are always granted the thing you seek?"

"Quite true," her mother reverently answered. "One desiring a favor who says her thousand Aves properly before midnight on Christmas Eve, very seldom fails to receive what she asks."

On Christmas Eve the weather was cold but windless. The two men went out betimes in another effort to beat down the road, with no great hope of success; but long before they left, and indeed long before daylight, Maria began to recite her Aves. Awakening very early, she took her rosary from beneath the pillow and swiftly repeated the prayer, passing from the last word to the first without stopping, and counting, bead by bead.

The others were still asleep; but Chien left his place at the stove when he saw that she moved, and came to sit beside the bed, gravely reposing his head upon the coverings. Maria's glance wandered over the long white muzzle resting upon the brown wool, the liquid eyes filled with the dumb creature's pathetic trustfulness, the drooping glossy ears; while she ceased not to murmur the sacred words:—"Hail Mary, full of grace..."

Soon Tit'Bé jumped from bed to put wood upon the fire; an impulse of shyness caused Maria to turn away and hide her rosary under the coverlet as she continued to pray. The stove roared; Chien went back to his usual spot, and for another half-hour nothing was stirring the house save the fingers of Maria numbering the boxwood beads, and her lips as they moved rapidly in the task she had laid upon herself.

Then must she arise, for the day was dawning; make the porridge and the pancakes while the men went to the stable to care for the animals, wait upon them when they returned, wash the dishes, sweep the house. What time she attended to these things, Maria was ever raising a little higher toward heaven the monument of her Aves; but the rosary had to be laid aside and it was hard to keep a true reckoning. As the morning advanced however, no urgent duty calling, she was able to sit by the window and steadily pursue her undertaking.

Noon; and already three hundred Aves. Her anxiety lessens, for now she feels almost sure of finishing in time. It comes to her mind that fasting would give a further title to heavenly consideration, and might, with reason, turn hopes into certainties; wherefore she ate but little, foregoing all those things she liked the best.

Throughout the afternoon she must knit the woollen garment designed for her father as a New Year's gift, and though the faithful repetition ceased not, the work of her fingers was something of a distraction and a delay; then came the long preparations for supper, and finally Tit'Bé brought his mittens to be mended, so all this time the Aves made slow and impeded progress, like some devout procession brought to halt by secular interruption.

But when it was evening and the tasks of the day were done, she could resume her seat by the window where the feeble light of the lamp did not invade the darkness, look forth upon the fields hidden beneath their icy cloak, take the rosary once more in her hands and throw her heart into the prayer. She was happy that so many Aves were left to be recited, since labor and difficulty could only add merit to her endeavor; even did she wish to humble herself further and give force to her prayer by some posture that would bring uneasiness and pain, by some chastening of the flesh.

Her father and Tit'Bé smoked, their feet against the stove; her mother sewed new ties to old moose-hide moccasins. Outside, the moon had risen, flooding the chill whiteness with colder light, and the heavens were of a marvelous purity and depth, sown with stars that shone like that wondrous star of old.

"Blessed art Thou amongst women . . ."

Through repeating the short prayer oftentimes and quickly she grew confused and sometimes stopped, her dazed mind lost among the well-known words. It is only for a moment; sighing she closes her eyes, and the phrase which rises at once to her memory and her lips ceases to be mechanical, detaches itself, again stands forth in all its hallowed meaning.

"Blessed art Thou amongst women . . ."

At length a heaviness weighs upon her, and the holy words are spoken with greater effort and slowly; yet the beads pass through her fingers in endless succession, and each one launches the offering of an Ave to that sky where Mary the compassionate is surely seated on her throne, hearkening to the music of prayers that ever rise, and brooding over the memory of that blest night.

"The Lord is with Thee . . ."

The fence-rails were very black upon the white expanse palely lighted by the moon; trunks of birch trees standing against the dark background of forest were like the skeletons of living creatures smitten with the cold and stricken by death; but the glacial night was awesome rather than affrighting.

"With the roads as they are we will not be the only ones who

have to stay at home this evening," said Madame Chapdelaine.
"But is there anything more lovely than the midnight mass at
Saint Coeur de Marie, with Yvonne Boilly playing the harmonium, and Pacifique Simard who sings the Latin so beautifully!" She was very careful to say nothing that might seem
reproachful or complaining on such a night as this, but in spite
of herself the words and tone had a sad ring of loneliness and
remoteness. Her husband noticed it, and, himself under the
influence of the day, was quick to take the blame.

"It is true enough, Laura, that you would have had a happier
life with some other man than me, who lived on a comfortable
farm, near the settlements."

"No, Samuel; what the good God does is always right. I
grumble . . . Of course I grumble. Is there anyone who hasn't
something to grumble about? But we have never been unhappy, we two; we have managed to live without faring over-
badly; the boys are fine boys, hard-working, who bring us
nearly all they earn; Maria, too, is a good girl . . ."

Affected by these memories of the past, they also were thinking of the candles already lit, of the hymns soon to be raised in
honor of the Savior's birth. Life had always been a simple and
a straightforward thing for them; severe but inevitable toil, a
good understanding between man and wife, obedience alike to
the laws of nature and of the Church. Everything was drawn
into the same woof; the rites of their religion and the daily
routine of existence so woven together that they could not
distinguish the devout emotion possessing them from the mute
love of each for each.

Little Alma Rose heard praises in the air and hastened to demand her portion. "I have been a good girl too, haven't I,
father?"

"Certainly . . . Certainly. A black sin indeed if one were
naughty on the day when the little Jesus was born."

To the children, Jesus of Nazareth was ever "the little Jesus,"
the curly-headed babe of the sacred picture; and in truth, for
the parents as well, such was the image oftenest brought to
mind by the Name. Not the sad enigmatic Christ of the Protes-

tant, but a being more familiar and less august, a new-born infant in his mother's arms, or at least a tiny child who might be loved without great effort of the mind or any thought of the coming sacrifice.

"Would you like me to rock you?"

"Yes."

He took the little girl on his knees and began to swing her back and forth.

"And are we going to sing too?"

"Yes."

"Very well; now sing with me:"

> Dans son étable,
> Que Jésus est charmant!
> Qu'il est aimable
> Dans son abaissement . . .

He began in quiet tones that he might not drown the other slender voice; but soon emotion carried him away and he sang with all his might, his gaze dreamy and remote. Telesphore drew near and looked at him with worshipping eyes. To these children brought up in a lonely house, with only their parents for companions, Samuel Chapdelaine embodied all there was in the world of wisdom and might. As he was ever gentle and patient, always ready to take the children on his knee and sing them hymns, or those endless old songs he taught them one by one, they loved him with a rare affection.

> . . . Tous les palais des rois
> N'ont rien de comparable
> Aux beautés que je vois
> Dans cette étable.

"Once more? Very well."

This time the mother and Tit'Bé joined in. Maria could not resist staying her prayers for a few moments that she might look and hearken; but the words of the hymn renewed her ardor, and she soon took up the task again with a livelier faith . . .

"Hail Mary, full of grace . . ."

> Trois gros navires sont arrivés,
> Chargés d'avoine, chargés de blé.
> Nous irons sur l'eau nous y prom-promener,
> Nous irons journer dans l'île ...

"And now? Another song: which?" Without waiting for a reply he struck in ...

"No? not that one ... *Claire Fontaine?* Ah! That's a beautiful one, that is! We shall all sing it together."

He glanced at Maria, but seeing the beads ever slipping through her fingers he would not intrude.

> A la claire fontaine
> M'en allant promener,
> J'ai trouvé l'eau si belle
> Que je m'y suis baigné ...
> Il y longtemps que je t'aime,
> Jamais je ne t'oublierai ...

Words and tune alike haunting; the unaffected sadness of the refrain lingering in the ear, a song that well may find its way to any heart.

> ... Sur la plus haute branche,
> Le rossignol chantait.
> Chante, rossignol, chante,
> Toi qui a le cœur gai ...
> Il y a longtemps que je t'aime
> Jamais je ne t'oublierai ...

The rosary lay still in the long fingers. Maria did not sing with the others; but she was listening, and this lament of a love that was unhappy fell very sweetly and movingly on her spirit a little weary with prayer.

> ... Tu as le cœur à rire,
> Moi je l'ai à pleurer,
> J'ai perdu ma maîtresse
> Sans pouvoir la r'trouver,
> Pour un bouquet de roses
> Que je lui refusai
> Il y a longtemps que je t'aime,
> Jamais je ne t'oublierai.

Maria looked through the window at the white fields circled by mysterious forest; the passion of religious feeling, the tide of young love rising within her, the sound of the familiar voices, fused in her heart to a single emotion. Truly the world was filled with love that evening, with love human and divine, simple in nature and mighty in strength, one and the other most natural and right; so intermingled that the beseeching of heavenly favor upon dear ones was scarcely more than the expression of an earthly affection, while the artless love songs were chanted with solemnity of voice and exaltation of spirit fit for addresses to another world.

> . . . Je voudrais que la rose
> Fût encore au rosier,
> Et que le rosier même
> A la mer fût jeté.
> Il y a longtemps, que je t'aime,
> Jamais je ne t'oublierai . . .

"Hail Mary, full of grace . . ."

The song ended, Maria forthwith resumed her prayers with zeal refreshed, and once again the tale of the Aves mounted.

Little Alma Rose, asleep on her father's knee, was undressed and put to bed; Telesphore followed; Tit'Bé arose in turn, stretched himself, and filled the stove with green birch logs; the father made a last trip to the stable and came back running, saying that the cold was increasing. Soon all had retired, save Maria.

"You won't forget to put out the lamp?"

"No, father."

Forthwith she quenched the light, preferring it so, and seated herself again by the window to repeat the last Aves. When she had finished, a scruple assailed her, and a fear lest she had erred in the reckoning, because it had not always been possible to count the beads of her rosary. Out of prudence she recited yet another fifty and then was silent—jaded, weary, but full of happy confidence, as though the moment had brought her a promise inviolable.

The world outside was lit; wrapped in that splendor which the night unrolls over lands of snow when the sky is clear and the moon is shining. Within the house was darkness, and it seemed that wood and field had illumined themselves to signal the coming of the holy hour.

"The thousand Aves have been said," murmured Maria to herself, "but I have not yet asked for anything . . . not in words." She had thought that perhaps it were not needful; that the Divinity might understand without hearing wishes shaped by lips—Mary above all . . . Who had been a woman upon earth. But at the last her simple mind was taken with a doubt, and she tried to find speech for the favor she was seeking.

François Paradis . . . Most surely it concerns François Paradis. Hast Thou already guessed it, O Mary, full of grace? How might she frame this her desire without impiety? That he should be spared hardship in the woods . . . That he should be true to his word and give up drinking and swearing . . . That he return in the spring . . .

That he return in the spring . . . She goes no further, for it seems to her that when he is with her again, his promise kept, all the happiness in the world must be within their reach, unaided . . . almost unaided . . . If it be not presumptuous so to think . . .

That he return in the spring . . . Dreaming of his return, of François, the handsome sunburnt face turned to hers, Maria forgets all else, and looks long with unseeing eyes at the snow-covered ground which the moonlight has turned into a glittering fabric of ivory and mother-of-pearl—at the black pattern of the fences outlined upon it, and the menacing ranks of the dark forest.

The Errors of Santa Claus

STEPHEN LEACOCK

IT WAS Christmas Eve.

The Browns, who lived in the adjoining house, had been dining with the Joneses.

Brown and Jones were sitting over wine and walnuts at the table. The others had gone upstairs.

"What are you giving to your boy for Christmas?" asked Brown.

"A train," said Jones, "new kind of thing—automatic."

"Let's have a look at it," said Brown.

Jones fetched a parcel from the sideboard and began unwrapping it.

"Ingenious thing, isn't it?" he said, "goes on its own rails. Queer how kids love to play with trains, isn't it?"

"Yes," assented Brown, "how are the rails fixed?"

"Wait, I'll show you," said Jones, "just help me to shove these dinner things aside and roll back the cloth. There! See! You lay the rails like that and fasten them at the ends, so—"

"Oh, yes, I catch on, makes a grade, doesn't it? Just the thing to amuse a child, isn't it? I got Willie a toy aeroplane."

"I know, they're great. I got Edwin one on his birthday. But

From *Wet Wit and Dry Humor* by Stephen Leacock. Copyright 1931, by Dodd, Mead & Co., Inc.

I thought I'd get him a train this time. I told him Santa Claus was going to bring him something altogether new this time. Edwin, of course, believes in Santa Claus absolutely. Say, look at this locomotive, would you? It has a spring coiled up inside the fire box."

"Wind her up," said Brown with great interest, "let's see her go."

"All right," said Jones, "just pile up two or three plates or something to lean the end of the rails on. There, notice the way it buzzes before it starts. Isn't that a great thing for a kid, eh?"

"Yes," said Brown, "and say! see this little string to pull the whistle. By Gad, it toots, eh? Just like real?"

"Now then, Brown," Jones went on, "you hitch on those cars and I'll start her. I'll be engineer, eh!"

Half an hour later Brown and Jones were still playing trains on the dining-room table.

But their wives upstairs in the drawing room hardly noticed their absence. They were too much interested.

"Oh, I think it's perfectly sweet," said Mrs. Brown, "just the loveliest doll I've seen in years. I must get one like it for Ulvina. Won't Clarisse be perfectly enchanted?"

"Yes," answered Mrs. Jones, "and then she'll have all the fun of arranging the dresses. Children love that so much. Look! there are three little dresses with the doll, aren't they cute? All cut out and ready to stitch together."

"Oh, how perfectly lovely," exclaimed Mrs. Brown, "I think the mauve one would suit the doll best—don't you?—with such golden hair—only don't you think it would make it much nicer to turn back the collar, so, and to put a little band—so?"

"*What* a good idea!" said Mrs. Jones, "do let's try it. Just wait, I'll get a needle in a minute. I'll tell Clarisse that Santa Claus sewed it himself. The child believes in Santa Claus absolutely."

And half an hour later Mrs. Jones and Mrs. Brown were so busy stitching dolls' clothes that they could not hear the roaring of the little train up and down the dining table, and had no idea what the four children were doing.

Nor did the children miss their mothers.

"Dandy, aren't they?" Edwin Jones was saying to little Willie Brown, as they sat in Edwin's bedroom. "A hundred in a box, with cork tips, and see, an amber mouthpiece that fits into a little case at the side. Good present for dad, eh?"

"Fine!" said Willie, appreciatively, "I'm giving father cigars."

"I know, I thought of cigars too. Men always like cigars and cigarettes. You can't go wrong on them. Say, would you like to try one or two of these cigarettes? We can take them from the bottom. You'll like them, they're Russian,—away ahead of Egyptian."

"Thanks," answered Willie. "I'd like one immensely. I only started smoking last spring—on my twelfth birthday. I think a feller's a fool to begin smoking cigarettes too soon, don't you? It stunts him. I waited till I was twelve."

"Me too," said Edwin, as they lighted their cigarettes. "In fact, I wouldn't buy them now if it weren't for dad. I simply *had* to give him something from Santa Claus. He believes in Santa Claus absolutely, you know."

And while this was going on, Clarisse was showing little Ulvina the absolutely lovely little bridge set that she got for her mother. "Aren't these markers perfectly charming?" said Ulvina, "and don't you love this little Dutch design—or is it Flemish, darling?"

"Dutch," said Clarisse, "isn't it quaint? And aren't these the dearest little things—for putting the money in when you play. I needn't have got them with it—they'd have sold the rest separately—but I think it's too utterly slow playing without money, don't you?"

"Oh, abominable," shuddered Ulvina, "but your mamma never plays for money, does she?"

"Mamma! Oh, gracious, no. Mamma's far too slow for that. But I shall tell her that Santa Claus insisted on putting in the little money boxes."

"I suppose she believes in Santa Claus, just as my Mamma does."

"Oh, absolutely," said Clarisse, and added, "What if we play a little game! With a double dummy, the French way, or Norwegian Skat, if you like. That only needs two."

"All right," agreed Ulvina, and in a few minutes they were deep in a game of cards with a little pile of pocket money beside them.

About half an hour later, all the members of the two families were down again in the drawing room. But of course nobody said anything about the presents. In any case they were all too busy looking at the beautiful big Bible, with maps in it, that the Joneses had bought to give to Grandfather. They all agreed that with the help of it, Grandfather could hunt up any place in Palestine in a moment, day or night.

But upstairs, away upstairs in a sitting room of his own, Grandfather Jones was looking with an affectionate eye at the presents that stood beside him. There was a beautiful whiskey decanter, with silver filigree outside (and whiskey inside) for Jones, and for the little boy a big nickel-plated Jew's harp.

Later on, far in the night, the person, or the influence, or whatever it is called Santa Claus, took all the presents and placed them in the people's stockings.

And, being blind as he always has been, he gave the wrong things to the wrong people—in fact, he gave them just as indicated above.

But the next day, in the course of Christmas morning, the situation straightened itself out, just as it always does.

Indeed, by ten o'clock, Brown and Jones were playing with the train, and Mrs. Brown and Mrs. Jones were making dolls' clothes, and the boys were smoking cigarettes, and Clarisse and Ulvina were playing cards for their pocket money.

And upstairs—away up—Grandfather was drinking whiskey and playing the Jew's harp.

And so Christmas, just as it always does, turned out all right after all.

The Waning Year

MAZO DE LA ROCHE

Now the December days marched coldly on toward Christmas. There were five children to consider. There had always been a Christmas Tree and a Santa Claus. Piers had marvelously well played the part and, since his departure, Nicholas. What he lacked in rosiness of countenance, Pheasant applied from a rouge pot. The sonorous jollity of his Santa Claus voice was contagious. But this year he declared that he no longer could do it. Something had gone out of him, he said. He was too old. He could not read the labels on the packages. Ernest or Finch must be Father Christmas.

But no one could, by any stretch of imagination, picture Ernest or Finch as Santa Claus. Nicholas must hold the Christmas fort till Piers came home. "Hmph, well," growled Nicholas, "he'd better hurry. I'm ninety-one."

"Why Uncle Nick," chided Meg, "think of Granny! She lived to be a hundred and two."

"She was a woman," said Nicholas, "and she hadn't gout. She was sound, you might say, to the last."

"And so are you!" cried Meg, kissing him. "You're just as sound as a dear old nut."

He was won over. He would do it, he declared, just this one time more.

The cloak of family custom hung heavy too on Finch's shoulders. From the time when the church was built, a Whiteoak had always read the Lessons at Morning Service. After Renny had gone to the war, Ernest had capably and with much more elegance filled this office, but for the past year it had obviously been too much for him to undertake. There were Sundays when the weather was not fit for him to venture out. So Mr. Fennel had himself read the Lessons. Now he and Meg and the two uncles had put their heads together and decided that Finch was next in order. He was to be home for some months and it would be good for him to fill the niche in the ordered sequence of things. Family custom must not be allowed to flag but must be kept firm and upright by Whiteoak mettle.

To Finch the idea of standing up behind the lectern and reading from the Bible was more intimidating than playing the piano in a concert hall. Yet he was pleased and even flattered by being chosen. He was thankful that neither Renny nor Piers would be there to see him. He could not have faced their amused gaze from the family pew.

The morning dawned cold and cloudy, with much snow in the sky but little on the ground. As he descended the stairs to breakfast, the resinous scent of the Tree filled the hall. Alayne and Pheasant had decorated it the day before and it was safely locked inside the library. On how many Christmas mornings had he come down those stairs, made dizzy by the wonder, the mysterious strangeness of that scent? He stood a moment alone in the hall. He was indeed alone, for Sarah had gone out of his life. He felt oddly young and untouched at this moment.

Alayne and the children were at the breakfast table. She was having a time of it to persuade Archer to eat anything. He desired only something that was not on the table. Finch looked at him severely.

"I can tell you this, young man," he said, "if I had demanded things like you do, I'd have been taken by the scruff and put out of the room."

"What's the scruff?" asked Archer.

"This." Finch laid a heavy hand on his neck. Archer wriggled away. "Who would have done it to you?" he asked.

"Your father."

"Mother wouldn't let him do it to me. She'd—"

"Archer," interrupted Alayne, "I want to hear nothing more from you."

Wragge entered the room with a portentous air. "Mrs. White-oak, please, my wife would like to see you in the kitchen as soon as convenient."

Alayne rose. "I have finished," she said, and went with him to the basement.

"I'm *not* going to church," said Archer, "and I *am* going to see the Tree. I'm going right now to get my presents off it."

Finch sprang up and lifted the small boy from his chair. He strode with him into the hall. Archer lay, stiff as a poker, in his arms.

"What are you going to do with him?" asked Roma.

"Open the door," ordered Finch.

Adeline opened the front door and Finch stepped onto the porch. All three dogs came into the house. Finch carried Archer to the steps and held him head downward over a snowdrift.

"Want to be dropped into that and left there?" he asked.

"I don't mind," answered Archer impassively.

"All right. Here goes!" He lowered Archer till his tow hair touched the snow. He lowered him till his head was buried. The little girls shrieked. Alayne could be heard talking, on her way up the basement stairs. The bell of Ernest's room was loudly ringing below. The two old men were having breakfast in bed, in preparation for a tiring day. Now Ernest wanted his. Two short rings meant that he wanted porridge, toast, and tea. One prolonged ring indicated that he wanted an egg. This was a prolonged ring. It went on and on.

Finch reversed Archer and stood him on his feet. His lofty white brow was surmounted by snowy locks.

"Now are you going to behave yourself?" asked Finch, grinning.

"I still don't want my breakfast," answered Archer. "And I still want to see the Tree."

"Wherever is that terrible draft coming from?" cried Alayne. "And who let the dogs in?"

Finch leaped up the stairs.

Oh, if Renny and Piers and Wake were home, how happy he could be! He pictured them, one after the other, at their various pursuits. What a Christmas it would be when they all were at Jalna once again! He knocked at Ernest's door and went in.

"Merry Christmas, Uncle Ernest!" He went to the bed and kissed him.

"Merry Christmas, my boy! Will you just prop those pillows behind me a little more firmly. How cold it is! Please don't touch me again with your hands. They're icy."

Finch tucked the eiderdown about him. "Is that better?"

The old gentleman looked nice indeed, with his lean pink face, his forget-me-not blue eyes and his silvery hair brushed smooth. Nicholas, when Finch visited him, was a contrast. His hair, his eyebrows, his moustache, still iron-gray, were ruffled. His bed was untidy and on the table at his side lay his pipe and tobacco pouch, with burnt matches strewn about.

After the season's greetings, Finch asked—"Have you rung for your breakfast yet, Uncle Nick?"

"No, no. I never ring till I've heard Rags bring your Uncle Ernest's. No matter how early I wake he always gets ahead of me. So now I just smoke a pipe and resign myself to waiting. How many times did he ring?"

"One long one."

"Means he wants an egg. Doesn't need an egg when he's going to eat a heavy dinner. To-morrow he'll be taking indigestion tablets, you'll see."

Nicholas stretched out an unsteady handsome old hand, found his pipe and a pigeon's feather with which he proceeded to clean it. What did it feel like to be ninety-one, Finch wondered. Very comfortable, to judge by the way Uncle Nick pulled contentedly at his pipe.

"So you're going to read the Lessons, eh?" the old man asked.

"Yes, and I'm scared stiff."

Nicholas stared. "You nervous—after all you've done!"

"This is different."

"I should think it is. A little country church, as familiar to you as your own home. Your own family there to support you."

"That's just it. When I see you all facing me while I read out of the Bible, it will seem preposterous. And I haven't had any practice. I don't know how to read out of the Bible."

"Good heavens, you've been often enough to church!"

"It's not the same."

Nicholas thought a minute, then he said, "I'll tell you what. You get my prayer book out of the wardrobe, then you can let me hear you read. I'll tell you how it sounds."

Finch went with alacrity to the towering walnut wardrobe that always had worn an air of mystery to him.

"Door to the left," directed his uncle. "Hatbox where I keep my good hat."

Finch opened the door. A smell which was a mixture of tobacco, old tweed, and broadcloth, came out. He took the lid from the large leather hatbox. There inside was his uncle's top hat and in its crown lay his prayer book, the gilt cross on its cover worn dim by the years.

"I remember," said Finch, "when you wore that silk hat every Sunday."

"Ah, there was dignity in those days! On this continent we shall sink before long to shirt sleeves and not getting to our feet when a woman comes into the room—to judge by what I see in the papers. Well, you boys weren't brought up that way. Now, let's hear you read."

Nicholas had in his younger days played the piano quite well. He was convinced that Finch had inherited his talent from him. Though his fingers had long been too stiff for playing, he still kept his old square piano in his room and sometimes when he was alone fumbled over the few stray bars he remembered. Now Finch sat down before the keyboard and placed the open book on the rack. He read the Epistle through. He looked inquiringly at his uncle.

"Too loud," said Nicholas.

"Not for the church, Uncle."

"You must learn to control your voice. It's a good one but it's erratic."

"I expect I'll make a mess of the whole thing."

"Nonsense. You read far better than old Fennel."

The jingling of dishes on Ernest's tray could be heard.

"There he is!" exclaimed Nicholas. He searched the top of his bedside table and found two envelopes. Wragge appeared at the door.

"Merry Christmas, sir!" His small gray face, with its jutting nose and chin, took on an expectant beam.

Nicholas handed him the envelopes.

"One for you—one for your wife. Merry Christmas to you both. Bring me porridge—thick toast, gooseberry jam. "

"Yes, sir. Thank you, sir. It's very nice to be remembered. Mr. Ernest did the sime for us. Mrs. Wragge will thank you later, sir."

When he had gone, Finch groaned. "Gosh, I completely forgot to give them anything! No wonder he gave me a chilly look. How much was in the envelopes, Uncle Nick?"

"Five in each. Ernest gives them the same. Well, it keeps 'em good-humored. They have a lot of trays to cope with."

Finch walked alone across the fields to church. A slight fall of snow had made them freshly white. There showed no human footprint, but the winding path was clearly defined among the tall dead grasses, the stalks of Michaelmas daisy and goldenrod. In and about ran the footprints of pheasants. Rabbits had been there too, leaving their Y-shaped prints, and field mice their tiny scratchings. From a twisted old thorn tree, a chickadee piped his last recollection of summer.

Now Finch could see the church tower rising from its knoll and in the graveyard two figures. They were Meg and Patience. As he drew near he saw that they were standing by the plot where the Vaughans were laid. It was the second Christmas that Meg's husband, Maurice Vaughan, had been gone from her. Yet Finch felt that it would scarcely be seemly to call out

"Merry Christmas" to Meg and Patience, mourning by his grave.

But Meg saved Finch embarrassment by at once seeing him and coming toward him with arms outstretched. She still wore black but to-day she had brightened it by pinning a little nose-gay of pink artificial daisies on the breast of her black lamb coat which had seen twelve seasons' wear.

"Merry Christmas!" she exclaimed, folding Finch to her bosom. "And many, many of them!"

Finch hugged them both, then, after an appreciative glance at the wreath on the grave, said:—

"Hadn't you better come into the church? You'll get cold standing here."

"Yes, we'll go at once. How do you like the wreath? I think it's marvelous the way they make these wreaths of bronze leaves. They look so natural. But they're terribly expensive."

"It's very nice, Meggie."

"I was saying to Patience, just as you came up, how strange it is to think that when I die I shall have to lie here among the Vaughans, instead of with the Whiteoaks, where I'd feel so much more at home."

"It seems strange."

"Do you think it might possibly be arranged that I should be buried among my own family?"

"Don't talk about it, Meggie."

Finch could not remember the time when death had not seemed real and terrible to him. The loss of both parents, when he was seven, had made an indelible impression on him. But Patience had the feeling that she could never die. Her mother too must live and live. She took Meg's hand and drew her toward the church. The last bell began to ring. People were mounting the icy steps—figures symbolic of the arduous Christian way. Finch hastened to the vestry. Patience called after him:—

"You'll find the surplices nice and clean, Uncle Finch. Mother and I washed and ironed them all."

"Good for you!"

As he passed the door he had a glimpse of Noah Binns ringing the bell, bending almost double to impart additional
Christmas fervor to the act. Bell ringer, gravedigger, farm
worker, he had been for many a year putting energy into only
the first two of these callings. Now that he was in his seventies,
he spared himself still more in farm work, yet demanded higher
wages—and got them. He had a patronizing and resentful attitude toward the Whiteoak family. He firmly believed that they
would like to put him out of his job of bell ringer and he had
made up his mind to hang on to it as long as he could hang
on to the bell rope.

Now his ferret eyes and Finch's large gray ones exchanged a
look of mutual challenge.

"Hurry up," said Binns's eyes, "or I'll stop ringing before
you get your danged surplice on."

Finch's eyes said—"If you let me down it will be the worse
for you."

The church was filled by the scent of greenery that was
twined about pulpit, font, and choir stalls. From his own body
there came to Finch the clean smell of his freshly laundered
surplice. Now he was in his seat near the steps of the chancel.
There was no escape. He was in for reading the Lessons. Miss
Pink, the organist, bent all her powers to the playing of the
opening hymn. Finch stole a sly look at the congregation. For a
brief moment his eyes rested on the family pews. There were
the dear old uncles, with Archer fenced in between them and
Adeline and Roma on the far side of Ernest. Alayne had not
come. In the pew behind were Pheasant and her three sons.
Across the aisle, in the Vaughan pew, Meg and Patience. All,
down to Archer, knew the Christmas hymn by heart, so they
were able to rivet their full attention on Finch. He began to
feel horribly nervous. His mouth felt dry. He was sure his voice
would come with a croak.

The calm tones of the Rector led the congregation through
the intricacies of the service. Finch watched him standing or
kneeling there, his brown beard streaked with silver, and
thought of his simple acceptance of the Christian faith and his

unostentatious adherence to it in his daily life. Finch felt calmed. After the singing of the *Venite Exultemus Domino* he moved with a kind of awkward dignity to his place behind the brass eagle. In a low voice he read:—

"Here beginneth the First Chapter of the Hebrews."

Meg's whisper, fierce in its intensity, came distinctly to him. *"Louder!"*

No one regarded this admonishment of Meg's as out of place. Those of the congregation who were near enough to hear her thought it well that she should make an effort to keep Finch up to the family's standard of reading the Lessons. As for Finch, he colored deeply, then really let his voice out. It was a strong and moving voice. It had power in it. No one could complain now that what he read was not audible.

"Here beginneth the first Chapter of St. Paul's Epistle to the Hebrews . . . 'God, who at sundry times and in divers manners spake in time past unto the fathers by the prophets, hath in these last days spoken unto us by his Son.' " And so proceeded till he came to the question—" 'For unto which of the angels said he at any time, Thou art my Son, this day have I begotten thee?' " Then his eyes rested for a moment on the congregation and he gathered the breast of his surplice in his hand and pulled at it as though he would rend it. He read on:—

" '. . . Thou, Lord, in the beginning hast laid the foundation of the earth; and the heavens are the works of thine hands: they shall perish; but thou remainest; and they all shall wax old as doth a garment; and as a vesture shalt thou fold them up, and they shall be changed: but thou art the same, and thy years shall not fail.' "

Surely Finch read the sombre words far too well. Surely his voice was too moving and the expression on his long face of too profound a melancholy. "As a vesture shalt thou fold them up!" It was not pleasant on a fine Christmas morning, thought Ernest. It was hardly decent. The little church had never heard the scriptures so read before. Even Mr. Fennel thought Finch was overdoing it.

But it was the way he tugged at his surplice that most worried the family. When he took his place behind the lectern to read the Second Lesson, his Uncle Nicholas clutched the lapel of his own coat, tugged at it, and shook his head so hard that his gray hair fell over his forehead. Finch wondered what was the matter with him. Then he perceived that his Uncle Ernest was doing the same. Startled, he clutched his surplice the tighter. He began to read in a loud nervous tone. Then he saw Meg. She was pulling at her fur collar as though she would pull it off! She was shaking her head! Now he understood. He released his surplice, controlled his voice. Suddenly he felt quite calm. He read the Second Lesson with credit and not too much feeling.

Pheasant's sons walked back with him across the fields. Rather they ran through the frosty air, drinking in its sweetness, rolling snowballs between their palms to hurl at each other. They were at Jalna as soon as the car which carried Nicholas and Ernest. Nicholas was somewhat disgruntled, for Ernest had insisted on his being bundled up in too many coats, mufflers, and rugs. He could not extricate himself from them. Twice he had tried to heave himself out of the seat and each time his heavy old body had sunk back on to the cushions. He had just got over a cold and Ernest was anxious about him.

"Dammit," growled Nicholas. "I feel like a feather bed. I'm stuck here. Tell the others. You must have dinner without me." He pushed out his lips beneath his gray moustache and blew angrily.

Wright now proffered his help. "Let me give you a hand, sir."

"No use trying, Wright. I'm stuck. Hullo, Finch! Tell them to have dinner without me—and the Tree without me."

Finch laughed and grasped him by the arms. Between them he and Wright got the old man out of the car and up the steps. The front door flew open and the children, still wearing their outdoor things, came tumbling out.

"Merry Christmas!" they shouted. "Merry Christmas, Uncle Nick!"

"You've wished me that three times already," growled Nicholas.

"It can't be wished too often, can it?" retorted Adeline.

All the way into the house Nicholas grumbled. He grumbled all the while he was being divested of his wraps. He was more and more depressed about playing the part of Santa Claus. The saint might be old but he had no gouty knee to hamper him. He was hale and hearty.

The three dogs had pushed their way into the house. The five children tore upstairs to take off their things, then tore down again. The rich smell of roasting turkey and stuffing rose from the basement. Through the keyhole and crevices of the library door the pungent scent of the Tree stole forth.

"Why are Alayne and Pheasant trying to restrain the children?" Nicholas thought. "Let 'em make all the noise they can. It will take a lot of noise to fill the void made by the absence of Renny and Piers and Wakefield."

At last they were seated about the table, with the massive turkey in front of Ernest. Rags had put an edge on the carving knife that might have divided a feather pillow at one stroke. Ernest faced the task with admirable calm. He twitched up his cuffs and took the knife and fork in hand. Alayne, facing him, sat very erect, a fixed smile on her lips. She did not see Ernest, but Renny, at the head of the table, the carving knife and fork poised, his bright gaze moving from the turkey to the face of the one he was about to serve, well knowing the particular choice of each member of the family. Pheasant must not let herself think of that prison camp in Germany! No—she must keep the thought of Piers far back in her mind, remembering only the children and that this was their day. But not so long ago—though sometimes it seemed half a lifetime—Piers had been Santa Claus, pink and white and jovial. She clenched her hands beneath the table till self-control came, then she laughed and chaffed with Finch and Mooey. Finch was in high spirits. He had come through his ordeal without disgrace, even with some credit. Physically he was feeling better than in years. He and Pheasant and Mooey never stopped laughing and talking.

Rags and his wife, she in a new black dress with snowy cuffs
and apron, bustled about the table. Bright sunlight, streaming
between the yellow velvet curtains, shone on the silver basket
mounded with bright fruit, the gay crackers, the shining heads
of the children.

But it touched something else. Nicholas bent forward to see.
He could scarcely believe his eyes. Grouped about the centre-
piece were three photographs framed in holly leaves. They were
of Renny, Piers, and Wakefield.

"Well," growled Nicholas, "I'll be shot!"

He looked down at the richly mounded plate in front of him,
at the mound of cranberry jelly Rags was offering him, in confusion and gloom.

"I don't like it at all," he muttered, but nobody heard him.
He raised his voice and repeated—"I don't like it at all."

"What don't you like, Uncle Nick, dear?" asked Meg.

He pointed three times. "These memorial pictures. They fuss
me. They take away my appetite. If they're left on the table I
shall be sick."

"That is just the way I feel, Uncle Nick," said Meg, with a
reproachful look at Alayne and Pheasant, whose idea it had
been.

"I think it's a grand idea," said Finch. "It makes you feel
that the chaps are almost with us in the flesh."

"I am sure they would be pleased," said Ernest.

"They'd hate it," muttered Nicholas. " 'Twould make 'em
feel dead."

"Nonsense," said his brother.

"The chaps would be pleased," said Finch.

"They'd feel dead," persisted Nicholas.

Tears began to run down Pheasant's cheeks.

Alayne rose and took the pictures from the table. She carried
them from the room with dignity, then with an impassive face
returned to her place at the table. Nicholas emptied his wine-
glass. He felt better now. He joined in the lively talk. He drank
a good deal and at last, when Finch and Meggie dressed him in
his Santa Claus costume, they declared they had never seen it

more becomingly worn. He forgot all about his gout. He was a noble, a magnificent Father Christmas. Everyone said so. At the last Adeline threw her arms about him and drew his head down to whisper:—

"You were splendid, Uncle Nick. Archer and Philip absolutely believed in you. Christmas is being almost as good as though Daddy were here."

So the year drew to its close. It was a mild winter. Yet there was enough snow to make it difficult for the birds to find food. Beneath Ernest's bedroom window there was a feeding table for birds on which Mrs. Wragge, three times a day, placed large bowlfuls of cut-up fresh bread. On it clustered the sparrows, getting more than their share of the food. But there were sleek, slate-colored little juncos too, and many a time the lively flash of a blue jay. The two old men watched them with never-failing interest. There was great excitement on the morning when a cardinal and his mate appeared. Shy at first, they soon grew bolder, till their coral-colored beaks pecked as intrepidly on the table as any sparrows. But when the pheasants trailed up out of the ravine the little birds gave way to them. Sparrows and juncos perched in the old hawthorn in which the table was built, to watch the great birds devour their bread, but a flash of blue and a flash of scarlet showed which way the blue jays and the cardinals had flown.

CZECHOSLOVAKIA

Sing Merrily

TRADITIONAL

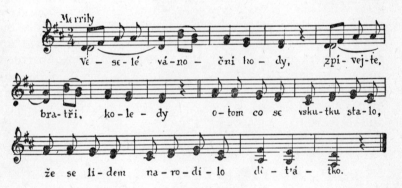

Merrily

Vé – se – lé vá – no – čni ho – dy, zpí – vej – te,
bra – tři, ko – le – dy o – tom co se vsku – tku sta – lo,
že se li – dem na – ro – di – lo di – ťá – tko.

Sing merrily this happy day.
Sing, brothers, sing this carol gay.
Gaily sing the truth adorning,
That to us on Christmas morning
Christ was born.

Babička

BOŽENA NÊMCOVÁ
(Translated by Václav Polák)

WHEN THE Christmas holidays were drawing near, the conversation was invariably interspersed with talks about the baking of Christmas rolls, discussions about the most desirable fineness of the flour and how much butter each intended to use. The girls also talked about the traditional "melting of lead"— usually tinfoil—and the children of the good Christ loaves, and about how these children sailed lighted candles in nut shells. The very little ones babbled of the Christ Child and the presents he would bring them.

It was the custom at the mill, the gamekeeper's lodge and the old bleachery that, whoever came on Christmas Eve or Christmas Day would get all he wanted to eat and drink. In fact, if no one would have shown up, Babička, the grandmother, would probably have gone to the crossroads to look for someone. Her joy can be imagined when, unexpectedly, her son Kašpar with her nephew from Olešnice arrived the day before Christmas! For an entire half day she wept with joy, and every few minutes she left her baking and ran back into the living room to look at them, and to ask her nephew how this one and that one were doing in her old home town.

"Your grandfather looked exactly like your uncle here, except he was a great deal taller," she'd say time after time.

The children examined their uncle and the new cousin from

all angles and were obviously much pleased with them, especially since they replied pleasantly to their endless questions.

Every year the children were firmly resolved to fast the day before Christmas so that, in the evening, they might see the promised golden pigs running about the room; but they never succeeded in keeping the fast all day long. Their intentions were good enough, but their flesh invariably proved too weak.

On Christmas Eve everybody received a goodly share of dainties; and even the poultry and the cattle were not forgotten when the Christmas loaves were cut. After supper the grandmother took a part of the contents from each dish and threw half of what she took into the brook in order that the water would remain pure, while she buried the rest under a tree in the orchard in order that the soil might prove fertile. She brushed the crumbs carefully off the table and threw them into the fire, so that no witch could do them any damage.

After all work was done, Betty took a branch of sweet elder outdoors and, shaking it, recited:

> "Sweet elder branch, I shake thee,
> Tell me, ye dogs who wake me,
> Where my intended might be!"

Then she listened to ascertain the direction in which the dogs were barking—for that's where her future husband was at that very minute!

In the living room the girls were melting a mixture of lead—or tinfoil—and wax, throwing the molten mass into cold water to divine the future from the bizarre shapes it assumed. The children were sailing lighted candles in nutshell-boats representing the ships of life. John secretly gave the pan of water a little push, and the shells merrily sailed from the edge to the center of the water. Then he cried joyfully:

"Look, I shall travel far, far into the world!"

"My dear boy," his mother said softly while peeling an apple for him, "once you get out into the stream of life, and the waves threaten to dash your boat on the rocks, you'll think longingly of the quiet haven from which you sailed." And she cut the

apple crosswise through its widest part, "for luck." The seeds
made a star, three of its rays clear and sound, but two were imperfect and worm-eaten. Laying the apple aside with a sigh, she
cut Barunka's, and again the star was imperfect. She thought,
"Neither one of them will ever be perfectly happy!" Then she
cut Willy's and Adélka's; and in those the stars were clear and
sound, but had only four rays.

"These two will probably be happier," she mused. Adélka
interrupted her by complaining that her nutshell-boat wasn't
going very far away· from the shore, and that her candle was
almost burned down.

"Mine isn't going very far, either!" said Willy.

At that moment someone pushed against the pan, the water
was all waves, and the boats in the center sank.

"See, see, you'll die before we do!" Adélka and Willy cried in
unison.

"That doesn't matter a bit, we're going to travel far anyway!"
Barunka replied, and John agreed with her. But the mother
stared sadly at the extinguished candles, and a presentiment
took possession of her soul that, perhaps, this innocent, childish
play might, after all, foreshadow the future.

"Will the Child Jesus bring us something?" the children
asked their "granny" in a whisper, after the table had been
cleared.

"Now, I don't know," she answered; "you will know when he
rings the bell."

So the smallest of the children took up their post at the window hoping that, when Jesus went by, they'd see him.

"Don't you know that Jesus can neither be seen nor heard?"
granny asked them. "He is in His heaven on a shining throne
and sends His gifts to good children by angels who bring them
down on golden clouds. All you'll hear is the bell."

Listening piously to what Babička said, the children still
kept staring out of the window. Just then a gleaming light became momentarily visible outside, and the tinkle of a bell was
heard. They clasped their hands, while Adélka whispered:

"Grandma, that was Child Jesus, wasn't it?"

Granny nodded. Then the door opened and the mother came in, telling the children that Child Jesus had left gifts for them in their grandmother's room. When they saw a beautiful lighted tree, their joy knew no bounds. Babička herself was not familiar with this custom since it was not a common one among the villagers, but she was much pleased with it and, long before Christmas, had seen to it that a proper tree was provided, and she herself had helped her daughter trim it.

"In Neisse and Kladrau they had had trees, too, do you remember, Kašpar?" Babička asked her son. "You were quite a boy when you left." She sat down beside him, leaving the children to enjoy their Christmas tree and the presents.

"Of course, I remember, *maminka,*" Kaspar replied. "It is a good custom, and you did well, Theresa, to introduce it here. The memory of Christmas will be dear to the children forever, once they find themselves adrift in the world. Away from home, one always loves to remember this day! Certainly *I* found this to be true. My master wasn't too strict, and I managed to have a good time during my apprentice years; and yet, I always thought, 'Oh, if I could only be home with my mother tonight, and eat pudding with honey, and buns with poppyseed sauce, and peas with cabbage!' I would have gladly exchanged all the good things I had for that homely fare!"

"Yes, our Christmas food!" granny smiled. "But didn't you forget the mixed dried fruit?"

"And so I did," he replied, nodding. "But, you know, I never did care for them. Though I thought of something else just now—in Dobrau they called it 'music.'"

"Oh, I know what you mean! The shepherds' Christmas carol! We sing that here, too; you'll hear it before long," his mother said, and she had hardly finished when the shepherd's horn was heard near the window. First the melody of the carol was played upon the horn, and then the shepherds sang:

"Arise, ye shepherds, arise!
Glad tidings to you we bring:
Today a savior was born to us
In a manger in Bethlehem."

"You're quite right, Kašpar," Babicka remarked. "If I didn't hear this song, it wouldn't seem like Christmas to me." Then she went outdoors and loaded the singers down with dainties.

On St. Stephen's Day the boys went out to sing carols at the mill and at the gamekeeper's. Indeed, if they hadn't shown up, the miller would have thought the ceiling must have dropped upon them, and she herself would have come around to the old bleachery to see what had happened. And afterwards other boys came to sing in return.

Now the Christmas holidays were over; and the children already began to talk of other holy days, such as that of the Wise Men from the East. And then the schoolmaster dropped in, sang a song of Christ's birth, and wrote the names of the three Wise Men on the door: Gaspar, Melchior, Balthasar. . . .

DENMARK

Ring Out, Ye Bells!

H. F. S. GRUNDTVIG　　　　　　　　　　　　　HENRIK RUNG

Ki-mer, i Klok ker, ja, ki-mer før Dag i det
dunk-le! tindrer, i Stjerner, som Englenes Øj-ne kan
funk — le! Fred kom til Jord, Him — melens
Fred med Guds Ord. Æ — ren er Guds i det høj — e!

Ring out, ye bells, in the darkness before the new day comes!
Sparkle, ye stars, in the morn ere the first sunny ray comes!
Peace be on earth! His word has given it birth!
Glory to God in the highest!

The Last Dream of the Old Oak-Tree

HANS CHRISTIAN ANDERSEN

IN THE forest, high up on the steep shore, hard by the open sea-coast, stood a very old oak-tree. It was exactly three hundred and sixty-five years old, but that long time was not more for the tree than just as many days would be to us men. We wake by day and sleep through the night, and then we have our dreams: it is different with the tree, which keeps awake through three seasons of the year, and does not get its sleep till winter comes. Winter is its time for rest, its night after the long day which is called spring, summer, and autumn.

On many a warm summer day the Ephemera, the fly that lives but for a day, had danced around his crown—had lived, enjoyed, and felt happy; and then rested for a moment in quiet bliss, the tiny creature, on one of the great fresh oak-leaves; and then the tree always said:

"Poor little thing! Your whole life is but a single day! How very short! It's quite melancholy!"

"Melancholy! Why do you say that?" the Ephemera would then always reply. "It is wonderfully bright, warm, and beautiful all around me, and that makes me rejoice!"

"But only one day, and then it's all done!"

"Done!" repeated the Ephemera. "What's the meaning of *done?* Are you *done,* too?"

"No; I shall perhaps live for thousands of your days, and my day is whole seasons long! It's something so long that you can't at all manage to reckon it out."

"No? then I don't understand you. You say you have thousands of my days; but I have thousands of moments in which I can be merry and happy. Does all the beauty of this world cease when you die?"

"No," replied the Tree; "it will certainly last much longer—far longer than I can possibly think."

"Well, then, we have the same time, only that we reckon differently."

And the Ephemera danced and floated in the air, and rejoiced in her delicate wings of gauze and velvet, and rejoiced in the balmy breezes laden with the fragrance of meadows and of wild-roses and elder-flowers, of the garden hedges, wild thyme, and mint, and daisies; the scent of these was all so strong that the Ephemera was almost intoxicated. The day was long and beautiful, full of joy and of sweet feeling, and when the sun sank low the little fly felt very agreeably tired of all its happiness and enjoyment. The delicate wings would not carry it any more, and quietly and slowly it glided down upon the soft grass-blade, nodded its head as well as it could nod, and went quietly to sleep—and was dead.

"Poor little Ephemera!" said the Oak. "That was a terribly short life!"

And on every summer day the same dance was repeated, the same question and answer, and the same sleep. The same thing was repeated through whole generations of ephemera; all of them felt equally merry and equally happy.

The Oak stood there awake through the spring morning, the noon of summer, and the evening of autumn; and its time of rest, its night, was coming on apace. Winter was approaching.

Already the storms were singing their "good-night, good-night!" Here fell a leaf and there fell a leaf.

"We'll rock you, and dandle you! Go to sleep, go to sleep! We sing you to sleep, we shake you to sleep, but it does you good in your old twigs, does it not? They seem to crack for very joy! Sleep sweetly, sleep sweetly! It's your three hundred and sixty-fifth night. Properly speaking, you're only a stripling as yet! Sleep sweetly! The clouds strew down snow, there will be quite a coverlet, warm and protecting, around your feet. Sweet sleep to you, and pleasant dreams!"

And the Oak-tree stood there, denuded of all its leaves, to sleep through the long winter, and to dream many a dream, always about something that had happened to it—just as in the dreams of men.

The great Oak had once been small—indeed, an acorn had been its cradle. According to human computation, it was now in its fourth century. It was the greatest and best tree in the forest; its crown towered far above all the other trees, and could be descried from afar across the sea, so that it served as a landmark to the sailors; the tree had no idea how many eyes were in the habit of seeking it. High up in its green summit the wood-pigeon built her nest, and the cuckoo sat in its boughs, and sang his song; and in autumn when the leaves looked like thin plates of copper, the birds of passage came and rested there, before they flew away across the sea; but now it was winter, and the tree stood there leafless, so that every one could see how gnarled and crooked the branches were that shot forth from its trunk. Crows and rooks came and took their seat by turns in the boughs, and spoke of the hard times which were beginning, and of the difficulty of getting a living in winter.

It was just at the holy Christmas time, when the tree dreamed its most glorious dream.

The tree had a distinct feeling of the festive time, and fancied he heard the bells ringing from the churches all around; and yet it seemed as if it were a fine summer's day mild and warm. Fresh and green he spread out his mighty crown; the sunbeams played among the twigs and the leaves; the air was full of the fragrance of herbs and blossoms; gay butterflies chased each other to and fro. The ephemeral insects danced as if all the world were created merely for them to dance and be merry in. All that the tree had experienced for years and years, and that had happened around him, seemed to pass by him again, as in a festive pageant. He saw the knights of ancient days ride by with their noble dames on gallant steeds, with plumes waving in their bonnets and falcons on their wrists. The hunting-horn sounded, and the dogs barked. He saw hostile warriors in colored jerkins and with shining weapons, with spear and halbert, pitching their tents and striking them again. The watch-fires flamed up anew, and men sang and slept under the branches of the tree. He saw loving couples meeting near his trunk, happily, in the moonshine; and they cut the initials of their names in the gray-green bark of his stem. Once—but long years had rolled by since then—citherns and Æolian harps had been hung up on his boughs by merry wanderers; and now they hung there again, and once again they sounded in tones of marvellous sweetness. The wood-pigeons cooed, as if they were telling what the tree felt in all this, and the cuckoo called out to tell him how many summer days he had yet to live.

Then it appeared to him as if new life were rippling down into the remotest fibre of his root, and mounting up into his highest branches, to the tops of the leaves. The tree felt that he was stretching and spreading himself, and through his roots he felt that there was life and motion even in the ground itself. He felt his strength increase, he grew higher, his stem shot up unceasingly, and he grew more and more, his crown became fuller, and spread out; and in proportion as the tree grew, he felt his happiness increase, and his joyous hope that he should reach even higher—quite up to the warm, brilliant sun.

Already had he grown high above the clouds, which floated past beneath his crown like dark troops of passage-birds, or like great white swans. And every leaf of the tree had the gift of sight, as if it had eyes wherewith to see; the stars became visible in broad daylight, great and sparkling; each of them sparkled like a pair of eyes, mild and clear. They recalled to his memory well-known gentle eyes, eyes of children, eyes of lovers who had met beneath his boughs.

It was a marvellous spectacle, and one full of happiness and joy! And yet amid all this happiness the tree felt a longing, a yearning desire that all other trees of the wood beneath him, and all the bushes, and herbs, and flowers, might be able to rise with him, that they too might see this splendor, and experience this joy. The great majestic oak was not quite happy in his happiness, while he had not them all, great and little, about him; and this feeling of yearning trembled through his every twig, through his every leaf, warmly and fervently as through a human heart.

The crown of the tree waved to and fro, as if he sought something in his silent longing, and he looked down. Then he felt the fragrance of thyme, and soon afterwards the more powerful scent of honeysuckle and violets; and he fancied he heard the cuckoo answering him.

Yes, through the clouds the green summits of the forest came peering up, and under himself the Oak saw the other trees, as they grew and raised themselves aloft. Bushes and herbs shot up high, and some tore themselves up bodily by the roots to rise the quicker. The birch was the quickest of all. Like a white streak of lightning, its slender stem shot upwards in a zigzag line, and the branches spread around it like green gauze and like banners; the whole woodland natives, even to the brown-plumed rushes, grew up with the rest, and the birds came too, and sang; and on the grass blade that fluttered aloft like a long silken ribbon into the air, sat the grasshopper cleaning his wings with his leg; the May beetles hummed, and the bees murmured, and every bird sang in his appointed manner; all was song and sound of gladness up into the high heaven.

"But the little blue flower by the water-side, where is that?" said the Oak; "and the purple bell-flower and the daisy?" for you see, the old Oak-tree wanted to have them all about him.

"We are here—we are here!" was shouted and sung in reply.

"But the beautiful thyme of last summer—and in the last year there was certainly a place here covered with lilies of the valley! and the wild apple-tree that blossomed so splendidly! and all the glory of the wood that came year by year—if that had only just been born, it might have been here now!"

"We are here, we are here!" replied voices still higher in the air. It seemed as if they had flown on before.

"Why, that is beautiful, indescribably beautiful!" exclaimed the old Oak-tree, rejoicingly. "I have them all around me, great and small; not one has been forgotten! How can so much happiness be imagined? How can it be possible?"

"In heaven, in the better land, it can be imagined, and it is possible!" the reply sounded through the air.

And the old tree, who grew on and on, felt how his roots were tearing themselves free from the ground.

"That's right, that's better than all!" said the tree. "Now no fetters hold me! I can fly up now, to the very highest, in glory and in light! And all my beloved ones are with me, great and small—all of them, all!"

That was the dream of the old Oak-tree; and while he dreamt thus a mighty storm came rushing over land and sea—at the holy Christmas-tide. The sea rolled great billows towards the shore; there was a crackling and crashing in the tree—his root was torn out of the ground in the very moment while he was dreaming that his root freed itself from the earth. He fell. His three hundred and sixty-five years were now as the single day of the Ephemera.

On the morning of the Christmas festival, when the sun rose, the storm had subsided. From all the churches sounded the festive bells, and from every hearth, even from the smallest hut, arose the smoke in blue clouds, like the smoke from the altars of the druids of old at the feast of thanks-offerings. The sea became gradually calm, and on board a great ship in the offing, that had fought successfully with the tempest, all the flags were displayed, as a token of joy suitable to the festive day.

"The tree is down—the old Oak-tree, our landmark on the coast!" said the sailors. "It fell in the storm of last night. Who can replace it? No one can."

This was the funeral oration, short but well meant, that was given to the tree, which lay stretched on the snowy covering on the sea-shore; and over its prostrate form sounded the notes of a song from the ship, a carol of the joys of Christmas, and of the redemption of the soul of man by His blood, and of eternal life.

"Sing, sing aloud, this blessed morn—
   It is fulfilled—and He is born;
   Oh, joy without compare!
      Hallelujah Hallelujah!"

Thus sounded the old psalm-tune, and every one on board the ship felt lifted up in his own way, through the song and the prayer, just as the old tree had felt lifted up in its last, its most beauteous dream in the Christmas night.

ENGLAND

Hark! The Herald Angels Sing

CHARLES WESLEY **FELIX MENDELSSOHN-BARTHOLDY**

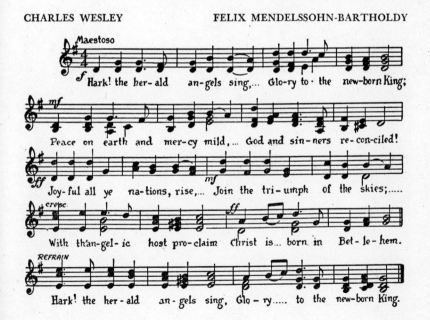

Hark! the her-ald an-gels sing,... Glo-ry to the new-born King;

Peace on earth and mer-cy mild,... God and sin-ners re-con-ciled!

Joy-ful all ye na-tions, rise,... Join the tri-umph of the skies;.....

With th'an-gel-ic host pro-claim Christ is... born in Bet-le-hem.

REFRAIN

Hark! the her-ald an-gels sing, Glo-ry..... to the new-born King.

A Christmas Carol

IN FOUR STAVES

CHARLES DICKENS

STAVE ONE: MARLEY'S GHOST

MARLEY was dead, to begin with. There is no doubt whatever about that. The register of his burial was signed by the clergyman, the clerk, the undertaker, and the chief mourner. Scrooge signed it. And Scrooge's name was good upon 'Change for anything he chose to put his hand to.

Old Marley was as dead as a door-nail.

Scrooge knew he was dead? Of course he did. How could it be otherwise? Scrooge and he were partners for I don't know how many years. Scrooge was his sole executor, his sole administrator, his sole assign, his sole residuary legatee, his sole friend, his sole mourner.

Scrooge never painted out old Marley's name, however. There it yet stood, years afterwards, above the warehouse door—Scrooge and Marley. The firm was known as Scrooge and Marley. Sometimes people new to the business called Scrooge Scrooge, and sometimes Marley. He answered to both names. It was all the same to him.

Oh! But he was a tight-fisted hand at the grindstone, was Scrooge! a squeezing, wrenching, grasping, scraping, clutching, covetous old sinner! External heat and cold had little influence on him. No warmth could warm, no cold could chill him. No wind that blew was bitterer than he, no falling snow was more intent upon its purpose, no pelting rain less open to entreaty.

Foul weather didn't know where to have him. The heaviest rain and snow and hail and sleet could boast of the advantage over him in only one respect,—they often "came down" handsomely, and Scrooge never did.

Nobody ever stopped him in the street to say, with gladsome looks, "My dear Scrooge, how are you? When will you come to see me?" No beggars implored him to bestow a trifle, no children asked him what it was o'clock, no man or woman ever once in all his life inquired the way to such and such a place, of Scrooge. Even the blind men's dogs appeared to know him, and when they saw him coming on, would tug their owners into doorways and up courts; and then would wag their tails as though they said, "No eyes at all is better than an evil eye, dark master!"

But what did Scrooge care! It was the very thing he liked. To edge his way along the crowded paths of life, warning all human sympathy to keep its distance, was what the knowing ones call "nuts" to Scrooge.

Once upon a time—of all the good days in the year, upon a Christmas eve—old Scrooge sat busy in his counting-house. It was cold, bleak, biting, foggy weather; and the city clocks had only just gone three, but it was quite dark already.

The door of Scrooge's counting-house was open, that he might keep his eye upon his clerk, who, in a dismal little cell beyond, a sort of tank, was copying letters. Scrooge had a very small fire, but the clerk's fire was so very much smaller that it looked like one coal. But he couldn't replenish it, for Scrooge kept the coal-box in his own room; and so surely as the clerk came in with the shovel, the master predicted that it would be necessary for them to part. Wherefore the clerk put on his white comforter, and tried to warm himself at the candle; in which effort, not being a man of a strong imagination, he failed.

"A Merry Christmas, uncle! God save you!" cried a cheerful voice. It was the voice of Scrooge's nephew, who came upon him so quickly that this was the first intimation Scrooge had of his approach.

"Bah!" said Scrooge; "humbug!"

"Christmas a humbug, uncle? You don't mean that, I am sure!"

"I do. Out upon merry Christmas! What's Christmas time to you but a time for paying bills without money; a time for finding yourself a year older, and not an hour richer; a time for balancing your books and having every item in 'em through a round dozen of months presented dead against you? If I had my will, every idiot who goes about with 'Merry Christmas' on his lips should be boiled with his own pudding, and buried with a stake of holly through his heart. He should!"

"Uncle!"

"Nephew, keep Christmas in your own way, and let me keep it in mine."

"Keep it! But you don't keep it."

"Let me leave it alone, then. Much good may it do you! Much good it has ever done you!"

"There are many things from which I might have derived good, by which I have not profited, I dare say, Christmas among the rest. But I am sure I have always thought of Christmas time, when it has come round—apart from the veneration due to its sacred origin, if anything belonging to it *can* be apart from that —as a good time; a kind, forgiving, charitable, pleasant time; the only time I know of, in the long calendar of the year, when men and women seem by one consent to open their shut-up hearts freely, and to think of people below them as if they really were fellow-travellers to the grave, and not another race of creatures bound on other journeys. And therefore, uncle, though it has never put a scrap of gold or silver in my pocket, I believe that it *has* done me good, and *will* do me good; and I say, God bless it!"

The clerk in the tank involuntarily applauded.

"Let me hear another sound from *you*," said Scrooge, "and you'll keep your Christmas by losing your situation! You're quite a powerful speaker, sir," he added, turning to his nephew. "I wonder you don't go into Parliament."

"Don't be angry, uncle. Come! Dine with us to-morrow."

Scrooge said that he would see him—yes, indeed he did. He

went the whole length of the expression, and said that he would see him in that extremity first.

"But why?" cried Scrooge's nephew. "Why?"

"Why did you get married?"

"Because I fell in love."

"Because you fell in love!" growled Scrooge, as if that were the only one thing in the world more ridiculous than a merry Christmas. "Good afternoon!"

"Nay, uncle, but you never came to see me before that happened. Why give it as a reason for not coming now?"

"Good afternoon."

"I want nothing from you; I ask nothing of you; why cannot we be friends?"

"Good afternoon."

"I am sorry, with all my heart, to find you so resolute. We have never had any quarrel, to which I have been a party. But I have made the trial in homage to Christmas, and I'll keep my Christmas humour to the last. So A Merry Christmas, uncle!"

"Good afternoon!"

"And A Happy New-Year!"

"Good afternoon!"

His nephew left the room without an angry word, notwithstanding. The clerk, in letting Scrooge's nephew out, had let two other people in. They were portly gentlemen, pleasant to behold, and now stood, with their hats off, in Scrooge's office. They had books and papers in their hands, and bowed to him.

"Scrooge and Marley's, I believe," said one of the gentlemen, referring to his list. "Have I the pleasure of addressing Mr. Scrooge or Mr. Marley?"

"Mr. Marley has been dead these seven years. He died seven years ago, this very night."

"At this festive season of the year, Mr. Scrooge," said the gentleman, taking up a pen, "it is more than usually desirable that we should make some slight provision for the poor and destitute, who suffer greatly at the present time. Many thousands are in want of common necessaries; hundreds of thousands are in want of common comforts, sir."

"Are there no prisons?"

"Plenty of prisons. But under the impression that they scarcely furnish Christian cheer of mind or body to the unoffending multitude, a few of us are endeavouring to raise a fund to buy the poor some meat and drink, and means of warmth. We choose this time, because it is a time, of all others, when Want is keenly felt, and Abundance rejoices. What shall I put you down for?"

"Nothing!"

"You wish to be anonymous?"

"I wish to be left alone. Since you ask me what I wish, gentlemen, that is my answer. I don't make merry myself at Christmas, and I can't afford to make idle people merry. I help to support the prisons and the workhouses,—they cost enough,—and those who are badly off must go there."

"Many can't go there; and many would rather die."

"If they would rather die, they had better do it, and decrease the surplus population."

At length the hour of shutting up the counting-house arrived. With an ill-will Scrooge, dismounting from his stool, tacitly admitted the fact to the expectant clerk in the tank, who instantly snuffed his candle out, and put on his hat.

"You want all day to-morrow, I suppose?"

"If quite convenient, sir."

"It's not convenient, and it's not fair. If I was to stop half a crown for it, you'd think yourself mightily ill-used, I'll be bound?"

"Yes, sir."

"And yet you don't think *me* ill-used, when I pay a day's wages for no work."

"It's only once a year, sir."

"A poor excuse for picking a man's pocket every twenty-fifth of December! But I suppose you must have the whole day. Be here all the earlier *next* morning."

The clerk promised that he would, and Scrooge walked out with a growl. The office was closed in a twinkling, and the clerk, with the long ends of his white comforter dangling below his waist (for he boasted no great-coat), went down a slide, at the end of a lane of boys, twenty times, in honour of its being Christmas eve, and then ran home as hard as he could pelt, to play at blindman's buff.

Scrooge took his melancholy dinner in his usual melancholy tavern; and having read all the newspapers, and beguiled the rest of the evening with his banker's book, went home to bed. He lived in chambers which had once belonged to his deceased partner. They were a gloomy suite of rooms, in a lowering pile of building up a yard. The building was old enough now, and dreary enough, for nobody lived in it but Scrooge, the other rooms being all let out as offices.

Now it is a fact, that there was nothing at all particular about the knocker on the door of this house, except that it was very large; also, that Scrooge had seen it, night and morning, during his whole residence in that place; also, that Scrooge had as little of what is called fancy about him as any man in the city of London. And yet Scrooge, having his key in the lock of the door, saw in the knocker, without its undergoing any intermediate process of change, not a knocker, but Marley's face.

Marley's face, with a dismal light about it, like a bad lobster in a dark cellar. It was not angry or ferocious, but it looked at Scrooge as Marley used to look,—ghostly spectacles turned up upon its ghostly forehead.

As Scrooge looked fixedly at this phenomenon, it was a knocker again. He said, "Pooh, pooh!" and closed the door.

The sound resounded through the house like thunder. Every room above, and every cask in the wine-merchant's cellars below, appeared to have a separate peal of echoes of its own. Scrooge was not a man to be frightened by echoes. He fastened the door, and walked across the hall, and up the stairs. Slowly too, trimming his candle as he went.

Up Scrooge went, not caring a button for its being very dark. Darkness is cheap, and Scrooge liked it. But before he shut his heavy door, he walked through his rooms to see that all was right. He had just enough recollection of the face to desire to do that.

Sitting-room, bedroom, lumber-room, all as they should be. Nobody under the table, nobody under the sofa; a small fire in the grate; spoon and basin ready; and the little saucepan of gruel (Scrooge had a cold in his head) upon the hob. Nobody under the bed; nobody in the closet; nobody in his dressing-gown, which was hanging up in a suspicious attitude against the wall. Lumber-room as usual. Old fire-guards, old shoes, two fish-baskets, washing-stand on three legs, and a poker.

Quite satisfied, he closed his door, and locked himself in; double-locked himself in, which was not his custom. Thus secured against surprise, he took off his cravat, put on his dressing-gown and slippers and his nightcap, and sat down before the very low fire to take his gruel.

As he threw his head back in the chair, his glance happened to rest upon a bell, a disused bell, that hung in the room, and communicated, for some purpose now forgotten, with a chamber in the highest story of the building. It was with great astonishment, and with a strange, inexplicable dread, that, as he looked, he saw this bell begin to swing. Soon it rang out loudly, and so did every bell in the house.

This was succeeded by a clanking noise, deep down below as if some person were dragging a heavy chain over the casks in the wine-merchant's cellar.

Then he heard the noise much louder, on the floors below; then coming up the stairs; then coming straight towards his door.

It came on through the heavy door, and a spectre passed into the room before his eyes. And upon its coming in, the dying flame leaped up, as though it cried, "I know him! Marley's ghost!"

The same face, the very same. Marley in his pigtail, usual waistcoat, tights, and boots. His body was transparent; so that Scrooge, observing him, and looking through his waistcoat, could see the two buttons on his coat behind.

Scrooge had often heard it said that Marley had no bowels, but he had never believed it until now.

No, nor did he believe it even now. Though he looked the

phantom through and through, and saw it standing before him, —though he felt the chilling influence of its death-cold eyes, and noticed the very texture of the folded kerchief bound about its head and chin,—he was still incredulous.

"How now!" said Scrooge, caustic and cold as ever. "What do you want with me?"

"Much!"—Marley's voice, no doubt about it.

"Who are you?"

"Ask me who I *was*."

"Who *were* you then?"

"In life I was your partner, Jacob Marley."

"Can you—can you sit down?"

"I can."

"Do it, then."

Scrooge asked the question, because he didn't know whether a ghost so transparent might find himself in a condition to take a chair; and felt that, in the event of its being impossible, it might involve the necessity of an embarrassing explanation. But the ghost sat down on the opposite side of the fireplace, as if he were quite used to it.

"You don't believe in me."

"I don't."

"What evidence would you have of my reality beyond that of your senses?"

"I don't know."

"Why do you doubt your senses?"

"Because a little thing affects them. A slight disorder of the stomach makes them cheats. You may be an undigested bit of beef, a blot of mustard, a crumb of cheese, a fragment of an underdone potato. There's more of gravy than of grave about you, whatever you are!"

Scrooge was not much in the habit of cracking jokes, nor did he feel in his heart by any means waggish then. The truth is, that he tried to be smart, as a means of distracting his own attention, and keeping down his horror.

But how much greater was his horror when, the phantom taking off the bandage round its head, as if it were too warm to wear indoors, its lower jaw dropped down upon its breast!

"Mercy! Dreadful apparition, why do you trouble me? Why do spirits walk the earth, and why do they come to me?"

"It is required of every man that the spirit within him should walk abroad among his fellow-men, and travel far and wide; and if that spirit goes not forth in life, it is condemned to do so after death. I cannot tell you all I would. A very little more is permitted to me. I cannot rest, I cannot stay, I cannot linger anywhere. My spirit never walked beyond our counting-house— mark me!—in life my spirit never roved beyond the narrow limits of our money-changing hole; and weary journeys lie before me!"

"Seven years dead. And travelling all the time? You travel fast?"

"On the wings of the wind."

"You might have got over a great quantity of ground in seven years."

"O blind man, blind man! not to know that ages of incessant labour by immortal creatures for this earth must pass into eternity before the good of which it is susceptible is all developed. Not to know that any Christian spirit working kindly in its little sphere, whatever it may be, will find its mortal life too short for its vast means of usefulness. Not to know that no space of regret can make amends for one life's opportunities misused! Yet I was like this man; I once was like this man!"

"But you were always a good man of business, Jacob," faltered Scrooge, who now began to apply this to himself.

"Business!" cried the Ghost, wringing its hands again. "Mankind was my business. The common welfare was my business; charity, mercy, forbearance, benevolence, were all my business. The dealings of my trade were but a drop of water in the comprehensive ocean of my business!"

Scrooge was very much dismayed to hear the spectre going on at this rate, and began to quake exceedingly.

"Hear me! My time is nearly gone."

"I will. But don't be hard upon me! Don't be flowery, Jacob! Pray!"

"I am here to-night to warn you that you have yet a chance and hope of escaping my fate. A chance and hope of my procuring, Ebenezer."

"You were always a good friend to me. Thank'ee!"

"You will be haunted by Three Spirits."

"Is that the chance and hope you mentioned, Jacob? I—I think I'd rather not."

"Without their visits, you cannot hope to shun the path I tread. Expect the first to-morrow night, when the bell tolls One. Expect the second on the next night at the same hour. The third, upon the next night, when the last stroke of Twelve has ceased to vibrate. Look to see me no more; and look that, for your own sake, you remember what has passed between us!"

It walked backward from him; and at every step it took, the window raised itself a little, so that, when the apparition reached it, it was wide open.

Scrooge closed the window, and examined the door by which the Ghost had entered. It was double-locked, as he had locked it with his own hands, and the bolts were undisturbed. Scrooge tried to say, "Humbug!" but stopped at the first syllable. And being, from the emotion he had undergone, or the fatigues of the day, or his glimpse of the invisible world, or the dull conversation of the Ghost, or the lateness of the hour, much in need of repose, he went straight to bed, without undressing, and fell asleep on the instant.

STAVE TWO: THE FIRST OF THE THREE SPIRITS

When Scrooge awoke, it was so dark, that, looking out of bed, he could scarcely distinguish the transparent window from the opaque walls of his chamber, until suddenly the church clock tolled a deep, dull, hollow, melancholy ONE.

Light flashed up in the room upon the instant, and the curtains of his bed were drawn aside by a strange figure,—like a child; yet not so like a child as like an old man, viewed through some supernatural medium, which gave him the appearance of having receded from the view, and being diminished to a child's proportions. Its hair, which hung about its neck and down its back, was white as if with age; and yet the face had not a wrinkle in it, and the tenderest bloom was on the skin. It held a branch of fresh green holly in its hand; and, in singular contradiction of that wintry emblem, had its dress trimmed with summer flowers. But the strangest thing about it was, that from the crown of its head there sprung a bright clear jet of light, by which all this was visible; and which was doubtless the occasion of its using, in its duller moments, a great extinguisher for a cap, which it now held under its arm.

"Are you the Spirit, sir, whose coming was foretold to me?"

"I am!"

"Who and what are you?"

"I am the Ghost of Christmas Past."

"Long Past?"

"No. Your past. The things that you will see with me are shadows of the things that have been; they will have no consciousness of us."

Scrooge then made bold to inquire what business brought him there.

"Your welfare. Rise and walk with me!"

It would have been in vain for Scrooge to plead that the weather and the hour were not adapted to pedestrian purposes; that bed was warm, and the thermometer a long way below freezing; that he was clad but lightly in his slippers, dressing-gown, and night-cap; and that he had a cold upon him at that time. The grasp, though gentle as a woman's hand, was not to be resisted. He rose, but finding that the Spirit made towards the window, clasped its robe in supplication.

"I am a mortal, and liable to fall."

"Bear but a touch of my hand *there*," said the Spirit, laying it upon his heart, "and you shall be upheld in more than this!"

As the words were spoken, they passed through the wall, and stood in the busy thoroughfares of a city. It was made plain enough by the dressing of the shops that here, too, it was Christmas time. The Ghost stopped at a certain warehouse door, and asked Scrooge if he knew it.

"Know it! I was apprenticed here!"

They went in. At sight of an old gentleman in a Welsh wig, sitting behind such a high desk that, if he had been two inches taller, he must have knocked his head against the ceiling, Scrooge cried in great excitement: "Why, it's old Fezziwig! Bless his heart, it's Fezziwig, alive again!"

Old Fezziwig laid down his pen, and looked up at the clock, which pointed to the hour of seven. He rubbed his hands; adjusted his capacious waistcoat; laughed all over himself, from his shoes to his organ of benevolence; and called out in a comfortable, oily, rich, fat, jovial voice: "Yo ho, there! Ebenezer! Dick!"

A living and moving picture of Scrooge's former self, a young man, came briskly in, accompanied by his fellow-apprentice.

"Dick Wilkins, to be sure!" said Scrooge to the Ghost. "My old fellow-'prentice, bless me, yes. There he is. He was very much attached to me, was Dick. Poor Dick! Dear, dear!"

"Yo ho, my boys!" said Fezziwig. "No more work to-night. Christmas eve, Dick. Christmas, Ebenezer! Let's have the shutters up, before a man can say Jack Robinson! Clear away, my lads, and let's have lots of room here!"

Clear away! There was nothing they wouldn't have cleared away, or couldn't have cleared away, with old Fezziwig looking on. It was done in a minute. Every movable was packed off, as if it were dismissed from public life for ever more; the floor was swept and watered, the lamps were trimmed, fuel was heaped upon the fire; and the warehouse was as snug and warm and dry and bright a ballroom as you would desire to see on a winter's night.

In came a fiddler with a music-book, and went up to the lofty desk, and made an orchestra of it, and tuned like fifty stomach-aches. In came Mrs. Fezziwig, one vast substantial smile. In came the three Miss Fezziwigs, beaming and lovable. In came the six young followers whose hearts they broke. In came all the young men and women employed in the business. In came the housemaid, with her cousin the baker. In came the cook, with her brother's particular friend the milkman. In they all

came one after another; some shyly, some boldly, some grace-
fully, some awkwardly, some pushing, some pulling; in they all
came, anyhow and everyhow. Away they all went, twenty couples
at once; hands half round and back again the other way; down
the middle and up again; round and round in various stages of
affectionate grouping; old top couple always turning up in the
wrong place; new top couple starting off again, as soon as they
got there; all top couples at last, and not a bottom one to help
them. When this result was brought about, old Fezziwig,
clapping his hands to stop the dance, cried out, "Well done";
and the fiddler plunged his hot face into a pot of porter especially provided for that purpose.

There were more dances, and there were forfeits, and more
dances, and there was cake, and there was negus, and there was a
great piece of Cold Roast, and there was a great piece of Cold
Boiled, and there were mince-pies, and plenty of beer. But the
great effect of the evening came after the Roast and Boiled,
when the fiddler struck up "Sir Roger de Coverley." Then old
Fezziwig stood out to dance with Mrs. Fezziwig. Top couple,
too; with a good stiff piece of work cut out for them; three or
four and twenty pair of partners; people who were not to be
trifled with; people who *would* dance, and had no notion of
walking.

But if they had been twice as many—four times—old Fezziwig
would have been a match for them, and so would Mrs. Fezziwig.
As to *her*, she was worthy to be his partner in every sense of
the term. A positive light appeared to issue from Fezziwig's
calves. They shone in every part of the dance. You couldn't have
predicted, at any given time, what would become of 'em next.
And when old Fezziwig and Mrs. Fezziwig had gone all through
the dance,—advance and retire, turn your partner, bow and
courtesy, corkscrew, thread the needle, and back again to your
place,—Fezziwig "cut,"—cut so deftly, that he appeared to wink
with his legs.

When the clock struck eleven this domestic ball broke up.
Mr. and Mrs. Fezziwig took their stations, one on either side the
door, and, shaking hands with every person individually as he

or she went out, wished him or her a Merry Christmas. When
everybody had retired but the two 'prentices, they did the same
to them; and thus the cheerful voices died away, and the lads
were left to their beds, which were under a counter in the back
shop.

"A small matter," said the Ghost, "to make these silly folks
so full of gratitude. He has spent but a few pounds of your mortal money,—three or four perhaps. Is that so much that he
deserves this praise?"

"It isn't that," said Scrooge, heated by the remark, and speaking unconsciously like his former, not his latter self,—"it isn't
that, Spirit. He has the power to render us happy or unhappy;
to make our service light or burdensome; a pleasure or a toil.
Say that his power lies in words and looks; in things so slight
and insignificant that it is impossible to add and count 'em up:
what then? The happiness he gives is quite as great as if it cost
a fortune."

He felt the Spirit's glance, and stopped.

"What is the matter?"

"Nothing particular."

"Something, I think?"

"No, no. I should like to be able to say a word or two to my
clerk just now. That's all."

"My time grows short," observed the Spirit. "Quick!"

This was not addressed to Scrooge, or to any one whom he
could see, but it produced an immediate effect. For again he
saw himself. He was older now; a man in the prime of life.

He was not alone, but sat by the side of a fair young girl in a
black dress, in whose eyes there were tears.

"It matters little," she said softly to Scrooge's former self.
"To you very little. Another idol has displaced me; and if it
can comfort you in time to come, as I would have tried to do,
I have no just cause to grieve."

"What idol has displaced you?"

"A golden one. You fear the world too much. I have seen
your nobler aspirations fall off one by one, until the master-
passion, Gain, engrosses you. Have I not?"

"What then? Even if I have grown so much wiser, what then? I am not changed towards you. Have I ever sought release from our engagement?"

"In words, no. Never."

"In what, then?"

"In a changed nature; in an altered spirit; in another atmosphere of life; another Hope as its great end. If you were free today, tomorrow, yesterday, can even I believe that you would choose a dowerless girl; or, choosing her, do I not know that your repentance and regret would surely follow? I do; and I release you. With a full heart, for the love of him you once were."

"Spirit! remove me from this place."

"I told you these were shadows of the things that have been," said the Ghost. "That they are what they are, do not blame me!"

"Remove me!" Scrooge exclaimed. "I cannot bear it! Leave me! Take me back. Haunt me no longer!"

As he struggled with the Spirit he was conscious of being exhausted, and overcome by an irresistible drowsiness; and, further, of being in his own bedroom. He had barely time to reel to bed before he sank into a heavy sleep.

STAVE THREE: THE SECOND OF THE THREE SPIRITS

Scrooge awoke in his own bedroom. There was no doubt about that. But it and his own adjoining sitting-room, into which he shuffled in his slippers, attracted by a great light there, had undergone a surprising transformation. The walls and ceiling were so hung with living green, that it looked a perfect grove. The leaves of holly, mistletoe, and ivy reflected back the light, as if so many little mirrors had been scattered there; and such a mighty blaze went roaring up the chimney, as that petrifaction of a hearth had never known in Scrooge's time, or Marley's, or for many and many a winter season gone. Heaped upon the floor, to form a kind of throne, were turkeys, geese, game, brawn, great joints of meat, sucking pigs, long wreaths of sausages, mince-pies, plum-puddings, barrels of oysters, red-hot chestnuts, cherry-cheeked apples, juicy oranges, luscious pears, immense twelfth-cakes, and great bowls of punch. In easy state upon this couch there sat a Giant glorious to see; who bore a glowing torch, in shape not unlike Plenty's horn, and who raised it high to shed its light on Scrooge, as he came peeping round the door.

"Come in,—come in! and know me better, man! I am the Ghost of Christmas Present. Look upon me! You have never seen the like of me before."

"Never."

"Have never walked forth with the younger members of my family; meaning (for I am very young) my elder brothers born in these later years?" pursued the Phantom.

"I don't think I have, I am afraid I have not. Have you had many brothers, Spirit?"

"More than eighteen hundred."

"A tremendous family to provide for! Spirit, conduct me where you will. I went forth last night on compulsion, and I learnt a lesson which is working now. To-night, if you have aught to teach me, let me profit by it."

"Touch my robe!"

Scrooge did as he was told, and held it fast.

The room and its contents all vanished instantly, and they stood in the city streets upon a snowy Christmas morning.

Scrooge and the Ghost passed on, invisible, straight to Scrooge's clerk's; and on the threshold of the door the Spirit smiled, and stopped to bless Bob Cratchit's dwelling with the sprinklings of his torch. Think of that! Bob had but fifteen "bob" a week himself; he pocketed on Saturdays but fifteen copies of his Christian name; and yet the Ghost of Christmas Present blessed his four-roomed house!

Then up rose Mrs. Cratchit, Cratchit's wife, dressed out but poorly in a twice-turned gown, but brave in ribbons, which are cheap and make a goodly show for sixpence; and she laid the cloth, assisted by Belinda Cratchit, second of her daughters, also brave in ribbons; while Master Peter Cratchit plunged a fork into the saucepan of potatoes, and, getting the corners of his monstrous shirt-collar (Bob's private property, conferred upon his son and heir in honour of the day) into his mouth, rejoiced to find himself so gallantly attired, and yearned to show his linen in the fashionable Parks. And now two smaller Cratchits, boy and girl, came tearing in, screaming that outside the baker's they had smelt the goose, and known it for their own; and, basking in luxurious thoughts of sage and onion, these young Cratchits danced about the table, and exalted Master Peter Cratchit to the skies, while he (not proud, although his collars nearly choked him) blew the fire, until the slow potatoes, bubbling up, knocked loudly at the saucepan-lid to be let out and peeled.

"What has ever got your precious father then?" said Mrs. Cratchit. "And your brother Tiny Tim! And Martha warn't as late last Christmas day by half an hour!"

"Here's Martha, mother!" said a girl, appearing as she spoke.

"Here's Martha, mother!" cried the two young Cratchits. "Hurrah! There's *such* a goose, Martha!"

"Why, bless your heart alive, my dear, how late you are!" said Mrs. Cratchit, kissing her a dozen times, and taking off her shawl and bonnet for her.

"We'd a deal of work to finish up last night," replied the girl, "and had to clear away this morning, mother!"

"Well! Never mind so long as you are come," said Mrs. Cratchit. "Sit ye down before the fire, my dear, and have a warm, Lord bless ye!"

"No, no! There's father coming," cried the two young Cratchits, who were everywhere at once. "Hide, Martha, hide!"

So Martha hid herself, and in came little Bob, the father, with at least three feet of comforter, exclusive of the fringe, hanging down before him; and his threadbare clothes darned up and brushed, to look seasonable; and Tiny Tim upon his shoulder. Alas for Tiny Tim, he bore a little crutch, and had his limbs supported by an iron frame!

"Why, where's our Martha?" cried Bob Cratchit, looking round.

"Not coming," said Mrs. Cratchit.

"Not coming!" said Bob, with a sudden declension in his

high spirits; for he had been Tim's blood-horse all the way from church, and had come home rampant,—"not coming upon Christmas day!"

Martha didn't like to see him disappointed, if it were only in joke; so she came out prematurely from behind the closet door, and ran into his arms, while the two young Cratchits hustled Tiny Tim, and bore him off into the wash-house, that he might hear the pudding singing in the copper.

"And how did little Tim behave?" asked Mrs. Cratchit, when she had rallied Bob on his credulity, and Bob had hugged his daughter to his heart's content.

"As good as gold," said Bob, "and better. Somehow he gets thoughtful, sitting by himself so much, and thinks the strangest things you ever heard. He told me, coming home, that he hoped the people saw him in the church, because he was a cripple, and it might be pleasant to them to remember, upon Christmas day, who made lame beggars walk and blind men see."

Bob's voice was tremulous when he told them this, and trembled more when he said that Tiny Tim was growing strong and hearty.

His active little crutch was heard upon the floor, and back came Tiny Tim before another word was spoken, escorted by his brother and sister to his stool beside the fire; and while Bob, turning up his cuffs,—as if, poor fellow, they were capable of being made more shabby,—compounded some hot mixture in a jug with gin and lemons, and stirred it round and round, and put it on the hob to simmer, Master Peter and the two ubiquitous young Cratchits went to fetch the goose, with which they soon returned in high procession.

Mrs. Cratchit made the gravy (ready beforehand in a little saucepan) hissing hot; Master Peter mashed the potatoes with incredible vigour; Miss Belinda sweetened up the apple-sauce; Martha dusted the hot plates; Bob took Tiny Tim beside him in a tiny corner at the table; the two young Cratchits set chairs for everybody, not forgetting themselves, and mounting guard upon their posts, crammed spoons into their mouths, lest they should shriek for goose before their turn came to be helped.

At last the dishes were set on, and grace was said. It was succeeded by a breathless pause, as Mrs. Cratchit, looking slowly all along the carving-knife, prepared to plunge it in the breast; but when she did, and when the long-expected gush of stuffing issued forth, one murmur of delight arose all round the board, and even Tiny Tim, excited by the two young Cratchits, beat on the table with the handle of his knife, and feebly cried, Hurrah!

There never was such a goose. Bob said he didn't believe there ever was such a goose cooked. Its tenderness and flavour, size and cheapness, were the themes of universal admiration. Eked out by apple-sauce and mashed potatoes, it was a sufficient dinner for the whole family; indeed, as Mrs. Cratchit said with great delight (surveying one small atom of a bone upon the dish) they hadn't ate it all at last! Yet every one had had enough, and the youngest Cratchits in particular were steeped in sage and onion to the eyebrows! But now, the plates being changed by Miss Belinda, Mrs. Cratchit left the room alone,—too nervous to bear witnesses,—to take the pudding up, and bring it in.

Suppose it should not be done enough! Suppose it should break in turning out! Suppose somebody should have got over the wall of the back yard, and stolen it, while they were merry with the goose,—a supposition at which the two young Cratchits became livid! All sorts of horrors were supposed.

Hallo! A great deal of steam! The pudding was out of the copper. A smell like a washing-day! That was the cloth. A smell like an eating-house and a pastry-cook's next door to each other, with a laundress's next door to that! That was the pudding! In half a minute Mrs. Cratchit entered,—flushed but smiling proudly,—with the pudding, like a speckled cannon-ball, so hard and firm, blazing in half of half a quartern of ignited brandy, and bedight with Christmas holly stuck into the top.

Oh, a wonderful pudding! Bob Cratchit said, and calmly too, that he regarded it as the greatest success achieved by Mrs. Cratchit since their marriage. Mrs. Cratchit said that now the weight was off her mind, she would confess she had had her doubts about the quantity of flour. Everybody had something to say about it, but nobody said or thought it was at all a small pudding for a large family. Any Cratchit would have blushed to hint at such a thing.

At last the dinner was all done, the cloth was cleared, the hearth swept, and the fire made up. The compound in the jug being tasted, and considered perfect, apples and oranges were put upon the table, and a shovelful of chestnuts on the fire.

Then all the Cratchit family drew round the hearth, in what Bob Cratchit called a circle, and at Bob Cratchit's elbow stood the family display of glass,—two tumblers, and a custard-cup without a handle.

These held the hot stuff from the jug, however, as well as golden goblets would have done; and Bob served it out with beaming looks, while the chestnuts on the fire spluttered and crackled noisily. Then Bob proposed:—

"A Merry Christmas to us all, my dears. God bless us!"

Which all the family re-echoed.

"God bless us every one!" said Tiny Tim, the last of all.

He sat very close to his father's side, upon his little stool. Bob held his withered little hand in his, as if he loved the child, and wished to keep him by his side, and dreaded that he might be taken from him.

Scrooge raised his head speedily, on hearing his own name.

"Mr. Scrooge!" said Bob; "I'll give you Mr. Scrooge, the Founder of the Feast!"

"The Founder of the Feast indeed!" cried Mrs. Cratchit, reddening. "I wish I had him here. I'd give him a piece of my mind to feast upon, and I hope he'd have a good appetite for it."

"My dear," said Bob, "the children! Christmas day."

"It should be Christmas day, I am sure," said she, "on which one drinks the health of such an odious, stingy, hard, unfeeling man as Mr. Scrooge. You know he is, Robert! Nobody knows it better than you do, poor fellow!"

"My dear," was Bob's mild answer, "Christmas day."

"I'll drink his health for your sake and the day's," said Mrs. Cratchit, "not for his. Long life to him! A merry Christmas and a happy New Year! He'll be very merry and very happy, I have no doubt!"

The children drank the toast after her. It was the first of their proceedings which had no heartiness in it. Tiny Tim drank it last of all, but he didn't care twopence for it. Scrooge was the Ogre of the family. The mention of his name cast a dark shadow on the party, which was not dispelled for full five minutes.

After it had passed away, they were ten times merrier than before, from the mere relief of Scrooge the Baleful being done with. Bob Cratchit told them how he had a situation in his eye for Master Peter, which would bring him, if obtained, full five and sixpence weekly. The two young Cratchits laughed tremendously at the idea of Peter's being a man of business; and Peter himself looked thoughtfully at the fire from between his collars, as if he were deliberating what particular investments he should favour when he came into the receipt of that bewildering income. Martha, who was a poor apprentice at a milliner's, then told them what kind of work she had to do, and how many hours she worked at a stretch, and how she meant to lie abed to-morrow morning for a good long rest; to-morrow being a holiday she passed at home. Also how she had seen a countess and a lord some days before, and how the lord "was much about as tall as Peter," at which Peter pulled up his collars so high that you couldn't have seen his head if you had been there. All this time the chestnuts and the jug went round and round; and by and by they had a song, about a lost child travelling in the snow, from Tiny Tim, who had a plaintive little voice, and sang it very well indeed.

There was nothing of high mark in this. They were not a handsome family; they were not well dressed; their shoes were far from being waterproof; their clothes were scanty; and Peter might have known, and very likely did, the inside of a pawn-broker's. But they were happy, grateful, pleased with one another, and contented with the time; and when they faded, and looked happier yet in the bright sprinklings of the Spirit's torch at parting, Scrooge had his eye upon them, and especially on Tiny Tim, until the last.

It was a great surprise to Scrooge, as this scene vanished, to hear a hearty laugh. It was a much greater surprise to Scrooge to recognize it as his own nephew's, and to find himself in a bright, dry, gleaming room, with the Spirit standing smiling by his side, and looking at that same nephew.

It is a fair, even-handed, noble adjustment of things, that while there is infection in disease and sorrow, there is nothing in the world so irresistibly contagious as laughter and good-humour. When Scrooge's nephew laughed, Scrooge's niece by marriage laughed as heartily as he. And their assembled friends, being not a bit behind-hand, laughed out lustily.

"He said that Christmas was a humbug, as I live!" cried Scrooge's nephew. "He believed it too!"

"More shame for him, Fred!" said Scrooge's niece, indignantly. Bless those women! they never do anything by halves. They are always in earnest.

She was very pretty; exceedingly pretty. With a dimpled, surprised-looking, capital face; a ripe little mouth that seemed made to be kissed,—as no doubt it was; all kinds of good little dots about her chin, that melted into one another when she laughed; and the sunniest pair of eyes you ever saw in any little creature's head. Altogether she was what you would have called provoking, but satisfactory, too. Oh, perfectly satisfactory.

"He's a comical old fellow," said Scrooge's nephew, "that's the truth; and not so pleasant as he might be. However, his offences carry their own punishment, and I have nothing to say against him. Who suffers by his ill whims? Himself, always. Here he takes it into his head to dislike us, and he won't come and dine with us. What's the consequence? He don't lose much of a dinner."

"Indeed, I think he loses a very good dinner," interrupted Scrooge's niece. Everybody else said the same, and they must be allowed to have been competent judges, because they had just had dinner; and, with the dessert upon the table, were clustered round the fire, by lamplight.

"Well, I am very glad to hear it," said Scrooge's nephew, "because I haven't any great faith in these young housekeepers. What do you say, Topper?"

Topper clearly had his eye on one of Scrooge's niece's sisters, for he answered that a bachelor was a wretched outcast, who had no right to express an opinion on the subject. Whereat Scrooge's niece's sister—the plump one with the lace tucker; not the one with the roses—blushed.

After tea they had some music. For they were a musical family, and knew what they were about, when they sung a Glee or Catch, I can assure you,—especially Topper, who could growl away in the bass like a good one, and never swell the large veins in his forehead, or get red in the face over it.

But they didn't devote the whole evening to music. After a while they played at forfeits; for it is good to be children sometimes, and never better than at Christmas, when its mighty Founder was a child himself. There was first a game at blind-man's buff though. And I no more believe Topper was really blinded than I believe he had eyes in his boots. Because the way in which he went after that plump sister in the lace tucker was an outrage on the credulity of human nature. Knocking down the fire-irons, tumbling over the chairs, bumping up against the piano, smothering himself among the curtains, wherever she went there went he! He always knew where the plump sister was. He wouldn't catch anybody else. If you had fallen up against him, as some of them did, and stood there, he would have made a feint of endeavouring to seize you, which would have been an affront to your understanding, and would instantly have sidled off in the direction of the plump sister.

"Here is a new game," said Scrooge. "One half-hour, Spirit, only one!"

It was a Game called Yes and No, where Scrooge's nephew had to think of something, and the rest must find out what; he only answering to their questions yes or no, as the case was. The fire of questioning to which he was exposed elicited from him that he was thinking of an animal, a live animal, rather a disagreeable animal, a savage animal, an animal that growled and grunted sometimes, and talked sometimes, and lived in London, and walked about the streets, and wasn't made a show of, and wasn't led by anybody, and didn't live in a menagerie, and was never killed in a market, and was not a horse, or an ass, or a cow, or a bull, or a tiger, or a dog, or a pig, or a cat, or a bear. At every new question put to him, this nephew burst into a fresh roar of laughter; and was so inexpressibly tickled, that he was obliged to get up off the sofa and stamp. At last the plump sister cried out:—

"I have found it out! I know what it is, Fred! I know what it is!"

"What is it?" cried Fred.

"It's your uncle Scro-o-o-o-oge!"

Which it certainly was. Admiration was the universal sentiment, though some objected that the reply to "Is it a bear?" ought to have been "Yes."

Uncle Scrooge had imperceptibly become so gay and light of heart, that he would have drank to the unconscious company in an inaudible speech. But the whole scene passed off in the breath of the last word spoken by his nephew; and he and the Spirit were again upon their travels.

Much they saw, and far they went, and many homes they visited, but always with a happy end. The Spirit stood beside sick-beds, and they were cheerful; on foreign lands, and they were close at home; by struggling men, and they were patient in their greater hope; by poverty, and it was rich. In almshouse, hospital, and jail, in misery's every refuge, where vain man in his little brief authority had not made fast the door, and barred the Spirit out, he left his blessing, and taught Scrooge his precepts. Suddenly, as they stood together in an open place, the bell struck twelve.

Scrooge looked about him for the Ghost, and saw it no more. As the last stroke ceased to vibrate, he remembered the prediction of old Jacob Marley, and, lifting up his eyes, beheld a solemn Phantom, draped and hooded, coming like a mist along the ground towards him.

STAVE FOUR: THE LAST OF THE SPIRITS

The Phantom slowly, gravely, silently approached. When it came near him, Scrooge bent down upon his knee; for in the air through which this Spirit moved it seemed to scatter gloom and mystery.

It was shrouded in a deep black garment, which concealed its head, its face, its form, and left nothing of it visible save one outstretched hand. He knew no more, for the Spirit neither spoke nor moved.

"I am in the presence of the Ghost of Christmas Yet to Come? Ghost of the Future! I fear you more than any spectre I have seen. But as I know your purpose is to do me good, and as I hope to live to be another man from what I was, I am prepared to bear you company, and do it with a thankful heart. Will you not speak to me?"

It gave him no reply. The hand was pointed straight before them.

"Lead on! Lead on! The night is waning fast, and it is precious time to me, I know. Lead on, Spirit!"

They scarcely seemed to enter the city; for the city rather seemed to spring up about them. But there they were in the heart of it; on 'Change, amongst the merchants.

The Spirit stopped beside one little knot of business men. Observing that the hand was pointed to them, Scrooge advanced to listen to their talk.

"No," said a great fat man with a monstrous chin. "I don't know much about it either way. I only know he's dead."

"When did he die?" inquired another.

"Last night, I believe."

"Why, what was the matter with him? I thought he'd never die."

"God knows," said the first, with a yawn.

"What has he done with his money?" asked a red-faced gentleman.

"I haven't heard," said the man with the large chin. "Company, perhaps. He hasn't left it to me. That's all I know. By, by."

Scrooge was at first inclined to be surprised that the Spirit should attach importance to conversation apparently so trivial; but feeling assured that it must have some hidden purpose, he set himself to consider what it was likely to be. It could scarcely be supposed to have any bearing on the death of Jacob, his old partner, for that was Past, and this Ghost's province was the Future.

He looked about in that very place for his own image; but another man stood in his accustomed corner, and though the clock pointed to his usual time of day for being there, he saw no likeness of himself amongst the multitudes that poured in through the Porch. It gave him little surprise, however; for he had been revolving in his mind a change of life, and he thought and hoped he saw his newborn resolutions carried out in this.

They left this busy scene, and went into an obscure part of the town, to a low shop where iron, old rags, bottles, bones, and greasy offal were bought. A gray-haired rascal, of great age, sat smoking his pipe. Scrooge and the Phantom came into the presence of this man, just as a woman with a heavy bundle slunk into the shop. But she had scarcely entered, when another woman, similarly laden, came in too; and she was closely followed by a man in faded black. After a short period of blank astonishment, in which the old man with the pipe had joined them, they all three burst into a laugh.

"Let the charwoman alone to be the first!" cried she who had entered first. "Let the laundress alone to be the second; and let the undertaker's man alone to be the third. Look here, old Joe, here's a chance! If we haven't all three met here without meaning it!"

"You couldn't have met in a better place. You were made free of it long ago, you know; and the other two ain't strangers. What have you got to sell? What have you got to sell?"

"Half a minute's patience, Joe, and you shall see."

"What odds then! What odds, Mrs. Dilber?" said the woman.

"Every person has a right to take care of themselves. *He* always did! Who's the worse for the loss of a few things like these? Not a dead man, I suppose."

Mrs. Dilber, whose manner was remarkable for general propitiation, said, "No, indeed, ma'am."

"If he wanted to keep 'em after he was dead, a wicked old screw, why wasn't he natural in his lifetime? If he had been, he'd have had somebody to look after him when he was struck with Death, instead of lying gasping out his last there, alone by himself."

"It's the truest word that ever was spoke, it's a judgment on him."

"I wish it was a little heavier judgment, and it should have been, you may depend upon it, if I could have laid my hands on anything else. Open that bundle, old Joe, and let me know the value of it. Speak out plain. I'm not afraid to be the first, nor afraid for them to see it."

Joe went down on his knees for the greater convenience of opening the bundle, and dragged out a large and heavy roll of some dark stuff.

"What do you call this? Bed-curtains!"

"Ah! Bed-curtains! Don't drop that oil upon the blankets, now."

"*His* blankets?"

"Whose else's do you think? He isn't likely to take cold without 'em, I dare say. Ah! You may look through that shirt till your eyes ache; but you won't find a hole in it, nor a threadbare place. It's the best he had, and a fine one too. They'd have wasted it by dressing him up in it, if it hadn't been for me."

Scrooge listened to this dialogue in horror.

"Spirit! I see, I see. The case of this unhappy man might be my own. My life tends that way, now. Merciful Heaven, what is this!"

The scene had changed, and now he almost touched a bare, uncurtained bed. A pale light, rising in the outer air, fell straight upon this bed; and on it, unwatched, unwept, uncared for, was the body of this plundered unknown man.

"Spirit, let me see some tenderness connected with a death, or this dark chamber, Spirit, will be for ever present to me."

The Ghost conducted him to poor Bob Cratchit's house,—the dwelling he had visited before,—and found the mother and the children seated round the fire.

Quiet. Very quiet. The noisy little Cratchits were as still as statues in one corner, and sat looking up at Peter, who had a book before him. The mother and her daughters were engaged in needlework. But surely they were very quiet!

" 'And he took a child, and set him in the midst of them.' "

Where had Scrooge heard those words? He had not dreamed them. The boy must have read them out, as he and the Spirit crossed the threshold. Why did he not go on?

The mother laid her work upon the table, and put her hand up to her face. "The colour hurts my eyes," she said.

The colour? Ah, poor Tiny Tim!

"They're better now again. It makes them weak by candle-light; and I wouldn't show weak eyes to your father when he comes home, for the world. It must be near his time."

"Past it rather," Peter answered, shutting up his book. "But I think he has walked a little slower than he used, these few last evenings, mother."

"I have known him walk with—I have known him walk with Tiny Tim upon his shoulder, very fast indeed."

"And so have I," cried Peter. "Often."

"And so have I," exclaimed another. So had all.

"But he was very light to carry, and his father loved him so, that it was no trouble,—no trouble. And there is your father at the door!"

She hurried out to meet him; and little Bob in his comforter —he had need of it, poor fellow—came in. His tea was ready for him on the hob, and they all tried who should help him to it most. Then the two young Cratchits got upon his knees and laid, each child, a little cheek against his face, as if they said, "Don't mind it, father. Don't be grieved!"

Bob was very cheerful with them, and spoke pleasantly to all the family. He looked at the work upon the table, and praised the industry and speed of Mrs. Cratchit and the girls. They would be done long before Sunday, he said.

"Sunday! You went to-day, then, Robert?"

"Yes, my dear," returned Bob. "I wish you could have gone. It would have done you good to see how green a place it is. But you'll see it often. I promised him that I would walk there on a Sunday. My little, little child! My little child!"

He broke down all at once. He couldn't help it. If he could have helped it, he and his child would have been farther apart, perhaps, than they were.

"Spectre," said Scrooge, "something informs me that our parting moment is at hand. I know it, but I know not how. Tell me what man that was, with the covered face, whom we saw lying dead?"

The Ghost of Christmas Yet to Come conveyed him to a dismal, wretched, ruinous churchyard.

The Spirit stood amongst the graves, and pointed down to One.

"Before I draw nearer to that stone to which you point, answer me one question. Are these the shadows of the things that Will be, or are they shadows of the things that May be only?"

Still the Ghost pointed downward to the grave by which it stood.

"Men's courses will foreshadow certain ends, to which, if persevered in, they must lead. But if the courses be departed from, the ends will change. Say it is thus with what you show me!"

The Spirit was immovable as ever.

Scrooge crept towards it, trembling as he went; and, following the finger, read upon the stone of the neglected grave his own name—EBENEZER SCROOGE.

"Am _I_ that man who lay upon the bed? No, Spirit! Oh no, no! Spirit! hear me! I am not the man I was. I will not be the man I must have been but for this intercourse. Why show me this, if I am past all hope? Assure me that I yet may change these shadows you have shown me by an altered life."

For the first time the kind hand faltered.

"I will honour Christmas in my heart, and try to keep it all the year. I will live in the Past, the Present, and the Future. The Spirits of all three shall strive within me. I will not shut out the lessons that they teach. Oh, tell me I may sponge away the writing on this stone!"

Holding up his hands in one last prayer to have his fate reversed, he saw an alteration in the Phantom's hood and dress. It shrunk, collapsed, and dwindled down into a bedpost.

Yes, and the bedpost was his own. The bed was his own, the room was his own. Best and happiest of all, the Time before him was his own, to make amends in!

He was checked in his transports by the churches ringing out the lustiest peals he had ever heard.

Running to the window, he opened it, and put out his head. No fog, no mist, no night; clear, bright, stirring, golden day.

"What's to-day?" cried Scrooge, calling downward to a boy in Sunday clothes, who perhaps had loitered in to look about him.

"*Eh?*"

"What's to-day, my fine fellow?"

"To-day! Why *Christmas day.*"

"It's Christmas day! I haven't missed it. Hallo, my fine fellow!"

"Hallo!"

"Do you know the Poulterer's, in the next street but one, at the corner?"

"I should hope I did."

"An intelligent boy! A remarkable boy! Do you know whether they've sold the prize Turkey that was hanging up there? Not the little prize Turkey,—the big one?"

"What, the one as big as me?"

What a delightful boy! It's a pleasure to talk to him. "Yes, my buck!"

"It's hanging there now."

"Is it? Go and buy it."

"Walk-*er!*" exclaimed the boy.

"No, no, I am in earnest. Go and buy it, and tell 'em to bring it here, that I may give them the direction where to take it. Come back with the man, and I'll give you a shilling. Come back with him in less than five minutes, and I'll give you half a crown!"

The boy was off like a shot.

"I'll send it to Bob Cratchit's! He sha'n't know who sends it. It's twice the size of Tiny Tim. Joe Miller never made such a joke as sending it to Bob's will be!"

The hand in which he wrote the address was not a steady one; but write it he did, somehow, and went down stairs to open the street door for the coming of the poulterer's man.

It *was* a Turkey! He never could have stood upon his legs, that bird. He would have snapped 'em short off in a minute, like sticks of sealing-wax.

Scrooge dressed himself "all in his best," and at last got out into the streets. The people were by this time pouring forth, as he had seen them with the Ghost of Christmas Present; and, walking with his hands behind him, Scrooge regarded every one with a delighted smile. He looked so irresistibly pleasant, in a word, that three or four good-humoured fellows said, "Good morning, sir! A merry Christmas to you!" And Scrooge said often afterwards, that, of all the blithe sounds he had ever heard, those were the blithest in his ears.

In the afternoon, he turned his steps towards his nephew's house.

He passed the door a dozen times, before he had the courage to go up and knock. But he made a dash, and did it.

"Is your master at home, my dear?" said Scrooge to the girl. Nice girl! Very.

"Yes, sir."

"Where is he, my love?"

"He's in the dining-room, sir, along with mistress."

"He knows me," said Scrooge, with his hand already on the dining-room lock. "I'll go in here, my dear."

"Fred!"

"Why, bless my soul!" cried Fred, "who's that?"

"It's I. Your uncle Scrooge. I have come to dinner. Will you let me in, Fred?"

Let him in! It is a mercy he didn't shake his arm off. He was at home in five minutes. Nothing could be heartier. His niece looked just the same. So did Topper when *he* came. So did the plump sister when *she* came. So did every one when *they* came. Wonderful party, wonderful games, wonderful unanimity, wonderful happiness!

But he was early at the office next morning. Oh, he was early there. If he could only be there first, and catch Bob Cratchit coming late! That was the thing he had set his heart upon.

And he did it. The clock struck nine. No Bob. A quarter past. No Bob. Bob was full eighteen minutes and a half behind his time. Scrooge sat with his door wide open, that he might see him come into the tank.

Bob's hat was off before he opened the door; his comforter too. He was on his stool in a jiffy; driving away with his pen, as if he were trying to overtake nine o'clock.

"Hallo!" growled Scrooge, in his accustomed voice, as near as he could feign it. "What do you mean by coming here at this time of day?"

"I am very sorry, sir. I *am* behind my time."

"You are? Yes. I think you are. Step this way if you please."

"It's only once a year, sir. It shall not be repeated. I was making rather merry yesterday, sir."

"Now, I'll tell you what, my friend. I am not going to stand this sort of thing any longer. And therefore," Scrooge continued, leaping from his stool, and giving Bob such a dig in the waistcoat that he staggered back into the tank again,—"and therefore I am about to raise your salary!"

Bob trembled, and got a little nearer to the ruler.

"A merry Christmas, Bob!" said Scrooge, with an earnestness that could not be mistaken, as he clapped him on the back. "A merrier Christmas, Bob, my good fellow, than I have given you for many a year! I'll raise your salary, and endeavour to assist your struggling family, and we will discuss your affairs this very afternoon, over a Christmas bowl of smoking bishop, Bob!

Make up the fires, and buy a second coal-scuttle before you dot another *i*, Bob Cratchit!"

Scrooge was better than his word. He did it all, and infinitely more; and to Tiny Tim, who did NOT die, he was a second father. He became as good a friend, as good a master, and as good a man as the good old city knew, or any other good old city, town, or borough in the good old world. Some people laughed to see the alteration in him; but his own heart laughed, and that was quite enough for him.

He had no further intercourse with Spirits, but lived in that respect upon the Total Abstinence Principle ever afterwards; and it was always said of him that he knew how to keep Christmas well, if any man alive possessed the knowledge. May that be truly said of us, and all of us! And so, as Tiny Tim observed, God Bless Us, Every One!

The Thieves Who Couldn't Help Sneezing

THOMAS HARDY

MANY years ago, when oak-trees now past their prime were about as large as elderly gentlemen's walking-sticks, there lived in Wessex a yeoman's son, whose name was Hubert. He

By Thomas Hardy. Reprinted by permission of, and by special arrangement with, Carl J. Weber, editor of the Colby College edition of this story, published in Waterville, Me., in 1942.

was about fourteen years of age, and was as remarkable for his candor and lightness of heart as for his physical courage, of which, indeed, he was a little vain.

One cold Christmas Eve his father, having no other help at hand, sent him on an important errand to a small town several miles from home. He travelled on horseback, and was detained by the business till a late hour of the evening. At last, however, it was completed; he returned to the inn, the horse was saddled, and he started on his way. His journey homeward lay through the Vale of Blackmore, a fertile but somewhat lonely district, with heavy clay roads and crooked lanes. In those days, too, a great part of it was thickly wooded.

It must have been about nine o'clock when, riding along amid the overhanging trees upon his stout-legged cob, Jerry, and singing a Christmas carol, to be in harmony with the season, Hubert fancied that he heard a noise among the boughs. This recalled to his mind that the spot he was traversing bore an evil name. Men had been waylaid there. He looked at Jerry, and wished he had been of any other color than light gray; for on this account the docile animal's form was visible even here in the dense shade. "What do I care?" he said aloud, after a few minutes of reflection. "Jerry's legs are too nimble to allow any highwayman to come near me."

"Ha! ha! indeed," was said in a deep voice; and the next moment a man darted from the thicket on his right hand, another man from the thicket on his left hand, and another from a tree-trunk a few yards ahead. Hubert's bridle was seized, he was pulled from his horse, and although he struck out with all his might, as a brave boy would naturally do, he was overpowered. His arms were tied behind him, his legs bound tightly together, and he was thrown into the ditch. The robbers, whose faces he could now dimly perceive to be artificially blackened, at once departed, leading off the horse.

As soon as Hubert had a little recovered himself, he found that by great exertion he was able to extricate his legs from the cord; but, in spite of every endeavor, his arms remained bound as fast as before. All, therefore, that he could do was to rise to his feet and proceed on his way with his arms behind him, and trust to chance for getting them unfastened. He knew that it would be impossible to reach home on foot that night, and in such a condition; but he walked on. Owing to the confusion which this attack caused in his brain, he lost his way, and would have been inclined to lie down and rest till morning among the dead leaves had he not known the danger of sleeping without wrappers in a frost so severe. So he wandered further onwards, his arms wrung and numbed by the cord which pinioned him, and his heart aching for the loss of poor Jerry, who never had been known to kick, or bite, or show a single vicious habit. He was not a little glad when he discerned through the trees a distant light. Towards this he made his way, and presently found himself in front of a large mansion with flanking wings, gables, and towers, the battlements and chimneys showing their shapes against the stars.

All was silent; but the door stood wide open, it being from this door that the light shone which had attracted him. On entering he found himself in a vast apartment arranged as a dining-hall, and brilliantly illuminated. The walls were covered with a great deal of dark wainscoting, formed into moulded panels, carvings, closet-doors, and the usual fittings of a house of that kind. But what drew his attention most was the large table in the midst of the hall, upon which was spread a sumptuous supper, as yet untouched. Chairs were placed around, and it appeared as if something had occurred to interrupt the meal just at the time when all were ready to begin.

Even had Hubert been so inclined, he could not have eaten in his helpless state, unless by dipping his mouth into the dishes, like a pig or cow. He wished first to obtain assistance; and was about to penetrate further into the house for that purpose when he heard hasty footsteps in the porch and the words, "Be quick!" uttered in the deep voice which had reached him when he was dragged from the horse. There was only just time for him to dart under the table before three men entered the dining-hall. Peeping from beneath the hanging edges of the tablecloth, he perceived that their faces, too, were blackened, which at once removed any remaining doubts he may have felt that these were the same thieves.

"Now, then," said the first—the man with the deep voice—"let us hide ourselves. They will all be back again in a minute. That was a good trick to get them out of the house—eh?"

"Yes. You well imitated the cries of a man in distress," said the second.

"Excellently," said the third.

"But they will soon find out that it was a false alarm. Come, where shall we hide? It must be some place we can stay in for two or three hours, till all are in bed and asleep. Ah! I have it. Come this way! I have learnt that the further closet is not opened once in a twelve-month; it will serve our purpose exactly."

The speaker advanced into a corridor which led from the hall. Creeping a little farther forward, Hubert could discern that the closet stood at the end, facing the dining-hall. The thieves entered it, and closed the door. Hardly breathing, Hubert glided forward, to learn a little more of their intention, if possible; and, coming close, he could hear the robbers whispering about the different rooms where the jewels, plate, and other valuables of the house were kept, which they plainly meant to steal.

They had not been long in hiding when a gay chattering of ladies and gentlemen was audible on the terrace without. Hubert felt that it would not do to be caught prowling about the house, unless he wished to be taken for a robber himself; and he slipped softly back to the hall, out at the door, and stood in a dark corner of the porch, where he could see everything without being himself seen. In a moment or two a whole troop of personages came gliding past him into the house. There were an elderly gentleman and lady, eight or nine young ladies, as many young men, besides half-a-dozen men-servants and maids. The mansion had apparently been quite emptied of its occupants.

"Now, children and young people, we will resume our meal," said the old gentleman. "What the noise could have been I cannot understand. I never felt so certain in my life that there was a person being murdered outside my door."

Then the ladies began saying how frightened they had been, and how they had expected an adventure, and how it had ended in nothing after all.

"Wait a while," said Hubert to himself. "You'll have adventure enough by-and-by, ladies."

It appeared that the young men and women were married sons and daughters of the old couple, who had come that day to spend Christmas with their parents.

The door was then closed, Hubert being left outside in the porch. He thought this a proper moment for asking their assistance; and, since he was unable to knock with his hands, began boldly to kick the door.

"Hullo! What disturbance are you making here?" said a footman who opened it; and, seizing Hubert by the shoulder, he pulled him into the dining-hall. "Here's a strange boy I have found making a noise in the porch, Sir Simon."

Everybody turned.

"Bring him forward," said Sir Simon, the old gentleman before mentioned. "What were you doing there, my boy?"

"Why, his arms are tied!" said one of the ladies.

"Poor fellow!" said another.

Hubert at once began to explain that he had been waylaid on his journey home, robbed of his horse, and mercilessly left in this condition by the thieves.

"Only to think of it!" exclaimed Sir Simon.

"That's a likely story," said one of the gentlemen-guests, incredulously.

"Doubtful, hey?" asked Sir Simon.

"Perhaps he's a robber himself," suggested a lady.

"There is a curiously wild wicked look about him, certainly, now that I examine him closely," said the old mother.

Hubert blushed with shame; and, instead of continuing his story, and relating that robbers were concealed in the house, he doggedly held his tongue, and half resolved to let them find out their danger for themselves.

"Well, untie him," said Sir Simon. "Come, since it is Christmas Eve, we'll treat him well. Here, my lad; sit down in that empty seat at the bottom of the table, and make as good a meal as you can. When you have had your fill we will listen to more particulars of your story."

The feast then proceeded; and Hubert, now at liberty, was not at all sorry to join in. The more they ate and drank the merrier did the company become; the wine flowed freely, the logs flared up the chimney, the ladies laughed at the gentlemen's stories; in short, all went as noisily and as happily as a Christmas gathering in old times possibly could do.

Hubert, in spite of his hurt feelings at their doubts of his honesty, could not help being warmed both in mind and in body by the good cheer, the scene, and the example of hilarity set by his neighbors. At last he laughed as heartily at their stories and repartees as the old Baronet, Sir Simon, himself. When the meal was almost over one of the sons, who had drunk a little too much wine, after the manner of men in that century, said to Hubert, "Well, my boy, how are you? Can you take a pinch of snuff?" He held out one of the snuff-boxes which were then becoming common among young and old throughout the country.

"Thank you," said Hubert, accepting a pinch.

"Tell the ladies who you are, what you are made of, and what you can do," the young man continued, slapping Hubert upon the shoulder.

"Certainly," said our hero, drawing himself up, and thinking it best to put a bold face on the matter. "I am a travelling magician."

"Indeed!"

"What shall we hear next?"

"Can you call up spirits from the vasty deep, young wizard?"

"I can conjure up a tempest in a cupboard," Hubert replied.

"Ha-ha!" said the old Baronet, pleasantly rubbing his hands. "We must see this performance. Girls, don't go away: here's something to be seen."

"Not dangerous, I hope?" said the old lady.

Hubert rose from the table. "Hand me your snuff-box, please," he said to the young man who had made free with him. "And now," he continued, "without the least noise, follow me. If any of you speak it will break the spell."

They promised obedience. He entered the corridor, and, taking off his shoes, went on tiptoe to the closet door, the guests advancing in a silent group at a little distance behind him. Hubert next placed a stool in front of the door, and, by standing upon it, was tall enough to reach to the top. He then, just as noiselessly, poured all the snuff from the box along the upper edge of the door, and, with a few short puffs of breath, blew the snuff through the chink into the interior of the closet. He held up his finger to the assembly, that they might be silent.

"Dear me, what's that?" said the old lady, after a minute or two had elapsed.

A suppressed sneeze had come from inside the closet.

Hubert held up his finger again.

"How very singular," whispered Sir Simon. "This is most interesting."

Hubert took advantage of the moment to gently slide the bolt of the closet door into its place. "More snuff," he said, calmly.

"More snuff," said Sir Simon. Two or three gentlemen passed their boxes, and the contents were blown in at the top of the closet. Another sneeze, not quite so well suppressed as the first, was heard: then another, which seemed to say that it would not be suppressed under any circumstances whatever. At length there arose a perfect storm of sneezes.

"Excellent, excellent for one so young!" said Sir Simon. "I am much interested in this trick of throwing the voice—called, I believe, ventriloquism."

"More snuff," said Hubert.

"More snuff," said Sir Simon. Sir Simon's man brought a large jar of the best scented Scotch.

Hubert once more charged the upper chink of the closet, and blew the snuff into the interior, as before. Again he charged, and again, emptying the whole contents of the jar. The tumult of sneezes became really extraordinary to listen to—there was no cessation. It was like wind, rain, and sea battling in a hurricane.

"I believe there are men inside, and that it is no trick at all!" exclaimed Sir Simon, the truth flashing on him.

"There are," said Hubert. "They are come to rob the house; and they are the same who stole my horse."

The sneezes changed to spasmodic groans. One of the thieves, hearing Hubert's voice, cried, "Oh! mercy! mercy! let us out of this!"

"Where's my horse?" said Hubert.

"Tied to the tree in the hollow behind Short's Gibbet. Mercy! mercy! let us out, or we shall die of suffocation!"

All the Christmas guests now perceived that this was no longer sport, but serious earnest. Guns and cudgels were procured; all the men-servants were called in, and arranged in position outside the closet. At a signal Hubert withdrew the bolt, and stood on the defensive. But the three robbers, far from attacking them, were found crouching in the corner, gasping for breath. They made no resistance; and, being pinioned, were placed in an outhouse till the morning.

Hubert now gave the remainder of his story to the assembled company, and was profusely thanked for the services he had rendered. Sir Simon pressed him to stay over the night, and accept the use of the best bedroom the house afforded, which had been occupied by Queen Elizabeth and King Charles successively when on their visits to this part of the country. But Hubert declined, being anxious to find his horse Jerry, and to test the truth of the robbers' statements concerning him.

Several of the guests accompanied Hubert to the spot behind the gibbet, alluded to by the thieves as where Jerry was hidden. When they reached the knoll and looked over, behold! there the horse stood, uninjured, and quite unconcerned. At sight of Hubert he neighed joyfully; and nothing could exceed Hubert's gladness at finding him. He mounted, wished his friends "Goodnight!" and cantered off in the direction they pointed out, reaching home safely about four o'clock in the morning.

Three Stockings

JAN STRUTHER

HOWEVER much one groaned about it beforehand, however much one hated making arrangements and doing up parcels and ordering several days' meals in advance—when it actually happened Christmas Day was always fun.

It began in the same way every year: the handle of her bedroom door being turned just loudly enough to wake her up, but softly enough not to count as waking her up on purpose; Toby glimmering like a moth in the dark doorway, clutching a nobbly Christmas stocking in one hand and holding up his pyjama trousers with the other. (He insisted upon pyjamas, but he had not yet outgrown his sleeping-suit figure.)

"Toby! It's only just after six. I did say not till seven."

"But, Mummy, I can't tell the time." He was barefoot and shivering, and his eyes were like stars.

"Come here and get warm, you little *goat*." He was into her bed in a flash, stocking and all. The tail of a clockwork dog scratched her shoulder. A few moments later another head appeared round the door, a little higher up.

"Judy, darling, it's *too* early, honestly."

"I know, but I heard Toby come in, so I knew you must be awake."

"All right, you can come into bed, but you've got to keep quiet for a bit. Daddy's still asleep."

And then a third head, higher up still, and Vin's voice, even deeper than it had been at Long Leave.

"I say, are the others in here? I thought I heard them."

He curled himself up on the foot of his father's bed. And by that time, of course, Clem was awake too. The old transparent stratagem had worked to perfection once more: there was nothing for it but to switch on the lights, shut the windows, and admit that Christmas Day had insidiously but definitely begun.

The three right hands—Vin's strong and broad, Judy's thin and flexible, Toby's still a star-fish—plunged in and out of the three distorted stockings, until there was nothing left but the time-hallowed tangerine in the toe. (It was curious how that tradition lingered, even nowadays when children had a good supply of fruit all the year round.) Their methods were as different as their hands. Vin, with little grunts of approval, examined each object carefully as he drew it out, exploring all its possibilities before he went on to the next. Judy, talking the whole time, pulled all her treasures out in a heap, took a quick glance at them and went straight for the one she liked best—a minikin baby in a wicker cradle. Toby pulled all his out, too, but he arranged them in a neat pattern on the eiderdown and looked at them for a long time in complete silence. Then he picked up one of them—a big glass marble with colored squirls inside—and put it by itself a little way off. After that he played with the other toys, appreciatively enough; but from time to time his eyes would stray towards the glass marble, as though to make sure it was still waiting for him.

Mrs. Miniver watched him with a mixture of delight and misgiving. It was her own favorite approach to life: but the trouble was that sometimes the marble rolled away. Judy's was safer; Vin's, on the whole, the wisest of the three.

To the banquet of real presents which was waiting downstairs, covered with a red and white dust-sheet, the stocking-toys, of course, were only an *apéritif*; but they had a special and exciting quality of their own. Perhaps it was the atmosphere in which they were opened—the chill, the black window-panes, the unfamiliar hour; perhaps it was the powerful charm of the miniature, of toy toys, of smallness squared; perhaps it was the sense of limitation within a strict form, which gives to both the filler and the emptier of a Christmas stocking something of the same enjoyment which is experienced by the writer and the reader of a sonnet; or perhaps it was merely that the spell of the old legend still persisted, even though for everybody in the room except Toby the legend itself was outworn.

There were cross-currents of pleasure, too: smiling glances exchanged by her and Vin about the two younger children (she remembered suddenly, having been an eldest child, the unsurpassable sense of grandeur that such glances gave one); and by her and Clem, because they were both grown-ups; and by her and Judy, because they were both women; and by her and Toby, because they were both the kind that leaves the glass marble till the end. The room was laced with an invisible network of affectionate understanding.

This was one of the moments, thought Mrs. Miniver, which paid off at a single stroke all the accumulations on the debit side of parenthood: the morning sickness and the quite astonishing pain; the pram in the passage, the cold mulish glint in the cook's eye; the holiday nurse who had been in the best families; the pungent white mice, the shrivelled caterpillars; the plasticine on the door-handles, the face-flannels in the bathroom, the nameless horrors down the crevices of armchairs; the alarms and emergencies, the swallowed button, the inexplicable earache, the ominous rash appearing on the eve of a journey; the school bills and the dentists' bills; the shortened step, the tempered pace, the emotional compromises, the divided loyalties, the adventures continually forsworn.

And now Vin was eating his tangerine, pig by pig; Judy had undressed the baby and was putting on its frock again back to front; Toby was turning the glass marble round and round against the light, trying to count the squirls. There were sounds of movement in the house; they were within measurable distance of the blessed chink of early morning tea. Mrs. Miniver looked towards the window. The dark sky had already paled a little in its frame of cherry-pink chintz. Eternity framed in domesticity. Never mind. One had to frame it in something, to see it at all.

FINLAND

Christmas Prayer

Z. TOPELIUS   JEAN SIBELIUS

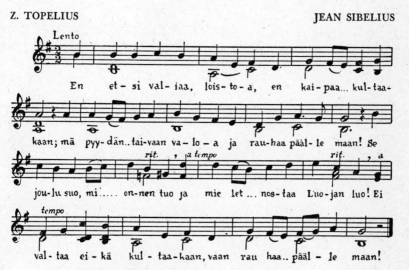

En et-si val-iaa, lois-to-a, en kai-paa... kul-taa-
kaan; mä pyy-dän..tai-vaan va-lo-a ja rau-haa pääl-le maan! Se
jou-lu suo, mi..... on-nen tuo ja mie let...nos-taa Luo-jan luo! Ei
val-taa ei-kä kul-taa-kaan, vaan rau haa..pääl-le maan!

Don't give us fame, oh Lord above,
Don't give us riches great.
We beg for peace, we long for love,
That stem from heaven's gate.
Let Christmas be,
Eternally,
The symbol of a world set free.
Not fame, nor pow'r, nor worldly worth,
But peace on earth!

A Long Way, Indeed

ARVID LYDECKEN
(Translated by K. C. Pihlajamaa)

Snow lay heavy in the valleys and on the hillsides. Its white blanket covered everything in sight, and the branches of the spruce trees bent low under its weight.

It was a bright cold winter eve, and the fire blazed merrily in the Pakkasvaara cabin. But little Annikin was sick abed with a high fever.

Mother was preparing supper. Father hadn't come home yet from work, nor had Ilmari returned from school. The school he attended was about six miles away; and the road the young lad had to take was rough and desolate so that he actually needed all his strength to make his way home. However, this evening the skis worked well in the powder-like snow, and soon red-cheeked Ilmari stepped briskly into the living room of the cabin, after having first brushed off the snow in the storm shed.

"Good evening, Mother," he called, rushing over to Annikin's bedside. "How do you feel, Sister?"

Annikin opened her eyes, and a slight smile played over her features; but she was too tired to speak. Wearily her head sank back into the pillow and she who was usually such a gay and cheerful playmate, slipped away asleep again almost immediately.

Soon Father, too, arrived, and they sat down to supper.

From *Arvilyn Satvja* by Arvid Lydecken. Reprinted by permission of the author.

"Is Annikin asleep?" Father asked under his breath, turning his head toward her bed. And when there was no reply, he continued: "It's too bad, but it just seems impossible to get money enough together to buy her the doll she wants so badly for Christmas."

"Oh, Father—can't you make it somehow?" Ilmari cried.

"I'm afraid I can't," Father sighed. "We'll be fortunate if we have enough to get through the winter."

As the days sped by, Ilmari kept on wondering how Annikin might yet get her doll. He was sure that, if she only could get it, joy would make her well over night. A happy person simply can't be sick, he told himself. The doll would be much better than all the medicines in the world. It would positively perform a miracle. He wracked his brain to find a way to earn a little money. But there just wasn't anything because they lived so far out of town.

Christmas drew ever closer. Now there was only a week to go, and still Ilmari hadn't been able to think of anything profitable. In fact, the situation seemed quite hopeless. At long last, however, he had a brilliant idea: he'd write the infant Jesus a letter! Since He was a child himself, He certainly loved children and would understand how important it was that his sister get her doll.

He wrote:—

"Dear Jesus: I take my pen in hand to write you this letter. I need your help, 'cause nobody else can help me. I am Ilmari and I live in the Pakkasvaara cabin. Annikin is sick. She is my sister. She wants a doll for herself. But we can't buy her one 'cause we are poor. If she only got the doll she would get well for sure. Dear Jesus, when you come to our place on Christmas Eve, please be sure to bring a doll. The Pakkasvaara cabin is six miles from the church in Siltasalmi. If you can only bring the doll I don't want nothing for myself. And I will be grateful to you all my life. Respectfully, Ilmari."

Christmas Eve had arrived. A lonesome candle burned on the table in the cabin and Father was reading from the bible.

Ilmari waited with bated breath for what would surely happen.

Suddenly there was a knock at the door.

"That's Him!" Ilmari cried. But it wasn't Jesus at all. It was only a young doctor from town. He had come on skis and carried a heavy knapsack on his shoulders. In it was a bag of coffee for Mother, and for Father some shining new money. Annikin got such a lovely blue-eyed doll that she was quite beside herself with joy. Nor had Ilmari been forgotten; he received a book which gave him greater pleasure than he had ever known.

Never before had there been so merry a Christmas in the Pakkasvaara cabin! Annikin's doll proved a wonderful medicine, and she became better day by day.

But only Ilmari knew who had sent the doctor on Christmas Eve. No doubt, Jesus hadn't had the time to come himself. And, besides, the way out to the Pakkasvaara cabin is a long one indeed. . . .

FRANCE

'Twixt Gentle Ox and Ass So Gray

TRADITIONAL

En - tre le bœuf et l'ân-e gris, Dors, dors, dors let pe-tit fils! Mille ang-es di - vins, mil-le se-ra-phins, Vo-lent à l'en-tour de ce grand Dieu.... d'a-mour .... Ro - i des anges, dors!

'Twixt gentle ox and ass so gray,
Sleep, sleep
On Thy bed of hay;
Thousand cherubim, thousand seraphim
Hover high above the mighty Lord of love.
Sleep, King of angels,
Sleep!

The Three Low Masses

ALPHONSE DAUDET
(Translated by Frank Hunter Potter)

"Two truffled turkeys, Garrigou?"

"Yes, father. Two splendid turkeys stuffed with truffles. I know something about it, because I helped to stuff them. You'd say their skins would burst in the roasting, they were so tight!"

"Jésu-Maria. And I'm so fond of truffles! . . . Give me my alb, Garrigou, quickly. . . . And besides the turkeys, what else have you seen in the kitchen up to now?"

"Oh, all sorts of good things. Ever since midday we've been doing nothing else but plucking pheasants, lap-wings, pullets, grouse; the air was thick with feathers. And then there are eels from the fishpond, and golden carp, and trout, and . . ."

"Trout? How big, Garrigou?"

"As big as that, father. . . . Huge!"

"I can almost see them. Have you put wine in the cruet?"

"Yes, father, I've put wine in the cruet. . . . But Lord! it isn't as good as the wine you'll be drinking pretty soon, at the end of Mass. If you could only see all the flasks and decanters in the Hall, full of wine of all colors . . . ! And the silver plate! And the epergnes, all chased! And the flowers, and the cande-labra! There'll never have been such a Réveillon! His lordship has invited all the gentry round; you'll be at least forty at table, not counting the bailiff and the notary. Ah, father, you're lucky to be one of them! Just a sniff of those lovely turkeys and the smell of truffles follows me everywhere . . . Y'm!"

"Come, come, my child. Let us beware of the sin of gluttony, and above all on this Eve of Christmas. Go now, light the candles and ring the first chime. It is nearly midnight. We must not be late."

This was the conversation which passed, on Christmas Eve of the year of grace 1649, between the reverend Dom Balaguère, one time prior of Barnabites but now chaplain to the Marquis de Trinquelage, and his young acolyte Garrigou—or at any rate what he thought was his acolyte Garrigou; for you are to know that the Devil this night had assumed the round and simple features of the young sacristan, the better to drag the good chaplain into temptation and induce him to commit the deadly sin of Gluttony. And while the seeming Garrigou (ha! ha!) was ringing the bells of the Castle chapel with all his might the priest finished vesting in the little sacristy; and with his imagination already perturbed by all these gastronomic rhapsodies, murmured absently to himself as he did so:

"Roast turkeys! Golden carp! And trout . . . as big as that!" Outside the night wind whistled, scattering the music of the bells. By degrees lights appeared in the darkness of the slopes of Mont Ventoux, crowned by the ancient towers of Trinquelage: the farmers and their families were coming to get their midnight Mass at the Castle. They climbed the hill in groups of five or six, singing, the father going first, lantern in hand, the women wrapped in their ample brown cloaks, their children clinging and sheltering. The late hour and the cold notwithstanding, all these honest folk went gaily, sustained by the thought that at the end of Mass there would be, as in every year, tables spread for them below, in the kitchens. From time to time on the rough hill the windows of some gentleman's coach, preceded by numerous footmen carrying torches, shimmered in the light of the moon. A trotting mule shook its bells, and by the light of lanterns half blotted out in the mist, the tenant farmers recognised their bailiff, and saluted him as he went by.

"Good night, Master Arnoton!"

"Good night, my children. Good night!"

The night was clear, the stars crackled with the cold: the winter blast blew shrewdly, and a fine sleet, slipping off cloaks without wetting them, faithfully upheld the tradition of a white Christmas. On the peak of the hill the Castle stood like a target with its huge mass of towers and gables, the spire of its chapel striking into the blue-black sky, a multitude of little winking lights coming and going and stirring at all the windows, glowing in the sombre outline of the great pile like sparks darting to and fro in the ash of burnt paper. Once over the drawbridge and through the postern the way to the chapel led through the outer courtyard, full of coaches, of servants, of sedan chairs, lit by the flame of torches and the blaze from the kitchens. One could hear the clinking of spits, the clang of frying-pans, the chiming of glass and of silver being set out for a banquet; and the warm mist, scented of roasting meats and strong herbs for subtle sauces, which hung over all inspired one reflection in the farmers, as in the bailiff, the chaplain, and everybody:

"What a Réveillon we shall have after Mass!"

TING-A-LING-A-LING-A-LING!

Midnight Mass is beginning. In the Castle chapel, a miniature cathedral with the interlaced vaulting of its roof, and its oaken panelling, high as the walls, the tapestries are hung, all the candles lit. And what a crowd! What costumes! Here, seated in the sculptured choir stalls, is the Marquis de Trinquelage in salmon-colored silk, and with him his noble guests. Opposite, kneeling on their velvet prie-Dieu, are the old dowager Marquise in flame-colored brocade and the young Marquise, wearing her high goffered tower of lace, in the last mode of the Court of France. Behind them in black, with their huge pointed perukes and clean-shaven visages, appear the bailiff, Master Thomas Arnoton, and the notary, Master Ambroy; two notes of gravity among all these flaming silks and figured damasks. Then come the stout butlers, the pages, the grooms, the stewards, and Dame Barbe, with her keys jingling at her side on a ring of fine silver. At the end, on the benches, are the lower servants, male and female, and the tenants with their families; and finally, right against the door, which they open and close discreetly, behold our friends the turn-spits, slipping in between two sauces to hear a scrap of Mass, bringing with them a breath of Réveillon into the festal air of the chapel, warm with so many lighted candles.

Is it the sight of the flat white caps which distracts the celebrant? Or is it not rather Garrigou's sacring-bell, this feverish little bell which is tinkling at the altar foot with infernal precipitancy, seeming to say all the time:

"Hurry up! HURRY up! The sooner we've done, the sooner to table!" The truth is that each time this diabolical little bell rings, the chaplain forgets his Mass and remembers only his supper. He sees in his mind's eye the bustling cooks, the blazing forge-like fires, the mist rising from uncovered pans . . . and in this mist two turkeys, superb, bursting, straining, mottled with truffles. . . . He sees the file of pages go by, bearing dishes enveloped in tempting odors, and goes in with them to the great hall, already prepared for the feast. O delicious! There is the enormous table, laden and sparkling; the peacocks roasted in their feathers; the pheasants spreading their golden wings; the ruby flasks; the pyramids of glowing fruit among green branches, the miraculous fish of Garrigou's story (ha! ha! Yes, Garrigou!) on their bed of fennel, their scales as iridescent as if they were just out of water, with bunches of fragrant herbs stuck in their monster gills. So vivid is his vision that Dom Balaguère can almost see these mirific dishes spread before him on the embroidered cloth of the altar, and twice or thrice, instead of DOMINUS VOBISCUM, he is astonished to find himself beginning the BENEDICITE. But beyond these trifling slips the good man says his Office most conscientiously without skipping one line or omitting one genuflexion: and all is well to the end of the first Mass: for as you know, on Christmas Day the same celebrant must celebrate three consecutive Masses.

"That's one!" says the chaplain to himself with a sigh of re-

lief: and then, without losing a moment, he signs to his clerk—
or the one he thinks is his clerk, and:

TING-A-LING-A-LING-A-LING-LING!

The second Mass begins, and with it the sin of Dom Balaguère. "Quick! Quick! Hurry!" screams Garrigou's little bell
in its shrill little voice. And this time the unhappy priest, giving himself over to the Demon of Gluttony flings himself on
his missal and devours its pages with all the avidity of his rag-
ing appetite. Furiously he bows, stands erect, makes sketchy
signs of the Cross, genuflects, shortening every gesture in order
to get through sooner. He hardly touches his breast at the CON-
FITEOR; at the Gospel he barely extends his arms. It becomes
a race between him and his clerk, which shall mumble through
the quicker. Verses and responses hurry along, bustling one another: words half-pronounced without opening the mouth
(which would take too much time) blur and melt away in in-
comprehensible murmurs.

"OREMUS PS . . . PS . . . PS . . ."
"MEA CULPA . . . PA . . . PA . . ."

They wallow in the Latin of the Mass like vintagers treading
the grape at harvest, splashing on every side.

"DOM . . . SCUM!" says Balaguère.

". . . STUTUO!" Garrigou answers him: and the whole time the
devilish little bell is clamoring in their ears like the bells on
post-horses galloping at top speed. You may imagine that at
this rate a low Mass is soon finished. . . . "And that's the second," says the chaplain, completely out of breath; and without waiting to recover, red in the face, sweating, he descends
the altar steps again and—

TING-A-LING-A-LING-A-LING-A-LING-A-LING!

The Third Mass begins. It is now but a few steps to the Hall;
but alas! as Réveillon comes nearer the miserable Balaguère
feels himself in the grip of a fury of impatience and greed. His
vision becomes sharper. The golden carp, the roasted turkeys
are there. . . . He is touching them. . . . He—O Heaven! the
dishes smoke, the scent of the wines is in his nostrils . . . and
the little bell cries to him furiously:

"Faster! Faster! **Much faster!**"

But how can he go any faster? His lips are now scarcely moving. He is not pronouncing any more words at all. He is within an ace of tricking the good God and filching His Mass from Him altogether. . . . And this is what he actually does, the unhappy sinner! Leaping from temptation to temptation he begins by jumping first one verse, then two; the Epistle is too long, he leaves it unfinished, skims through the Gospel, passes by the Creed, gives the Preface a distant salute, skips the Pater, and by hops, leaps, and bounds hurls himself thus into eternal damnation, at his heels the devilish Garrigou (vade retro, Satanas!) egging him on with cordiality, holding up the chasuble, turning the pages two at a time, jostling the lectern, upsetting the cruet, incessantly ringing and ringing his little bell, louder and louder, faster and faster. You should see the aghast faces of the congregation! In their endeavor to follow the priest's movements in this Mass, of which they cannot distinguish one single word, some stand when the rest are kneeling, some sit when the others stand: all the succeeding phases of this singular Office jostle one another among the congregation in a dozen different attitudes. The Star of Bethlehem, marching across the skies on its journey to the Stable far away, turns pale with fear on seeing such confusion. . . .

"Really, the abbé is going too fast! It is impossible to follow him," murmurs the old dowager Marquise, shaking her coif in bewilderment.

Master Arnoton, his great steel spectacles on his nose, tries in vain to discover where the deuce he is in his missal. . . . But at heart all these honest folk are fixed equally on Réveillon, and are not too seriously perturbed at the post-haste speed of Mass. And when Dom Balaguère with shining face turns him at last and intones with all the force of his lungs "ITE, MISSA EST!" his flock with one voice answers with a "DEO GRATIAS" so joyous and so overpowering that one would think oneself already at table, drinking the first toast.

Five minutes afterwards the assembled gentry took their seats in the great hall, the chaplain in their midst. The castle, illuminated from top to bottom, resounded with songs, with shouts, and laughter, and merriment; and the venerable Dom Balaguère planted his fork in a wing of pullet, washing away the remorse for his sin in a flood of Clos du Pape and rich gravy. He ate and drank so heartily, the poor worthy man, that he died that night of a terrible apoplexy, without time to repent, and in the morning arrived in Heaven still flushed from the night's feasting: and I leave you to imagine what sort of a reception he got.

"Out of My sight, bad Christian!" ejaculated the Sovereign Judge, Master of all mankind. "Your sin is great enough to efface a whole lifetime of goodness. You have robbed Me of a midnight Mass. Very well! You shall repay Me three hundred in its place, and you shall not enter My Paradise until you have celebrated, in your own chapel, these three hundred Christmas Masses in the presence of all those who have sinned with you and through your example."

And this is the true legend of Dom Balaguère, as they tell it in the olive country. To-day the castle of Trinquelage is no more; but the chapel still stands on the peak of Mont Ventoux, in a clump of green oaks. The wind shakes its ruined door; grass grows on the threshold; birds have built their nests at the angles of the altar and in the embrasures of the high windows, whence the colored glass disappeared ages ago. But it seems that every year at Christmas a supernatural light glints among the ruins, and the country people going to Mass and Réveillon see this spectre of a chapel lighted up with invisible candles burning in the open air, even in snow and wind. Laugh if you like, but a vine-grower of the neighborhood, one Garrigue (doubtless a descendant of Garrigou) has sworn to me that one Christmas Eve, having a little drink taken, he lost himself in the mountain near Trinquelage; and this is what he saw. Before eleven o'clock, nothing. All was silent and dead. Then suddenly, near midnight, a peal which sounded as if it were ten leagues away; and very soon, on the hill road, Garrigue saw lights trembling and vague moving shadows. Under the chapel porch there was movement. There were whispers.

"Good night, Master Arnoton!"

"Good night, my children. Good night."

When all had entered my vine-grower, a courageous fellow, crept up gently and, peeping through the broken door, saw a singular sight. The people he had seen were all grouped around the choir and in the ruined nave, as if the old benches were still there: fair ladies in brocade with lace head-dresses, seigneurs bedizened from head to foot, peasants in flowered jackets, such as our ancestors wore, all appearing strangely old, faded, dusty, and weary. From time to time the night-birds who inhabit the chapel, awakened by so many lights, flew round the candles, whose flames stood up straight and dim, as if they burned behind a veil: and what highly amused Garrigue was the spectacle of a personage with huge steel glasses who incessantly shook at intervals his tall peruke, on which one of these birds was perched, its feet entangled, silently flapping its wings.

And at the East end a little old man with the figure of a child, kneeling in the centre of the choir, desperately rang a little silent bell, while a priest vested in ancient gold moved to and fro at the altar, reciting prayers in a soundless voice. . . .

Without doubt it was Dom Balaguère saying his third Low Mass.

Cosette

VICTOR HUGO
(Translated by Isabel F. Hapgood)

THE INN-KEEPER retired to his room. His wife was in bed, but she was not asleep. When she heard her husband's step she turned over and said to him:—

"Do you know, I'm going to turn Cosette out of doors to-morrow."

Thénardier replied coldly:—

"How you do go on!"

They exchanged no further words, and a few moments later their candle was extinguished.

As for the traveller, he had deposited his cudgel and his bundle in a corner. The landlord once gone, he threw himself into an arm-chair and remained for some time buried in thought. Then he removed his shoes, took one of the two candles, blew out the other, opened the door, and quitted the room, gazing about him like a person who is in search of something. He traversed a corridor and came upon a staircase. There he heard a very faint and gentle sound like the breathing of a child. He followed this sound, and came to a sort of triangular recess built under the staircase, or rather formed by the staircase itself. This recess was nothing else than the space under the steps. There, in the midst of all sorts of old papers and pot-sherds, among dust and spiders' webs, was a bed—if one can call by the name of bed a straw pallet so full of holes as to display the straw, and a coverlet so tattered as to show the pallet. No sheets. This was placed on the floor.

In this bed Cosette was sleeping.

The man approached and gazed down upon her.

Cosette was in a profound sleep; she was fully dressed. In the winter she did not undress, in order that she might not be so cold.

Against her breast was pressed the doll, whose large eyes, wide open, glittered in the dark. From time to time she gave vent to a deep sigh as though she were on the point of waking, and she strained the doll almost convulsively in her arms. Beside her bed there was only one of her wooden shoes.

A door which stood open near Cosette's pallet permitted a view of a rather large, dark room. The stranger stepped into it. At the further extremity, through a glass door, he saw two small, very white beds. They belonged to Éponine and Azelma. Behind these beds, and half hidden, stood an uncurtained wicker cradle, in which the little boy who had cried all the evening lay asleep.

The stranger conjectured that this chamber connected with that of the Thénardier pair. He was on the point of retreating when his eye fell upon the fireplace—one of those vast tavern chimneys where there is always so little fire when there is any fire at all, and which are so cold to look at. There was no fire in this one, there was not even ashes; but there was something which attracted the stranger's gaze, nevertheless. It was two tiny children's shoes, coquettish in shape and unequal in size. The traveller recalled the graceful and immemorial custom in accordance with which children place their shoes in the chimney on Christmas eve, there to await in the darkness some sparkling gift from their good fairy. Éponine and Azelma had taken care not to omit this, and each of them had set one of her shoes on the hearth.

The traveller bent over them.

The fairy, that is to say, their mother, had already paid her visit, and in each he saw a brand-new and shining ten-sou piece.

The man straightened himself up, and was on the point of withdrawing, when far in, in the darkest corner of the hearth, he caught sight of another object. He looked at it, and recognized a wooden shoe, a frightful shoe of the coarsest description, half dilapidated and all covered with ashes and dried mud. It was Cosette's sabot. Cosette, with that touching trust of childhood, which can always be deceived yet never discouraged, had placed her shoe on the hearth-stone also.

Hope in a child who has never known anything but despair is a sweet and touching thing.

There was nothing in this wooden shoe.

The stranger fumbled in his waistcoat, bent over and placed a louis d'or in Cosette's shoe.

Then he regained his own chamber with the stealthy tread of a wolf.

A Christmas Story

GUY DE MAUPASSANT
(Translated by Lafcadio Hearn)

DR. BONENFANT was cudgeling his brain, repeating to himself, "A Christmas story? a Christmas story?" when all at once he exclaimed: "Why, of course, I know one, and a very strange one, too; it is a fantastic tale. I saw a miracle! Yes, ladies, a miracle on a Christmas eve.

It astonishes you to hear me speak thus, me, who believe in

nothing. And yet, I saw a miracle! I saw it, saw it with my own eyes, I tell you, as plain as could be.

Was I greatly surprised? No, not in the least, for, although I do not take much stock in your doctrines, I still believe in faith, and I know that it can move mountains. I might even cite many examples of this, but then I would run the risk of arousing your indignation and of lessening the effect of my story.

I shall acknowledge at the start that, though not convinced and converted by what I witnessed, I was, to say the least, deeply moved, and I will try to relate to you the whole occurrence with the artless simplicity of a credulous native of Auvergne.

I was at the time a country doctor, inhabiting the little market town of Rolleville, Normandy.

That year we had a most awful winter. Toward the end of November it began snowing, after a week of heavy frosts. The dark clouds were seen from afar, coming from the north, and shortly after the fall of the white flakes began.

A single night was sufficient to cover the whole country as with a shroud.

The farmhouses, isolated in their square yards, surrounded by their screens of great trees powdered over with rime, seemed slumbering beneath this thick but light froth-like substance.

No noise resounded across the lifeless plains. The crows alone gave evidence of life as, moving in flocks, they described long festoons across the sky, ineffectually seeking food, and swooping down all together on the ghost-like fields, pecking at the snow with their big bills.

Nothing could be heard but the uncertain sound made by the continued fall of this icy dust, dropping without intermission.

For eight long days this weather lasted. When the avalanche ceased the earth was covered with a pall five feet thick.

During the three weeks that followed, a sky as clear as a blue crystal during the day, and at night all sprinkled with frosty-looking stars, extended over the hard and glistening bed of snow.

Fields, hedges, elm trees, all seemed dead, killed by the cold. Neither man nor beast dared venture out, and the chimneys of the cottages, in white shirts, alone gave signs of the hidden life below by the thin streaks of smoke which they sent straight up through the nipping air.

From time to time a tree was heard to snap, as if its wooden limbs were breaking beneath the bark, and now and then a large branch broke off and fell to the ground, the irresistible cold solidifying the sap and tearing the fibres asunder.

The dwelling-houses set down, here and there throughout the fields, seemed distant a hundred leagues from each other. I, alone, would go out occasionally to see my nearest patients, running the risk at every step of being buried in a snowdrift.

I soon noticed that a mysterious terror hovered over the country. Every one imagined that such a scourge must be supernatural. Some even pretended that, at night, they would hear out of doors strange voices, shrill whistles, or unearthly shrieks.

These noises were undoubtedly made by birds of passage, traveling in the twilight toward the south. But it was useless to try to explain this to the terrified peasants. Every one seemed scared to death and all thought something extraordinary was going to happen.

Old Vatinel's smithy was situated at the farther end of the hamlet of Epivent, on a highway which is now abandoned and lost to sight. As the bread was giving out, he resolved to take a trip to the village. After remaining some hours, talking in the principal houses of the place, he took up his provisions, and chock-full of news, he set out for home before dark.

All of a sudden, while plodding along by the side of a hedge, he thought he spied an egg on the snow; yes, an egg, lying there, all white, just like everything around it. He stooped and saw that it was really an egg. Where did it come from? What hen could have left the warm hen-house to come and lay in such a place? The blacksmith was astounded; he could not make it out at all; still he picked up the egg and he carried it to his wife.

"Here, old lady, here's an egg I found in the road."

The woman shrugged her shoulders. "An egg in the road? In this weather; pshaw! you must be drunk."

"No, indeed, old woman. I found it near a hedge; it was still quite warm, not chilled at all. Here it is; I put it inside of my shirt to keep it from freezing. It will do for your dinner."

The egg was slipped into the pot where the soup was simmering, and the blacksmith began to tell his wife all the news he had picked up on his journey. The woman listened, pale as a ghost, with fright. "Surely," said she, "I heard that whistling myself, the other night, and it even seemed to me to come from the chimney."

They sat down to table, where, after finishing the soup, the blacksmith buttered his bread, while his wife took up the egg and examined it suspiciously.

"Suppose there was something in this egg?"

"What do you want there to be in it?"

"Do I know?"

"Well, then, eat the egg and don't be making a fool of yourself."

She broke the egg. It looked just like any other egg and very fresh.

She began to eat it with some hesitation, tasting it, laying it aside and taking it up again.

The husband asked, "Well, what taste do you find to that egg?"

She did not answer, but on finishing the egg she suddenly stared at her husband with a wild, fixed, terrified look, and, raising her arms, she twisted them around and then rolled to the floor in convulsions, shrieking in the most horrible manner. All night she writhed in dreadful spasms, shaken by a frightful tremor and almost deformed by her hideous convulsions.

The blacksmith, unable to manage her, was at length obliged to tie her down.

And she yelled at the top of her voice, never ceasing to cry out. "The devil has got me! The devil has got me!"

The next morning I was called in. I prescribed all the anodynes known to the profession without obtaining the slightest result. She was insane.

Then, notwithstanding the depth of the snow, the news spread from farmhouse to farmhouse that the blacksmith's wife was bedeviled. From every direction people came, not to enter the house, for this was more than they dared do, but to stand at a distance and listen to the mad woman's voice, so strong that one could not believe it human.

The village curate was notified. He was a plain old priest. He came in haste, his surplice on, as if to administer the last sacraments to a dying person. Extending his hands he thundered forth the words of exorcism over the foaming, writhing woman, held down in bed by the united strength of four men.

But the evil spirit would not be cast out.

Christmas came around without any change in the weather.

On Christmas eve the priest came to me saying, "Doctor, I feel like having that unfortunate woman attend service to-night. Maybe God will work a miracle in her behalf at the very hour in which he was born of a woman."

I replied, "I approve your plan fully, father. If her mind be struck by the holy rites, and nothing is more likely to make an impression on her, she may be cured without the aid of any other remedy."

The old divine murmured, "You are no believer, Doctor; still you will assist me, will you not? You will take charge of the poor creature and bring her to me?"

I promised my assistance.

When evening gave way to night the bell of the church began ringing out its doleful notes, sounding through the gloomy space far over the frozen white spread of snow.

Dark forms came slowly along, obeying the belfry's brazen summons. The wan moon shed her soft light over the landscape, rendering the pallid desolation of the fields more visible.

Taking four men with me I went to the forge. The bedeviled woman, tied down to her bed, shrieked continuously. Notwithstanding her strenuous resistance we dressed her neatly and carried her away.

When I arrived at the cold-looking, illuminated church, I found it full of people. The assistants were chanting their monotonous notes; the brazen horn was resounding throughout the edifice, while the tinkling bell of the acolyte directed the movements of the believers.

Shutting up the woman and her keepers in the kitchen of the parsonage I awaited the moment which I judged most favorable for the success of the experiment. I chose the instant following the communion. All the peasants, in the hope of tempering His severity, had been to receive their God. An impressive stillness reigned over all while the priest was terminating the sacred mystery.

At a given signal, the church door was flung open and my four assistants entered dragging the crazy woman.

As soon as her eyes fell upon the shining lights, the blazing choir, the golden tabernacle and the kneeling crowd, she struggled so fiercely that she nearly slipped away from us. She shrieked so shrilly that everybody in the church trembled, and many even took flight in terror.

My patient no longer had the semblance of a woman, drawn up as she was, her body twisted around, her head thrown back and her eyes wildly staring about her.

We dragged her to the steps of the chancel, and there held her squatted on the floor.

The priest was awaiting us at the altar. As soon as he saw the woman somewhat quieted, he took up the monstrance with its bright golden rays encircling the snow-white host in its centre, and, coming forward a few steps, he raised it with both hands above his head, presenting it to the wild gaze of the shrieking she-devil.

The woman kept on screaming, her staring eyes fixed on the shining object, while the priest stood so still that one might have taken him for a statue.

And this lasted a long, long time.

The fascinated woman now seemed stricken with fear. She gazed steadfastly at the monstrance, trembling violently and shrieking all the time, but in a manner far less heart-rending. And this still lasted a long, long time.

One would have supposed she could no longer close her eyes, so riveted on the host were they. Then she began to moan, and her rigid body seemed to unbend, to give way.

Every being in the church was prostrated, face to the floor.

The possessed woman now began to drop her eyelids rapidly and to raise them again immediately, as if unable to bear the sight of her God. She had become quiet, and all at once I noticed that her eyes remained closed. She was in a somnambulistic trance, hypnotised. I beg your pardon, she was conquered by the persistent contemplation of the monstrance with its golden rays, overpowered by the victorious Christ.

They carried her out, an inert body, while the priest returned to the altar.

The agitated assistants intoned a Te Deum hymn of thanksgiving.

The wife of the blacksmith slept during forty whole hours, and when she awoke she had not the slightest recollection of having been possessed with and delivered of a devil.

This, ladies, is a true account of the miracle I saw.

Dr. Bonenfant ceased speaking for awhile and then added in a slightly irritated tone:

"I could not help attesting the truth of the occurrence in writing."

GERMANY

O Come, Little Children

CHRISTOPH VON SCHMID   J. A. P. SCHULZ

Ihr Kin-der-lein, kom-met, O kom-met doch all! Zur krip-pe her kom-met in Bet-le hem's Stall, und seht, was in die-ser hoch-bei - li-gen Nacht der Va ter im Him-mel für Freu-de uns macht.

O come, little children, O come one and all!
O come to the cradle in Bethlehem's stall!
Come, look in the manger! There sleeps on the hay
An infant so lovely, in light bright as day.

Christmas at the Buddenbrooks'

THOMAS MANN
(Translated by H. T. Lowe-Porter)

IT WAS under these circumstances that the Christmas feast
drew near, to which little Hanno was counting the days,
with a beating heart and the help of a calendar manufactured
by Ida Jungmann, with a Christmas tree on the last leaf.

The signs of festivity increased. Ever since the first Sunday
in Advent a great gaily colored picture of a certain Ruprecht
had been hanging on the wall in grandmamma's dining-room.
And one morning Hanno found his covers and the rug beside
his bed sprinkled with gold tinsel. A few days later, as Papa was
lying with his newspaper on the living-room sofa, and Hanno
was reading "The Witch of Endor" out of Gerock's "Palm
Leaves," an "old man" was announced. This had happened
every year since Hanno was a baby—and yet was always a surprise. They asked him in, this "old man," and he came shuffling
along in a big coat with the fur side out, sprinkled with bits of
cotton-wool and tinsel. He wore a fur cap, and his face had
black smudges on it, and his beard was long and white. The
beard and the big, bushy eyebrows were also sprinkled with

Reprinted from *The Buddenbrooks* by Thomas Mann, translated by H. T.
Lowe-Porter, by permission of Alfred A. Knopf, Inc. Copyright 1936 by Alfred A.
Knopf, Inc.

tinsel. He explained—as he did every year—in a harsh voice, that *this* sack (on his left shoulder) was for good children, who said their prayers (it contained apples and gilded nuts); but that *this* sack (on his right shoulder) was for naughty children. The "old man" was, of course, Ruprecht; perhaps not actually the real Ruprecht—it might even be Wenzel the barber, dressed up in Papa's coat turned fur side out—but it was as much Ruprecht as possible. Hanno, greatly impressed, said Our Father for him, as he had last year—both times interrupting himself now and again with a little nervous sob—and was permitted to put his hand into the sack for good children, which the "old man" forgot to take away.

The holidays came, and there was not much trouble over the report, which had to be presented for Papa to read, even at Christmas-time. The great dining-room was closed and mysterious, and there were marzipan and gingerbread to eat—and in the streets, Christmas had already come. Snow fell, the weather was frosty, and on the sharp clear air were borne the notes of the barrel-organ, for the Italians, with their velvet jackets and their black moustaches, had arrived for the Christmas feast. The shop-windows were gay with toys and goodies; the booths for the Christmas fair had been erected in the market-place; and wherever you went you breathed in the fresh, spicy odor of the Christmas trees set out for sale.

The evening of the twenty-third came at last, and with it the present-giving in the house in Fishers' Lane. This was attended by the family only—it was a sort of dress rehearsal for the Christmas Eve party given by the Frau Consul in Meng Street. She clung to the old customs, and reserved the twenty-fourth for a celebration to which the whole family group was bidden; which, accordingly, in the late afternoon, assembled in the landscape-room.

The old lady, flushed of cheek, and with feverish eyes, arrayed in a heavy black-and-gray striped silk that gave out a faint scent of patchouli, received her guests as they entered, and embraced them silently, her gold braceles tinkling. She was strangely excited this evening—"Why, Mother, you're fairly trembling," the Senator said when he came in with Gerda and Hanno. "Everything will go off very easily." But she only whispered, kissing all three of them, "For Jesus Christ's sake—and my blessed Jean's."

Indeed, the whole consecrated program instituted by the deceased Consul had to be carried out to the smallest detail; and the poor lady fluttered about, driven by her sense of responsibility for the fitting accomplishment of the evening's performance, which must be pervaded with a deep and fervent joy. She went restlessly back and forth, from the pillared hall where the choir-boys from St. Mary's were already assembled, to the dining-room, where Riekchen Severin was putting the finishing touches to the tree and the table-full of presents, to the corridor full of shrinking old people—the "poor" who were to share in the presents—and back into the landscape-room, where she rebuked every unnecessary word or sound with one of her mild sidelong glances. It was so still that the sound of a distant hand-organ, faint and clear like a toy music-box, came across to them through the snowy streets. Some twenty persons or more were sitting or standing about in the room; yet it was stiller than a church—so still that, as the Senator cautiously whispered to Uncle Justus, it reminded one more of a funeral!

There was really no danger that the solemnity of the feast would be rudely broken in upon by youthful high spirits. A glance showed that almost all the persons in the room were arrived at an age when the forms of expression are already long ago fixed. Senator Thomas Buddenbrook, whose pallor gave the lie to his alert, energetic, humorous expression; Gerda, his wife, leaning back in her chair, the gleaming, blue-ringed eyes in her pale face gazing fixedly at the crystal prisms in the chandelier; his sister, Frau Permaneder; his cousin, Jürgen Kröger, a quiet, neatly-dressed official; Friederike, Henriette, and Pfiffi, the first two more long and lean, the third smaller and plumper than ever, but all three wearing their stereotyped expression, their sharp, spiteful smile at everything and everybody, as though they were perpetually saying "Really—it seems incredible!" Lastly, there was poor, ashen-gray Clothilde, whose thoughts were probably fixed upon the coming meal.—Every one of these persons was past forty. The hostess herself, her brother Justus and his wife, and little Therese Weichbrodt were all well past sixty; while old Frau Consul Buddenbrook, Uncle Gotthold's widow, born Stüwing, as well as Madame Kethelsen, now, alas, almost entirely deaf, were already in the seventies.

Erica Weinschenk was the only person present in the bloom of youth; she was much younger than her husband, whose cropped, graying head stood out against the idyllic landscape behind him. When her eyes—the light blue eyes of Herr Grünlich—rested upon him, you could see how her full bosom rose and fell without a sound, and how she was beset with anxious, bewildered thoughts about usance and book-keeping, witnesses, prosecuting attorneys, defense, and judges. Thoughts like these, un-Christmaslike though they were, troubled everybody in the room. They all felt uncanny at the presence in their midst of a member of the family who was actually accused of an offense against the law, the civic weal, and business probity, and who would probably be visited by shame and imprisonment. Here was a Christmas family party at the Buddenbrooks'—with an accused man in the circle! Frau Permaneder's dignity became majestic, and the smile of the Misses Buddenbrook more and more pointed.

And what of the children, the scant posterity upon whom rested the family hopes? Were they conscious too of the slightly uncanny atmosphere? The state of mind of the little Elisabeth could not be fathomed. She sat on her bonne's lap in a frock trimmed by Frau Permaneder with satin bows, folded her small hands into fists, sucked her tongue, and stared straight ahead of her. Now and then she would utter a brief sound, like a grunt, and the nurse would rock her a little on her arm. But Hanno sat still on his footstool at his mother's knee and stared up, like her, into the chandelier.

Christian was missing—where was he? At the last minute they noticed his absence. The Frau Consul's characteristic gesture, from the corner of her mouth up to her temple, as though putting back a refractory hair, became frequent and feverish. She gave an order to Mamsell Severin, and the spinster went out through the hall, past the choir-boys and the "poor" and down the corridor to Christian's room, where she knocked on the door.

Christian appeared straightway; he limped casually into the landscape-room, rubbing his bald brow. "Good gracious, children," he said, "I nearly forgot the party!"

"You nearly forgot—" his mother repeated, and stiffened.

"Yes, I really forgot it was Christmas. I was reading a book of travel, about South America.—Dear me, I've seen such a lot of Christmases!" he added, and was about to launch out upon a description of a Christmas in a fifth-rate variety theatre in London—when all at once the church-like hush of the room began to work upon him, and he moved on tip-toe to his place, wrinkling up his nose.

"Rejoice, O Daughter of Zion!" sang the choir-boys. They had previously been indulging in such audible practical jokes that the Senator had to get up and stand in the doorway to inspire respect. But now they sang beautifully. The clear treble, sustained by the deeper voices, soared up in pure, exultant, glorifying tones, bearing all hearts along with them: softening the smiles of the spinsters, making the old folk look in upon themselves and back upon the past; easing the hearts of those still in the midst of life's tribulations, and helping them to forget for a little while.

Hanno unclasped his hands from about his knees. He looked very pale, and cold, played with the fringe of his stool, and twisted his tongue about among his teeth. He had to draw a deep breath every little while, for his heart contracted with a joy almost painful at the exquisite bell-like purity of the chorale. The white folding doors were still tightly closed, but the spicy poignant odor drifted through the cracks and whetted one's appetite for the wonder within. Each year with throbbing pulses he awaited this vision of ineffable, unearthly splendor. What would there be for him, in there? What he had wished for, of course; there was always that—unless he had been persuaded out of it beforehand. The theatre, then, the long-desired toy theatre, would spring at him as the door opened, and show him the way to his place. This was the suggestion which had stood heavily underlined at the top of his list, ever since he had seen *Fidelio;* indeed, since then, it had been almost his single thought.

He had been taken to the opera as compensation for a particularly painful visit to Herr Brecht; sitting beside his mother, in the dress circle, he had followed breathless a performance of *Fidelio,* and since that time he had heard nothing, seen nothing, thought of nothing but opera, and a passion for the theatre filled him and almost kept him sleepless. He looked enviously at people like Uncle Christian, who was known as a regular frequenter and might go every night if he liked: Consul Döhlmann, Gosch the broker—how could they endure the joy of seeing it every night? He himself would ask no more than to look once a week into the hall, before the performance: hear the voices of the instruments being tuned, and gaze for a while at the curtain! For he loved it all, the seats, the musicians, the drop-curtain—even the smell of gas.

Would his theatre be large? What sort of curtain would it have? A tiny hole must be cut in it at once—there was a peephole in the curtain at the theatre. Had Grandmamma, or rather had Mamsell Severin—for Grandmamma could not see to everything herself—been able to find all the necessary scenery for *Fidelio?* He determined to shut himself up tomorrow and give a performance all by himself, and already in fancy he heard his little figures singing: for he was approaching the theatre by way of his music.

"Exult, Jerusalem!" finished the choir; and their voices, following one another in fugue form, united joyously in the last syllable. The clear accord died away; deep silence reigned in the pillared hall and the landscape-room. The elders looked down, oppressed by the pause; only Director Weinschenk's eyes roved boldly about, and Frau Permaneder coughed her dry cough, which she could not suppress. Now the Frau Consul moved slowly to the table and sat among her family. She turned up the lamp and took in her hands the great Bible with its edges of faded gold-leaf. She stuck her glasses on her nose, unfastened the two great leather hasps of the book, opened it to the place where there was a bookmark, took a sip of *eau sucrée,* and began to read, from the yellowed page with the large print, the Christmas chapter.

She read the old familiar words with a simple, heart-felt accent that sounded clear and moving in the pious hush. " 'And to men good-will,' " she finished, and from the pillared hall came a trio of voices: "Silent night, holy night!" The family in the landscape-room joined in. They did so cautiously, for most of them were unmusical, as a tone now and then betrayed. But that in no wise impaired the effect of the old hymn. Frau Permaneder sang with trembling lips; it sounded sweetest and most touching to the heart of her who had a troubled life behind her, and looked back upon it in the brief peace of this holy hour. Madame Kethelsen wept softly, but comprehended nothing.

Now the Frau Consul rose. She grasped the hands of her grandson Johann and her granddaughter Elisabeth, and proceeded through the room. The elders of the family fell in behind, and the younger brought up the rear; the servants and poor joined in from the hall; and so they marched, singing with one accord "Oh, Evergreen"—Uncle Christian sang "Oh, Everblue," and made the children laugh by lifting up his legs like a jumping-jack—through the wide-open, lofty folding doors, and straight into Paradise.

The whole great room was filled with the fragrance of slightly singed evergreen twigs and glowing with light from countless tiny flames. The sky-blue hangings with the white figures on them added to the brilliance. There stood the mighty tree, between the dark red window-curtains, towering nearly to the ceiling, decorated with silver tinsel and large white lilies, with a shining angel at the top and the manger at the foot. Its candles twinkled in the general flood of light like far-off stars. And a row of tiny trees, also full of stars and hung with comfits, stood on the long white table, laden with presents, that stretched from the window to the door. All the gas-brackets on the wall were lighted too, and thick candles burned in all four of the gilded candelabra in the corners of the room. Large objects, too large to stand upon the table, were arranged upon the floor, and two smaller tables, likewise adorned with tiny trees and covered with gifts for the servants and the poor, stood on either side of the door.

Dazzled by the light and the unfamiliar look of the room, they marched once around it, singing, filed past the manger where lay the little wax figure of the Christ-child, and then moved to their places and stood silent.

Hanno was quite dazed. His fevered glance had soon sought out the theatre, which, as it stood there upon the table, seemed larger and grander than anything he had dared to dream of. But his place had been changed—it was now opposite to where he had stood last year, and this made him doubtful whether the theatre was really his. And on the floor beneath it was something else, a large, mysterious something, which had surely not been on his list; a piece of furniture, that looked like a commode—could it be meant for him?

"Come here, my dear child," said the Frau Consul, "and look at this." She lifted the lid. "I know you like to play chorals. Herr Pfühl will show you how. You must tread all the time, sometimes more and sometimes less; and then, not lift up the hands, but change the fingers so, *peu à peu.*"

It was a harmonium—a pretty little thing of polished brown wood, with metal handles at the sides, gay bellows worked with a treadle, and a neat revolving stool. Hanno struck a chord. A soft organ tone released itself and made the others look up from their presents. He hugged his grandmother, who pressed him tenderly to her, and then left him to receive the thanks of her other guests.

He turned to his theatre. The harmonium was an overpowering dream—which just now he had no time to indulge. There was a superfluity of joy; and he lost sight of single gifts in trying to see and notice everything at once. Ah, here was the prompter's box, a shell-shaped one, and a beautiful red and gold curtain rolled up and down behind it. The stage was set for the

last act of *Fidelio*. The poor prisoners stood with folded hands.
Don Pizarro, in enormous puffed sleeves, was striking a perma-
nent and awesome attitude, and the minister, in black velvet, approached from behind with hasty strides, to turn all to happiness. It was just as in the theatre, only almost more beautiful.
The Jubilee chorus, the finale, echoed in Hanno's ears, and he
sat down at the harmonium to play a fragment which stuck in
his memory. But he got up again, almost at once, to take up the
book he had wished for, a mythology, in a red binding with a
gold Pallas Athene on the cover. He ate some of the sweetmeats
from his plate full of marzipan, gingerbread, and other goodies,
looked through various small articles like writing utensils and
school-bag—and for the moment forgot everything else, to examine a penholder with a tiny glass bulb on it: when you held
this up to your eye, you saw, like magic, a broad Swiss landscape.

Mamsell Severin and the maid passed tea and biscuits; and
while Hanno dipped and ate, he had time to look about. Every
one stood talking and laughing; they all showed each other
their presents and admired the presents of others. Objects of
porcelain, silver, gold, nickel, wood, silk, cloth, and every other
conceivable material lay on the table. Huge loaves of decorated
gingerbread, alternating with loaves of marzipan, stood in long
rows, still moist and fresh. All the presents made by Frau Permaneder were decorated with huge satin bows.

Now and then some one came up to little Johann, put an
arm across his shoulders, and looked at his presents with the
overdone, cynical admiration which people manufacture for
the treasures of children. Uncle Christian was the only person
who did not display this grown-up arrogance. He sauntered over
to his nephew's place, with a diamond ring on his finger, a
present from his mother; and his pleasure in the toy theatre
was as unaffected as Hanno's own.

"By George, that's fine," he said, letting the curtain up and
down, and stepping back for a view of the scenery. "Did you ask
for it? Oh, so you did ask for it!" he suddenly said after a pause,
during which his eyes had roved about the room as though he

were full of unquiet thoughts. "Why did you ask for it? What made you think of it? Have you been in the theatre? *Fidelio*, eh? Yes, they give that well. And you want to imitate it, do you? Do opera yourself, eh? Did it make such an impression on you? Listen, son—take my advice: don't think too much about such things—theatre, and that sort of thing. It's no good. Believe your old uncle. I've always spent too much time on them, and that is why I haven't come to much good. I've made great mistakes, you know."

Thus he held forth to his nephew, while Hanno looked up at him curiously. He paused, and his bony, emaciated face cleared up as he regarded the little theatre. Then he suddenly moved forward one of the figures on the stage, and sang, in a cracked and hollow tremolo, "Ha, what terrible transgression!" He sat down on the piano-stool, which he shoved up in front of the theatre, and began to give a performance, singing all the rôles and the accompaniment as well, and gesticulating furiously. The family gathered at his back, laughed, nodded their heads, and enjoyed it immensely. As for Hanno, his pleasure was profound. Christian broke off, after a while, very abruptly. His face clouded, he rubbed his hand over his skull and down his left side, and turned to his audience with his nose wrinkled and his face quite drawn.

"There it is again," he said. "I never have a little fun without having to pay for it. It is not an ordinary pain, you know, it is a misery, down all this left side, because the nerves are too short."

But his relatives took his complaints as little seriously as they had his entertainment. They hardly answered him, but indifferently dispersed, leaving Christian sitting before the little theatre in silence. He blinked rapidly for a bit and then got up.

"No, child," said he, stroking Hanno's head: "amuse yourself with it, but not too much, you know: don't neglect your work for it, do you hear? I have made a great many mistakes.— I think I'll go over to the club for a while," he said to the elders. "They are celebrating there to-day, too. Good-bye for the present." And he went off across the hall, on his stiff, crooked legs.

They had all eaten the midday meal earlier than usual today, and been hungry for the tea and biscuits. But they had scarcely finished when great crystal bowls were handed round full of a yellow, grainy substance which turned out to be almond cream. It was a mixture of eggs, ground almonds, and rose-water, tasting perfectly delicious; but if you ate even a tiny spoonful too much, the result was an attack of indigestion. However, the company was not restrained by fear of consequences—even though Frau Consul begged them to "leave a little corner for supper." Clothilde, in particular, performed miracles with the almond cream, and lapped it up like so much porridge, with heart-felt gratitude. There was also wine jelly in glasses, and English plum-cake. Gradually they all moved over to the landscape-room, where they sat with their plates round the table.

Hanno remained alone in the dining-room. Little Elisabeth Weinschenk had already been taken home; but he was to stop up for supper, for the first time in his life. The servants and the poor folk had had their presents and gone; Ida Jungmann was chattering with Riekchen Severin in the hall—although generally, as a governess, she preserved a proper distance between herself and the Frau Consul's maid.—The lights of the great tree were burned down and extinguished, the manger was in darkness. But a few candles still burned on the small trees, and now and then a twig came within reach of the flame and crackled up, increasing the pungent smell in the room. Every breath of air that stirred the trees stirred the pieces of tinsel too, and made them give out a delicate metallic whisper. It was still enough to hear the hand-organ again, sounding through the frosty air from a distant street.

Hanno abandoned himself to the enjoyment of the Christmas sounds and smells. He propped his head on his hand and read in his mythology book, munching mechanically the while, because that was proper to the day: marzipan, sweetmeats, almond cream, and plum-cake; until the chest-oppression caused by an over-loaded stomach mingled with the sweet excitation of the evening and gave him a feeling of pensive felicity. He read about the struggles of Zeus before he arrived at the headship of the gods; and every now and then he listened into the other room, where they were going at length into the future of poor Aunt Clothilde.

Clothilde, on this evening, was far and away the happiest of them all. A smile lighted up her colorless face as she received congratulations and teasing from all sides; her voice even broke now and then out of joyful emotion. She had at last been made a member of the Order of St. John. The Senator had succeeded by subterranean methods in getting her admitted, not without some private grumblings about nepotism, on the part of certain gentlemen. Now the family all discussed the excellent institution, which was similar to the homes in Mecklenburg, Dobberthien, and Ribnitz, for ladies from noble families. The object of these establishments was the suitable care of portionless women from old and worthy families. Poor Clothilde was now assured of a small but certain income, which would increase with the years, and finally, when she had succeeded to the highest class, would secure her a decent home in the cloister itself.

Little Hanno stopped awhile with the grown-ups, but soon strayed back to the dining-room, which displayed a new charm now that the brilliant light did not fairly dazzle one with its splendors. It was an extraordinary pleasure to roam about there, as if on a half-darkened stage after the performance, and see a little behind the scenes. He touched the lilies on the big fir-tree, with their golden stamens; handled the tiny figures of people and animals in the manger, found the candles that lighted the transparency for the star of Bethlehem over the stable; lifted up the long cloth that covered the present-table, and saw quantities of wrapping-paper and pasteboard boxes stacked beneath.

The conversation in the landscape-room was growing less and less agreeable. Inevitably, irresistibly, it had arrived at the one dismal theme which had been in everybody's mind, but which they had thus far avoided, as a tribute to the festal evening. Hugo Weinschenk himself dilated upon it, with a wild levity of manner and gesture. He explained certain details of the pro-

cedure—the examination of witnesses had now been interrupted by the Christmas recess—condemned the very obvious
bias of the President, Dr. Philander, and poured scorn on the
attitude which the Public Prosecutor, Dr. Hagenström, thought
it proper to assume toward himself and the witnesses for the
defense. Breslauer had succeeded in drawing the sting of several of his most slanderous remarks; and he had assured the
Director that, for the present, there need be no fear of a conviction. The Senator threw in a question now and then, out of
courtesy; and Frau Permaneder, sitting on the sofa with elevated shoulders, would utter fearful imprecations against Dr.
Moritz Hagenström. But the others were silent: so profoundly
silent that the Director at length fell silent too. For little
Hanno, over in the dining-room, the time sped by on angels'
wings; but in the landscape-room there reigned an oppressive
silence, which dragged on till Christian came back from the
club, where he had celebrated Christmas with the bachelors
and good fellows.

The cold stump of a cigar hung between his lips, and his
haggard cheeks were flushed. He came through the dining-room
and said, as he entered the landscape-room, "Well, children, the
tree was simply gorgeous. Weinschenk, we ought to have had
Breslauer come to see it. He has never seen anything like it, I
am sure."

He encountered one of his mother's quiet, reproachful side-
glances, and returned it with an easy, unembarrassed questioning look. At nine o'clock the party sat down to supper.

It was laid, as always on these occasions, in the pillared hall.
The Frau Consul recited the ancient grace with sincere conviction:

> "Come, Lord Jesus, be our guest,
> And bless the bread thou gavest us"

—to which, as usual on the evening, she added a brief prayer,
the substance of which was an admonition to remember those
who, on this blessed night, did not fare so well as the Budden-

brooks family. This accomplished, they all sat down with good consciences to a lengthy repast, beginning with carp and butter sauce and old Rhine wine.

The Senator put two fish-scales into his pocket, to help him save money during the coming year. Christian, however, ruefully remarked that he hadn't much faith in the prescription; and Consul Kröger had no need of it. His pittance had long since been invested securely, beyond the reach of fluctuations in the exchange. The old man sat as far away as possible from his wife, to whom he hardly ever spoke nowadays. She persisted in sending money to Jacob, who was still roaming about, nobody knew where, unless his mother did. Uncle Justus scowled forbiddingly when the conversation, with the advent of the second course, turned upon the absent members of the family, and he saw the foolish mother wipe her eyes. They spoke of the Frankfort Buddenbrooks and the Duchamps in Hamburg, and of Pastor Tibertius in Riga, too, without any ill-will. And the Senator and his sister touched glasses in silence to the health of Messrs. Grünlich and Permaneder—for, after all, did they not in a sense belong to the family too?

The turkey, stuffed with chestnuts, raisins, and apples, was universally praised. They compared it with other years, and decided that this one was the largest for a long time. With the turkey came roast potatoes and two kinds of compote, and each dish held enough to satisfy the appetite of a family all by itself. The old red wine came from the firm of Möllendorpf.

Little Johann sat between his parents and choked down with difficulty a small piece of white meat with stuffing. He could not begin to compete with Aunt Tilda, and he felt tired and out of sorts. But it was a great thing none the less to be dining with the grown-ups, and to have one of the beautiful little rolls with poppy-seed in his elaborately folded serviette, and three wine-glasses in front of his place. He usually drank out of the little gold mug which Uncle Justus gave him. But when the red, white, and brown meringues appeared, and Uncle Justus poured some oily, yellow Greek wine into the smallest of the three glasses, his appetite revived. He ate a whole red ice, then half a white one, then a little piece of the chocolate, his teeth hurting horribly all the while. Then he sipped his sweet wine gingerly and listened to Uncle Christian, who had begun to talk.

He told about the Christmas celebration at the club, which had been very jolly, it seemed. "Good God!" he said, just as if he were about to relate the story of Johnny Thunderstorm, "those fellows drank Swedish punch just like water."

"Ugh!" said the Frau Consul shortly, and cast down her eyes.

But he paid no heed. His eyes began to wander—and thought and memory became so vivid that they flickered like shadows across his haggard face.

"Do any of you know," he asked, "how it feels to drink too much Swedish punch? I don't mean getting drunk: I mean the feeling you have the next day—the after-effects. They are very queer and unpleasant; yes, queer and unpleasant at the same time."

"Reason enough for not describing them," said the Senator.

"*Assez,* Christian. That does not interest us in the least," said the Frau Consul. But he paid no attention. It was his peculiarity that at such times nothing made any impression on him. He was silent awhile, and then it seemed that the thing which moved him was ripe for speech.

"You go about feeling ghastly," he said, turning to his brother and wrinkling up his nose. "Headache, and upset stomach—oh, well, you have that with other things, too. But you feel *filthy*"—here he rubbed his hands together, his face entirely distorted. "You wash your hands, but it does no good; they feel dirty and clammy, and there is grease under the nails. You take a bath: no good, your whole body is sticky and unclean. You itch all over, and you feel disgusted with yourself. Do you know the feeling, Thomas? you do know it, don't you?"

"Yes, yes," said the Senator, making a gesture of repulsion with his hand. But Christian's extraordinary tactlessness had so increased with the years that he never perceived how unpleasant he was making himself to the company, nor how out of place his conversation was in these surroundings and on this evening. He continued to describe the evil effects of too much Swedish punch; and when he felt that he had exhausted the subject, he gradually subsided.

Before they arrived at the butter and cheese, the Frau Consul found occasion for another little speech to her family. If, she said, not quite everything in the course of the years had gone as we, in our short-sightedness, desired, there remained such manifold blessings as should fill our hearts with gratitude and love. For it was precisely this mingling of trials with blessings which showed that God never lifted his hand from the family, but ever guided its destinies according to His wise design, which we might not seek to question. And now, with hopeful hearts, we might drink together to the family health and to its future—that future when all the old and elderly of the present company would be laid to rest; and to the children, to whom the Christmas feast most properly belonged.

As Director Weinschenk's small daughter was no longer present, little Johann had to make the round of the table alone and drink severally with all the company, from Grandmamma to Mamsell Severin. When he came to his father, the Senator touched the child's glass with his and gently lifted Hanno's chin to look into his eyes. But his son did not meet his glance: the long, gold-brown lashes lay deep, deep upon the delicate bluish shadows beneath his eyes.

Therese Weichbrodt took his head in both her hands, kissed him explosively on both cheeks, and said with such a hearty emphasis that surely God must have heeded it, "Be happy, you good che-ild!"

An hour later Hanno lay in his little bed, which now stood in the ante-chamber next to the Senator's dressing-room. He lay on his back, out of regard for his stomach, which feeling was far from pleasant over all the things he had put into it that evening. Ida came out of her room in her dressing-gown, waving a glass about in circles in the air in order to dissolve its contents. He drank the bicarbonate of soda down quickly, made a wry face, and fell back again.

"I think I'll just have to give it all up, Ida," he said.

"Oh, nonsense, Hanno. Just lie still on your back. You see, now: who was it kept making signs to you to stop eating, and who was it that wouldn't do it?"

"Well, perhaps I'll be all right. When will the things come, Ida?"

"To-morrow morning, first thing, my dearie."

"I wish they were here—I wish I had them now."

"Yes, yes, my dearie—but just have a good sleep now." She kissed him, put out the light, and went away.

He lay quietly, giving himself up to the operation of the soda he had taken. But before his eyes gleamed the dazzling brilliance of the Christmas tree. He saw his theatre and his harmonium, and his book of mythology; he heard the choir-boys singing in the distance: "Rejoice, Jerusalem!" Everything sparkled and glittered. His head felt dull and feverish; his heart, affected by the rebellious stomach, beat strong and irregularly. He lay for long, in a condition of mingled discomfort, excitement, and reminiscent bliss, and could not fall asleep.

Next day there would be a third Christmas party, at Fräulein Weichbrodt's. He looked forward to it as to a comic performance in the theatre. Therese Weichbrodt had given up her *pensionat* in the past year. Madame Kethelsen now occupied the first story of the house on the Mill Brink, and she herself the ground floor, and there they lived alone. The burden of her deformed little body grew heavier with the years, and she concluded, with Christian humility and submission, that the end was not far off. For some years now she had believed that each Christmas was her last; and she strove with all the powers at her command to give a departing brilliance to the feast that was held in her small over-heated rooms. Her means were very narrow, and she gave away each year a part of her possessions to swell the heap of gifts under the tree: knick-knacks, paper-weights, emery-bags, needle-cushions, glass vases, and fragments of her library, miscellaneous books of every shape and size. Books like "The Secret Journal of a Student of Himself," Hebel's "Alemannian Poems," Krummacher's "Parables"—

Hanno had once received an edition of the "Pensées de Blaise Pascal," in such tiny print that it had to be read with a glass.

Bishop flowed in streams, and Sesemi's ginger-bread was very spicy. But Fräulein Weichbrodt abandoned herself with such trembling emotion to the joys of each Christmas party that none of them ever went off without a mishap. There was always some small catastrophe or other to make the guests laugh and enhance the silent fervor of the hostess' mien. A jug of bishop would be upset and overwhelm everything in a spicy, sticky red flood. Or the decorated tree would topple off its wooden support just as they solemnly entered the room. Hanno fell asleep with the mishap of the previous year before his eyes. It had happened just before the gifts were given out. Therese Weichbrodt had read the Christmas chapter, in such impressive accents that all the vowels got inextricably commingled, and then retreated before her guests to the door, where she made a little speech. She stood upon the threshold, humped and tiny, her old hands clasped before her childish bosom, the green silk cap-ribbons falling over her fragile shoulders. Above her head, over the door, was a transparency, garlanded with evergreen, that said "Glory to God in the Highest." And Sesemi spoke of God's mercy; she mentioned that this was her last Christmas, and ended by reminding them that the words of the apostle commended them all to joy—wherewith she trembled from head to foot, so much did her whole poor little body share in her emotions. "Rejoice!" said she, laying her head on one side and nodding violently: "and again I say unto you, rejoice!" But at this moment the whole transparency, with a puffing, crackling, spitting noise, went up in flames, and Mademoiselle Weichbrodt gave a little shriek and a side-spring of unexpected picturesqueness and agility, and got herself out of the way of the rain of flying sparks.

As Hanno recalled the leap which the old spinster performed, he giggled nervously for several minutes into his pillow.

Fifty Marks

HANS FALLADA
(Translated by Eric Sutton)

WE WERE newly married, Itzenplitz and I, and to all intents and purposes we possessed absolutely nothing. Now when you are very young and newly married and very much in love into the bargain, this doesn't matter a very great deal. True, we had our wistful moments, but always one of us would laugh and say: "Why, there's no reason for everything to come all at once! We've got all the time in the world!" And the wistful moment was over.

Yet I do remember one particular conversation of ours in the Park, when Itzenplitz sighed and said, "Oh, if only we hadn't to watch every penny so carefully!"

I sought enlightenment. "Well?" I asked, "What then?"

"I'd buy myself something!" said Itzenplitz dreamily.

"Well, and what would you buy?"

Itzenplitz reflected. Believe it or not, she had to think before she said, "For instance, a pair of warm woolly slippers!"

"Well, I'll be darned!" I said, completely staggered, and was filled with awe at the remarkable reasoning of my wife Elizabeth, alias Ibeth, alias Itzenplitz; for it was midsummer, the sun was beating down, and for my part I wanted nothing better

Reprinted by permission of the estate of Hans Ditzen-Fallada.

at the moment than a cool shower and a cigarette. Yet it must have been as the aftermath of this midsummer colloquy that our Christmas Wish-List came into being.

"You know, Tim," said Itzenplitz, thoughtfully rubbing her long, sharp nose, "we ought to start now putting down everything that comes into our heads. Afterward, at Christmas, it'll be an awful scramble and we shall quite probably give each other silly things we don't need at all."

Accordingly we wrote down our first Christmas wish on a piece of paper torn from my order-book: "1 pair of warm woolly slippers for Itzenplitz"; and since we always made a point of being strictly impartial, I wrote underneath after much thought and frowning: "1 good book for Tim." "That's fine!" said Itzenplitz, and stared rapturously at the Wish-List as if slippers and book might pop out of it at any moment.

Midsummer gave place to late autumn; after the first slushy snow came the Christmas shop-windows, and all the time our Christmas Wish-List grew and grew and grew.

"What does it matter if there is a terrible lot?" consoled Itzenplitz. "Then we shall have our choice. It's really more of a crossing-out list. Just before Christmas we'll cross out everything we can't manage, but wishing's still free, surely?" She reflected a moment and said, "I can wish what I like, can't I, Tim?"

"Yes," I said recklessly.

"Fine!" she said, and in a twinkling she had written: "1 blue silk evening frock (latest model)." She regarded me challengingly.

"Well, you know, Itzenplitz . . ." I observed.

"You said wishing was free!"

"All right," I said, and wrote: "1 radio." And now I gave *her* a challenging look. Then we began a lively dispute, conducted with Machiavellian ingenuity, as to which we needed more, an evening frock or a radio—and all the time we were both perfectly well aware that for the next five years neither would even bear consideration.

But all this took place much later. For the time being we

were still in the park, and it was summer, and we had written down our first two wishes. Now Itzenplitz has a rather long, mischievous nose, which easily goes red with joy or indignation, hence her nose-rubbing; and on top of that she has the quickest eyes in the world. She is always finding something, and sure enough, at this moment she called: "Here it is! Oh, Tim, Tim, here's our first Christmas *groschen!*" And she touched it with her toe.

"Christmas *groschen?*" I said, picking it up, "I'm off right now to buy three cigarettes with it."

"You give it to me! It's our Christmas *groschen,* it's for our Christmas Savings Box!"

"*Have* you a Christmas Savings Box?" I asked derisively. "I've never seen you with one."

"I'll find something all right. Just let me look!" And her eyes darted about under the trees as if the search were due to start right away.

"We'll do it like this," I suggested. "We'll make a rough estimate of how much we want to spend on each other at Christmas, say for instance fifty marks . . ."

"You poor goop!" she said pityingly.

". . . and there'll be six pay-days before Christmas, and each time we'll put by eight marks, no, eight marks fifty. That'll do the trick!"

"And now I'm off for my three cigarettes."

"No, you don't! That *groschen* belongs to me!"

"Really!" I jeered.

"Oh you're a stupid boy and I shan't speak a word to you for three days, and I won't walk with you at all, ever!"

Thereupon, snorting with rage, she left me standing and walked on alone. I followed her slowly; but when after a while we came to the streets, she walked on one side and I on the other as though we were perfect strangers. Only when a troop of really fat, respectable, Sunday-clad citizens came along, I was thoroughly low and called across the street: "Hey, miss! I say, miss!" The people made goggle-eyes, and she turned crimson and threw back her head.

But suddenly I had an idea, and I raced across and shouted: "Itzenplitz, we'd quite forgotten, there's a fifty-mark bonus at Christmas, of course!"

Her first impulse was to bite my head off, and she did begin by inquiring who on earth would dream of giving a bonus to an idiot like myself; then, however, we considered our case seriously, deliberating whether, with times so bad, there would be any bonus at all, and the final verdict was: "We'll pretend there won't be one. But oh, it would be lovely . . . !"

Now I have still to relate why we were obliged to be so economical, and what we lived by, and what prospects we really had for the Christmas bonus. It is not at all easy to explain what I did. Recent as it all is, I shake my head and wonder how I managed to combine my manifold duties. At all events I spent all morning from seven o'clock onward in the editorial office of a local rag and wrote up half the local page, while Herr Pressbold, the Editor, sat opposite me, filling up the whole of the rest of the paper with the aid of pictures, matrices, correspondence, broadcasting programs and a very defective typewriter. For this I was paid eighty marks a month, and that was our only regular source of income. However, having survived the morning, I set out to solicit subscribers and advertisements on a commission basis, 1.25 Reichsmarks per subscriber, and ten per cent of every advertisement. I was also treasurer of a voluntary sick-fund (three per cent of all subscriptions), entrusted by an athletic club with the collection of members' subscriptions, and to crown all, I functioned as secretary of the Town Improvements and Tourist Board. For this last, however, I got nothing save the glory and the somewhat remote prospect of these gentlemen doing something for me should anything ever happen to turn up.

Thus there was no lack of employment, only the depressing thing about the whole business was that all these combined activities hardly yielded enough to keep Itzenplitz and me alive. The verb "to buy" might have been Chinese for all it meant to us. Many were the times I came home listless and despondent, having tramped about the whole afternoon, knocked at fifty doors, and earned not fifty pfennigs. Today I am firmly convinced (however vehemently she may still deny it) that Itzenplitz's merry conceits were solely for the purpose of taking my mind off my troubles.

It must have been some time in the autumn—wet, foggy weather, and myself in the worst of humors, and our Christmas Box still a thing of fancy, when I came home and found Itzenplitz with a kitchen knife in one hand and a briquette, sawed through long-ways, in the other.

"What on earth are you up to?" I asked in astonishment, for she was engaged in hollowing out this half-briquette with the end of the knife. The other half lay before her on the table.

"Sh-h, Tim!" she whispered darkly, "the world is full of evil-doers!" And she pointed with her knife to the door, pasted up with wall-paper, behind which dwelt the neighbor we referred to between ourselves as Jolly Roger.

"Well, what's the matter?" And then, in conspiratorial tones, she enlightened me; she had halved the briquette and was going to hollow it out and make a slit in it, and stick it together again with glue, and that was to be our Christmas Savings Box, and the idea was to put it among the other briquettes, for—"There are lots and lots of great, big, savage villains, all panting after our poor little money!" And her eyes sparkled.

"And you're as mad as a hatter!" I said. "Besides, talking of Christmas, Heber says there's absolutely no question of any bonus this year. The chief is as savage as the devil because business is bad!"

"That's fine!" she said. "Oh, Timothy-Titus, tell me all, so I'll know who gets the briquette at his head on Christmas Eve."

I have already mentioned that our editor was Herr Pressbold. A fine fellow he was too, pugnacious, blustering, daily increasing in girth; but he had no say. Herr Heber was the man. He kept the cash and the books, and had the ear of the Big Noise on whom we only set eyes once every six months. He spent his life being trundled about the country in his Rolls Royce, and had here a sawmill and there a little provincial paper and here some real estate and there a farm.

But on the paper his right-hand man was Herr Heber, a dry, bony, long-shanked man of figures, and him I had tried to pump in a certain matter of Christmas bonuses and fifty marks. As well try to pump the Sahara desert! He had inquired whether the first cold spell had gone to my head, and whether I realized what it meant to work in a losing concern; and I could consider myself lucky if by the New Year the rotten rag wasn't washed out altogether.

And the worst of it was that Pressbold, on whom I was counting for support, had piped the same tune and actually reproved me for my "inflated ideas," telling me I ought to be glad if we weren't axed and that whatever we did we mustn't aggravate the Big Noise. And while the two of them jawed me, I thought that the losing concern and the boss's troubles were nothing to me, and the Wish-Lists sailed past my mind's eye like leaves in the wind, and away danced the warm woolly slippers and the evening frock and the good book and the Christmas Duck.

Ah, yes, the Christmas Duck! That reminds me. This is the moment for the official introduction of our neighbor beyond the wall-paper door, friend Jolly Roger. I don't suppose we ever knew Jolly Roger's real name, but he had the northern garret while we occupied the southern. He was a really black man. Indeed, I can only describe him by saying that he produced an effect of complete blackness; he had black bristly hair, black eyes that glittered wildly, and an untidy black beard. In town, and especially with the police, he was well-known and well-feared as a drunkard and a rowdy. In his spare time he was also a stoker at the Municipal Electricity Works. We could hardly have been closer neighbors; even when he turned over in bed we heard him, and so no doubt he heard all our business too.

At all events he heard our Christmas discussion about the duck. At her house, as in mine, the traditional Christmas fare had been goose, but in the course of the debate it occurred to us that a twelve-pound goose ("if it weighs less it's nothing but skin and bone") was rather a lot for two. So we decided on a duck—goose, so to speak, in octavo instead of folio. It would be just right for the two of us; but where to buy it and for how much. . . ?

At this moment a roar, a hoarse, unintelligible bellowing, issued from Jolly Roger's room, and a minute afterward a fist descended on our door. Swaying, but wild to look upon as a beast of the jungle, Jolly Roger stood in the doorway; he had come straight out of bed and was clad only in shirt and trousers, which he held up with a firm grip of the left hand.

"I'll get the Christmas bird for you!" croaked Jolly Roger, glaring from one to the other.

We were not a little startled and embarrassed. Itzenplitz rubbed her nose and kept on murmuring, "Very kind of you" and "Very nice of you," and I tried to explain that we were still rather undecided—perhaps we should plump for a goose or a turkey after all.

"Fools!" roared Jolly Roger, and the plaster flew from the ceiling, so hard did he slam the door. However, he evidently bore us no malice. He did not, it is true, renew his offer of a duck, but when, a week before Christmas, he met Itzenplitz on the landing endeavoring to nail two boards together as a stand for the Christmas tree, he took the boards away and declared: "I'll see to that. I've got a board ready planed in the boiler room; make you a present of it for Christmas. Peach of a stand!"

But to return to the bonus question—my first attack then had been repulsed, and partly to console ourselves, we held an inquiry into our financial position. We ascertained what exactly we had put by since the great Christmas-Saving-Resolution. This was no easy task, for Itzenplitz had quite a system of separate funds—Housekeeping Money, Pocket Money, Tim's Money, the Fuel Fund, New Purchases Fund, Rent Fund and Christmas Fund, and since, thanks to our financial state, it was usually ebb-tide in most of the pots and tins, the few coins wandered from one fund to another and where they originally belonged it was impossible to tell.

Itzenplitz rubbed at her nose, which was growing rapidly redder, added a little here and a little there, abstracted a *groschen* and replaced a mark, while I leaned on the stove and made sarcastic remarks. Finally it seemed clear that within a period of three months the Christmas Fund had swollen to 7.85 Reichsmarks, always assuming that the briquettes would last out the month. If not, then another two marks fifty would go to the Fuel Fund.

We looked at each other; but it never rains without pouring, and so in this moment of complete insolvence who should strike a chord in Itzenplitz's brain but my mother-in-law, and then Tutti and Johnny, nephew and niece. "I've always given Mummy and the children something for Christmas. We *must* manage it, I tell you!"

"Quite, quite; but you might tell me how!"

Itzenplitz disclosed nothing; instead she pulled off a masterstroke. She called on me one fine day at the paper, and engaged our old stick-in-the-mud of a Heber in a positively enchanting conversation. I still see him, with his long, dismal, horse-face, his cheeks actually tinged with red, sitting behind the city desk, and Itzenplitz on the other side on our one cane chair; Itzenplitz in kid gloves—a pinafore frock with dotted silk blouse and a cheap summer coat. She put it over. She talked, she chatted, she prattled and she gossiped. She gave him the dope he wanted. She fed his old, dried-up, bachelor's heart with small talk. No sooner did a name fall than she invented the most intriguing stories on the spur of the moment. She chattered about people she had never seen, sealed engagements, broke them off, brought children into the world, killed off rich aunts, and as for Paradieser's cook. . . !

Heber's fishy old eyes grew really animated and down came his bony fist on the counter. "I've always had my ideas about that feller! Well, I never!" And ever so gradually she worked her way from love to money, from Spieckermann's expensive new curtains and how on earth they could afford them and we certainly could not, and the Leisegang's were a bit shaky too, so people said, but here, God be praised, everything looked a mar-

vel of prosperity, and no wonder with such a management!
"And we're counting on you, you know, to put in a good word
for us over the Christmas bonus. *You* can work the miracle,
Herr Heber!"

But Heber, the six feet of misery, was, of course, quite unmoved; he merely cleared his throat and with a side glance at
me loudly declared that he knew which way the wind blew,
that good bait caught fine fish but not him, and that anyone
anxious to burn his fingers was at perfect liberty to go to the
Chief himself!

It was defeat, complete and ignominious. We fled with feeble
stammerings from the News Room and I was terribly sorry for
Itzenplitz. For at least five minutes she said nothing, but merely
snuffled disconsolately to herself, she was so crushed.

But however depressing this may have been, and however
remote the prospect of a bonus, however gloomy our Christmas outlook, on the thirteenth of December it snowed for the
first time that year. It was real dry, powdery snow that fell on
frozen ground and stayed, and needless to say we could not
bear to stay indoors, but went out into the frost and swirling
flakes.

Oh, that dreary, miserable little one-horse town! The gas-
lamps burned in vain in the falling snow, and in our out-lying
street the people passed by like pale phantoms. When, however,
we reached Main street, everything lay bathed in a magic light
from the shop-windows, and the Christmas candles (electric
ones) were burning, and we leaned our foreheads on the plate-
glass and discussed this and pointed out that. "Look! That
would be just right for us!" (Ninety-seven per cent of the
articles exhibited were just right for us.)

And then we came to the worthy, old-established firm of
Harland's the grocer's, and a wave of recklessness lifted us and
carried us in, and we bought half a pound of hazel-nuts, half
a pound of walnuts and half a pound of Brazil nuts: "Just to
make it a bit Christmassy at home. No need for nut-crackers—
we'll crack them in the door." Then we passed Ranf's the book-
seller's, and there we saw a miracle: *Buddenbrooks* for two

marks eighty-five. "Why, Itzenplitz, it's bound to have cost twelve before. Two marks eighty-five—that's a net economy of nine marks fifteen—and we're *bound* to land some Christmas ads!" So we bought *Buddenbrooks;* and passing Hämel's, we went in just to get some ideas for mother-in-law, Tutti and Johnny. For mother we bought a pair of very warm black gloves (five marks fifty); for Tutti a ball of remarkable size at one mark, and for Johnny a scooter (one mark ninety-five). And still the wave lifted and swept us on. I still see Itzenplitz standing before the mirror in a swarm of shoppers, trying on the little lace collar over her coat, her face a picture of happy absorption. "And you'll be giving me something for Christmas in any case, won't you, Tim? And perhaps later on the collar'll be gone. Isn't it sweet?"

It was still snowing as we strolled home: we walked close together, arm-in-arm, her hand in mine in my coat-pocket, and we had an armful of parcels as behooved true Christmas shoppers. And we were incredibly happy, and the advertisements would come—that was certain!

Being a man of almost meticulous tidiness, I undid the parcels and stacked our purchases while Itzenplitz fried the potatoes for supper. I then stuffed all the wrappings into our little cooking-stove called Roaring Rupert, and he roared and crackled exceedingly. But while we were happily lost in our fried potatoes, Itzenplitz suddenly sprang to her feet and called, "Don't be cross, Tim, but I really must try on that sweet little collar!"

I gave my consent, but—where was the collar? We searched and searched in vain.

"Oh, Tim, you must have burnt it with the wrappings!"

"I'm not such an idiot as to burn collars. You simply didn't bring it, that's all!"

She jerked open the stove, and stared and stared into the blaze—("It was *so* sweet") but I dashed back to the store, forced my way in long after closing-time and worried tired shop-girls in their packing-up for a vanished parcel—and went slowly and sadly home. And until bedtime we crept about the garret subdued and wordless.

But the new day came, and the snow still lay glistening and sparkling under a bright winter sky, and anyway, what's a collar? "Just wait and see how many collars we shall be able to buy before we're through! We're the right sort of people, aren't we! So rich that we can feed the fire with three-mark collars!"

My account of our first Christmas would not be complete without children to figure in it. If ever Itzenplitz and I talked of former Christmasses, it was those of our childhood that came back most vividly. The later ones were blurred and confused; never again had the Christmas tree sparkled so brightly. But I could still tell Itzenplitz exactly how it was when I got the doll's theater, and, two years later, the lead figures for Robinson Crusoe.

"There must be children for a really proper Christmas. It'll be lonely here, you know."

However, just before Christmas we got our baby after all. It was the eighteenth of December. Snow had turned to slush, frost to unpleasant, penetrating dampness—dismal days of fog that would not lift. On one of these afternoons that were neither day nor night, there had come a wailing, almost like a baby's cry, outside our door, and when Itzenplitz opened it, something cowered there, half-dead with wet and cold—a dirty-white kitten.

I did not see our guest till some hours later, when I came home from my advertisement-hunting. He was already fairly dry and not so rumpled, but even then it was plain that this dirty-white little fellow with the black patch half across his face was nothing but a common alley-cat. "Rumpelstiltskin," said Itzenplitz. "Our Rumpelstiltskin."

Well, there it was and there it stayed, and as Itzenplitz said, we had at least one youngster to share our Christmas.

On the twenty-third I hung round Heber as a bridegroom

round his bride, but he was quite inscrutable and as bony and codlike as ever, and on the evening of the twenty-third Itzenplitz and I had our first real row; primarily because I had said nothing, secondly because Rumpelstiltskin had pulled out all the stalks of our one and only pot of heather, a present from Frau Pressbold—and thirdly because Jolly Roger, instead of delivering the Christmas-tree stand, had again put Itzenplitz off till the next day.

The new day dawned—December the twenty-fourth and Christmas Eve—an ordinary, gray, opaque winter day, neither warm nor cold. At ten o'clock Heber went to see the chief. As I sat there and waited for his return I wrote a stinking notice of the Christmas film running at the Cinema de Luxe and put my whole soul into it. Back came Heber, looking as bony and codlike as ever, sat down at his place and grumbled across at me: "Müller, you'll have to go at once to Ladewig's. He says he only took a quarter page and you wrote up half a page. Another of your muddles, I suppose!"

And as I trailed through the streets, my one thought was: "Poor Itzenplitz—poor Itzenplitz." All the life had gone out of me; but really, deep down, I had never believed in the Christmas bonus. When you really need something it never comes.

At Ladewig's I, of course, was right, and he remembered and was decent enough to admit it. I crept slowly back to the paper and told Heber, who said: "There you are! That's what I'm always saying. Those people call themselves business men! And by the way, just sign this receipt, will you? I've talked the Chief round again after all."

For one moment I felt giddy, and then everything grew bright, the sun shone, and I very nearly kissed the old shark on both cheeks. Then, with a shout of—"Just a second, Herr Heber," I signed for the fifty-mark note and raced, without hat or coat, the note in my hand, down Main Street into the Neuhäuserstrasse, over the Kirchplatz, through the Reepschläger-gangsse to the Stadtrat-Hempel-Strasse, charged up the staircase, burst like a hurricane into our room, banged the note on the table and cried: "Make a list of what we're buying, Itzenplitz! Call for me at two!" And I kissed her and twizzled her round and was downstairs and back in the office before you could say "Knife!" Heber, the old fishface, had not yet recovered from his stupefaction and kept on muttering plaintively to himself: "I wouldn't like to be as crazy as you are even for an hour on Sundays, Müller!"

But at two o'clock, when Heber had departed, she came. And this is the list, our final Christmas Purchases List, that she gave me to read:

FOOD

1 Duck	R. M. 5.–
Red Cabbage	–.50
Apples	–.60
Nuts	2.–
Figs, dates and raisins	3.–
Sundries	5.–
	16.10

FOR THE TREE

Our tree	R. M. 1.–
12 Candles	–.60
Candle-holders	–.75
Tinsel	–.50
Magic candles	–.25
	3.10

FOR RUMPELSTILTSKIN

1 Bucket fresh sand	R. M. –.25
1 Fish	–.15
	–.40

For Tim

Gloves	R. M.	4.–
Cigarettes		2.–
1 Shirt		4.–
1 Tie		2.–
Something else		2.–
		——
		14.–

For Itzenplitz

1 Lottery ticket	R. M.	1.–
1 Pair scissors		2.50
1 LACE COLLAR (!)		3.–
1 Shawl		6.–
1 Permanent		2.–
		——
		14.50
		——

OUR CHRISTMAS   48.10

"Listen!" began Itzenplitz at top speed (Heber's lunch hour was over at four and everything had to be done by then). "Listen, I know it's a terrible lot to spend on eating, but the duck'll last at least four days and there's only one Christmas a year. I *must* have some proper scissors for sewing now."

"What's 'something else'?" said I, interrupting her torrent of words.

"Oh, that means a little surprise for you."

"I want a couple of marks for 'something else' too!" I announced threateningly.

"Oh, Tim, we shall have only five marks left, and suppose the gas man comes? And I should be two marks fifty up on you then! Besides, it's not necessary, really it isn't—we're going to have *such* a merry Christmas!"

"I don't care, I'm having those two marks!" I persisted.

Then off went Itzenplitz to fetch old Lenzy, who had promised to deputize for me till four o'clock. For who was likely to come to the paper on the afternoon of the twenty-fourth? So off we dashed, and of course none of the prices were right.

Needless to say we were not finished by four; but we arranged that, having dashed back to the paper so that Heber might not notice my absence, I should ask leave to knock off at half-past. Meanwhile Itzenplitz would have her hair done, and afterward we would do the rest of the shopping together.

At five minutes to four I arrived at the office to find that old Lenzy had actually got an engagement announcement from a young couple for nine marks eighty; that woman could do anything! When Heber came I gave him no peace till he handed over 98 pfennigs commission. He was horrified at my needing money so soon after my bonus; but I must admit that in the end he showed the true Christmas spirit and gave me a whole mark.

Soon after half-past four I really did get away and dashed off to the Steinmetzstrasse; and the worthy Unger, who three weeks before had broken off his engagement and retrieved his presents, was actually at home. So we came to terms and I bought the fine gold chain with the aquamarine pendant—three marks down (two marks "something else" plus one mark engagement commission) and fifteen weekly instalments of one mark as from the first of January.

My fears that Itzenplitz would be standing waiting for me outside the barber's were not realized. On this day of all days every woman and girl appeared to be having her hair done. Yet in spite of my frozen feet I was not angry when she emerged with her waves and curls and ringlets, and we flung ourselves once more into the maelstrom of Christmas shoppers. And on my manly bosom reposed the aquamarine pendant.

It was long after nightfall when we arrived home. I seized the bucket and dashed off to the new building site for sand, and the caretaker growled mightly at me for turning up at a quarter to seven with such an order—sand for the cat, forsooth! But at home I found Itzenplitz in despair. Jolly Roger had still not reported with the Christmas-tree stand—and he was at home for we could hear noises. We crept out hand in hand to the dark landing and knocked at his door. We heard him tossing about in bed, heard sounds of snoring and opened softly. In an old bottle a cheap candle was burning, and over another half-empty one (the whole garret reeked of schnapps) Jolly Roger had dozed off. We were, of course, terribly afraid of him, but nevertheless we crept like Indians into his room to search for that stand. The search was soon over—it simply wasn't there. But just as Itzenplitz, with true feminine persistence, was engaged in opening a drawer which could never in this world secrete a Christmas-tree stand, there came a hoarse croak from the bed, "Well, yer young scallywags? Chrishmash-tree shtand? T'morrow fer certain!" He spoke—and slept again.

Five minutes to seven found me racing townward. At Günther's, the iron-monger's Christmas stands were sold out; at Mamlock's the iron shutters rattled down in front of my nose.

At ten minutes past seven I arrived home empty-handed, and there in Rumpelstiltskin's sand bucket, triumphantly draped with a white tablecloth, sparkling and radiant, stood our little Christmas-tree.

Wonderful Christmas, glorious Christmas . . . and Itzenplitz actually began to cry over the aquamarine pendant—"I haven't got anything nearly as nice for you, you know." But the lighter was a good one for all that. And then we stood and looked on while Rumpelstiltskin, with much cracking and tearing, worried his fish; and Itzenplitz said softly: "We shan't need him next year."

A Christmas Party

GERHART HAUPTMANN
(Translated by Eric Posselt)

AGAIN CHRISTMAS was approaching. Its arrival was announced by the decision of the National Ladies' Society to hold their Christmas party for the poor that year at the Casino. Since Mrs. Enke was president of the organization, my father conferred repeatedly with her and Deacon Spahner.

Two tremendous Christmas trees, the topmost candles of which blackened the ceiling, had been set up in the smaller ballroom. The presents were arranged in neat little piles on the white-covered horseshoe table. During the celebration each one of the poor, old men and careworn women stood before the proper pile. They stood and were ashamed, hardly daring to open their mouths for the songs, especially since the two shining trees displayed their physical misery in such a glaring light.

We—my father, my mother and I—watched this, for us, new spectacle with distaste. Old Mrs. Menzel, genteelly poor, had found refuge with us; the old lady couldn't stop shivering.

Deacon Spahner availed himself of the rare occasion to let his talent as a preacher shine, while the poor were still not permitted to touch their gifts but could only devour them with their eyes. The sermon lasted twice as long as was necessary. But at last they apparently were ready.

From *Das Abenteuer meiner Jugend* by Gerhart Hauptmann. Printed by permission of Margarete Hauptmann.

Madam Enke rose—every inch a Maria Theresa—the Order of Queen Louise on her pompous bosom. Her impressive head with the button nose and the two shining dark eyes belonged to the Slavic rather than the German race. In keeping with the festive spirit of the evening, she had bedecked herself with the most beautiful pieces from the family heirlooms of the Hindemiths—earrings, brooches, necklaces and, as stated before, the Order of Queen Louise, the decoration most cherished by herself and most envied by all.

But did the Child in the cradle, did Mary and Joseph, did ox and ass ever hear such words, in such tones, as issued from the mouth of the bearer of the Order of Queen Louise? Indeed, the very first utterances of that benevolent lady seemed to justify the little mustache sprouting on her upper lip.

"You know, of course, that you are receiving presents donated by charitable people," she said, "and I suppose you realize that and are properly grateful." It sounded resolute, and every one knew immediately that to reason with Mrs. Enke would require a great deal of courage.

Whereupon she poured out, occasionally reaching the heights of brusque command, a plethora of moral demands which had to be digested by the befuddled guests of the Christ Child before they were permitted to reach for their gifts.

Suddenly, to our surprise and consternation, we heard something like a heated exchange of words, but realized a moment later that it was quite one-sided, inasmuch as Madam Enke gave a hollow-cheeked miner's wife a terrible tongue lashing. They had, we learned, the previous year given her some children's clothes which she hadn't used. She had sold them. Actually, she was told, she didn't belong here at all, and wasn't really entitled to further presents. And mark Mrs. Enke's word for it, this was absolutely the last time, in case she again proved herself unworthy of charity!

This incident, so raw, so despicable and repulsive, has remained in my mind through all the years as a paradigm of Christmas parties as they certainly should not be. . . .

Twilight Hour

THEODOR STORM
(Translated by Eric Posselt)

IT WAS the study of an official. Its occupant—a man of about forty, with sharply cut features but mild, light blue eyes under the straight, light blond hair—sat at his desk which was covered with books and papers. He was signing the documents which the old office orderly put before him. The December afternoon sun was casting its last rays on the inkpot into which he occasionally dipped his pen. At last everything had been signed.

"Is there anything else, Judge?" the old man asked, folding the papers.

"No, thank you."

"Then I have the honor of wishing you a Merry Christmas."

"The same to you, my dear Erdmann."

The orderly spoke one of the southern German dialects; in the voice of the judge was something of the harshness of that more northerly German tribe which, only a few years before, had again bled in vain in one of its age-old battles with a hostile neighbor.

When his subordinate had left, the judge took from among his papers a letter he had started and slowly went on writing.

The shadows in the room grew darker. He didn't notice the slim figure of the woman who, behind him, had noiselessly entered the room; only when she put her arms around his shoulder did he know she was there. Her face was not young; but in her eyes was that expression of girlishness which is apparent in women who know themselves loved even when they have passed their first youth.

"Are you writing to my brother?" she asked, and her voice, though somewhat softer, had the same timbre as her husband's.

He nodded. "Go ahead, read it," he replied, putting aside his pen and looking up at her.

She bent over him in the twilight and read slowly.

"I am well again and able to work—fortunately, for this is the trouble with being away from home—one is forced to reconquer ever anew and from hour to hour the ground on which one stands. Bad as it may be at home, you're still better off in this respect. And who wouldn't have liked to stay behind if he could only have saved a piece of bread and that essential soft pillow which, according to the old proverb, a clean conscience always is."

Silently she placed her hand on his forehead while he, having followed her reading, turned the page. Then she read on:

"The good and clever woman whom you met last Christmas at our home I've been able to do a real service by arranging a compromise with her neighbor's estate. The beautiful forest which she wanted so badly finally became hers a short time ago. If we only had a hemlock from it for your friend Harro for tomorrow! Hereabouts, for miles around, no evergreens can be found. And what is Christmas without a tree and its scent whispering of secrets and miracles?"

"You, though," the judge remarked after his wife had finished reading, "you do bring with you in your clothes the scent of a true Christmas Eve."

With a smile she reached into her pocket and put a big piece of brown Christmas cake on the table.

"It just came from the baker," she said. "Go ahead, taste it— your mother never baked a better one for you."

He broke off a small piece and inspected it carefully; he found everything that had given him pleasure as a boy: it was hard as glass and the pieces of sugar in it were well melted and candied.

"What good spirits rise from such cakes," he mused, leaning back in his armchair. "Suddenly I see again how Christmas came in the old stone house at home. The brass door handles are perhaps gleaming still more than usual; the big lamp in the vestibule throws its light even more brightly on the plaster curlicues of the whitewashed wall: a group of children pushes through the door, singing and begging; from the large kitchen in the cellar the fragrance of the dainties being prepared in the huge copper kettles tickles their nostrils. . . . I *see* all that. I see my father and mother—thank God, they are both still alive! But the time into which I look rests deep in the twilight of the past. I am still a boy. The rooms on both sides of the vestibule are lighted. The one to the right is the Christmas room. While I stand before the door listening to the rustle in the gold leaf and the hemlock branches in the room beyond, the drayman comes up the stairs from the yard, a wax candle in his hand.

"He shakes his head with a grin and disappears into the Christmas room. But where is Uncle Erich? There he comes up the stairs from outside. The door is flung open. No, it's only an apprentice, carrying the long stemmed pipe of the *Herr Ratsverwandter*. Yet another horde of childen presses in behind him. The little throats recite: *Vom Himmel hoch da komm ich her!* And grandmother is already among them, the busy old lady, the pantry key hanging from her little finger, a plate full of dainties in her hand. How quickly they disappear! I, too, get my share, and just then my sister arrives with the nurse, all dressed up, her long hair freshly braided. But I refuse to stay: three steps at a time I run down into the yard."

It had gradually grown dark. Silently the wife of the judge had removed a bundle of documents from a chair and sat down beside her husband.

"In the side-wing is my father's study. Today no light comes from the writing room into the front vestibule; the old miracle-maker is being employed inside by my mother with the Christmas secrets. But I grope my way along the opposite wall into my father's room. I hear his footsteps: he is no longer working. Softly I open the door. How clearly I see him before me, and the smoke-stained big room in which the hard tick of the old clock can be heard. Festively restless, he paces to and fro among the tables covered with papers, in one hand the brass candle-stick with the lighted candle, the other hand stretched out as if he were trying to ward off every disturbing element. He opens the drawer of his old stand-up desk and takes from its fishskin cover the large gold snuff-box, once a gift of great grandmother to her intended, and later, after grandfather's death, a valued present to father. But he isn't through yet; from the money-basket he selects shining silver coins for the servants, a gold one for the secretary.

" 'Has Uncle Erich arrived?' he asks without turning toward me.

" 'Not yet, father. May I go and call for him?'

" 'Yes, you might do that.'

"And I run through the house to the street, around the corner and along the docks. From below in the dusk I hear the whistling of the wind in the tackle of the sailing ships as I arrive at the old gabled house with its porch. The door is flung open so violently that the doorbell re-echoes through vestibule and hall. In front of the counter stands the old clerk in charge of the retail business. He looks at me somewhat gloomily.

" 'The master is in his office,' he says dryly. He does not care much for the noisy wild brat. But that doesn't bother me.

"I fly on my way through the back door and across two dark yards, for it is in an age-old queer side wing that my uncle's sanctum is located. I negotiate the narrow hallway without mishap and knock on a door.

" 'Come in!'

"There he sits, the fine little man in his elegant brown coat, before his immense working table. The light of the office lamp falls on his friendly small eyes and on the huge family nose sticking out over the freshly laundered stand-up collar.

"Uncle, I—we wanted to know whether you were ready to come," I stammer after having caught my breath.

" 'Don't we want to sit down first for a moment?' he replies, letting his pen glide in summation over the open page of the ledger. I feel quite at ease and I am not getting a bit impatient; but I don't sit down. I remain standing and notice the picture of the merchantmen plying the routes to England and the West Indies that hangs on the wall. The ships are all owned by my uncle. And it isn't very long before the ledger is slammed shut and the key ring rattles.

" 'There we are,' my uncle says, 'now we are ready.'

"While he gets his bamboo cane from the corner, I am already at the door. But he holds me back.

" 'Just you wait a little. We must fetch several things along from here.' Saying which he produces from a dark corner of the room two mysterious, sealed packages. I know them well: such packages always contain a real piece of Christmas, for uncle has a brother in Hamburg and he never steps under the Christmas tree with empty hands. Such never-before-seen dainties as he often places, right in the middle of the celebration, on the Christmas plates of my sister and myself I will never again see anywhere the rest of my life.

"Soon, leading my uncle by the hand, I am climbing the wide stone steps to our house. For a few moments he disappears with his packages into the Christmas room; the tree isn't lit yet, but through the half-open and quickly closed door something glitters from the promising darkness inside. I close my eyes because I don't want to see anything yet, and enter the opposite, festively lighted room filled with the fragrance of the brown cake and today's specially mixed tea. His hands behind his back, father is walking up and down.

" 'Well, did you come?' he asks. And the next instant Uncle Erich, too, is with us, and it seems as if the room has become twice as bright after he enters. He greets my grandmother and father, he accepts the cup which my sister offers him on the yellow checkered tray.

" 'What do you think,' he says, trying to give his eyes a rather worried expression, 'probably there won't be much for us to-night.' But withal he laughs so comfortingly that his words ring like a golden promise.

"Then, while the brass teakettle hums and sings, he starts one of his little tales about the things that have happened since we saw him last. Perhaps it is the purchase of a new walking stick or the unfortunate breaking of a cup. It all flows along so gently that it soothes! And particularly if he pauses to re-enjoy the tale told with comfortable laughter, who then wouldn't join in? In vain my father takes his critical pinch of snuff—even he has to laugh. It is in this harmless chattering—something that I didn't realize until much later—that that ever-busy man finds relaxation after a day's toil. I still remember it fondly and it seems to me that today nobody understands this any more. But while my uncle thus unwinds his tales, mother, who has been invisible since noon, suddenly sticks her head through the door. Uncle bows and stops in the middle of a sentence. The door and its counterpart in the opposite room are opened wide. Hesitatingly we enter. And, facing us, reflected by the huge wall mirror, stands the lighted tree with its little banners of gold leaf, its white net bags and the golden eggs hanging like children's dreams in the branches . . .''

"Paul," the wife affirms, "no matter how far we have to go to get it, we simply must have a hemlock tree again. The poor boy has built himself a Christmas garden—he just went out again to fetch some more moss from the oak grove."

For a moment the judge is silent.

"It isn't a good thing to go abroad," he said then, "once you have sat at your own hearth at home. I still feel as if I were a mere guest here, and tomorrow or the day after the time will be up and we will all have to return home."

She took her husband's hand and held it firmly; but she didn't answer.

"Do you still remember this one Christmas?" he began once more. "I had finished school and, once again, for the last time, I was living for a while in my father's house. True, it wasn't any longer as gay there as it had been. Unforgettable things had occurred and the old family burial plot under the huge linden tree had been opened a few times. My mother, a restlessly active woman, frequently let her hands fall in the midst of her work and stood motionless as if she had forgotten herself. As our old Margret used to say: she carried a little room in her head in which a dead child was playing.

"Only Uncle Erich, a little grayer to be sure, still told his friendly little tales, and sister and grandmother, too, were still alive. That was the Christmas Eve I am speaking of, when a young, beautiful girl was visiting my sister. Do you remember her name?"

"Ellen," she said softly, leaning her head against his shoulder. The moon had risen and was highlighting a few silvery threads in the silky brown hair worn severely parted and wrapped around a tortoise-shell comb in a smooth braid.

His hand caressed her head.

"Ellen, too," he went on, "had received presents. They were lying on a small mahogany table, gifts from my mother and whatever her parents had sent from home. She stood with her back against the lighted tree, her hand resting on the table, and stayed there for a long while. I can still see her—" and he let his eyes rest silently for a moment on his wife's beautiful face— "when my mother came over to her, unnoticed. She took her hand and looked questioningly into her eyes. Ellen didn't turn, she merely bowed her head, only to straighten up suddenly and rush into the next room. Do you remember? While mother was shaking her head, I followed the girl because, after a little quarrel the night before, we had become fast friends. Ellen had seated herself in a chair in the corner near the oven; it was almost dark in there, and only a solitary candle with a neglected 'thief' was burning.

" 'Are you homesick, Ellen?' I asked.

" 'I don't know.'

"For a while I stood silent by her side.

" 'What have you got there?'

" 'Do you want it?'

"It was a purse of dark red silk.

" 'If you made it for me,' I replied. I had seen her working on it during the last few days and had noticed that she always hid it in her sewing basket whenever I came close. But Ellen refused to answer. She got up and cleaned the candle so that it suddenly grew quite light in the room.

" 'Come along,' she said, 'the candles are burning down and Uncle Erich still wants to distribute his dainties.' And so saying she brushed her eyes lightly with her handkerchief and returned to the Christmas room. Later, when we sat around the dice game, she was the gayest of them all. Nor was there another word about my Christmas present.

"Do you know, woman—" and he let go of her hand which he had held firmly all this time—"girls shouldn't be so stubborn. This interlude just wouldn't let me rest. I simply had to have that purse, and because. . . ."

"Because—what, Paul? Go ahead, speak up!"

"Well, didn't you hear about it? Because of that incident I suddenly got the girl in my head, too."

"I know," she said, and in the bright moonlight he saw something bright in her eyes that reminded him of the willful girl she had once been. "Of course I know the story, and could even tell it myself. But this was a year later, and not on Christmas but on New Year's Eve; nor was it here but across the border."

She shoved aside the inkstand and a few papers and sat down on the desk facing her husband. "This cousin was visiting with Ellen's father, the marvelous old churchwarden who, at that time, was still an enthusiastic nimrod. Ellen had never before had such a beautiful long letter as the one in which the cousin announced his arrival. But he wasn't so clever with the gun as with the pen. And yet—was it the country air or the beautiful gun chest in the churchwarden's room?—he had to go out hunting every day. And when he returned at night, soaked through and empty-handed, and placed the gun silently back on its rack—how sweetly taunting the speech of the old gentleman: 'This year the hares seem to be particularly shy.' Or: 'My boy, what will Diana think of you?' But, most of all—are you listening, Paul?"

"I am listening, woman."

"Most of all it was Ellen who tormented him. She put a straw wreath on his head, she tied a goose wing to his gun. And one day—do you remember? snow had fallen—she took a hare the handyman had shot from the larder, and a little while later he sat on his old feeding spot in the garden, just as if he were still alive, a cabbage leaf in his mouth. Then she called her cousin and pulled him to the open yard door.

" 'Do you see him, Paul? Back there among the cabbage heads! The ears are sticking out of the snow.'

"He saw him, too. His hands were trembling.

" 'Hush, Ellen. Don't talk so loud. I'll get the gun.' "

"But before the door to his room fell shut, Ellen had run out into the snow again and when he finally came sneaking up with the loaded gun, the hare was once again hanging on his safe hook in the larder. But the cousin patiently permitted her to keep on teasing him."

"Certainly," the judge said, resting his arms comfortably on the armrests of his chair. "He still didn't have the purse."

"Exactly. That was still lying untouched in the lowboy in Ellen's attic room. But, wherever Ellen was, the cousin was, too, that is, whenever he wasn't out hunting. When she sat at her sewing table, he surely had to fetch the book he was reading to her. If she was in the kitchen baking waffles, he stood beside her, watch in hand, to make sure the waffle iron was turned at the right time. And thus New Year's Eve arrived. During the afternoon the two of them had shot at golden eggs with her father's pistols in the yard, eggs she had cut off the Christmas tree. And applauded by the handclapping of the little ones, the cousin had actually hit two of the eggs. But was it because he had to leave the next day—or was it because Ellen ran away? —when he called for her in the little room he was no longer the patient cousin, he seemed grouchy and hardly looked at her. He stayed that way all afternoon, and even when they sat down at table. Ellen's mother looked at them questioningly once or twice, but didn't say anything. The churchwarden had other concerns, he poured the punch he had brewed himself. And when the clock down in the village struck twelve, he sang the old New Year's carol by Johann Heinrich Voss that was sung through all its stanzas. Then they cried, 'Prosit New Year!' and shook hands all around. And Ellen, too, held out her hand to the cousin; but he hardly touched it with his fingertips. And this was true also when, shortly thereafter, they said good night. But when the girl was alone upstairs in her attic room—and now, mark well how honestly I tell my story!—she was too restless to sleep. She sat quietly on the edge of her bed, not undressing and not paying any attention to the cold of the unheated room. She was hurt and after all she hadn't hurt him, really. To be sure, he had asked her only yesterday whether she had again put the hare in the cabbage field, and she had just shaken her head. Was it that, perhaps, and did he know that he had already helped eat up that hare three days ago? She decided to read once more that beautiful letter of the cousin's. But when she put her hand into the pocket, the key to her lowboy was not there. Taking the candle, she went down to the living room and from there, when she didn't find the key, to the kitchen where she had worked a little while ago. What with all the cooking and baking of the previous evening, it was still warm in the large dark room. And, right enough, there was the key on the window sill. But she remained standing there awhile, looking through the window into the night. Far and light the snow field stretched out before her eyes; down there, scattered, were the black straw roofs of the village. Near the house, among the bare branches of the silver poplar, she could clearly make out the big crow's nests. The stars gleamed. She remembered an old rhyme, a sorcerer's plea, which she had learned years and years ago from the daughter of the schoolmaster. Behind her the house was quiet and empty. She shuddered, and yet the temptation to have a try at eerie things grew within her. So she stepped back a little, quietly pulled one shoe off her foot, took a deep breath, turned her eyes to the stars and said: 'God greet thee, evening star!'

"But what was that? Wasn't that the yard door opening? She went to the window and listened. No, it was probably only the creaking of the old poplar at the gable side of the house. And again she said under her breath:

> " 'God greet thee, evening star!
>   You're shining so bright from afar
>   Over east and west
>   And over the crow's nest.
>   Is there one born for my love?
>   Is there one picked from above?
>   Let him come, as he stands,
>   Let him hold out his hands,
>   In his workaday dress . . .' "

"Then she twirled the shoe around her head and threw it over her shoulder. But she waited in vain—she didn't hear it fall. She began to feel queer: so this was what she got for her being so rash! What uncanny thing could have caught her shoe before it fell to the floor? For a minute she stood there and then, with the last ounce of her courage, she managed to slowly turn her head. There was a man standing in the dark doorway, and it was Paul. He actually had been out again after some hapless hare."

"No, Ellen," the judge said then, "you know well enough that wasn't really it. Just like her, he had merely not been able to sleep—and now he held the girl's small shoe in his hand. Ellen sat down on a chair near the hearth, sat there with closed eyes and her hands folded in her lap. There was no doubt about it, she was giving herself up for lost; for she knew well enough that her cousin had heard everything. Do you still remember what he said to her?"

"Yes, Paul, I remember. And it was very cruel and not at all noble of him. 'Ellen,' he said, 'isn't my purse ready yet?' But Ellen refused to be taken in. She got up and opened the window so that the night air and all that starry glitter came in to join them in the room."

"But," he interrupted, "Paul had come close, and so she

quietly put her head on his shoulder, and I still hear how sweetly her voice sounded when she said out into the night: 'God greet thee, evening star!' "

The door was thrown open; a healthy boy of about ten came into the room carrying a candle.

"Father! Mother!" he shouted, shading his eyes with his hand. "Here are moss and ivy and another juniper sprig!"

The judge had risen.

"So you finally got here, my boy?" he said, taking the collection box and the treasures the boy had brought home.

Ellen quietly slid off the table and shook herself a little as if awakening from a dream. She put her hands on her husband's shoulders and gazed into his eyes for a moment. Then she took the boy by his hand.

"Come, Harro," she said, "let's build Christmas gardens."

HOLLAND

Rejoice, O Rose of Jericho

TRADITIONAL

Toen aan de roos van Je-ri-cho, De
Zoon van God werd af-ge-staan, Ver-blijdde zich haar
har-te zeer, De hem-mel werd haar op-ge-daan.

Rejoice, O Rose of Jericho,
The Son of God will come to thee!
Thy heart will sing in jubilo
And heavenly felicity.

Thus spake the angel of Our Lord
To Mary once in Galilee
And brought the tidings, so adored,
Of how He would set mankind free.

The Godchild of the Highwayman

ANTOON COOLEN
(Translated by Alexander Gode)

MANY YEARS ago there lived a poor Dutch shoemaker with a wife and eleven children. All day long the good man worked in his shop till his hands were full of blisters. He cut and shaped sturdy, handsome clogs of willow wood. The shavings and cuttings positively flew about, but even so he just couldn't make ends meet. The shoes he turned out and the money he earned simply were not enough to keep all their mouths fed and their bodies clothed. So they were always hard up, and when winter came and times were bad and the number of customers dwindled, they lived through troubled days and had to be content with bread and water or a thin broth, and in their threadbare clothes they huddled together about their wood fire lest they freeze.

One winter, on Christmas Eve, the wife went to bed early. Well now, that is the way it is, she had told her husband, using the identical expression he had known her to use all through the years. The children, all eleven of them, were hurriedly placed with some neighbors. And when, late that night, they were called back and came in, their father told them that Kriss Kringle had been there. Of course, they couldn't believe that and came to see for themselves. And then they did see it and

From *Kerstvertellingen* by Antoon Coolen. Printed by permission of the author.

crowded around the wooden crib which their father had fixed and in which the child lay all bundled up. The boys stood open-mouthed in the light of the lamp like singing angels, and the father behind the children nervously knitted his brow and wheezed through his nose, looking worried and greatly troubled.

The next day the neighbors came to admire the child. They were all enraptured because it was such an uncommonly beautiful child. The mother had little attention to spare for her other boys, she was so very happy and absorbed with her baby, and lay there in quiet bliss giving it her breast. When the people asked what the newborn's name was to be, the parents couldn't answer. The father just said: "We have no godparents yet."

Thereupon the neighbors became less talkative, looking at each other for, indeed, they all were godfathers or godmothers of one or another of the children. They pondered at length whether there wasn't someone about the place who hadn't yet served as godparent for one of the cobbler's children. And lo, there stepped forth from among their ranks an unmarried old woman who had never been asked. To be sure, she was very poor, but if need be, she said, she was willing to be the god-mother.

Fine, so they had a godmother. But a godfather! That was a much weightier and more significant problem. For the god-father had to go along to the baptism and answer the prayers so that the child would grow up in the faith and forsake the devil and his vanities. But where was there a godfather to be found? All the men turned away and left.

"We are already godfathers of your children!" they said.

And sure enough, they were indeed. For if you are a god-father, no matter how little you have, in good old custom you are expected to give your godchild some present, small if need be; at first on the day of the Christening and later on anniver-saries. And that, of course, was an added difficulty, although they all knew the father would not be too particular about that part of it. Indeed not, for all his eleven children, quite against good usage, were generally forgotten on their anniversaries by their poor godfathers.

Yet, as long as there was no godfather, the child could not be baptized and made into a Christian. There he lay, guarded by his mother but forsaken by God and screaming heathenish complaints about being hungry or about being surfeited when his belly was swollen and could not get rid of the tension. But that wasn't the worst of it. Just think, if the little fellow were to die in his state of wickedness and damnation in consequence of the original sin! Then his little soul would be cast out from heaven and barred irrevocably and for all time from eternal bliss. Of course, if the worst came to the worst, the father himself could christen the child; he could take water and pour it over his head and say: "I christen thee in the name of the Father, the Son and the Holy Ghost," provided he could keep his hands steady enough during the excitement. But what if the sad event were to happen quite suddenly or at night when everybody was asleep? It really was very risky for the child's salvation and not at all advisable to let him be long without the holy sacrament of baptism; and for this reason the neighbors advised the father to go and see the baron about it in his castle. Of course, he wasn't exactly the best Christian you could think of, but for a real and life-sized godfather he would do, after all, and if he didn't forget the anniversaries, the presents he gave would at any rate not be the smallest.

Now the baron! He sat there behind his walls and ditches outside the village. It was all very forbidding and out of this world. And how could you go there and keep breathing and not sink into the ground? But in the father's mind the child's salvation outweighed the world and the grandeur of all its barons taken together. And so he put on his faded Sunday suit and started on the long way out.

But as he approached the castle and reached the awe-inspiring height of the wind-swept beech copse, his heart grew heavy with fear. He had to collect all his courage, and actually there wasn't a shred of it left to help him cross the old weather-beaten, ivy-covered stone bridge. He hardly knew how he had got there when he found himself standing between the wrought-iron lanterns in front of the heavy door. His heart was thumping in his throat when he pulled the iron chain of the bell. Good God, his pauper's hand had sufficed to start a tocsin of alarm in there! A little later, a butler in blinding splendor arrived wearing a blue and silver livery. You just could not imagine how he managed to get into it and out again.

Later on the shoemaker did not even know whether or not he had asked his question and explained the difficult situation. All he could remember was the giant figure in blue and silver, with white stockings, gray hair, a tight mouth and raised eyebrows. And the head of this figure shook slowly and silently from side to side.

Then the shoemaker left. His nose was running and he sniffled with worry, and there were deep wrinkles in his forehead. But as he took the way back and passed through a wood, his heart full of sadness, he suddenly noticed a mighty horseman sitting in the saddle slightly bent over and making straight for him. The cobbler stopped and so did the rider. He raised his head and looked into a friendly though old and wrinkled face. The horseman asked him:

"My good man, why do you look so sad?"

The cobbler felt immediately at his ease when he heard the friendly voice. Sniffling he replied:

"I cannot find a godfather for my twelfth child."

"How about a godmother?"

"Oh, a godmother I have But how can the boy be christened as long as there is no godfather?"

"It's a boy, you say?"

"Yes."

"What if I became his godfather?"

The shoemaker could hardly trust his ears. Completely bewildered, he looked up at the stranger and found no reply. The horseman noticed the good fellow's embarrassment and said:

"You need but say 'yes' or 'no.' "

"Yes," said the father as quickly as if he were afraid that the next moment he might not be able to utter any word at all.

"Fine," said the horseman. "That's settled. You get the ceremony arranged and be sure to be at the church tomorrow at twelve o'clock. I'll be there."

Without more ado he wheeled around his horse, gave it the spurs, and though he obviously was an old man he rode off like a bold and spirited youth. His bent back was no longer noticeable, for as he galloped along he leaned forward over the neck of his steed.

When the father reached home he was overjoyed, and when his wife saw him she thought that the thing they had anxiously hoped for, yet didn't dare expect, had actually come to pass. So she asked quickly:

"The baron, is he going to be godfather?"

"No," replied her husband; "but I am happy just the same because I've found another godfather who is better than all barons."

The woman was very much amazed and asked:

"Who is the godfather?"

That was surely the simplest and most natural question to ask, but it nevertheless made her husband speechless for a few seconds. For now it suddenly occurred to him that he had actually forgotten to ask the horseman's name. The shock kept him silent for a while, but then he admitted:

"I don't know who he is."

Now this matter was not one to laugh at and so the woman didn't laugh, but took quite an effort to restrain herself. She asked:

"What am I supposed to believe now? How can you have found a godfather without knowing who he is?"

"Well," said the man, "you see, there was a man on horseback, a real gentleman. He came riding through the wood and asked why I looked so downcast. I told him we had no godfather for our twelfth child. He wanted to know whether or not it was a boy, and then he said that he was willing to be the godfather and that he would be at church tomorrow at twelve o'clock. Now I must go and tell the pastor about it."

"Don't do it," said the wife.

"Well now," he replied, "how is this? Why shouldn't I do it? I promised I would."

"Don't do it," repeated the woman. "For who can tell that he isn't just trying to make fun of you in your misery, you simple soul, you! And if he isn't trying to make a fool of you, how can you be sure what sort of a man he is? What if he isn't even a Christian? What if he is a wicked man or a murderer or a highwayman? Perhaps he has sold his soul to the devil and wants to be the godfather of your child in order to do the devil a good turn. He was on horseback, you say? What if the horse was stolen?"

"Good Lord," thought the shoemaker, "when I was talking to the man, my heart was thumping with joy and delight that everything was so smooth and simple. And now that I am talking to my wife, everything gets so involved and troublesome." But he refused to give up his happiness and so he decided to give his wife an answer. He thought the matter over for a while and said:

"Wife," he said, "God forgive me that I must say this so shortly after the birth of our child; but you are just talking according to your lights and your little courage. That he should not be a good Christian is quite impossible. He was much too kind and acted in a spirit of brotherly love in dealing with poor me. Wicked he cannot be, for it was of his own free will that he was trying to do good. He cannot be a robber because he looks like a gentleman and has gray hair. That he should be a murderer is still more impossible, for he was extremely delicate and full of compassion for a totally unknown poor devil such as I undoubtedly am for him."

Now this was surely a very fine answer, and his wife thought about it for a while in silence. But she was not entirely satisfied yet, and finally said:

"That is all well and good, but why don't you say anything about the horse?"

"The horse?"

"Yes, the horse! If he stole it, nothing but trouble and shame will come to our boy."

"No," answered the shoemaker. "His horse was surely not stolen. For it was so quiet and obeyed him so readily that you could see how it trusted its master and how accustomed it was to him."

Again the woman kept silent for a while before she said:

"But what if you are wrong in any of these things?"

Then the man's patience gave out.

"Now listen," he said. "Then we'll still have found a god-father who offered himself of his own free will and kindness and therefore shouldn't first be looked at from all sides. Our child is to be christened, and that is the most important thing."

With that the conversation came to an end. That was good, for now the children came in and there was a great deal of noise. The father told them what had happened. He spoke about the fine and wealthy gentleman he had met and said:

"Now your little brother will be christened tomorrow."

"And what is he going to be called?" they asked.

"Now, you must not worry about that. Wait till tomorrow," said the father. And that settled that.

The following day, just before twelve o'clock, the shoemaker and a woman, carrying the child in his baptismal dress under a veil of fine muslin, went to church and the horseman from the wood arrived, too. He dismounted, tied his horse to a linden tree in front of the inn called At the Sign of the Golden Pitcher located opposite the church, and came over to join them. He greeted them most civilly, bowing and touching his horseman's cap in a very dignified and well-bred manner. Then he looked at the child. The woman lifted the muslin for him and he looked underneath it for half a second. At the same time he put his finger where the child's neck must have been and made a little clicking noise with his tongue. Then he stared dreamily across the square in front of the church, beat his switch against his leggings and said:

"Well, what are we waiting for?"

The father thought, "Now I must ask his name!" and said: "Look here, you are so very kind and have offered to be the child's godfather. I am very grateful and much obliged to you, and have no right to ask you who you are. But, on account of the child, I've got to know. What name are you going to give him?"

"Francis," replied the stranger.

Thereupon they entered the church, and when they came to the rear the little boy began to cry. It sounded very strange in the church, like the bleating of a lamb when it reaches its pen. Then the old pastor and the sexton came along and everything went off smoothly according to the established custom. The stranger looked on as the pastor touched the child's ears with spittle, as he used his neatly washed finger-tips to dub its quavering tongue with salt, as he anointed his breast and poured cold water over his little red head. The sexton had a towel ready, and the woman rubbed the child dry so that it wouldn't catch cold. When everything was finished, they all left the church and the stranger turned immediately towards his horse. But before walking away he took a purse out of his pocket and put it into the father's hand. The poor shoemaker had indeed been hoping that it would be to his good luck and advantage that this unknown gentleman was to be his child's godfather; but such a big and heavy purse full of money as he now held in his hand, that was more than he had expected, and it took him unawares. In his confusion he could not think what to do first: look into the purse or thank the stranger. He felt a shiver go through him from the great and wonderful surprise, and in his heart it grew into a great joy. He turned pale and then red and did not know what to stammer. Then the horseman said:

"This money is for a christening party. Have a good time!"

And then it was too late to say "Thank you," for the horseman had already gone back to his horse. He put his foot into the stirrup, jumped into his saddle and rode off.

The woman who carried the child had seen that the shoemaker had been given a purse. Now she was in a hurry to get back home, for in the neighborhood of the church were a few inns. Now, this does not mean that the woman would have been averse to drinking the infant's health in a little brandy and sugar, but she was afraid that the shoemaker, drunk with

joy at suddenly owning so much money, might not know when
to stop and might get out of control; and when and how would
they ever manage under such conditions to get home with the
baptized child?

They set out immediately. But even before they had left the
square, an old woman with a black bonnet on her head came
rushing toward them. She motioned to the shoemaker and took
him a few steps aside. Then she whispered:

"I was in the church when your child was christened. Do you
know that your child's godfather is a highwayman who lives in
the woods with his gang and waits for travellers to pass in order
to rob and murder them?"

The old woman didn't wait for an answer but disappeared
like a black spook. The shoemaker was frightened and dismayed
by what she had whispered in his ear. He didn't want to believe
it and told himself that it couldn't be true. But he could not
help being scared by his own doubts. Yet he had come to like
the godfather very much and so he told himself:

"Now, that is the way women are. The one troubles you with
her questions; the other comes along with her silly talk and kills
your fun. And both put you in doubt and uncertainty."

But what if what she had said was true and this money in his
hand had been acquired by theft? Well, he thought, even then
he wouldn't have to bother about it too much for, as to the
old woman's tale, he had no certainty whatever. In any case,
the horseman, even if he were actually a highwayman, could
very well have given him a purse that was *not* acquired by theft
or some other dishonest means. Yes, that must be the way it was,
for you could see by just looking at him how sensitive and
righteous this stranger was. But the very fact that he had to
reason with himself in this manner made it plain that the great
joy which one person had given him through a purse filled
with money was badly disturbed and marred by another who
could not repress the pleasure of giving him so terrible a disappointment.

The shoemaker and the woman with his child arrived finally
at his house. The christened boy was handed over to his mother.

Her childbed days were over, but not her forty days; and she had not yet been to church to make the offering which had to precede her cleansing. Yes, and she also had to wait for the christening to thank God that her child had been saved, for it was now accepted into the faith. But now she had her child back, and the shoemaker showed her the purse.

"Look," he said, "this is what his godfather gave us as a present so that we can celebrate."

The mother was very frightened when she saw the purse.

"God help us," she said. "We should keep this money for our child, but I am afraid it won't prove a blessing."

"Why not?" asked the father.

"Well," answered the mother, "I have been told that the godfather of our child is a highwayman."

Thus the shoemaker learned that evil talk is faster than a happy father who carries his child home from church.

"How do you know?" he asked.

"A little old woman I don't know came here and told me."

"So," said the father, "you trust a little old woman you don't know more readily than your own husband? And if this money, as you say, will not prove a blessing, why then should we keep it to bring bad luck to our child? It is much better to use it up for a party. That, after all, is what it was given for."

"Oh my," replied the wife, "now you are getting to be a spendthrift, too!"

The shoemaker concluded that there is just no getting along with women, no matter what you say or do. But he preferred the certain to the uncertain. He was going to use this money. Then nobody could claim it back from him because it had been stolen. It had been meant and was given for a party. If the godfather had thought of the possibility that it would not be used for a celebration, he obviously would not have given so much. Of course, it need not all be used. If they wished they could put aside enough to keep for days when great need or other adversities might overcome them.

Thereupon the father called his boys together and distributed money among them to go to the butcher's and baker's and get good tender meat and fine white bread, and one of his boys he sent to the Golden Pitcher to get a jug of good wine. This boy came right back with a message from the innkeeper who wanted to know whether there wasn't some mistake and whether it wasn't a jug of barley beer that was wanted. This made the father doubtful in spite of himself. Perhaps it was better to get barley beer for reasons of economy. After all, barley beer was a delicious and wonderful drink, too. But then, suddenly, the shoemaker took offense to the nettling lesson which the innkeeper apparently meant to read to him in so hateful and venomous a way.

"You run back to the innkeeper," he said to his boy, "and tell him that there was no mistake. What we want are two jugs of wine, and of the best. And tell the innkeeper to treat himself at my expense to a tankard of barley beer to drink to the health of our newly christened child."

With this message the boy went back and returned home with two jugs of wine. Of course it wasn't the best. The innkeeper had given him an inferior vintage—for the price he got for his best. Why, actually, it was a very common kind of wine he had sent along; but that sort of people just wouldn't know the difference. When everything was in the house, when the cooking and frying was done and finished, the feast got into full swing. Never before had there been such a wonderful smell in this house, of meat and wine and other good things. They all ate and drank. Neighbors came in to join them and make merry. Only the mother, busy at her stove, kept a little aside, and she it was who overheard how the neighbors talked about her and her husband.

"Now you see," she heard them say under their breath when they had to pause in their feasting and go outside for a moment, "now you see how they spread themselves on the highwayman's money!"

This was a great and heavy burden weighing upon the mother's heart. She did not take part in the merriment of her spouse. On the contrary, when she saw and heard him in such a state of elation, his head drunk, and red with wine, assuring every comer that all his neighbors were his beloved friends, she grew very sad. She blamed him for his extravagances, and the wasting of the ill-gotten money which thus had to be ill-spent as well.

"For once I am enjoying myself," her husband cried. "The food and the wine are wonderful! The horseman must have been a nobleman, indeed, to let us have this celebration."

When the feast was over, a little money was left and that was kept against bad times. The shoemaker stood again in his shop with his willow and poplar wood, his crotchets and chisels.

The little boy, after his christening, remained a puny and pitiful child. True, he grew a little bigger, but he did not really thrive and prosper. Even when he could sit up, he remained pale and sickly. And the mother, with fear in her heart, would often think that her child was so weak because of his un-Christian godfather whom they had accepted in thoughtless haste, blinded by the temptation of money. With bitterness she remembered the celebration they had had in their house, for it was something that people of their kind, poor and frugal as their lives were, were not meant to enjoy.

"We shouldn't have done it," she said plaintively to her husband as she sat there with her pale little boy whose eyes looked so cheerless and tired.

"Oh," said the man, "you keep imagining things." But as he looked into the boy's face, he couldn't help but sniffle with nervousness and worry.

The women from the neighborhood came around suggesting what could be done for the child. They knew a great many remedies, but none did any good. Soon all of the people were convinced that the woman would not keep her child for long.

No, she didn't keep it. It was Christmas Eve again, and the countryside was cold and covered with snow. A biting north wind blew out the quavering lamp of life. And the little boy died in his mother's arms. The poor woman was inconsolable.

"But you have eleven more," said the people.

"Yes, but none is so weak and dear as this little one was," the mother replied. "And he was the most beautiful of them all."

"And now he is one of Christ's children in heaven," a woman from the neighborhood consoled her.

"Yes, yes. But it was so wonderful when he arrived here as our own Kriss Kringle," said the mother. "And it was so happy a birthday on Christmas Eve."

"You have such a large family. Haven't you worries enough as it is, and isn't it a God-send that there is at least one mouth less to feed?" said the people.

But she always had the last word and found a reply to every-thing that was said to console her. The people seemed to respect that, and pitied her. But when they left the house they remem-bered, whispering ominously as though they were called upon to judge, that the godfather had not been a good Christian and that this was the reason, no doubt, that the innocent little child had to suffer such punishment.

But by then the pure and blameless little soul had been carried by his guardian angel up the golden ladder to heaven high above the clouds. It passed hosts and hosts of heavenly angels, splendid and white as snow, proclaiming peace on earth in this bright night. The guardian angel carried it farther along to the golden portal of eternal bliss. When a child arrives there, the portal opens by itself. St. Peter came to welcome the young-ster.

"Dear little angel," he said, "come inside; the gates of heaven are open before you."

"Indeed," said the little boy boldly, "I am most eager to enter, if only my good godfather can come in too."

"Your godfather?" asked Peter, knitting his brow. "That I must first look up in the book of life. We shall see how he stands."

St. Peter went over to the heavenly archives and looked up the life of the child's godfather in the big book. And when he came back after a while, he looked very worried and sad and said:

"My dear little boy, your godfather is unfortunately a very great sinner, a highwayman and a murderer who persists in the way of wickedness. That's why his name is down in the book as one who must be turned away from heaven and transferred to the eternal fire. But for you, dear boy, the bliss of paradise is waiting. Now come in quickly."

"No, thank you," said the child. "If my godfather can't come to heaven, I won't come in either." And saying so, he slipped away from the hand of his guardian angel who was about to lead him in.

St. Peter was greatly disturbed by what the boy had said. For if a child destined to be received into the Kingdom of Heaven spurns it because his innocent soul rebels against God's unfathomable justice and attempts to force Him to greater leniency with such impudent insistence, how can heaven endure such violence? St. Peter tried to convince the boy that, really, he should come in and assured him that it was in the nature of heavenly bliss that there would be no unpleasantness for him even if his godfather were not there, nor even if his own father and mother were condemned to suffer the most horrible pains of hell's eternal and unquenchable fire. But the boy refused to be persuaded. He would not yield or change his mind and kept on repeating:

"I won't go to heaven if my godfather doesn't come too."

Now Jesus happened to come walking along, and He was walking in a circle of light from a thousand stars, each one of which was a thousand times brighter than the sun. Everything was so permeated with the brilliance of this strong white glow that St. Peter, the guardian angel, and even the boy himself began to radiate great beauty from its reflection. Jesus came forward to the portal and inquired what was happening, and for what reason St. Peter looked so perturbed.

"Lord Jesus," said St. Peter, "this child refuses to enter heaven unless his godfather can come in, too. But his godfather is a hardened and obdurate sinner who doesn't want to reform and belongs among those for whom you decree the punishment of hell."

"But my dear little boy, my innocent little angel," said Jesus, "you must come in quickly. Those who have attained the bliss of heaven mustn't worry about the others whose faults con-

demn them to suffer the punishment of hell. That must not and
does not interfere with the eternal joy which I have prepared
for those who follow me."

"No, thank you, dear Jesus," said the child, unmoved even
by Him. "I won't go to heaven without my godfather." And he
stood there so frank and free and determined in the presence of
Jesus, St. Peter and the guardian angel, that none of them could
convince him to walk inside.

"Alas," said Jesus, "your godfather is a very wicked man who
has many sins on his conscience. My paradise of righteous and
holy people and children is not for him and his like."

"My godfather," said the boy, "may be all you say he is, but
when I could not find a godfather, it was he whose pity and
love moved him to show us a way out of our trouble. He gave
me a name and helped to give me a Christian soul so that I
might win the rewards of heaven. And that is why I won't go
inside if he isn't allowed."

Jesus thought for a spell and said:

"My dear child, today earth and heaven are celebrating my
birthday as a son of man. So I shall do something, something
for your sake alone, and something that I can do only for a
child. I shall make an exception to the eternal rules and laws
which are valid for good and evil and which decide about
heaven and hell."

Then he motioned to a tiny angel who came flying by in high
spirits, singing softly of the glory of heaven.

"Bring me an earthen jar," said Jesus. And He had hardly
spoken before the little angel, fast as light, was back with an
earthen jar. Jesus took it and handed it to the boy. It was
bigger than he and he had to spread his arms wide to carry it.

"Here," said Jesus, "take this jar and go back to earth. Your
guardian angel will go with you. Look up your godfather and
tell him that I am sending him this jar and that I shall take
him to paradise together with you when he has filled it with
the tears of his penitence."

The child took the earthen jar and, carried and guarded by
the wings of his angel, he descended along the golden ladder of

heaven through stars and clouds down to earth. He was very
happy. Thought he, if I moved Jesus to do this, how then can
I fail to get the tears of my godfather?

On earth, in night-covered towns and villages and all through
the countryside, rang the bells of God's human birth, and men
came to kneel by the side of the Christ-child who had come to
save the earth from its wickedness. In his hideout in the woods
the child's godfather heard the soughing of the wind and the
rustling of the snow against the darkened window in back of
him. He sat there staring into the wavering glow and the dancing flames of the beechwood fire in the fireplace. He, too, heard
the Christmas bells echoing through the tree tops, but his soul
was touched by nothing beyond a pleasant nostalgia that awoke
in him as he remembered his distant childhood and how, as a
child, he had celebrated Christmas. He got up to pour himself
a goblet of wine. Then he sat down again by the fire and
dreamily took a deep draft. And while the bells were softly
tolling through the night, he thought back over his life. He still
managed to feel courageously that he had achieved a great deal
through his intrepidity and that he had a perfect right to rest
content and calm. But then his entire life, his wickedness and
mischief, swept past his vision in a hasty mist as though it were
far away and quite unimportant and as though now, toward
the close of his life, it were obliterated by the long intervening
span of time. And then of a sudden this and that particular
detail of his life of sin stood out boldly in his memory and he
was startled by the oppressive distinctness with which one followed the other. He could neither deny nor reject them nor
ease his mind of the weight they suddenly assumed. So he drank
greedily, for he longed for that slight state of intoxication
which, together with the pleasant sound of the nocturnal bells,
would lull him into his former state of pleasant indifference.

But outside the dark blue window pane in back of him a
strange thing happened. Out of the night and through the
falling snow a small child's hand reached out and knocked on
the glass, nay, it knocked on the door of his heart. The window
opened under this pressing urge and, together with a gust of

snow, admitted a tiny angel carrying a jar in his arms. The highwayman felt as though he were listening to a beautiful song, and as though a soothing light were passing over him. The window closed again, all by itself and without a sound. Down near the feet of the highwayman a small voice said:

"Oh, how glad I am to be with you, my dear godfather."

It took the highwayman a few moments before he discovered where the small voice came from. Then he saw a child sitting by the fire at his feet, so very lovely that the sight moved him deeply. Had this little creature called him godfather? Then he remembered that he had, indeed, been the godfather to a poor shoemaker's child. And now he was very much upset; but when he saw the smile on the child's face, a soothing quietude came over him. Then the child said:

"You see, I died."

With this the highwayman's heart was filled with a strong feeling of foreboding.

"Yes," said the child, "I died, and when I got to heaven I heard that you wouldn't go there because you are a sinner. But I said that I was your godchild and didn't want to go to heaven if you weren't allowed to go there, too."

These words found an echo in the highwayman's heart, an echo that said: how strong is a child!

"Then," said the boy, "I induced Jesus to send me here with this message: if you fill this jar with the tears of your penitence, you will be permitted to enter heaven together with me."

And a lofty phrase rang in the highwayman's heart, a phrase that said: how strong is a child!

The highwayman felt that his heart would break, and in mortification he wept before the child over his own wickedness, and wept burning tears of penitence. The child caught them carefully in the jar. When the jar was filled to the brim, the child carried them above the clouds and the stars to the feet of Lord Jesus.

At that moment the heart of the highwayman ceased beating.

And there was greater rejoicing over his repentance than over ninety-nine of the righteous. For they are not in need of mercy.

HUNGARY

Blessed Be the Birth

TRADITIONAL

mf Krisz-tus U - runk - nak ál - dott szü - le - té - sén,

an - gya - li ver - set mond-junk szent ün - ne - pén, mely Beth-le-

hem - nek me - ze - jé - ben ré - gen zen-gett e - ké - pen.

Bless'd be the birth of God, our Lord and Master!
Let us intone the greeting of the angels
Which, long ago, at Bethlehem was spoken,
There in the pasture.

Praise be unto Lord God in the highest,
And here below be peace unto all mankind,
Good will to all and sundry tribes and peoples,
Races and nations.

Which of the Nine?

MAURUS JÓKAI
(Translated by Monique Jean)

ONCE UPON a time in the city of Budapest there lived a poor shoemaker who simply couldn't make ends meet. Not because people had suddenly decided to give up wearing boots, nor because the city council had passed an ordinance directing that shoes be sold at half price, nor even because his work was not satisfactory. Indeed, the good man did such excellent work that his customers actually complained that they couldn't wear out anything he had once sewed together. He had plenty of customers who paid him promptly and well enough; not one of them had run away without settling his bill. And yet Cobbler John couldn't make both ends meet.

The reason was that the good Lord had blessed him all too plentifully with nine children, all of them as healthy as acorns.

Then, one day, as if Cobbler John hadn't already had trouble enough, his wife died. Cobbler John was left alone in this world with nine children. Two or three of them were going to school; one or two were being tutored; one had to be carried around; gruel had to be cooked for the next; another had to be fed, the next one dressed, yet another washed. And on top of all this he had to earn a living for all of them. Verily, brethren, this was a big job—just try it in case you doubt it!

When shoes were made for them, nine had to be made all at once; when bread was sliced, nine slices had to be cut all at one time. When beds were made ready, the entire room between window and door became one single bed, full of little and big blond and brunette heads.

"Oh my dear Lord God, how Thou hast blessed me," the good artisan often sighed while even after midnight he still worked and hammered away at his lasts in order to feed the bodies of so many souls, stopping occasionally to chide now one, now another tossing restlessly in a dream. Nine they were —a round number nine. But thanks be to the Lord, there was still no cause for complaint, because all nine were healthy, obedient, beautiful and well-behaved, blessed with sound bodies and stomachs. And rather should there be nine pieces of bread than one bottle of medicine; rather nine side by side than coffins between them. But none of Cobbler John's children had the slightest intention of dying. It was already fated that all nine of them should fight their way through life and not yield their places to anybody. Neither rain nor snow nor dry bread would ever hurt them.

On Christmas Eve, Cobbler John returned late from his many errands. He had delivered all sorts of finished work and had collected a little money which he had to use to buy supplies and to pay for their daily needs. Hurrying homeward, he saw stands on every street corner, loaded with golden and silver lambs and candy dolls which pushcart women were selling as gifts for well behaved children. Cobbler John stopped before one or two of the carts. . . . Maybe he ought to buy something. . . . What? For all nine? That would cost too much. Then for just one? And make the others envious? No, he'd give them another kind of Christmas present: a beautiful and good one, one that would neither break nor wear out, and which all could enjoy together and not take away from each other.

"Well, children! One, two, three, four . . . are you all here? he said when he arrived home within the circle of his family of nine. "Do you know that this is Christmas Eve? A holiday, a very gay holiday. Tonight we do not work, we just rejoice!"

The children were so happy to hear that they were supposed to rejoice that they almost tore down the house.

"Wait now! Let's see if I can't teach you that beautiful song I know. It's a very beautiful song. I have saved it to give it to you all as a Christmas present."

The little ones crawled noisily into their father's lap and up on his shoulders, and waited eagerly to hear the lovely song.

"Now what did I tell you? If you are good children . . . just stand nicely in line! . . . there . . . the bigger ones over here and the smaller ones next to them." He stood them in a row like organ pipes, letting the two smallest ones stay on his lap.

"And now—silence! First I'll sing it through, then you join in." Taking off his green cap and assuming a serious, pious expression, Cobbler John began to sing the beautiful melody: "On the blessed birth of Our Lord Jesus Christ. . . ."

The bigger boys and girls learned it after one rendition, though the smaller ones found it a bit more difficult. They were always off key and out of rhythm. But after a while they all knew it. And there could be no more joyous sound than when all the nine thin little voices sang together that glorious song of the angels on that memorable night. Perhaps the angels were still singing it when the melodious voices of nine innocent souls prayed for an echo from above. For surely there is gladness in heaven over the song of children.

But there was less gladness immediately above them. There, a bachelor was living all by himself in nine rooms. In one he sat, in the other one he slept, in the third one he smoked his pipe, in the fourth he dined, and who knows what he did in all the others? This man had neither wife nor children but more money than he could count. Sitting in room number eight that night, this rich man was wondering why life had lost its taste. Why did his soft spring bed give him no peaceful dreams? Then, from Cobbler John's room below, at first faintly but with ever increasing strength, came the strains of a certain joy-inspiring song. At first he tried not to listen, thinking they would soon stop. But when they started all over for the tenth time, he could stand it no longer. Crushing out his expensive cigar, he went down in his dressing gown to the shoemaker's flat.

They had just come to the end of the verse when he walked

in. Cobbler John respectfully got up from his three-legged stool and greeted the great gentleman.

"You are John, the cobbler, aren't you?" the rich man asked.

"That I am, and at your service, Your Excellency. Do you wish to order a pair of patent leather boots?"

"That isn't why I came. How very many children you have!"

"Indeed, I have, Your Excellency—little ones and big ones. Quite a few mouths to feed!"

"And many more mouths when they sing! Look here, Master John—I'd like to do you a favor. Give me one of your children. I'll adopt him, educate him as my own son, take him travelling abroad with me, and make him into a gentleman. One day he'll be able to help the rest of you."

Cobbler John stared wide-eyed when he heard this. These were big words—to have one of his children made into a gentleman! Who wouldn't be taken by such an idea? Why, of course, he'd let him have one! What great good fortune! How could he refuse?

"Well, then, pick out one of them quickly, and let's get it over with," said the gentleman. Cobbler John started to choose.

"This one here is Alex. No, him I couldn't let go. He is a good student and I want him to become a priest. The next one? That's a girl, and of course Your Excellency doesn't want a girl. Little Ferenc? He already helps me with my work. I couldn't do without him. Johnny? There, there—he is named after me. I couldn't very well give him away! Joseph? He is the image of his mother—it's as if I saw her every time I look at him. This place wouldn't be the same without him. And the next is another girl—she wouldn't do. Then comes little Paul: he was his mother's favorite. Oh, my poor darling would turn in her grave if I gave him away. And the last two are too small —they'd be too much trouble for Your Excellency. . . ."

He had reached the end of the line without being able to choose. Now he started all over; this time beginning with the youngest and ending with the oldest. But the result was still the same: he couldn't decide which one to give away because one was as dear to him as the other and he would miss them all.

"Come, my little ones—you do the choosing," he finally said. "Which one of you wants to go away to become a gentleman and travel in style? Come now, speak up! Who wants to go?"

The poor shoemaker was on the verge of tears as he asked them. But while he was encouraging them, the children slowly slipped behind their fathers' back, each taking hold of him, his hand, his leg, his coat, his leather apron, all hanging on to him, and hiding from the great gentleman. Finally Cobbler John couldn't control himself any longer. He knelt down, gathered them all into his arms and let his tears fall on their heads as they cried with him.

"It can't be done, Your Excellency! It can't be done. Ask of me anything in the world, but I can't give you a single one of my children so long as the Lord God has given them to me."

The rich gentleman said that he understood, but that the shoemaker should do at least one thing for him: would he and his children please not sing anymore? And for this sacrifice he asked Cobbler John to accept one thousand florins.

Master John had never even heard the words, "One thousand florins," spoken, never in all his life. Now he felt the money being pressed into his hand.

His Excellency went back to his room and his boredom. And Cobbler John stood staring incredulously at the oddly shaped banknote. Then he fearfully locked it away in the wooden chest, put the key into his pocket and was silent. The little ones were silent, too. Singing was forbidden. The older children slumped moodily in their chairs, quieting the smaller ones by telling them they weren't allowed to sing anymore because it disturbed the fine gentleman upstairs. Cobbler John himself was silently walking up and down. Impatiently he pushed aside little Paul, the one who had been his wife's favorite, when the boy asked that he be taught again that beautiful song because he had already forgotten how it went.

"We aren't allowed to sing anymore!"

Then he sat down angrily at his bench and bent intently over his work. He cut and hammered and sewed until suddenly he caught himself humming: "On the blessed birth of Our Lord

Jesus Christ. . . ." He clapped his hand over his mouth. But then all at once he was very angry. He banged the hammer down on the workbench, kicked his stool from under him, opened the chest, took out the thousand florin bill and ran up the stairs to His Excellency's apartment.

"Good, kind Excellency, I am your most humble servant. Please take back your money! Let it not be mine, but let us sing whenever we please, because to me and my children that is worth much more than a thousand florins."

With that he put the bill down on the table and rushed breathlessly back to his waiting family. He kissed them one after the other; and lining them up in a row just like organ pipes, he sat himself down on his low stool, and together they began to sing again with heart and soul: "On the blessed birth of Our Lord Jesus Christ. . . ." They couldn't have been happier if they had owned the whole of the great big house.

But the one who owned the house was pacing through his nine rooms, asking himself how it was that those people down below could be so happy and full of joy in such a tiresome, boring world as this!

IRELAND

Christmas Song

FITZPATRICK WARD, JR.

O. PETRI

"Mór Cluaniʒ."

♩ = 80

Slóir is mol do Duit, a Dé! Tú an flaiteas dá bruil buan-ró,

Tú do bí ʒan cli ʒan cóir. Tú an Rí ós na ríʒ --- tib.

Glory be to Thee, O Lord,
Thou art our eternal aim.
In our hearts we carry Thee,
King of Kings we Thee proclaim.

It was Thee who made the world,
Elder, Thou, Superior,
It was Thee who died for us,
Haven, Thou, and Savior.

Let Thy love shine on us all,
Thou, who didst descend to hell,
When the Day of Judgment dawns,
Prophet, Thou, and Warning Knell.

Turkey and Ham

LYNN DOYLE (Leslie Alexander Montgomery)

WHEN WEE Mr. Anthony the solicitor was courtin' Mr. Livingston's daughter, Miss Betty, he had only the one trouble. It wasn't his girl; she was a quiet simple affectionate slip of a grey-eyed girl, an' thought the sun riz an' set on him. The bother was, Mr. Anthony was so pleased about it that he begun to put on fat. He told me his trouble, one day we were out shootin' over the Bermingham estate, that Miss Betty's father was agent for; an' I only laughed at him.

"What odds does it make," says I, "if your young lady takes no notice?"

That comforted him for a while; but the followin' week a thunderbolt fell on him.

"George," sez Miss Betty to him one evenin', very timid, "I'm thinkin' of tryin' to slim. It would never do for the two of us to get fat," sez she. "People would look after us as we went down the street."

Mr. Anthony jumped as if he had touched an electric wire.

"That settles it," sez he. "I needed that jog. Not that I'm greedy, dear; but I'm a great judge of food and wine, and it seemed a pity not to exercise my talent. Now, my mind is made up. As and from the end of tonight's dinner—I'll have to eat that, since it's cooked—I go on a diet till I've lost a stone and a half. I will not have you slimming, Betty. Curse it," says he,

From *Shake of the Bag* by Lynn Doyle. Reprinted by permission of A. P. Watt & Son and Gerald Duckworth & Co. Ltd.

"I don't care if you grow as round as a dumpling. I love you. But we mustn't become ridiculous. Listen to me, darling," he says, warmin' up; "from to-night I go on to Dr. Thompson's diet. It's a corker, mind you, It slimmed old Mrs. McGimpsey till she rattled in her coffin; and it may kill me, too; but my word is my oath. Damme, if it wasn't boiled chicken and bacon I'd give tonight's dinner to the dog."

"Don't overdo it, George," sez Miss Betty, a trifle frightened. "You might injure your health. And you forget that to-morrow's Christmas Day, and you're dining with us."

"I was doing more than that," sez Mr. Anthony. "I was dining in the middle of the day as well, just to spite my old housekeeper. She has my Christmas dinner bought, a turkey and a ham, and sausages and chestnuts and heaven knows what; and I got a present of two bottles of champagne from Mr. Bermingham—the Widow Clicquot, 1921—that would make a tombstone angel play jazz tunes."

"But George, darling," says Miss Betty, "were you going to eat and drink all that? And I was sympathizing about your figure!"

"Confound it, no," says Mr. Anthony. "I never get anything but a morsel, a couple of slices of breast, and maybe a wing and a sausage or two; and then off goes the rest to her relations. She has a sister married to the gamekeeper of the Bermingham estate, and another to the keeper of the back lodge-gate, and you'd think she was married to them herself. They get about two-thirds of all the food I pay for; and now they're going to get the whole of my Christmas dinner."

"But it's a shame," says Miss Betty, "an imposition!"

Mr. Anthony stopped on the road.

" 'Gad," says he, "I never thought of that. It *is* an imposition. I've been weak, Betty," sez he, "and that's not like me. I can't eat my Christmas dinner—grape-fruit and toast, the doctor's diet says—and I can't drink my Christmas champagne; but, begad, if I fast the housekeeper's relatives may fast, too. Pat Murphy's coming round this evening after dinner to fix up some shooting for St. Stephen's Day. I'll give my dinner to him. Not a word!"

says he. "I want to show you that you're getting a man that loves
you better than his meals. It's a point of honor with me, now.
Damme," sez he, "I'll stick to the diet should I go up the aisle
with you, and the people looking through me as if I was a rain-
bow."

But when Mr. Anthony offered me the dinner that evening
it was far too late.

"I just daren't take it, Mr. Anthony," says I. "We have a
turkey of my wife Mollie's rearin' that she cried over when she
was killin' it, as if it was a child; an' the least I can do is to
attend the funeral. An' as for Champagne, I wouldn't have the
wee bubbles out of my system before the New Year. Eat an'
drink the whole lot yourself," says I. "Miss Betty'll never
know."

"I wouldn't do that," says Mr. Anthony. "Is it deceive poor
Betty even before I'm married to her? Never!" says he. "I'm a
man of principle. Beyond what the doctor's diet permits—not a
crumb," says he, "not the pop of a cork. I suppose the housekeeper's clan will have to get the dinner after all."

"Give it to some decent poor family," says I. "It'll be a
friendly turn. An' if a solicitor's soul *can* be saved it may do
somethin' in that direction as well."

"Tell me the name of a family," says he, "and if the champagne goes to heads unaccustomed to anythin' but porter,
damme, I'll defend them myself."

"The O'Greens of Creel's Row are decent people that would
be glad of an extra bit an' sup on a day like that," says I; "but,
sure, if you sent your Christmas dinner to a Nationalist family
there'd be a revolution."

"This is where brains and experience come in," says Mr.
Anthony, all pleased with himself. "There's an Orange family
called Williamson on the far side of the Row. We'll split the
dinner between the two families, an' I'll throw in a drop of
whiskey, each, to warm their stomachs after the champagne."

"If you do that," says I, "your soul an' body are safe for the
Christmas holidays, anyway. But if your whiskey is so plenty
could you not spare me a drop, now?"

"I can," says he, "and will."

He took down a bottle an' filled out about half a glass.

"Isn't it an extraordinary thing, Pat," says he, twirlin' the glass in his hand, "the way people let drink get a hold of them. Now here I am," says he, takin' a sip, "that have given up this stuff maybe for ever, and I don't care a fig. There's nothin' to give up," says he, takin' another sup. "I've lost the taste for it already. Bless my soul!" he says, emptyin' down the last drop, "I've dirtied your glass. Wait till I get another."

"All the same, Mr. Anthony," says I, "you'll find it a long Christmas day."

"It can't be helped," says he, lookin' a bit glum. "Principle is principle. But, do you know, Pat; I think it would be a kindly act if you and I dropped round to the houses of these two poor fellows to-morrow. They'd like to see the giver of the feast; and it might console me under the diet if I saw other people doing themselves harm instead of me."

"I'm with you," says I, "if you'll make it early. We're not eatin' our dinner till four. The brother-in-law and his wife are comin' down on the afternoon train from Belfast."

"Good," says Mr. Anthony. "What time do these unfortunate people dine?"

"They don't dine at all," says I. "As soon as the grub is cooked they eat it."

"Very well," says Mr. Anthony. "I'll not be up myself; but I'll tell the housekeeper to send the stuff off about ten. And three hours will cook a ham."

"It doesn't take near as long to cook drink," says I.

"We'll have to take our chance of that," says Mr. Anthony. "I can put a flask in my pocket. Let us say half-past twelve at Johnson's corner. Oh, just a minute," says he. He tossed up a shilling. "The turkey goes to the O'Greens, and the ham to the Williamsons. We'll call on the Williamsons first, to accustom me to the smell of food. If I encounter the turkey first I might be tempted to taste the stuffing. Don't be surprised if you find me thinner in the morning, Pat. There'll be nothing in me but half a grape-fruit and some kind of sawdust toast. Curse that

doctor fellow," says he, forgettin' himself a little. "And to think
that he'll be eating bacon and eggs."

The next day about a quarter to one o'clock Mr. Anthony
an' I walked up the path to Robert Williamson's cottage. About
six feet away from the door Mr. Anthony stopped me.

"Do you smell it, Pat?" says he.

"What?" says I, after a hard sniff.

"The ham," says he. "Pure Limerick. I would know it a mile
away. They're a queer lot in the South of Ireland, but damme,
they can make ham. Lovely," says he, takin' a sniff himself. "I
feel well paid already for my little bit of self-sacrifice. Don't let
me stay too long. That smell is making me ravenous."

When we went into the Williamsons' kitchen there was nobody there but Mrs. Williamson, an' the two children. The fire
was barely in, an' there wasn't even a saucepan on it. Mrs.
Williamson was blowin' the bellows; an' she looked up all surprised. Mr. Anthony stammered a little.

"I was just taking a Christmas morning walk with my friend
Pat Murphy," says he; "and we thought we'd call and wish you
a Happy Christmas."

"Thank you, sir," says Mrs. Williamson, well pleased, "you
were always very kind. Shake hands with the gentleman," says
she to the children, "and say 'Thank you'."

It's very hard to have a child sayin' "Thank you" for nothin'.
Mr. Anthony put his hand in his pocket and fetched out some
silver. I looked, an' the divil a thing smaller was among it than
two-shillin' bits. He gave the children one apiece; but you could
see by his face he was addin' it to the cost of the ham.

Mrs. Williamson thanked him herself with the tears in her
eyes.

"The boss got half a day's work this mornin' at double pay,"
says she, "an' he'll not be back till half-past two, so I haven't a
bite cooked in the house that I could offer you."

Mr. Anthony's face fell, an' he gave a very straightforward
sniff. Mrs. Williamson took the hint.

"You've said it, sir," sez she. "It's a bit on the elderly side,
sure enough; but maybe you would take a morsel."

She went to the cupboard an' fetched out a piece of very broadminded-lookin' cheese; though the green was beginnin' to get the better of the Orange.

"Try a piece of that an' a sup of whiskey, sir," says she, "you an' Pat Murphy; just for the credit of the house."

Mr. Anthony turned his back on the cheese, an' filled himself out a stiffish glass. It pulled him together a good deal, for he faced round manful again.

"Thank you, mem," says he; "but I'm on a diet, and cheese is specially forbidden. But you're right to eat that piece at half-past two; for I doubt it will be past its best by three o'clock.—Now don't be drinking all the woman's whiskey, Pat," says he to me, that was barely takin' a poor man's drink. "I thought we were neither to eat nor wet our lips till we got home."

But I lingered a minute to speak to Mrs. Williamson.

"You should have thanked him for the dinner," says I. "He's not well pleased."

"What dinner?" says she, gapin' at me.

"It was half his dinner was sent you this mornin'," says I. "He's on a diet an' didn't want the good food wasted. A whole Limerick ham, an' whiskey an' champagne wine. Did you not open the parcel yet?"

"If there was a parcel sent me it must have gone astray," says she; "for as true as I'm here I never got a crumb."

"That's queer," says I. "The housekeeper was to send it— half to you an' half to the O'Greens."

Mrs. Williamson looked very hard at me, an' the color riz in her face.

"Oh, 'fare ye well, Killeavey'," says she. "That's all we'll ever hear of it. The ould faggot," says she. "Not that I would give offence to anybody of your persuasion, Mr. Murphy; but I expect she has gone an' sent the whole jing-bang to the O'Greens because they're her own sort. Run away, dear!" she says to the little boy that was hangin' round her. "Not a word, mind you, to Mr. Anthony. I'll say nothin' to my man. He'd want to stand on his rights; an' there's no use havin' a row between neighbors on this of all days in the year. But it's not very Christmas be-

havior of her, I'll say that. An' I haven't tasted a bit of Limerick
ham since I was at service in the Berminghams! Never mind,
Mr. Murphy. It's not your fault. But there'll no blessin' follow
it."

I suppose the whiskey did all the better work on Mr. Anthony
on account of him bein' near empty; but when I caught up on
him it was beginning to lift his heart a little.

"Now not one syllable out of you," says he, "about the tea-
spoonful of whiskey I had. If that cheese wasn't an excuse for
at least half a pint I'll go back and eat the stuff. Isn't it a pity
we went into the house at all? If I hadn't this cold in my head
I'd have smelt it at the gate. Are we near the O'Greens?"

"It's somewhere about this part of the Row," says I. "Take
a sniff an' try if you can smell a turkey."

"There's Mrs. O'Green just gone into the door," says he,
very hasty. "Come on. I don't want the neighbors to think I'm
serving a writ. You haven't four sixpences for a two-shilling
piece Pat, have you? No? Curse it," says he, "I must have put
in my pocket the money I had for the Bermingham servants instead of what I got for the poor. How many young O'Greens
are there?"

"Seven," says I, "an' three dead."

"Thank heavens," says Mr. Anthony. "I mean for the three
dead. My goodness," says he, fishing among his change, "this is
going to cost me fifteen-and-sixpence. Can they all walk?"
lookin' at me with a bit of hope in his eye.

"There's two of them can't, Mr. Anthony," says I; "but I
doubt they could hold on tight enough to a couple of two-
shillin' bits if they were put in their hand."

"D—n them," sez he, good-natured enough. "But I'll give the
Berminghams' butler sixpence, and have my revenge."

Mr. and Mrs. O'Green an' the seven children were all in the
wee kitchen; an' the five that could walk fell on Mr. Anthony
an' near tore him to bits.

"An' very kind of you, sir," shouts Mrs. O'Green through the
noise. "You were always gentry, Mr. Anthony, an' had somethin'
in the heel of your hand for the poor man; an' God bless you

an' the purty girl you're goin' to marry, an' may you raise as hearty an' healthy a flock as my own an' as many of them, though I doubt the mistress is a bit light in the make for it."

Mr. Anthony had been holdin' on to his money so far; but this was too much for him. He hauled out the silver, an' in his splutter began at the half-crown end, an' cost himself an extra sixpence. There was great enthusiasm; an' Mr. Anthony's Sunday breeches aged six months in about three minutes.

"We're just goin' to have our Christmas dinner," roars Mrs. O'Green. "You'll have a bite with us. Hold on till I try the pot."

"Good gracious," says Mr. Anthony in my ear, "I hope they haven't put in the champagne, too."

She laid a big dish on the table. The boilin' pot cleared a way through the crowd for itself, an' out tumbled a stew of rabbits an' bacon an' vegetables that would have tempted a sick millionaire let alone a man on a diet.

"It's hardly done yet, but take that in your fingers, sir," says she, handin' him the leg of a rabbit, "an' just pick it as you stand there. Now, take it! It won't talk to you—barrin' you prosecute my man for shootin' it accidentally in Mr. Bermingham's demesne, an' a gentleman like you won't do that. Fetch the whiskey, Michael," she shouts at her husband. "I'll hold the twins. There's plenty more where that bottle came from," says she, slippin' the twins' two two-shillin' bits into her husband's hand with a wink; "but porter'll be better for you."

Mr. Anthony leaned over to me as he was standin' with a glass in one hand an' the leg of a rabbit in the other.

"Take this bone out of my mouth," he mumbles. "I've near swallowed it twice; an' it would be sure to go down with the whiskey. I can't refuse to eat with these poor people," says he. "The Irish are very proud, and it would be taken as a deadly insult. And, curse it, I'm entitled to somethin' for my sixteen bob. By the way, did you see any sign of the turkey, or has it got lost in the stew?"

I shook my head as if I didn't hear him, for, troth, I'd been wonderin' about the turkey myself. An' when we were goin' out of the house, after me an' Mr. Anthony had drunk another

couple of sups of whiskey an' Mr. Anthony had bought two reserved tickets for a concert in aid of the new chapel, I drew
Mrs. O'Green behind the open cupboard door.

"What became of the turkey?" says I.

"What turkey?" says she. "My man shot no turkey, or if he
did it was an accident."

"Mr. Anthony is on a diet," says I in her ear; "but had his
Christmas dinner bought, an' sent you an' your family half of
it, a turkey an' dear knows what besides. The housekeeper was
to bring or send it, an' Mr. Anthony came round hopin' for a
wing or a leg, so that he could eat an' still keep his conscience
clear."

Mrs. O'Green took a look at me, an' then a half-scared look
over her shoulder at her husband.

"Come outside," says she.—"It's that ould witch of a housekeeper," says she. "Oh, well I know where our turkey is gone.
It's decoratin' the insides of her an' her two sticks of sisters that
hasn't chick or child between them, an' me with five hungry
children an 'two I'm feedin' myself an' wouldn't have a bite in
the house this day if my hard-workin' man hadn't shot three
rabbits an' a water-hen yesterday evenin' an' him skulkin' behind hedge an' ditch to keep out of sight of the gamekeeper
that's leatherin' into our turkey this minit—an' I wish he had
shot *him,* too. But, for the love of mercy, Pat Murphy, say
nothin' to nobody; for Michael has a wee sup of drink on him,
this bein' Christmas mornin'—that was why I gave him the
twins to hold, to keep him at peace—an' if he hears this news
there'll be the siege of Athlone! Away with you," says she; "for
he has his eye on me, an' for all he's a good faithful husband
he's wicked in drink, an' might do somebody a mischief if he
found out. God send I'll be able to keep it from him an' save
his soul from sin this holy day, an' me with a couple of mouth-
fuls of whiskey in me, too, an' long-tongued with it, that the
like never crossed my lips since the two blessed twins were
christened Aloysius an' Timothy by Father O'Leary in this
very house an' them dyin' but lived since, an' we had half a
pint of whiskey that isn't paid for yet, an' I hope that ould

extortioner down the street won't keep Mr. Anthony's two shillin'-bits again 'it an' not let us have the porter."

Mr. Anthony was a temperate man, generally, more used to eatin' than drinkin'; an' when I caught up with him I found him two or three notes higher in the tune than when we left Williamson's, an' a little inclined to hiccough, though he handled it in a very gentlemanly way.

"There's a native courtesy about the Irish people, Pat," says he, "a fine old standard of princely hospitality—*hmph!* I beg your pardon," says he.—"Look at that poor creature with one miserable rabbit in a pot along with very bad company, and, damme, she was handing round legs of it as if it was a centipede. She wanted me to take whiskey, too. I wish I had. There's something sticking in my gizzard about half-way down, blast me but I think it's a claw. She should have cut the claws off, shouldn't she, Pat? No system about the Irish, all happy-go-lucky. Now I'm a me-methodical man," says he, takin' it in a rush. "It runs in my mind—" he stopped in the middle of the road an' began to grope in his pockets—"that I've lost somethin'. —What do you think, Pat?"

"What do you think you've lost?" says I.

He looked at me a bit wanderin' an' peevish.

"I don't *think* I've lost," says he. "I know.—Wait till I think what it was. I have it," says he. "What became of the turkey? An' if it comes to that——" he looked at me all surprised, "what became of the Limerick ham?"

An' then the divil entered into me.

"Mr. Anthony," says I, "should we not call round by the gamekeeper's house? Your old housekeeper is sure to be there, an' she would take it as a great compliment."

"So she would," says Mr. Anthony, stoppin' in the middle of the road again, an' forgettin' all about the turkey an' the ham for the time. "A very proper thing, too. Lord of the Manor visits old retainer—what? Lead on, Macduff. Wait a minute," says he, wrinklin' up his forehead as if he was still tryin' to remember somethin', "do I look like a man that was on a strict diet?"

"You look like a man that will be on a quare strict diet to-morrow," sez I.

An', sure enough, the whiskey was gettin' more of a hold of him every second.

"I don't mind about to-morrow," says he, devil-may-care all at once, "so long as I'm all right to-day. And I don't care for any keeper—gatekeeper, gamekeeper, or housekeeper. If she opens her mouth to say the word 'diet'—if I even see it in her eye—I'll give her a month's notice without the option of a fine. Come along!

"Wait a minute," says he again; an' this time he looked worrieder than ever. "If we should meet Betty! *That* would be awkward, Pat. I couldn't give *her* a month's notice, could I?" He wagged his head very solemn as if there was nothing to be said for the opposite side. "And she could give *me* notice on the spot. Hold on," says he. "What day is this? Christmas Day. And she'll have had her lunch. She couldn't come out full of lunch on Christmas Day and sack poor Anthony that has nothing inside him at all—at any rate nothing that's doing him any good. No, no. Posterous.— I mean," says he, pickin' his steps through the syllables very carefully, "*Pre*-pos-terous.

"Now, listen to me, Pat," says he when we got under way once more, "we must do this in style. The old castle—the gamekeeper's house is the old castle. The wicked Baron—that's the housekeeper; and very wicked she was this day when she found I'd given away the family's dinner. The gallant knight—quite clearly that's G. Anthony, Esq., solicitor-at-law except on Christmas Day. And the beautiful damsel is Betty."

"But she isn't here," says I.

"I know that," says he, shakin' his head very mournful. "It's just as well."

"An' where does Pat Murphy come in?" says I, humourin' him.

"You don't come in at all," says he, "if you have any sense. For, there's going to be bloody wars. Do you think," says he, lookin' at me as if he was an owl that had sat up playin' cards till night-time, "that I didn't spot what that old deceiver had done with my Christmas gifts? Well, I did *not* spot it. I'm a man that makes so few blunders that I can acknowledge when I do make one. The whole way along there was something appearing and disappearing in my mind. I thought for a while it was my eyeglass. It was fluttering about me like a butterfly; but I caught it at last. And then all at once I saw that old harridan of a housekeeper carrying away my good dinner to her friends and leaving the poor and hungry with nothing to cover their nakedness but some d——d bad whiskey. Halt!" says he, pulling up on his toes. "We're at the gate. Form fours! Do you see that?" says he, pullin' a wee tin-trumpet out of his pocket. "The youngest walking O'Green child gave me that—and I'm still two and fourpence down over the transaction. When I blow three blasts on that—over the top!"

He blew three blasts on the wee trumpet—the first two were misfires—an' away up the path with me a good distance behind him—for the whiskey was beginnin' to die in me, an' I was feelin' a trifle ashamed of the whole transaction. When I got into the eatin'-room he was standin' at the head of the table holdin' a champagne bottle by the neck. The gamekeeper an' his wife, the lodge-keeper an' *his* wife, an' the housekeeper were all seated round such a spread as you never saw, bar in a picture—a turkey, a ham, plum puddin', cakes, sweets, bottles, an' glasses. They were just goin' to begin. There was a big salmon trout in front of the gamekeeper, an' he had dealt it all round the party an' given himself the ace.

Mr. Anthony was lookin' down on them with what would have been a frown if his features could have kept their places in the class.

"It *is* my dinner," says he, catchin' a hiccough just as it was tryin' to escape. "'S *all* my dinner. That's my trout you're eating. You might think that's boiled trout; but it's not. It's poached trout. And I got a present of it because I proved to the satisfaction of a magistrate that it wasn't poached trout. *So, where are you?*" says Mr. Anthony so loud all of a sudden that the gamekeeper raised his knife an' fork to protect himself.

You never saw five people as willin' to be in another place as the party round that table. But the gamekeeper gathered himself together.

"You're wrong, sir," says he, very soothin', a thing that didn't help his case at all. "I got this fish from Big Billy Lenahan of the Hills."

"So did I," says Mr. Anthony; an' the gamekeeper didn't know the answer.

"The fish was a present to me," says he at last. "That it may choke me if it wasn't," says he, gettin' desperate.

"Very good," says Mr. Anthony with great satisfaction. *"Let* it choke you. Stand up and swallow a mouthful; and if the fish doesn't choke you I'll make it apologize."

The gamekeeper looked at his wife most pitiful, but she had nothin' to say; an' Mr. Anthony seemed very determined. So the gamekeeper stood on his feet with the plate of fish in one hand, balanced about a couple of ounces on the blade of his knife, an' made a shot at his mouth. He half caught the piece of fish, saw it was slippin', took a sudden suck; an' between that an' six pairs of eyes watchin' him, two of them in hope, sure enough he choked. An' the right name of it was chokin'. He was a short-necked, red-faced man when he started, but before you could count three he was purple, an' the eyes were comin' out of his head. I think it was his bad conscience more than the fish; but one or other looked like bein' the death of him. The three weemin let a combined family yell an' gathered round him cryin' an' lamentin'; the brother-in-law got him under the arms; an' between pullin' an' haulin' they had him out of the room an' into the kitchen in a twinklin', an' the door shut. I didn't know till the next day whether he lived or died.

For Mr. Anthony wasn't a bit put about, but laid down the bottle of champagne an' took up a whiskey-bottle.

"Seeing I'm on a diet, Pat," says he, "and have to deny myself, and you don't like champagne, we'd better begin the wake with whiskey."

He poured out two tough ones; an' he had finished first.

"Now, Pat," says he, "do you take the turkey an' I'll take the ham."

But I was beginnin' to feel the weather a bit myself, now; an' somehow it didn't seem right that I should have the honor of carryin' the turkey.

"No, no, sir," says I. "I take the ham."

We didn't get it settled; for, just as I spoke, a big boulder of a stone came flying through the window an' carried about a quarter of the plates an' glasses to their long home.

Mr. Anthony seized the champagne bottle again, an' dived under the table-cloth.

"Take cover," says he. "He isn't dead yet."

I got behind a chair, waitin' for the second bomb. An' as Mr. Anthony poked his head out from the folds of the table-cloth, holdin' the champagne-bottle at the "Present," in rushes Michael O'Green with his two eldest boys on his heels, an' him wild-lookin'. He didn't even hear the pop as Mr. Anthony fired.

"Yez stole me Christmas dinner," says he, "but yez'll never eat it."

An' with that he lays hands on the turkey.

"Grab all you can, lads," says he. "What's not ours we'll make ours."

But even in the state he was in by this time Mr. Anthony was still the legal man.

"Justice and fair-play," says he, risin' to his feet, with his thumb in the champagne bottle, an' it thinkin' it was tryin' to put out a fire. "Take what you like; but leave the ham."

It was like a ghost risin' before Michael. He let half a prayer, half an apology, out of him, lifted the turkey, called off the family with what plunder they'd laid hands on, an' away down the road, gallopin'.

But nothin' could shake Mr. Anthony by this time.

"You were quite right, Pat," says he as solemn as if he was on the Bench; "you do take the ham. I'll carry the champagne, if I can get it to my head without being drowned. Fetch one of those bottles of whiskey as well, or the battle of the Boyne will be fought over again in Creel's Row this day."

He wasn't far out. Robert Williamson was a quiet determined man that liked to get to the bottom of things, an' insisted on what was his due. When he came home his wee son told him enough about the dinner he had missed for him to get the whole story out of his wife. He put on his hat.

"Leave the dinner till I come back," says he. "I'll either have that ham with me or Michael O'Green by the hair of his head."

When he got to O'Green's the family was just takin' their places in triumph for such a feed, between rabbit stew an' the turkey, as would go down in the family history for generations to come. Robert wasted no words.

"I see you have your turkey," says he to Michael. "An' that old bigot of a housekeeper let you have our ham as well. If I don't get it in two minits, I'll kick the stuffin' out of you an' the turkey both."

Any other time, Michael would have asked nothin' better than to let him try. But he had been greatly soothed by his victory about the turkey.

"Mr. Anthony kept the ham, Robert," says he. "As true as death I haven't got it."

"Then I'll have the turkey," says Williamson, quite simple an' straightforward; lays hold of it by the legs, an' lifts it from the dish.

"Will you, by my sowl?" roars Michael, flamin' all at once, an' lays hold of the turkey by the neck; an' in a minute the two of them was pullin' tug-of-war all over the kitchen floor, with the family yellin' to raise the thatch. There was already a fair knot of Creel's Row people gathered since word had gone round about Michael O'Green arrivin' with a whole cooked turkey in his hand; so Mr. Anthony an' I got through unbeknownst, an' into the kitchen just in time for Robert Williamson to miss Michael with the turkey an' hit Mr. Anthony in the face. It was the first time I saw Mr. Anthony real vexed the whole day. He brushed the loose bits of the turkey off his face, snatched the ham from me, an' liftin' it with his two hands felled Robert like a sheep. Then he came to himself again.

"There's your ham, Robert," says he in his ear, as Robert stood up half-dazed. "I'm sorry it slipped out of my hand. But I'm on a diet; and a trifle weak with the hunger."

The sergeant of police had got wind of the turkey, an' came in with two constables just in time to prevent a European war; for Michael an' his family weren't too well pleased with the condition the turkey was in by this time, an' wanted to lay claim to the ham. But the trouble was settled, for the time bein', with the help of the bottle in my pocket. The sergeant sent Williamson an' the ham home under escort, an' volunteered to drive Mr. Anthony an' me back in his own wee car; an' when we got there Mr. Anthony got round him to fetch word to Mr. Livingston's that Mr. Anthony had been slightly injured while heroically separatin' two men engaged in a party fight, an' wouldn't be able to go for dinner.

As my head began to clear I could see that he was wrong.

"You'll have Miss Betty back here as sure as eggs are eggs," says I; "an' where'll you be, then, with the state you're in?"

Mr. Anthony looked at me, an' would have turned pale but for the gravy of the turkey that was crusted on his face.

"Curse it," says he: "isn't it hellish the way a fine brain like mine is blunted by even the smell of drink. Come up to the bathroom with me, quick, and do you pour water on my head. I'd miss myself with Niagara Falls."

I thawed the gravy off him with hot water, an' had got him into purty fair order with cold, when sure enough we heard wheels; an' the next minute Miss Betty was in the hall.

"He's puttin' on his dressin'-gown, Miss Betty," says I, runnin' out with a towel in my hand, "an' will speak to you over the banisters." "Don't let her within ten steps of the stairs of you," says I to Mr. Anthony before he went out; "for between wet an' dry that you've put into you this day your breath'll be like a pole-cat."

So Mr. Anthony perjured himself from the top of the stairs, an' made it all sound like sober truth, though it was neither; an' Miss Betty's eyes near lit up the stair-rods she was so proud of him for reddin' the party row when the police couldn't do it.

"You'll be able to come to dinner," says she, coaxin'.

"I think I will, after all," says Mr. Anthony, never heedin' the kick I gave him. "But, mind you, Betty, not even my injuries are to be an excuse for breaking the diet. I'm a man of my word should it snow turkeys."

"Oh, *George*," says Miss Betty, "how obstinate you are—and how dear. I think I'll have to run up and kiss you."

Mr. Anthony cursed under his breath, an' took a very frightened skelly at me.

"Just a minute, darling," says he, lettin' on to wrap the dressin'-gown tighter round him. "Has Stubbs the chemist anything?" he whispers to me.

"He has capsules," says I, "would make violets of a bad egg; but they take a while to work."

"Betty, dear," says Mr. Anthony—"it sounds very unromantic, I know—the truth is my lips are a good deal bruised. But Pat Murphy is getting me something from the chemist; and I think, darling"—his voice would have lubricated a stripped bearing— "I think they'll be healed by dinner-time."

ITALY

The Jesus Child Is Comen

TRADITIONAL

Moderato

Ge- sù Bam — bin l'è na.— to, ... l'è nato in

Be —te - lem .... l'è sopra un po'' di pa — ia,...

.... l'è sopra un po' di .fien! L'è sopra un po' di

fien, s'a j'è'l bambin ch'a piu - ra, sôa ma - ma ch'a lo a-

do - ra, ... l'è sopra un po' di fien! ....

The Jesus Child is comen,
Is comen to Bethlehem.
He sleeps on a bit of bedding,
That looks like an anadem.
He sleeps in His anadem,
His mother looks at Him, adoring,
Her spirit to heaven soaring,
In the manger at Bethlehem.

The Golden Crucifix

GRAZIA DELEDDA
(Translated by Eric Posselt)

I WAS living in Sardegna at the time and I wanted to unearth some Christmas story about the island. I used to know an old peasant who knew many of them—a tenant on one of our small holdings down in the valley.

He used to come to visit us in the summer and fall, hunched over his walking stick, a sack slung around his neck, his wispy grey beard dropping into the open end of the bag. He always came to see us late in the afternoon, when the evening star was smiling at us children through the purple twilight. The old peasant seemed like one of the Three Wise Men who had taken the wrong turn and had lost his companions. But he offered things more precious to us than gold and the Wise Men's crown—fruits and strange tales.

He very seldom came to see us in the winter, and was not so interesting then because he carried only olives, and olives are bitter. Therefore we often went to visit him down in the valley. It was comfortable there, sheltered from the cold wind, with the clouds spreading like a veil over a crib, the water withdrawn and the mountain slopes dry. When the weather was good it seemed like spring. Almond trees were blooming, deceived by the mildness like dreamers, and the olives glistened in the grass like purple pearls.

From *Romanzi e Novelle* by Grazia Deledda. Printed by permission of Arnoldo Mondadori Editore, Milano.

The old man lived in a tiny hut in the midst of an olive grove that rested on a small plateau protected by harsh grey stones and wild bushes. He had a primitive bee-hive that had long since been abandoned by the bees. The wild cats loved to lie in it, beautiful like little tigresses.

When we came to see him this time, the enclosure was warmed by the sun, the olives were silvery, and the afternoon so limpid that on the slopes of the opposite mountain one could see shining rivulets and the women collecting acorns hidden in the grass.

The little old man had spread the olives on the ground to let them dry and was picking up those that seemed a little spoiled. He didn't feel like talking. His tongue had grown stiff from solitude and silence. However, the servant had brought a good medicine to free the rusty words. So the old man drank deeply and began to complain.

"What kind of a tale do you want me to tell? I am old and speak only to the earth that calls me. If you want stories, you know how to read. Why don't you look for them in the books?"

"Drink some more," said the servant, bending down to select some olives. "Tell us about the time you were going to get married, why don't you?"

"That's a true story, not a legend," he replied. "I'll tell you that one because it happened around this time, on Christmas Eve. I was twenty years old then, and was engaged. Of course, I was very young to get married, but my father had died, and my mother was always ill. She had heart trouble and was God-fearing, so she said to me: 'Get married so that when I die you will not have to carry the cross of life alone, or fall in the clutches of the first woman you meet.'

"But whom to choose? I wasn't rich and I really didn't care about wealth. All I wanted was a wife who would be honest and God-fearing. We thought this over, asking ourselves who she should be.

"There was a very respectable family living near us, father, mother and seven children. They were all good workers and went to church and confession as God decrees. Three of the seven children were girls, beautiful, tall and slim with waists you could span with your two hands. They kept their eyes lowered, the bodices buttoned tightly and their hands under their aprons. Nor did they walk like you modern girls, looking at people as if you were going to eat them. My mother asked the youngest for me, and I was accepted. When Christmas time came, I had to give her the present with which, as is customary, I engaged myself to marry her. By accepting it she agreed to take me as her husband.

"We thought and thought about that present. Sitting opposite each other near the fire, my mother and I debated as to whether the present should be a gold coin, an embroidered scarf, or a ring. Finally my mother said: 'Listen, son, I have only a few more days to live and every step is a farewell to the things of this earth. Take this golden crucifix and give it to her.'

"She gave me her cross together with the mother of pearl rosary to which it was attached. But her eyes were glistening with tears, and her lips were parted with emotion and the aching of her heart. I was so troubled that I tried to give it back to her; but unable to speak she merely pushed my hand back.

"I wrapped the rosary and the cross in a handkerchief, wrapped the little bundle in yet another handkerchief, and carried it in my pocket for three days like a relic. From time to time I touched it for fear of losing it and felt, I don't know why, a strange anxiety, although my heart swelled with love.

"On Christmas Eve I went to call on my intended. Two other young men were there too, to whom her sisters were betrothed. The kitchen, with so many people in it, looked very festive. But everybody was serious because of the presence of the in-laws with their serene but rather somber miens. We felt the same respect for them that one has for the saints over the altar, and the girls came and went with lowered eyes, offering wine and cookies to their young men, answering the compliments paid them in low voices and without smiling.

"I felt at home in such surroundings because I was a serious boy, an orphan accustomed to look upon life seriously. It made me happy to steal an occasional glance at my future wife and whenever she raised her eyes and looked at me, as often as her back was turned to her father and mother, it was as though the sky had opened. The kitchen with the old people, the young men and their betrothed, and the four brothers who were busy skinning a couple of goats for dinner, was like a Holy Court in the presence of God, the saints and the angels. How happy I was that evening! I have never been so happy since. I was anxiously waiting for the moment when we would return from mass, and I could present my gift to the girl and so be bound to her.

"Suddenly somebody knocked at the door. One of the brothers went to open it and came back with a stranger, a tall man with a sack over his shoulders, a twisted walking stick in his hand. I looked him over carefully as he advanced silently on soft shoes like those worn by the people of Oliano. At first glance he seemed very old, with a short white beard and light colored eyes; but then I realized that he was young, fair-haired and tired as though he had come from very far away.

"None of us knew him, and the women stared at him curiously. Everyone thought he was a friend of the father who received him with dignified cordiality.

" 'Take a seat,' he said. 'Where do you come from?'

"The stranger sat among us without removing his sack, the stick on his knees, his legs stretched out toward the fire. He looked at us, one after the other, smiling as if we were old acquaintances.

" 'I come from very far and am just passing through the village,' he said in a voice even calmer than that of my future father-in-law. 'I thought I'd step in, because I see you are having a celebration.'

" 'Yes, indeed, we are celebrating, as you can see,' my father-in-law-to-be replied. 'Our girls are engaged, and here are the young men, strong and handsome as young lions. We are in want of nothing.'

" 'Of nothing, indeed,' cried the young men, nudging each other with their elbows and laughing. The girls, after so much gravity, also burst into laughter and could not stop. I laughed, too, and so did father and mother. It was like an infectious disease. The only one who remained quiet was the stranger, looking at us like a child, neither surprised nor displeased. Then, when everybody had become serious again, he turned to the women and said:

" 'Many years ago I passed through this same village and happened, as tonight, to come to a house where there was a young engaged couple. And everybody was happy and gay as you are now. But the bride stared at me intently, and when I was about to leave she followed me to the door and said: "You are my true love. I have been waiting for you. Stay here and give me the present." I gave her the gift, and although I went away and she married another, I was her true husband. Her son will give to you young brides the gift I gave her, and you in turn will pass it on to your sons for their brides.'

"We looked at each other and weren't laughing and smiling any longer. The man seemed odd to us, almost mad. And after our merriment we almost began to fear him.

"My mother-in-law said: 'Tell us, what was thy present?'

" 'A golden crucifix.'

"At that I felt shivers run down my back. The son of the stranger's true love could only be I. I was the only one who had brought my mother's golden cross as a gift for my bride. I couldn't open my mouth. My head was whirling. I saw everything confusedly. My ears were buzzing and I couldn't hear the words exchanged between the stranger and the others. I felt a terrible pain in my heart, and a weight, a weight was breaking my back, just as if the crucifix in my pocket had suddenly become tremendously heavy and were pulling down my shoulders.

"Having warmed his feet at the fire, the stranger rose quietly. Tall and silent, his stick in his hand and the sack on his back, he opened the door and went out into the darkness.

" 'Who was he?' asked my mother-in-law.

" 'And who would know that?' answered my father-in-law. 'I never met the man, though his face seems familiar. Probably I saw him years ago when he came calling on his true love.'

"I remained silent, and once more all of us were as we had been before, serious and grave. The girls went swiftly to and fro preparing dinner; but my betrothed was pale and kept her eyes averted. No longer did she look at me. My heart was beating rapidly, and through the haze that still shrouded my head it seemed to me that the eyes of all those in the room stared at me with distrust. And thus it remained until the time came for us to go to mass. We arose, but I felt heavy and unsteady and moved as though I had drunk too much. We walked in single file, the women in front and then the men.

"When we arrived at the church the others mixed with the crowd, but I stood apart. Slowly I moved back, back to the basin with the holy water, back to the door and down the steps. At the entrance I turned my back on God's house and ran, ran as if chased by demons. I wandered among the fields like a madman until the sun rose. Then I returned to my house.

"Mother was already up. She was lighting the fire and she looked tranquil, but pale as though she hadn't slept all night. Seeing me in my dishevelled state, she thought I had been drinking and spread my straw pallet on the floor for me to lie on. Her only words were: 'A fine figure you're cutting, son!'

"I threw myself on the floor, beating my fists against the pallet. Then I got to my knees, took the crucifix out of my pocket and twisted it. The rosary snapped, and the beads scattered over the floor. It seemed they, too, were afraid of me. My mother gasped. A great lump of pity rose in my throat, and I told her everything. 'What else could I do?' I moaned. 'You were the stranger's true love. You were that woman. But how could I give your crucifix to my bride? They all looked at me as if they had guessed. I ran away from shame.'

"My mother remained silent. She gathered up the beads in her apron and began to thread them, one by one, on the rosary. She waited until I had calmed down. Then she said:

" 'Why couldn't the two other young men have been the sons of the stranger's beloved?'

" 'Because they had gold coins to give to their brides, and not golden crucifixes,' I replied.

" 'The gold coins also have crosses on them,' she replied. 'Listen to me. That stranger comes to the house of each bride, giving her a cross to bear. Do you think that last night the three young girls did not go out after him? Yes, and he gave each one of them a cross, and their sons will be his sons. How simple you are! Don't you believe in God? Yes, you do believe in God and in Jesus, and you know that Jesus is not dead. He is alive. He is in this world with us, and he enters the homes of those who are charitable, to bless and multiply their loaves of bread. He blesses and turns into sweet wine the water for those of good heart. And to all brides he gives a crucifix, a golden one, but always a cross. He was that stranger and you simpleton, you didn't recognize him.'

"So," the old man said, finishing his story, "the crucifix remained my own."

POLAND

Christmas Lullaby

TRADITIONAL

Lu-la-jże Je-su-niu mo-ja per — et-ko,

Lu — laj.... u — lu-bi-one moj pieś-ci-det-ko.

REFRAIN

Lu-la-jże... Je-zu-niu.. lu-la-jże lu-laj,

A ty.. go ma-lu-lu wpła-czu u — tu-laj.

Hush-a-bye, Baby, my heart's loveliest treasure,
Hush-a-bye, Jesus, sweet beyond measure,
Hush, and Thy mother will sooth all Thy sorrow,
Baby will smile on us all of tomorrow.

Winter

LADISLAS REYMONT
(Translated by M. H. Dziewicki)

SINCE DAYBREAK on Christmas Eve, the whole village was in a state of feverish excitement and bustling activity.

It had again frozen during the night, and as the frost came after a couple of mild days and damp fogs, the trees were all covered over with a moss-like growth of glassy crystals. The sun had come out of the clouds, and shone in a clear blue sky, with only the thinnest and most transparent veil of haze; but it shone palely, coldly, like the Host in the Monstrance, warming nothing. The frost had grown harder as the day advanced, and of such severity and penetration that it almost took the breath away, and raised a cloud of condensed vapor round every living being. Yet the world was steeped in bright sunshine, and radiant with glittering splendor; on every side the sparkling snow seemed oversprinkled with a dew of diamond-like scintillation. The surrounding fields, buried under their white pall, lay refulgent, but dead. Now and then a bird passed, flapping over their pure expanse, while its black shadow glided along the ground below; or a covey of partridges clucked amongst the snow-laden bushes, with timorous watchfulness and stealth, drawing near to the dwellings of men and their cornstacks

Reprinted from *The Peasants* by Ladislas Reymont, translated by Michael H. Dziewicki, by permission of Alfred A. Knopf, Inc. Copyright 1924, 1925, by Alfred A. Knopf, Inc.

crammed with grain. Elsewhere a hare would show its dark form, leaping through the drifts, or standing on its hind legs, or gnawing to get at the garnered corn, but—alarmed by the barking of the dogs,—scamper back to the great forest, where every tree was tufted with hoar-frost.

A keen piercing cold, luminous with glacial sheen, now shimmered over the whole world, and plunged it in ice-bound stillness.

Not a single cry broke the hard silence of the countryside, no living voice resounded, no breath of wind whispered amongst those glistening arid fields of snow. Only at rare intervals, from the roads half buried in the drifts, did faint-voiced bells and the stridulous creaking of a sledge strike the ear, so feeble and so far off that they were all but inaudible, and no one could tell whence it came or whither it went, ere the sound again faded into utter silence.

But all along the Lipka roads, on either side of the pond, the folk were noisy and swarming. The air itself wafted something of festive joy, and the people, nay, even the cattle, were full of the same. Through the frozen air that carried sound so well, there floated cries like musical tunes; laughter out of many a merry throat echoed from one end of the hamlet to the other, awakening like gaiety of heart; dogs rolled madly about on the snow, and bayed with glee, and pursued the crows that hung about the cabins; horses whinnied in unseen stalls; and cows in their byres bellowed tunefully. One might almost fancy that the snow crackled more crisply and briskly underfoot, while the sledge-runners sounded sharp along the hardened and glass-smooth roads, and the smoke went up in blue pillars straight as arrows, and the cabin-windows winked in the sun till they fairly dazzled you. Noisy children were all about, and the hum of talk was heard, and the cackling of geese that swam about in the holes made in the ice; and people were calling, calling to one another. On the roads, round about the homesteads and their belongings, folk were passing everywhere; and through the snow-whitened orchards gleamed the red petticoats of women going from hut to hut and, as they went and grazed the trees or shrubs, receiving a shower of silvery dust.

On this day, even the mill did not clatter. Indeed, it was silent during the whole festival; but a pellucid ice-cold stream, led out by the sluices, ran with babbling melody; and beyond this, somewhere far away, the cries of a flock of wild ducks, wheeling in the air, arose from marshes and moors.

Every cabin—Machek's, Simon's, the Voyt's, and who can say how many more?—was now being aired and scoured and scrubbed, and the rooms, the passages, and even the snow in front of the huts, were strewn with fresh pine-needles; in some dwellings the hearths, grown black and dingy, had also been whitewashed. In all the huts they were busy making bread, especially the *strucle,* or wheaten bread, with poppy-seed-sprinkled crust; and this seed was also being pounded in mortars for other much-liked dainties.

Yes, Yule-tide was at hand: the feast of the Divine Child, the joyful day of wondrous goodwill to men; the blessed respite from the long never-ending round of labor, to arouse the souls of men from their wintry torpor, and shake off the gray dullness of everyday life, and make them go forward joyfully and with a glad thrill of the heart, to meet the day of our Lord's Nativity.

At Boryna's, too, the same activity, and quick going to and fro, and bustling preparation, prevailed as elsewhere.

Boryna himself had been in town since the morning, to make purchases. Pete, a man whom he had taken as groom after Kuba's death, accompanied him.

They all were very busy inside the cabin. Yuzka, humming a tune, was cutting out of colored paper some of those curious figures which they stick for decoration either on the beams or on the picture-frames, making them look as if painted in brilliant colors. Yagna, her sleeves turned up almost to her shoulders, was kneading in the trough with her mother's aid; now preparing the long *strucle,* and loaves of the finest flour (she was hurrying, for the dough had already risen, and she had to fashion the loaves instantly); now casting an eye on Yuzka's work; now seeing to the honey-and-cheese-cakes, that were rising under warm coverings, and awaiting their turn for the baking-oven; and now flying round to where the fire roared up the chimney.

Vitek had been ordered to see to the fire and keep it well fed with logs; but they had seen him only at breakfast: afterwards, where was he?—Both Yagna and Dominikova looked for him about the premises, and called him, but in vain; he never answered. The naughty lad was away beyond the haystack, out in the fields, under the bushes where he was setting snares to catch partridges, and covering these over with thick layers of chaff, both to conceal them, and as a bait. Lapa accompanied him, and also Bociek, the stork that he had taken care of, and healed, and fed, and taught a number of tricks, and made such a friend of that he had only to whistle in a peculiar manner for it to come to him as obediently as Lapa—with whom, besides, it got on in perfect harmony, and they used to hunt rats together in the stable.

Roch, whom Boryna had taken to his home for the holidays, had been and was still in church, where, in company with Ambrose, he had spent the morning decorating the altar and the walls with pine-branches that the priest's servant brought to them.

It was near noon when Yagna had finished kneading all the loaves, and was now placing them on a board, patting them into shape, and daubing them over with white of egg, lest they should crack in the oven. Just then Vitek came in, crying out: "They are bringing us the Kolendy!"

Since early dawn, Yanek, the organist's eldest son—the one who was at school—had been taking altar-breads round, in company with his younger brother.

When they came in, and said: "Praised be Jesus Christ!" Yagna turned and saw them.

She was greatly confused at the room being in such disorder and, hiding her bare arms beneath her apron, asked them to sit down and rest, as they had heavy baskets, and the younger one bore several packages besides.

They said they could not. "We have still to go over half the village, and but little time for that."

"At least stay awhile, Mr. Yanek, and warm yourself: it is so bitterly cold!"

"And," Dominikova proposed, "perhaps you will both take a little hot milk."

They made excuses, but at last rested themselves close to the window. Yanek was unable to take his eyes off Yagna, till she hurriedly pulled her sleeves down over her arms: at which he turned crimson like a beet-root, and fumbled in his basket for the altar-breads. He took out the finest and largest packet, in a gilt paper wrapper, and containing several colored wafers, also shaped like altar-breads. Yagna, holding her hands under her apron, took the packet, laid it on a plate beneath the crucifix, and then brought him a good gallon measure of linseed, and six eggs.

"Have you been back here long, Mr. Yanek?"

"Only three days: since Sunday."

"Is not that book-learning a very tedious thing?" Dominikova inquired.

"Not very; but then it is only to last till spring."

"Your mother told me—I remember 'twas on my wedding-day—you were going to prepare for the priesthood."

"Yes, I—I am.—After Eastertide," he answered, in a low tone and with downcast eyes.

"Lord, what a consolation that will be to your parents! To have a priest in the family! And what an honor to the parish!"

"Have you any news?"

"None; and that is good news. Everything goes on quietly with us, as is usual amongst farmers."

"Yagna, I should willingly have come over for your wedding, but they would not let me."

"Oh," Yuzka exclaimed, "what a merry-making that was! Why, there was dancing for three days running!"

"Kuba died then, I am told."

"Yes, he did, poor wretch! Lost so much blood, he passed

away before the priest came to shrive him. They say in the village that his soul is doing penance—that there is now some creature wandering about and groaning by night along the ways and where four roads meet, and hard by crosses, waiting for God to have mercy on it. It must be Kuba's soul: whose else?"

"What is this you say?"

"Naught but the truth. I myself have seen nothing, and so cannot swear to it. But there may be things in the world that man's mind is unable to see through, no matter how keen. For these are the works of God, not of man."

"I am sorry Kuba died. The priest himself wept when he told me."

"A most upright servant he was: quiet, religious, hard-working, never taking what was not his, and always ready to share his last garment with a poor man."

"Continual changes in Lipka. Every time I come back here, I find things quite altered.—I was at Antek's to-day. His children are ill, misery is knocking at their door, and he himself is so changed, so thin, I hardly knew him."

To these words there was no answer. Yagna quickly turned her face away, and set about putting the loaves on the shovel, whilst her mother darted him such a glance that he felt he had touched on an unpleasant subject. With a wish to mend matters, he was seeking to start another, when Yuzka addressed him with a blush, and asked for some of his colored wafers.

"I want them for the 'globes' we hang up. We had some from last year, but they were quite spoiled in the racket of the wedding-feast."

Certainly he would; and he gave her more than a dozen, of five different tints.

"So many! O Lord! I shall have enough to make not only 'globes,' but 'moons' too, and 'stars'!" she cried in great glee. Yagna whispered to her, and she came, blushing, her apron over her face, to offer him six more eggs in return for his gift.

Boryna had meanwhile returned, and came in, Lapa and Bociek following him, along with Vitek.

"Shut the door this instant," cried Dominikova, "or the cakes will get cold!"

"When women set to putting things in order," Boryna said jocosely, as he warmed his freezing hands, "men must seek lodgings, even at the tavern. The road was like glass, the sledge ran splendidly, but it was so cold we were nearly frozen in our seats.—Yagna, give Pete something to eat. He has been nigh freezing to the marrow in his soldier's greatcoat.—Tell me, Yanek, are you home for long?"

"Till Twelfth Night."

"You must be a great help to your father, both at the organ and in his office. It is so cold, he can hardly wish to leave his warm bed, now that he is getting on in years!"

"But that's not why he did not come to you himself: our cow has calved to-day, and he is forced to stay and tend her."

"That's good for you: you will have milk all the winter through."

"How now, Vitek, have you watered the colt?"

"I have myself," said Yagna, "but it would not drink at all, only frisked about; and it teased the mare so, I had to take it away to the biggest stall."

Yanek and his brother took their leave, but the former had his eyes fixed on Yagna to the very last: he saw she was still more lovely than in autumn, when yet unmarried.

It was therefore no wonder that she had so completely overcome her old husband, who could see nothing in the world but her. They said truly in the village that his love had made a dotard of him. Hard and unyielding as he was to everyone else, Yagna could do with him whatever she pleased; he obeyed her in everything, saw things only through her eyes, and took her advice, and her mother's too. Nor had he any reason to regret the results. His farm was in good order, everything prospered, he had every comfort, someone to complain to and talk things over with; and his only care in the world was now Yagna, to whom he cast up his eyes as to some holy image.

Even now, whilst warming himself by the fire, he looked lovingly in her direction, and had ready, just as before the wedding, sweet affectionate words for her; all his thoughts were to give her pleasure.

Yagna, indeed, cared as much for his love as for last year's snow. Just now she was moody, and out of patience with his transports of tenderness. Everything harried her, and she went about, angry and cold as a February wind, throwing work on her mother, or on Yuzka, and spurring her husband himself to exertions by some sharp word: she herself went to the other lodgings, she said, to see about the stove, and to the stable to tend the colt; but, in reality, to be alone and think of Antek.

For Yanek had reminded her of him, and now Antek was as present to her mind's eye as if he were there before her in the flesh. During hard upon three months she had seen nothing of him—except that once, when she was driving out along the Poplar-road. Yes, time had flowed by like a river: the wedding, the home-coming, her various occupations and the cares of her household duties, had left her no time to think of him. Out of sight, out of mind; and her acquaintances had avoided all mention of his name. And now, she knew not why, he had surged up suddenly before her with so sad and reproachful a look that her very soul within her was shaken and distressed.— "I have done no harm to you," she said within herself; "why, then, are you haunting me thus, like a spectre, like a ghost?" And she attempted to wrestle with her memories of the past. She marvelled why his figure alone came back to her so—not Matthew's, not Staho Ploshka's, not any of the others—only his! Had he given her a love-charm that was now putting her beside herself, and tormenting her with the pangs that she felt?

"What is he doing now, poor fellow? what is he thinking of? . . . And there is no means of having speech with him, none!— Certainly, it is a grievous sin.— Dear Jesus! It is a thing forbidden; so the priest told me in confession.— Oh, but if I could only speak to him once more—speak even in presence of a third person!— No, no: never, never, never! . . . I am Boryna's until death!"

"Yagna!" her mother called; "do come: we have to take the loaves out."

She ran back to the house, hurrying and bustling, and seeking to forget. But in vain: everywhere she saw his eyes, and those black overshadowing brows of his—and those red, red lips . . . how ravenously eager, and how sweet!

She set to work with feverish activity, putting the place in order; and in the evening she went to the byre, a place she scarcely ever visited. But all would not do. He was always there —there before her.—A great craving arose within her, tearing her heart to shreds; and her soul was so sorely tempest-tossed that she at last came to Yuzka, sedulously at work making "globes," and, sitting down upon the chest by her side, burst into a passion of tears.

Her mother and her husband were alarmed and sought to calm her; they tried to soothe her as one soothes a spoiled child; they caressed her, they looked lovingly into her eyes: all was of no avail. She cried till she could cry no longer. And then, suddenly, she felt a change and, rising from her seat in a strange humor of merriment, began to talk and laugh, and almost burst into song.

Boryna stared at her in wonder, and so did her mother. Then they exchanged glances full of meaning, and went out to whisper together in the passage. They came back gay and joyful, and embraced and kissed her with the most tender affection.

"Do not lift that kneading-trough!" exclaimed Dominikova earnestly; "you must not. Matthias will do that for you!"

"Why, I have often lifted and carried many a heavier thing!" She did not understand.

Boryna would not let her touch the trough; he carried it himself. And a little later, when she was in the bedroom, he took the opportunity of taking her in his arms and telling her something that Yuzka was not to hear.

"Both mother's head and yours are turned! What you suppose is not the case: you are both wrong."

"These are things that we know something about, and there is no mistake here.—Let me see. It is Yule-tide now. . . . Then—then it will be only in July.—Dear, dear! in harvest-time!—Yet let us thank God that it has come to pass in any case." He

would have embraced her again, but she shrank away from him
in a temper, and ran to her mother to protest. The old dame,
however, asserted that there was no mistake.

"There is, there is! 'tis naught but your fancy!" Yagna cried
in hot denial.

"You are not glad of this, it seems?"

"And why should I be glad? Have we not enough troubles,
without this too thrown in?"

"Do not complain, or the Lord will punish you!"

"Let Him, let Him!"

"But what have you to complain of?"

"That I do not wish it: that is all!"

"Look, Yagna: if you have a child, then, in the case of your
husband's death (which Heaven forfend!) it would have an
equal part with the other children as his heir; and possibly all
the land might come to it in the end. . . ."

"Land, land, land! Ye think of naught else; and to me it is
naught!"

"Because you're as yet a silly child, and your head is full of
nonsense. A man without land is like a man without legs: he
crawls about and cannot get anywhere.—But, at any rate, say
nothing of this to Matthias; it would vex him."

"I shall say whatever I like. What do I care for him?"

"Then do so, if you are such a fool; yes, tell everybody about
it!—Go rather, set to work; take the herrings out of the water
to soak them in milk; it will make them less salt. And tell
Yuzka to pound some more poppy-seed; there is yet much
work, and the day is far spent."

So it was. Evening approached, the sun had sunk behind the
forest; its setting glow stretched along the sky in blood-red
streaks, and all the snows were fiery and as if over-sprinkled
with live coals. The hamlet had quieted down. Folk were still
fetching water from the pond, and chopping firewood; at times
sledges went past like a whirlwind, men ran across the pond,
gates creaked on their hinges, and voices were heard here and
there; but the movement was slowing down as the fires of sun-
set died out: with the pallid livid hues now overspreading the

plain, the quiet also spread, the land sank to rest, and the ways had fewer and fewer passers-by. The far-off fields now lost in murky darkness, the winter evening reigned over the country; the cold increased, the snow crackled louder underfoot, and all the panes were embellished with frost-patterns and fantastic traceries.

Slowly the village was vanishing in gray snowy shadows, melting away; neither huts nor fences nor orchards could be made out; only a few lights twinkled, more thick than usual, because everyone was busy preparing the meal of Christmas Eve.

In every cabin, from the richest to the very poorest of all, preparations were being zealously made; in each family room, at the corner next the east, they had placed a sheaf of corn; the tables were strewn with hay beneath bleached linen napery; and they looked out eagerly through the windows for the appearance of the first star.

The sky, as is often the case when it freezes, was not very clear when evening began to fall; it had seemed to veil itself as soon as the last glow had burned out, and was hidden in the gloom of many a dusky wreath.

Yuzka and Vitek, terribly chilled, were standing outside the porch, on the watch for the appearance of the first star.

"There it is!" Vitek suddenly exclaimed. "There it is!"

Boryna and the others, and Roch last of them all, came out to see.

Yes, it was there, and just in the east, having pierced through the sombre curtains which hung round about it: it shone forth from the dark-blue depths, and seemed to grow larger as they gazed upon it; gleaming brighter and brighter, nearer and nearer, till Roch knelt down in the snow, and the others after him.

"Lo, 'tis the star of the Three Wise Men," he said; "the Star of Bethlehem, in whose gleaming our Lord was born.—Blessed be His Holy Name!"

These words they piously repeated after him, gazing up with eager eyes at the bright far-off witness of the miraculous Birth —the visible token of God's mercy, visiting the world.

Their hearts throbbed with tender gratitude and glowing faith, while they received and absorbed into their hearts that pure light, the sacred fire—the sacrament to fight with and to overcome all evil!

And the star, seeming to grow larger still, rose up like a ball of fire, from which beams of azure brightness shot down like the spokes of a mystic wheel, darting its rays upon the snows, and twinkling with radiant victory over darkness. Then after it there came forth other stars, its faithful attendants, peering out in innumerably dense multitudes—filling all the heavens, covering them with a dew of light, and making them, as it were, a mantle of dark azure, strewn with silver motes.

"And now that the Word is made Flesh," said Roch, "it is time to take our meal."

They went in, and took seats for supper at a high long bench.

Boryna occupied the first place, then Dominikova and her sons (for they had arranged to eat together); Roch sat in the middle, Pete, Vitek, and Yuzka after him, and Yagna at the very end; for she had to see about the service.

The family room was now in utter and solemn silence.

Boryna, having made the sign of the Cross, divided an altar-bread with each of those present, and all partook of it with reverence, as representing the Bread of Life.

"Christ," then said Roch, "was born at this hour; therefore let every creature feed upon this holy bread!"

And though they had eaten all day long only a little dry bread, and were very hungry, they all ate slowly and with due decorum.

The first dish consisted of sour beet-root soup, with mushrooms and potatoes in it. After this came herrings, rolled in flour and fried in oil. Then there was a dish of cabbage and mushrooms, also seasoned with oil. And, to crown the feast, Yagna had prepared a most dainty dish—buckwheat meal, mixed with honey and fried in oil of poppy-seed! With all these dishes, they ate common dry bread: it was not becoming, on such a great fast-day, to eat either cakes or *strucle,* these containing butter or milk.

They ate for a considerable time, and there was but little conversation; only spoons clattered and lips were smacked. Boryna wanted to get up and help Yagna, but her mother would not have it.

"Let her be," she said; "it will do her no harm. 'Tis the first Yule-tide at which she presides; she must learn and accustom herself."

Lapa, whimpering at times, was poking its head against thighs and knees, fawning and wagging its tail, in hope of getting sooner fed. Bociek the stork, whose place was in the passage, ever and anon pecked at the wall, or uttered its *klek-klek-klek*, to which the hens at roost responded.

The meal was not over yet, when someone tapped at the window.

Dominikova cried out: "Let no one in, no, nor even look that way! It is the Evil One: he will enter, and then stay here all the year round!"

The spoons dropped, and they listened in dismay, as the tapping was repeated.

"It is Kuba's soul!" Yuzka whispered.

"Say no foolish things: someone in need is there. On this day, none should suffer hunger, or be without a roof over him." So saying, Roch got up and opened the door.

It was Yagustynka, standing humbly on the threshold, who wept abundantly, and begged to be let in.

"Oh, give me but a corner, and what you leave your dog! Have pity on a poor old woman! . . . I was waiting for my children to ask me; I waited in vain, starved with cold in my hut. . . . O Lord! I am now a beggar-woman; and they leave me here, forlorn, without a morsel of bread—worse off than a dog! . . . And their cabin is full of people and of noise. I crept thither, looked round the corner and in at the window. . . . It was all of no use."

"Well, sit ye down with us. Better had it been to come when evening fell, and not expect favors from your children.—They will rejoice when they drive a last nail into your coffin, to make sure you will not come back to them." Thus Boryna spoke, and very kindly made a place for her by his side.

But she was unable to eat anything, however heartily Yagna, the least stingy of housewives, pressed her to take some food. It was impossible; she sat drooping, bent, crouching, taciturn, her trembling body showing how much she suffered.

The place was now cozy and quiet, pervaded by an atmosphere of kindliness and of solemn piety, as if the Holy Child were lying in the midst of them.

A huge fire, continually supplied with fresh fuel, was droning up the chimney, lighting the whole apartment; against its blaze the glazed images shone dazzlingly, the panes loomed black in the night. And now they seated themselves in front of the fire, on the long bench, and talked together in hushed and serious tones.

Presently Yagna made coffee, with plenty of sugar in it, which they sipped at leisure.

After a pause, Roch took out a book, round which he had wound his rosary, and began to read to them in a low voice that was full of deep emotion:

"Lo, a new thing hath come to pass to-day: a Virgin hath brought forth a Son: our Lord hath in the town of Bethlehem, not least of Judah's cities, entered this our world in poverty, within a wretched byre, on hay, amongst the cattle, which were all His brethren on this night. And that same star, which now is gleaming, gleamed upon the Child, showing the way unto the Three Wise Men: who, albeit black and heathens, yet were kind of heart, and came from far-off lands, across wide rolling seas with gifts; and thus bore witness to the Truth. . . ."

He continued reading a long time and his voice took the intonations of a prayer, almost of a chant or the singing of some holy litany. They listened to him in pious stillness, their souls silent and attentive, their hearts thrilling under the fascination of the miraculous, with the sincerest gratitude to God for the favors conferred upon them.

"Ah, sweet Jesus! Didst Thou then deign to be born in a stable, in that far-off country, amongst cruel heretics—and in

such poverty—and in such wintry frost! O poor, poor Holy One,
O sweet Child!"—Such were their thoughts, and their bosoms
throbbed with pity, and their souls flew away like birds, over
land and sea, to the place of the Nativity, to the Manger and
the Crib over which the Angels sang—and to the Sacred Feet of
the Child Jesus. There they fell, with all the might of their
fiery faith and trust in Him; and they surrendered themselves
to Him—His faithful servants for ever and ever. Amen!

As Roch went on reading, Yuzka, who was a good, kind, im-
pressionable girl, fell to weeping copiously over our Lord's unhappy lot. Yagna, too, wept with her face in her hands and her
head hidden behind Andrew, who was listening close by, with
mouth wide open, and so greatly struck by what he heard, that
he repeatedly pulled Simon by his sleeve, saying: "Lo! do you
hear that, Simon?"

When it was over, some remarks were dropped:

"Poor Child! not even a cradle!"

"I marvel that He did not freeze."

"And that our Lord was willing to bear so much pain."

"Because," Roch answered, "it was only by His sufferings
and sacrifice that He could save His people: which had He not
done, Satan would assuredly have been master of the world and
lord of every soul."

"Of this and these he is pretty much master and lord as it
is," Yagustynka muttered.

"Sin is master, wickedness lord; and these are the helpers of
Satan."

"Ah, well, whosoever it may be, one thing is sure: an ill fate
has power over man."

"Speak not thus, lest ye sin: ye are blinded by wrath against
your children."

The rebuke was stern, and she did not dispute its justice.
The others also were silent, and Simon rose to withdraw; but
his mother, attentive to everything, noticed him.

"Wither away so fast?" she hissed.

"Out—I feel too hot in here," he faltered, taken aback.

"Going to Nastka—to divert yourself, hey?"

"Would ye forbid, or hold me back?" he growled, but threw his cap back on to the chest where it had been.

"Return with Andrew to our hut: we have left the place to the care of Providence. See to the kine, and stay there for me; when I have rejoined you, we shall all go together to church." These were her orders; but as the lads were slow to obey, she did not repeat them; rising at once, she took an altar-bread from the table.

"Vitek, light the lantern; we are going to the kine. In this Yule-tide night, all the animals understand what men say, because our Lord was born in their midst. And whosoever shall, being without sin, speak unto them then, him will they answer with a human voice: this day they are the equals of man, and they are our fellows. And therefore we shall go and share the altar-bread with them."

All made for the byre, Vitek leading, lantern in hand.

The cows were lying in a row, leisurely chewing the cud; but the approach of the lantern and the voices caused them to snort and scramble heavily to their feet, turning their great heads away from the light.

"You, Yagna, are mistress here; it is yours to divide this bread amongst them: so will they thrive and not take any sickness. But let them not be milked till to-morrow evening, or they will give no more milk at all."

Yagna broke an altar-bread into five pieces, made the sign of the cross over each cow between her horns, and laid the thin bit of wafer upon her broad rough tongue.

Yuzka wanted to know whether the horses were also to get their share of the bread.

"It must not be; there were no horses in the byre where Christ was born."

When they had returned, Roch spoke thus:

"Every being, every meanest blade of grass, every little pebble, nay, even the star that is all but unseen to the eye—everything feels to-day, everything knows that the Lord is born."

"My God!" Yagna exclaimed. "What! even clods and stones?"

"I speak sooth: it is so. Everything has its soul. All beings in the world have feeling, and await the hour when Jesus, taking pity on them, shall say:

"'Awake, O soul, and live, and merit Heaven!'—Yes, and the tiniest worm, the swaying grass even, can after its fashion have merit, and praise the Lord in its own way. . . . And to-night, of all nights in the year, they all rise up, full of life, and listen, waiting for His Word!

"And to some it comes now, but to others not yet: they lie patient in the dark, expecting the dawn; stones, waterdrops, clods, trees, and whatever God has appointed each of them to be!"

Mute, they all pondered over the words he said; for he had spoken, and in sapient wise, and words which touched the heart. Yet both Boryna and Dominikova had doubts as to the truth of these; and, much as they turned them over and over in their minds, they could not clear up the matter. For, though God's Omnipotence was indeed marvelous and beyond all thought, still—that everything should have a soul!—this was what they could not grasp. But now, the smith having come in with his family, they set these thoughts aside.

"We shall sit up with you, Father, and then go together to midnight mass," he said.

"Sit down," said Boryna; "it will be more pleasant with you. We shall be all together, save for Gregory."

Yuzka looked indignantly at her father, for she thought of Antek: but she durst not say anything.

Once more they took their seats on benches by the fire; but Pete went out into the yard to chop fire-wood against the coming great Day of Rest, Vitek taking the chopped wood in his arms and piling it up in the passage.

"Ah! but I had forgotten!" cried the smith. "The Voyt ran and asked me to tell Dominikova she was to come at once; for his wife is in travail and screams so that she is likely to be confined this very night."

"I would have liked to go to church with you all; but since you say she screams, I must look in."

Having whispered with the smith's wife, she hastened away,

for she was an expert in these matters, and to many had done more good than the doctors.

Various legends relating to the day were told by Roch: one of them was as follows:

"Long ago—as many years back as from now to Christ's Birth —a certain wealthy husbandman was walking home from market, where he had sold a couple of fatted calves, and had the money concealed in one of his boots. He bore a stout cudgel and was stout himself—perhaps the strongest fellow in his village. But he was in a hurry to get home ere nightfall, because in those days thieves used to hide in the woods and waylay true men.

"This must have been in summer, for the greenwood was fragrant and resounded with many a sweet song; a mighty wind rocked the trees, and there was an uproarious rustling overhead. Now, therefore, the man went along in haste, looking around him and fearing. But he saw only young and old pines and oaks standing side by side, and never a living soul. Yet he feared, for he was approaching a cross, and close by was so dense a thicket, the eye could not see to pierce it: there thieves were mostly wont to hide. So he crossed himself and, saying prayers in a loud voice, ran on as fast as he could.

"He had without hurt passed out of the wood of tall trees, and had gone through the undergrowth of dwarf pines and of juniper-bushes. Already he could see the green of the open country, hear the streamlets babbling and gurgling along and the lark singing on high; and he noted men ploughing and flocks of storks winging their way over the marshes; nay, he had even caught the scent of the cherry-orchards in blossom: when out of the last of the thickets the robbers came leaping upon him! They were twelve, all armed with knives. Bravely he fought, and though they soon overpowered him, he would not give up his money, and shrieked for help. So they threw him down, put their knees on his chest, and were going to slay him. Suddenly, they were all struck motionless, and remained so— bending over him, knives in air, full of rage, but, as it were, turned to stone!—And at that same instant all things around also became still as death. The birds, silent, floated moveless in air—the streams rested—the sun rolled on no more—the wind fell dead—the trees remained as they were bent by the wind—and the corn also. And the storks seemed fixed in the sky, with outstretched wings . . . and the ploughman remained with whip raised over his horse where it stood . . . and the whole region, as if terror-struck, became immobile like a picture.

"How long this lasted, none can tell, but it endured until men heard upon earth the Angels' chant:

'Christ comes: fear Him, O ye Mighty!'

when immediately all things began to move again. But the thieves took the warning given them by this prodigy, and released their victim; and they went together, following the voices they heard, to the stable; there they paid homage to the new-born Babe, along with all the creatures which lived on earth or in air."

They wondered much at the legend told them; but presently Boryna and the smith began to talk of other matters.

After a time, too, Yagustynka, who had all the time sat silent, spoke out, and with no pleasant words.

"Oh, ye talk, ye talk, ye talk: and wherefore, but only to make time pass? Were it true that of old there came from heaven those who protected the wretched and saved them from the oppressor: then why do they not come now too? Is there now less of poverty, less of misery, less of torture and of pain? Man is like a poor bird, unarmed, and let loose to fly about the world. The hawk, the beasts of prey, and want of food slay it; and him Crossbones always takes in the end.—And ye prate of mercy, and feed fools with promises, deluding them and saying that salvation is at hand!—Ah, who is at hand?—Antichrist! and he will deal out justice, and He will have mercy, even as the hawk has mercy on the chickens!"

Roch started up. "Woman!" he cried in a thundering voice; "do not blaspheme! do not hearken sinfully to the whispers of the Wicked One, that will drag you down to your damnation and to everlasting fire!"—But he fell back upon the bench, and could speak no more for the sobs that choked his voice, and shuddered from head to foot with horror and with sorrow for that lost soul. And when somewhat calmer, he set the truth before her with all the power of a firm believer, striving to bring her back into the right way.

He spoke to her long—very long; and as well as a priest in the pulpit.

Meanwhile Vitek, having been greatly struck to hear that cattle possessed human speech on Christmas Eve, called Yuzka away quietly, and they went both of them to the cow-house.

Holding each other by the hands, trembling with awe, and crossing themselves more than once, they slipped in amongst the cows.

Down they knelt by the side of the largest one, that they looked on as the Mother of the Byre. Out of breath, agitated, with tears in their eyes and dread in their hearts, as if they were in church and during the Elevation—they nevertheless were upheld by strong trust and a lively faith. Vitek put his mouth to her ear, and quavered in a low voice:

"Hist! Gray One! Gray One!"

But she only gurgled inaudibly, and went on chewing with a roll of her tongue and a smack of her lips.

"Something strange has come upon her: she answers naught!"

Then they knelt by the next cow, and Vitek, who by this time was on the verge of weeping, called earnestly to her:

"Spotted One! Spotted One!"

They both approached very close to her mouth, and listened, holding their breath; but never, never a word!

"Ah! no doubt we have sinned, so we shall not hear her speak. They answer only such as are sinless; and we are sinners!"

"True, Yuzka, true! we are sinful, we have sinned. O Lord! so it is! Aye, I stole some bits of string from master once. And an old strap besides. . . . Yes, and also. . . ." He could go no farther; remorse and repentance for his faults shook the lad with a convulsion of tears and sobs; and Yuzka, following his example, wept from the bottom of her heart. They cried together, and would not be comforted till they had laid bare before each other all their "manifold sins and offences."

At home, no one remarked their absence, for all were piously singing hymns—not Christmas carols, which it was not deemed proper to strike up until after midnight.

On the other side of the house, Pete was having a wash and making a grand toilet. He had completely changed his clothes, Yagna having brought him another suit of his, that he had put by in the store-room.

But what a cry arose when he appeared before them, clad—no longer in his military cloak and gray uniform—but in the usual garb of a peasant!

"They laughed at me and nicknamed me Gray Dog," he faltered; "so I have changed my clothes."

"Change your speech, and not your garments!" Yagustynka snarled.

"That likewise he will get back, since his soul has remained Polish."

"And what marvel if he should forget something, after five years far away, never once hearing his mother-tongue spoken?"

Here they broke off their talk; the high-pitched tinkle of the mass-bell was now heard in the chamber.

"We must be off: it is ringing for the shepherd's mass!"

And in a very short time all had set out, save Yagustynka. She stayed to watch the house, and still more to loose the reins in solitude to the bitterness of her heart.

The mass-bell meantime rang, rang, rang, like the quick twitter of a bird, calling them to church.

Out of their cabins they poured; now and then a ruddy refulgence shone from the opening and closing doors, with a flash as of lightning. In some huts, the fire was put out or covered. In the dark night, as they hurried on, a voice would be heard, or a cough, and the crunching of shoes on the snow, and the holy words of mutual greeting: and on they went, deeper and deeper into the dark-gray blackness, till only their footsteps sounded in the frozen air.

From afar they now began to perceive the glowing church-windows, and the great door thrown open and pouring forth light, and the people surging in—billows on billows, slowly filling the aisle, decorated with Christmas trees of many a kind; crowded along the white walls, swarming in front of the altar, filling the pews in an ever-rising flood, rolling and undulating to and fro with the incoming human tide, which brought in along with it a fog of condensed breath-vapor, so thick that the altar-lights shone dim and scarcely seen through its folds.

And still the people came in, came in continually.

They arrived from Polne Rudki in a compact mass, great tall fellows, ponderous, yet active, all flaxen-haired, all clad in blue-black capotes; their women comely, every one of them, adorned with "double" aprons, and having for headgear caps underneath red kerchiefs.

Next came in straggling knots of twos and threes, the men of Modlitsa: poor sickly wretches, strengthless creatures, in gray patched capotes, and all bearing sticks, for they had come on foot. Of these the common tavern joke was that they lived on mud-fishes only, because their lands were miry and intersected with marshes, and their garments smelt of the peat they used for fuel.

From Vola, too, came some, by separate families, like the juniper-bushes that always grow in thick clumps and close together: none of them tall, but all of middle height, stumpy and not unlike sacks of corn, yet lively fellows: great talkers, most stubbornly litigious, given to fighting, and spoilers of the forests. They were in gray capotes, with facings of black braid, and red girdles.

There, too, was the "nobility" of Rzepki, which, as evil tongues say, "has only a bag and a bundle, one cow for five and one cap for three"; they came all in one band, taciturn, looking down and askance at everyone they met. Their womenfolk, dressed like manor-people, very much pranked out, very handsome, white of complexion and voluble of tongue, walked in their midst, and were treated by them with the utmost courtesy.

Directly after them entered the men of Przylek, tall, slender and strong as trees in a pine-forest, and so decked out as to make the eye water: white capotes, red waistcoats, shirts adorned with green ribbons, breeches striped with yellow bands; and they pushed forwards, giving way to no one, till they got quite close to the altar.

And then, almost the last of all, like so many squires, in walked the people of Debie. They were but few; each went apart from the others, strutting proudly forwards, and took his place in the pews next to the high altar, having precedence of everyone; self-confident, because wealthy. Their womenfolk carried prayer-books, and wore white caps tied under the chin, and jackets of dark-colored cloth.—And then there were also men from the more remote hamlets, from many a little cluster of huts, from sawmills, and from manors too—but who could count them all?

And in this multitude, pressed and surging and rustling like a wood in a breeze, the white capotes of the Lipka men and their women's red kerchiefs were conspicuous.

The church was full, even to the very last place in the porch, and anyone who came late had to pray outside under the trees in the cold.

Now the priest began the first mass, and the organ pealed forth, while all the people swayed to and fro, and bowed down, and knelt before the Divine Majesty.

There was a deep hush; fervent prayers went up; every eye was fixed on the priest, and on the one taper that burned high above and in the middle of the altar. The organ played soft music, fugues and harmonies so touchingly sweet that they sent a thrill to the very heart. At times the priest turned to the people with outstretched hands, uttering aloud certain sacred Latin words; and the people too extended their arms, sighing audibly, and, bending down in deep contrition, struck their breasts and prayed with fervor.

Then, when the first mass was over, the priest mounted the pulpit, spoke of the sacred festival, and exhorted them to flee all things evil: his words went to their hearts like fire, and sounded like thunder through the church. Of his hearers, some sighed, some beat their breasts; others were sharply stung by remorse,

and others again—those in particular who were of amatory dis-
position—fell a-weeping. For the priest spoke with true zeal and
eloquence, his words went straight to the heart and mind; and
however drowsy the heat in the church had made more than
one, even these could not but listen to him.

Just before the second mass, the organ pealed out again, and
the priest intoned the famous carol:

"Come to meet Him—come to greet Him!"

and the people started up from their knees as one man, with a
billowing swirl, took up the tune, and roared in unison, with
a loud blast from each man's lungs:

"Jesus in the manger laid!"

The Christmas trees vibrated and shook with the din, and the
lights flickered in the enormous volume of sound.

So united were they, in souls and faith and voices, that it
seemed as if a giant were trolling forth that tremendous chant
that rolled, carrying every heart along with it, to the sacred feet
of the Divine Child!

When the second mass was over, the organist struck up one
Christmas carol after another, and to such lively leaping meas-
ures that it was all they could do to hold back from leaping too;
but at any rate they all turned round to the organ-loft, and
shouted the words in tune and time with the music.

Antek alone was not singing with the others. He had come
with his wife and with Staho's family, but had let them go on
before him, he himself standing close to the pews. He had no
mind to take his old place among the farmers in front of the
altar, and was looking for a place somewhere else, when he perceived his father coming in with all his family, pushing forward
to the centre of the nave, with Yagna going first of them all.

He shrank back behind a young fir-tree, and thenceforward
never took his eyes off her. She sat down at the end of a pew
close to the side gangway; and he, unconsciously obeying in-
stinct, pressed forward with stubborn jostling, till he was close
to her; and when all knelt down during mass, he too knelt and
bent forward so that his head touched her knees.

She at first took no notice of him: the rushlight she was using to read by shed so faint a glimmer round, and the fir boughs concealed him so well that he could not be seen. It was only at the Elevation, when, going down on her knees, she beat her breast and bowed her head in adoration, that she happened to look in his direction—and her heart suddenly stopped beating, and she was petrified with joy.

She durst not look a second time. What she had seen was but a dream to her; a vision—a "false creation," and no more.

She closed her eyes and remained long on her knees, with head bowed down, and body bent forward—almost beside herself with excitement. At last, however, she seated herself and looked him straight in the face.

Yes, it was really he—Antek—his face very haggard and bronzed; and those eyes of his, so bold and daring, now looked into hers with such sorrowful tenderness that her heart was smitten through and through with affectionate apprehension, and the tears came to her eyes.

Like the other women there, she sat stiffly, apparently reading in her book in which she saw not a single letter, nor even the page before her. What she did see was his face—his eyes, so sad, so full of appeal, flashing, blazing, bright as stars, coming between her and the rest of the world. She felt lost and helpless —and he was kneeling by her side; and she heard his quick breath and felt it hot, and was aware of the dear, yet awful might which went forth from him, seized upon her heart, bound it to him as with cords, thrilling her at once with pleasure and dismay—with a vertiginous shuddering, and a cry for love so potent that her every limb quaked, and her heart beat wildly like some poor bird nailed in sport by the wings to a barndoor!

The second mass was now over, and the people were all singing together, and praying and sighing and weeping; but these two, as if beyond this world, heard nothing, saw nothing, thought of nothing but each other.

Dread—joy—affection—remembrance—enchantment—desire!— all these feelings alternately glowed within them, passing from one to the other, and knitting them in one, so that they felt themselves one being, and their two hearts throbbed in unison, and one fire flamed in the eyes of each.

Antek came yet a little nearer, leaned his shoulder against her hip (and a hot flush surged over her, and she was nigh to swooning); and as she knelt again, he flung these words— words that might have been brands of fire—into her ear:

"Yagna! Yagna!"

She shook, and almost fell fainting; his voice pierced her through and through with keen rapture—with a sharp-edged delight.

"Come out some evening . . . come out . . . behind the hay-stack . . . I shall be waiting there every night. . . . Fear not . . . I must speak to you. . . . 'Tis urgent.—Come." This he said in an impassioned whisper, very close to her—so close that his breath was like a flame upon her face.

She replied nothing: the words stuck in her throat. Her heart was palpitating so violently that she thought everyone near her must have heard it. But she made a gesture as if she would go that very instant where he wished, where her love was urging her . . . behind the haystack.

The church was resounding with the joyful thunder of the carols, when she came a little to her senses, and looked round at the people and the sanctuary.

Antek was there no more. He had withdrawn unnoticed, and was slowly walking out into the churchyard.

There he stood in the frost a long time, beneath the belfry, that he might cool down a little and breathe some fresh air. But his bosom was so overflowing with gladness, there was in him such an exultation, such a triumph of power, that he never even heard the chant that welled out from the open church door, nor the faint echoes which repeated it from the bells above. No, he took no heed of anything whatsoever. . . .

Seizing a handful of snow, and swallowing it greedily, he leapt over the wall and into the road—rushing away, out on to the countryside, wayward as the blast.

Portugal

The Jesus Child

TRADITIONAL

En - trae, en - trae pas-to - ri - - 'nhos, Per es - sa
por - tal sa - gra - - do; Vin - de ver o Deus Me - ni -
ni, Nu - mas pa - lhi - nhas dei - ta - do. gri - nó

Oh enter, enter dear shepherds
And come through that sacred portal
To see the Little God Jesus,
Who lies on straw though immortal.

For He has redeemed all of mankind
By coming down to this earth,
And Bethlehem, blessed be its memory,
To-night saw the Savior's birth.

The Mass of the Cock

AQUILINO RIBEIRO
(Translated by Eric Posselt)

THE GOD-CHILD was about to be born. Already pious Clarinha and her husband, João Lájeas, were building him a house with a thatch roof and a moss floor, and a crib for the donkey and the ox with the hump. For the walls they used old sheets, and around the manger they placed the shepherds on horseback, the kings with their bursting gift hampers, and all the rabble of the highways. Faithfully each year Clarinha had Glòrinhas with her skillful fingers sew a new dress for the infant, of finest Dutch linen, its little ruffled collar stiffly starched. And the Child, who was really a lump of sugar, laughed and laughed as if someone were tickling his navel. Lovingly, later on, in the soothing shadows of the Mass of the Cock, by the golden light of the candles, the padre would lift Him to be kissed, piously murmuring: *"Venite adoremus!"*

The God-child was showered with kisses, but of gifts there were none. Down in the valley He was bribed with a tray richly filled with succulent fruit and sticky sweets that was auctioned off at the plaza to whoever offered most. But in the mountains nobody gave presents since money was scarce, though the Savior welcomed the hills people just as cheerfully as if each one of them were carrying all the gold, the incense and the myrrh of the Wise Men from Egypt.

From *Terras do Demo* by Aquilino Ribeiro. Printed by permission of Livraria Bertrand, S.A.R.L., Lisbon.

Now, while the women of the house prepared Christmas Eve supper, João Lájeas kept on putting the finishing touches to the manger.

The wine cart came down from the hills and in the distance the barking of the dogs with the herds sounded as though it came from the end of the world. In obedience to the Lord and in celebration of this great day of precepts, João decided to eat less and drink more. For doesn't the Church, the holy mother and benefactor of mankind, command: Go hungry, but never, never thirsty! So, while fetching a hammer, or nails, or water to wash the dirty face of the black king, he frequently found his way to the inn.

"What bad breath you have, *Tio* João!" exclaimed the pious Clarinha, turning her nose away. "If someone put a light to your mouth, you'd flare up like a torch!"

"Now, look here, I haven't drunk too much . . . And may the Infant accept my sacrifice!"

The night came, cloaked in mist, bringing with it another turn of the wheel of time and another year as welcome, indeed, as the log crackling in the fireplace, the simmering pots and pans, as peace and good will toward men. At the next turn of the wheel, many would be truly fertilizing the earth, while others might yet have a way to go. So, fall to and eat and drink, and welcome Christmas Eve!

There was rejoicing in every home, from the most sumptuous to the most humble, from that of Padre Francisco and his sacristan, who also wore a tonsure on his head, to the lowly Rôlas. And Luis Moneta who was mad at his wife, who threatened to regale him with a stingy feast of corn pone, also went to Cláudio's store.

"Do you still have some codfish?" he asked from the doorway, in a half-hearted, sort of tentative way. His cloak was thrown over his arm and he was shoeless, as a visible sign that it wasn't the stones in the road that cost him his money.

"I've some left."

Alonzo's Zefa with the chicken neck, though otherwise fat and rosy, had brought a jug to be filled.

"Your turn," she said as she made her way out; "do you want a sip, Luis Rôla?"

"Sure enough, sure enough, seeing that you've got some."

"Go ahead, then."

"Sure enough, and good luck to you!"

Meantime, Cláudio made two chalk marks on the slate fixed to the beam where he listed his accounts.

"So you want a little fish, eh?" he said to Rôla, anxious to make a sale.

"Let's see what there is."

Cláudio put the fish on the counter and displayed them one by one. But Rôla turned up his nose; they were either too big or too small, or, in his opinion, the expense would be more than the pleasure they'd give his household.

"*Meu rico,* what I have is right here."

His eyes on the fish, Rôla kept weighing the pros and cons.

"These are monsters!" he said, scratching the nape of his neck with a ratlike claw.

"That's all there is."

"Cut me off an *arratel* and a half, or two. . . ."

"Nothing doing, that'd spoil the fish. You know I can't cut them up."

People came and people left. Glòrinhas wanted some cigarettes for her father. Claudina's Zé came rushing in on clattering wooden shoes and also wanted a fish, one of the medium ones. And then Rôla quickly selected his before she could snap it up.

"What the . . . just for once! Weigh me this elephant," he said, pointing his forefinger at the likeliest one.

"Two kilos and a quarter," declared Cláudio after an attentive and silent weighing.

"*Apre!* then it weighs more than my money. Two kilos and a quarter? How come that in this poverty stricken land of ours things never come at our terms when they come at all?!"

"Hell's bells, don't you know, the bigger they come the better they taste?"

"Listen, I've got to fill my belly cheaply!"

"Go ahead and eat horsemeat!"

Claudina's Zé broke into guffaws as Rôla, grabbing another fish, said:

"This one looks smaller."

"It may look smaller, but it isn't. And the quality is the same."

He put the fish on the scales, balanced it, counterweighed it, and finally declared that it was an ounce heavier than the first, but recommended it as bright colored, without blemish, and having firm thorny bones, the sign of an adult and well-made fish. But Rôla rejected it without blinking an eyelash since it cost a few *reis* more.

"I'll take this one," declared Claudina's Zé.

"And well served you are," Rôla remarked, expectorating. "My own purse doesn't go that far. . . . Listen, why haven't you got smaller ones for people who aren't as greedy?"

"Why be fussy? Eat whiting!" Zé rebuffed him.

"And how much is that?"

"One hundred and ten for the *arratel*—the usual price."

"*Irra!*" he said, clicking his tongue against his palate. "That's more expensive than chicken, and that's for the sick."

"And for them who like it."

"Sure enough. Nobody is forced to eat it. But since these are left-overs, you ought to give more for the price. . . ."

"Left-overs! You're mad! I've always known you were a cheapskate. Is that what you learned from the padres?"

Rôla laughed uproariously to take the sting out of Cláudio's biting words.

"They sure taught you your lesson!"

"Well, see what you can do."

"What do you mean? Pay up or shut up! I could easily get seven *vinténs* and still sell all I've got. Listen to that bird!"

"In Barrelas you get it for a *tostão* from the English."

"Go ahead and buy it from them! What's stopping you? The road is free."

"But that's way down at the port. I like to help our own people make a living."

"I'll bet you'd like to see all of us hung. You'd even pull the trap. What a beast!"

The shopkeeper shook his head violently from side to side, a sign that he was becoming annoyed.

"Well, how much will you take for two kilos and a quarter?" Rôla asked tensely, realizing that the joke had gone too far.

"The scales will tell you. Four times a hundred and ten— four hundred and forty, plus thirty *réis* for the quarter—four hundred and seventy."

"Listen, *Tio* Cláudio, in round figures, how about four hundred and forty?"

"If you want round figures, pay up five *tostões*."

"Man, and what about the change?"

"That won't kill you."

And so the whelp continued to whine and deplore this miserable life until Cláudio was so bored that he was about to throw the codfish back into the chest.

"Thirty *réis* is all I make. And you, a man who went to school, trying to squeeze the gizzards out of me. Shame on you!" Finally he let him have the codfish out of sheer embarrassment.

"Do use it carefully," Rôla said to his wife when he brought it home. "That ought to last until Lent."

"Divide it yourself, by the soul of the Lord!"

"Go on, take the tail and two hind pieces. That makes six *arráteis* . . . and keep your eye on Bispo!"

Florinda prepared a portion with chopped colewort, wheat dumplings, stewed onions, oil and a touch of garlic—a dish fit for a new born babe. From the rest she made fish balls with sauce and potatoes and seasoned them with vinegar—enough to make a saint break his fast. With the result she filled two earthen porringers, one for herself, the other for her mother and Bispo. And thus, in the light of the burning log in the fireplace, began for them the feast of the Good Night.

The wind howled outside the door like a pack of hounds racing after the dead leaves around the cornice of the roof. From the stand of pines near the cemetery came a whining so high pitched, so furious, that the lamentations of the damned in hell coming from the open pit must sound like it. Heavy rain squalls drenched the roofs. The water dripping from the eaves played a dolorous and bored ping-ping on the stones and the drying-racks outside. The river in the skies came down upon the houses so ruthlessly as if the world were to be drowned, little by little; and in this onslaught of destruction, time tumbled noiselessly into the bottomless abyss.

Some years bring snow, clothing the earth in white and celebrating the coming of the Savior in purity and innocence. In the sunshine the snowy traceries shine brighter than the ancient high altar with the candles all aglow at the *salutaris*. On the threshing floors hungry birds look among the straw for the grains that have escaped the hands of the threshers and send up to God their *kyries* that sound like chirping only to heretics. In the homes the wheel keeps on turning, and Safardinho who digs graves for the dead now plays gay tunes for the living.

With the storm still growling over the mountain ranges and the snow covering peaks and dales with kerchiefs of white linen, at the hour when Our Lady writhes in the pangs of childbirth, there is the age-old roar in the crackling log in the house of the Gaudêncios. Let winter do its worst: the walls are secure and the log comes from the old chestnut tree that once gave shade and shelter, which Gaudêncio had felled. Thus even the consumption of the codfish feast becomes a song to heaven.

But it didn't last long. For Rôla and his wife were hardly half through their meal when Bispo and the old woman were already licking up the gravy on their plates with pieces of bread.

"You seem to be hungry as wolves," growled Rôla to the tune of their smacking.

"Here comes the fish tail," Florinda announced, ladling out a second portion. "And don't you say we are starving you to death!"

The old woman speared, Bispo speared, and both began to fight like two dogs over a single bone. Luis Rôla broke into loud guffaws.

"Don't fight, you two!" he said. "Take my portion. I've had

my fill." He acted as though he wanted to push his plate in their direction.

With greedy eyes Bispo stretched out his paw; but the old woman who seemed to be less eager and apparently content with what she had, suddenly snatched the plate from under his nose and gorged herself on what was left.

"Mil diabos!" her son complained when he saw himself cheated out of his share. "All you have to do is to turn your head, and you're already robbed!"

Rôla laughed and guzzled. His mother had sent him a pitcher of wine from her vineyard that tickled the gullet. He swallowed, and swallowed again, leaving hardly a drop for Bispo whose glances could have killed him.

"Don't drink all of it!" he exclaimed, raising his arms in protestation.

Now Florinda put the codfish balls in front of her husband and doled out one each to her mother and her brother. Then she wanted to know:

"You tell me whether anyone else has had such a feast! Not even our *Tio* Padre, no matter how much money he makes with his chanting!"

Dying to leave, for at this hour the village lads went out looking for wood for the bonfire on the Square of St. João, Bispo got up.

"The prayers come first!" his brother-in-law barked at him.

"But the boys will go and cut in our pine stand at Corgas!"

"Let them! At such an occasion not even I could stop them, nor will little you who is nothing but an ass. Let them cut where they want to."

Rôla stuck out his feet toward the brazier, the old woman reached for her distaff, and the ensuing silence was interrupted only by the roar of the wind and the clatter of the pots and pans under Florinda's nimble hands.

"There's just one thing missing to make this feast complete," Rôla remarked.

"I know, the pancakes; but eggs are too expensive. . . ."

"Not that. . . ."

Florinda understood; they all understood. And like crawling maggots their most secret and most intimate thoughts crept on.

"What's missing is that this old woman give us the money she has scratched together."

"The devil take you, that red-headed woman simply wants to hoard it!"

"Forty pounds would make a nice little pile!"

"Go get it from your father who keeps on robbing the world!"

"She's got it, that much is certain. Perhaps she even showed it to Jaime. But where is it?"

"Jaime has seen nothing but lice and bedbugs—of all things God has cursed us. *Boca-rota!* That's the way God helps them. He went to Rio. Alonso is the one who says. . . ."

While these thieving thoughts flitted mutely from one to the other, Rôla kicked the brazier in helpless rage, folded his hands and prayed:

"We thank Thee, oh Lord, for Thy great gifts. P.N. and Av.M."

His voice was hoarse and his face showed plainly that his mind wasn't on his prayer. The devil blinked an eye. He rattled off invocations to St. John, St. Martin, St. Peter, St. Paul and the Virgin Mary faster even than Padre Francisco could have read the mass, and was about to wind up without a last Our Father for the house, as custom demands, when Florinda took over at the proper moment.

"For the soul of Manuel Libânio, may God rest his soul in peace, P.N. and Av.M."

At the end of the supplication the old woman chimed in:

"For the souls of my father José Gaudêncio and my mother Custódia, P.N. and Av.M."

The prayer rolled rapidly and like a hiss from their lips.

"For the soul of my sister Rosalina, God grant her eternal rest, P.N. and Av.M."

The fire crackled. The wind was like a neighing horse.

"Santa Eufemia, have pity on my brother Augusto and intercede for him, Av.M."

Finally Rôla let his folded hands fall on his knees; but the old woman was apparently set to go on for a long time. He finally put a stop to it.

"Oh Lord, these prayers are said in all humility on earth, accept them as much in heaven . . . !"

And all having said their, "Jesus, Amen!" they proceeded to ask for the blessing of the old woman. Florinda and Bispo in clear voices as is the custom, and Rôla with a mumbled snarl. Then Bispo asked Rôla for his blessings as the head of the household and, wrapping himself in his cloak, ran out.

"Go on, go on, *bigorrilhas!* And see to it that they won't have to carry you home!" Rôla cried as Bispo broke helter-skelter from the house, in a hurry to join the gang and help build the bonfire in the village square.

The sheen of the buried money had cost Rôla his good humor, so he proceeded to take a nap since the Mass of the Cock was still hours away. The old woman moved closer to the fire and, fingering her beads, silently communed with all those who had long since been laid to rest in the cemetery.

Then the bells awoke to call the people to the Mass of the Cock. It was just when the snorer in his dream was about to dig up the hidden treasure.

"Light that lantern!" Rôla ordered his wife. "That padre must be in a hurry to collect his coppers."

They all dressed hastily and Florinda, putting on a new skirt her cousin Glorinhas had made for her, nicely full at the hips, had hardly the patience to comb her hair. The old woman who had spent the last hours sitting in the ash pit, her teeth chattering with the cold, searched the corners for some old rag to warm her bones.

"The bonfire will soon be lit," her son-in-law grumbled. "Get going!"

Florinda gave him a taper, and they left. It was dark with the darkness before dawn; the stars were curdled in the heavy fog. But the rain had stopped and the wind had moved on to other parts except for the short gusts that were reminders of the departed storm. At the inn they ran into Clarinha who was also on her way to mass, all bundled up, holding her lantern before her to light her steps.

"Good morning, and a Merry Christmas that brings us the Infant!"

And so they proceeded, the two old women in front, the others in the rear.

"Maybe our Padre Francisco is even now at the altar," Clarinha said. "You simply can't trust that little bell. If you hadn't made so much noise at your house, I probably wouldn't have awakened at all."

"The bell rang all right," Rosa replied. "I was just dreaming of my father, God keep him! What a funny thing a person's head is! I dreamed that we were all at the farm at Faia and going to the Mass of the Cock at the convent of Freixinho. We had passed Távora above Pontigo, when—listen to this!—some men grabbed me and wanted to throw me in the water. But my father wouldn't let them, and so we came to mass. Friar José da Lapa was reading it, and there were so many people that we couldn't find a decent spot. The manger was a sight, all silk and all lace; the nuns had made it with their clever fingers and plenty of leisure. The candles were burning as bright as the sun, and there was such a smell of wax you could have suffocated. The whole crowd of people fell on their knees. And suddenly these men appeared again and grabbed me by the hair and began to choke me. What a nightmare, Clara, what a nightmare! My father said: Let the girl be, she is my daughter! But they wouldn't let go of me. I tried to shriek, but I couldn't. I wanted to run away, but I didn't have the strength. God bless my brother, the padre, for ringing the bell when he did! What snakes and lizards there are in a person's head!"

"Sometimes they represent the temptation of the demon!" Clara suggested.

"Sure . . . or a portion of codfish lying in your stomach," Rôla added moodily.

They were only a few steps away from the square. In its center the enormous pyre of pine logs was burning and managed,

in the gusts of wind, to paint the walls blood-red in the pre-
dawn gloom. Beyond it bustled the young men of the village,
holding out their paws to the blast and engaged in noisy conversation.

Like two sentinels guarding the square fluttered the two new
flags with the cross at the top. They were made of freshly cut
pines, still dripping with resin and tall like masts, and had been
brought from the forest by the lads. Nobody dared say, "You
can't trespass on my property! The young men picked and
chose any conveniently located trees. That was the custom. On
their shoulders they carried them to the square, while the girls
prepared the bread with the tassels, a cross on each door latch
to stave off the demons. And here then, again, was the wheel
of the year, turning; here were the butcher and the beggar and
the muleteer, going and coming on these roads to Christ.

People with wooden-soled sandals passed, lanterns in their
hands since it was still extremely dark. From within the little
chapel, from across the multitude of peaked hoods, shone the
candles on the altar. The wicks had been lit one by one and
looked like tiny stars that had fallen into a cistern. Assisted by
Lájeas, Padre Francisco was already donning the white surplice
to be properly garbed for the feast of glory.

The entire parish was arriving and the excitement rose until
a whole sea of heads crowded around the door to hear the mass.
Then Rôla, too, came up to wedge himself in near the friar
who stood ready to ring the bell. With his cloak thrown over
his arm, he prepared himself to follow the ritual and the trou-
blous sights of the holy sacrifice. He felt a premonition that the
young rascals feeding the pyre in the square might very easily
sneak over to his cowshed and steal the slabs he had lying there.
And his fears were only too justified. Just when Clara was about
to open her mouth to say an Our Father for the soul of her de-
funct husband, Narinho jumped over a fence at Barralha's farm
and other youngsters slunk away in the direction of Rôla's
house. So Rôla tore himself away from his devotion and followed them. He had guessed the intention of the young rap-

scallions quite correctly, and caught up with them at his door.

"Nothing doing," he told them quite friendly like. "You can't take that!"

They burst out laughing.

"What shall we take then?"

"Go somewhere else."

"May the wolves take you, *Tio* Rôla. You're too stingy."

"What do you want? I simply haven't got any wood."

"Not even a few pieces of kindling?"

"I don't know that there is any in the kitchen. And if there is, it isn't enough to make a box. Let's see."

The three of them entered.

"*Arre!* he says he has no wood!" exclaimed the one pointing to a kitchen corner piled high with kindling.

"Now, wait a minute, that's all I have in reserve."

As they turned to leave, the one in front grabbed a block of wood standing near the spinning wheel and started to run. With one leap Rôla had him by the collar of his coat.

"Leave that block alone!"

"There are plenty of blocks. . . ."

"This one is chestnut; that's where the old woman sits."

"It's rotting anyway."

"Wouldn't you like to live as long as this block will last?"

The youngster tried to get away with the block, but Rôla hung on to it, bracing himself against the door post.

"You're just an old pig!" the two lads shouted as they finally disappeared.

Rôla bent down to put the block back where it belonged, two or two and a half spans of worm-eaten chestnut wood, as wide as a medium sized man around the waist, upon which the old woman was in the habit of perching like a raven. During the struggle a piece of the heart of the tree trunk had broken off. Really, it wasn't as good any more as he had thought, but . . . ah! ah!

Rôla pulled out his pocket knife and tugged at the corner of a rag somehow inside the block: wrapped in a piece of half rotted cloth he discovered forty *peças,* yellow like the sun, shining like polished brass and as pleasant to the touch as the finest oil!

He ran out to the cowshed, tore a stone from the wall and hid his booty behind it. All the holy morning long he laughed in the Square of St. João, drank, smeared the faces of the passing girls with charcoal and treated them to wine, chicken and sweets. He behaved like a fool.

At breakfast time he was back at the house. Florinda gave him a goodly portion of smoked sausage with fried potatoes, but he couldn't eat, he had no appetite.

"The old woman," he said, "will have a fit. Where is she?"

"She went to the vegetable garden and hasn't returned yet. I've already asked João to call her."

They ate and drank and talked; more than an hour had passed when Bispo came in to tell them that nobody knew anything about his mother.

"*Ai!* by the soul of Barzabu!" Rôla exclaimed.

Florinda stared at him with veiled eyes. He ran over to the spinning wheel and looked at the mysterious block. He couldn't swear to it, but it seemed to him someone must have been fussing around with it after he had put it back in its place.

"Did she snoop around here?"

"She did."

Then they rushed out to look for the old woman. They ran into the vegetable garden and to the threshing floor, where she was most likely to be. They asked people at the dance and looked for her in the chapel; they sent a messenger to the house of her son at Lamosa. Nothing! The old woman had simply disappeared and nobody could tell them anything about it. At nightfall a cowherder came running to their house and shouted:

"*Tia* Rosa lies drowned in Cláudio's well!"

They went there. It was she all right, lying at the bottom of the pit two *varas* deep. They fished her out with some ropes. Her belly was quite bloated, and her feet, legs and face nibbled by fish.

"*Ai,* little mother of God, I loved her so!" Florinda shrieked in a high pitched voice. "The light of my eyes has gone out!

Oh my darling little mother! May the swine eat whoever hurt her! She never hurt anyone with a single word! Oh mother, mother!"

With big tears in the corners of his eyes, Rôla murmured:

"Nobody esteemed her higher than I did . . . nobody! I told my brother-in-law João only the other day. . . ."

His deed caught up with his voice. Actually he was terribly worried over the poor creature who had thus delivered to Lucifer the soul God had given her. The undertaker came to the village. Afraid of a scandal, Padre Francisco applied simultaneously to the authorities and his prelate for permission to bury the old woman in sacred soil.

Recalling her nightmare, Clarinha blamed the Temptor for it all; but just to make sure Rôla secretly carted a few calf's legs to Moimenta anyway to squelch all gossip.

"That cursed money!" Florinda said to her husband.

"Cursed, indeed! I wouldn't want it in my pocket. . . ."

"Why not spend it for a couple of masses for her poor soul?"

"I don't like that either!"

Early one morning when everyone was still snoring, he took the stage coach from Barrelas to Viseu. And returned from there with a nice bundle of banknotes, new ones, between his heart and his shirt. . . .

ROMANIA

Christmas

TRADITIONAL

O, ce ves-te mi-nu-na-tă In Vif-le-iem ni.... s'a-ra — — tă, As-tăzi s'a năs-cut Cel făr de'n-ce-put, Cum au spus pro-ro — cii.

Oh, to hear the wondrous tiding
Come to us from Bethlehem:
He without beginning,
In the prophet's way,
He was born today!

A Christmas Tale

QUEEN MARIE OF ROMANIA

THIS IS A very strange tale I have got to tell you to-day. It is about a mysterious well—a deep, deep well which lay in the centre of a dark forest. It is also a Christmas tale.

No one knew why that well was there, nor who had dug it, nor how old it was.

The peasants from the villages around stood in great awe of this well, because from its depth a weird sound could be heard, a sort of moan, half sob, half gurgle, and sometimes a sound as though someone were knocking against its sides, which made you think of a lost soul in distress, perhaps held captive down there and unable to get out.

The village nearest the forest was called Galea. It was a very poor little village, its cottages small and miserable, with tiny gardens in which the flowers always looked sad and anæmic, for the ground was stony and unfruitful.

In the centre of the village stood a little wooden church. It was ancient and rather shaky, its huge roof looked too big for it, but the passing seasons had toned it down to a rich brown with a gray shimmer, which was pleasant to the eye.

Old stunted lilac bushes clustered round it, protecting the humble graves which lay scattered about beneath their shade, like a forlorn flock of sheep.

The peasants were rather ashamed of their tiny dilapidated church, and dreamed of building a fine edifice, all white with a tin roof, that would shine like silver in the sun, and not let the

rain nor the snow through in the bad seasons, a church with
stout columns in front, all decorated in bright colors, and with
God's eye painted over the door.

You and I would probably have infinitely preferred the
crooked little wooden church with its over-large roof, but then
you see, each community has its ambition and its pride, and
does not want to stand behind other communities. Bostea, the
village on the other side of the forest, had a beautiful new big
church of the kind that Galea coveted. But Galea was a much,
much poorer village than Bostea, and it sadly felt its inferiority.

But it was about the mysterious well I was going to tell you,
was it not?

The villagers for some reason had conceived the idea that the
unknown being who was held captive in that well, could become a danger to the country-side if it ever managed to get out,
and that the only way to keep it contented was by throwing
small offerings down into its depth.

The poor often think that they must make sacrifices to God
or to any power greater than themselves; it is a sort of way of
keeping off ill-luck from their thresholds. And yet God knows
their lives are full enough of sacrifices from beginning to end.

There were certain feast-days on which the villagers had the
habit of taking their offerings to the dreaded well, and these
were especially St. Maria Mare and St. Dumitru.

The moment Mass was over, before any dancing or drinking
could begin, they would collect in groups and start off into the
forest with their queer little offerings.

Some brought flowers or colored eggs, others flat breads
sprinkled with poppy seeds; some brought bunches of corn tied
with bright ribbons. Little children would sacrifice their first
ripe plums, cherries, or nuts, also the precious little pebbles
picked up in the river-bed, and which became a lovely bright
pink when you licked them.

The maidens made sacrifice of beads from their girdles and
little painted cards with pictures of the saints or small holy
medals, or of trinkets bought at the "moshi." [1] The young men

---

[1] "Moshi," fair.

would throw down small coins, buttons from their military tunics, or the bright red carnation they so fondly wore stuck behind their left ear.

Even quite old women would go limping through the sunshine, distaff in hand. Quite exhausted they would sink down on the well's edge and pronounce strange wishes over the water, throwing in wisps of wool or flax, whilst they murmured prayers, watching the while with one eye what the young ones were doing, always ready to criticize or to disapprove.

But in winter the well was almost quite forsaken, for no one particularly cared to go through the forest in that season. Right on the outskirts of Galea, lived a widow in a cottage so small and humble that it was really hardly more than a hut. In all the village she was known as poor Maria, and she had but one little boy, Petru, who had large gray eyes set in a pale, anxious small face.

Petru had had two little sisters, but both of them lay under the lilac bushes of the churchyard, and so poor was Maria that she had not even been able to mark the spot with crosses, and this made Petru very sad.

Petru was pious and an ardent believer. He faithfully observed all the precepts of the Church; he was a conscientious faster, though verily at all times Petru had but little to eat.

He would devoutly listen to all that old Popa Toader had to say, though sometimes he did not properly understand what it meant, and certain scraps of his exhortations would remain sticking in his mind, taking undue proportions.

Amongst others, Petru had conceived an uncomfortable belief that because the church of Bostea was larger and newer than their poor little wooden church, it was, therefore, also a holier place.

This idea had come to him because, on Easter Sunday, Popa Toader had spoken about collecting money for building a new church, and had held up as example the Bostea church which God would surely bless, as it had been erected by sacrifices made by every inhabitant, who each year had offered part of his hard-earned economies for the honor of God.

Petru of course had no money, not even the poorest little farthing; certainly if he had, he would have gladly given it for the building of the new church.

Petru had never been to Bostea, and just because of that, he had created in his imagination a wonderful vision of its church, which must have all the beauties and qualities Galea's poor little sanctuary never possessed.

Petru was about seven years old when his mother fell very ill indeed; it was just at the beginning of winter, which that year had set in with unusual severity. Petru loved his mother beyond all things on earth, and his poor little heart was wrung with terrible grief, seeing her thus pining away, and he so utterly helpless before her suffering.

Maria was a very patient woman, she never complained; it was from her that Petru had his big gray eyes and pathetic face.

There was no real bed in Maria's hovel; she lay on a sort of wooden bench over which a few ragged rugs had been spread, and upon this miserable pallet she lay all shaken by fever, her lips blue and cracked. A large earthen oven took up part of the hut; it had all sorts of shapes so as to fit into the crooked little room. Maria lay behind this oven, which Petru tried to keep as warm as he could by going each day to fetch wood on the outskirts of the forest, whence he would wearily return carrying on his back as many dry branches as he could. Petru was small, so that the weight was almost too much for him, and would quite bend him in two until he looked like a giant porcupine crawling home through the snow.

Petru would also try to cook. A few strings of dry onions hung against the wall behind the oven, and in a wooden bowl on the floor was their meagre provision of "malaiu." [1]

Probably Petru was not a very successful cook; anyhow Maria turned away with a weary sigh from the daily mess he so anxiously offered her.

This made Petru terribly unhappy and great round tears would roll down his pinched little face. He would hide away in a corner and say his prayers over and over again, all the

---

[1] "Malaiu," meal, maize.

prayers Popa Toader had ever taught him, even if they had no connection with his trouble—but they were prayers, therefore of course acceptable to God.

After that the little boy would crawl on to the wooden pallet beside his mother, nestling close up to her, hoping to keep her warm with the embrace of his skinny little arms.

Alas, God did not seem to listen to Petru's prayers, because his mother grew worse and worse instead of better, till Petru began tormenting himself, imagining that he must have displeased God in some way. Yet worry his head as he would, he could not remember a single occasion upon which he had broken the law, for Petru was an almost painfully well-behaved little boy, who never had any time to enjoy life or to be naughty, having had to work and make himself useful, ever since he had been able to stand on his feet. He had always been an anxious little soul, ever ready to carry burdens too heavy for his frail shoulders.

It was Christmas Eve, and still poor Maria lay on her pallet, sick unto death, when an idea came into Petru's head.

Petru had ideas sometimes, but they would not always work out, because no one had ever time to bother about his mind, nor to help it to expand. But this idea had grown and grown till it had become a fixture, and then, when it was quite ripe, Petru set about carrying it out, and this is what it was:

He knew that when one desires something very, very much, one must offer a taper to some blessed image, more especially to that of the Mother of God. Those little lights have a wonderful way of reinforcing prayer. Now Petru had obtained one of these little tapers from the old village chanter, as recompense for small services rendered last Sunday during Mass. It was certainly a very thin, fragile-looking little taper, a thing to be treated with infinite care, but the old man had also given him a smashed old match-box, in which there were still five unused matches, and if he could keep them from the damp, they certainly would light his little taper for him when he placed it before the icon of his choice.

All might have been quite simple, had not Petru been pos-

sessed with the idea that he must carry his candle to the Bostea
church, for, with the other villagers, he shared the mistaken
idea that their own old wooden church was not quite an entirely worthy House of God—poor dear crooked little church.

Now to get to Bostea, you had either to take a very, very
long road, or you had to take the short-cut through the dark
forest where the mysterious well stood.

Even in summer-time Petru dreaded the groaning, moaning
well; how much more, therefore, in winter, when the forest
was all black and when wolves might be prowling about. Yet
he dare not remain away too long from his mother's bedside,
so in spite of his fear he made up his mind that he must face
that grim path through the wood.

Petru put on his rough, well-used "suman" [1] and the old
"caciula" [2] which had once been his father's, and which gave
him the quaint appearance of a wandering fungus, slipped on
his fingerless gloves, which were so much darned that there was
more darn about them than glove, and having hidden the precious taper and matches in his pocket, he was ready to start.

Before slipping outside, however, he did not forget to pile
all the reserve of dried sticks upon the fire, and to place a small
mug of water beside his mother, who lay with her face turned to
the wall, mumbling all sorts of strange things which had no
sense and which filled poor little Petru's soul with dread.

Dusk was already gathering, but Petru had not been able to
get off sooner. He felt nervous, but now that his mind was made
up he meant to carry out his plan, never matter what the effort
might cost him.

Soon he reached the edge of the forest and bravely plunged
into its shade, but his heart beat like a heavy hammer in his
breast.

"Perhaps I shall be able to avoid the well," thought the boy.
"I know there are two paths—one is a little longer, but it does
not go past the well. . . ."

The wind was howling through the branches; in the still-

---

[1] "Suman," cape, overcoat.
[2] "Caciula," peasant's fur cap or bonnet.

ness of the forest it sounded like an angry voice. Petru shivered, it was terribly cold. But luckily the snow was not very deep, except in places where it lay in drifts.

Hurry as he would, night seemed to be pursuing him, gaining on him, catching him up. His breath came in hard gasps which hurt him at the bottom of his throat. What a terribly big forest, and how tall the trees were! Never had poor Petru felt so small.

"I hope, oh, I do hope I am on the right road," said the child almost aloud, "I do not want to come past that terrible old well."

And just as he said this, thump, thump, he heard an uncanny sound that made his heart jump into his mouth.

Thump—thump, and then came another sound more like a moan rising from the very bosom of the earth.

Perspiration broke out on poor Petru's forehead in spite of the cold. How dark it was getting, the trees had become walls of darkness shutting him in on all sides. . . .

Thump—thump . . . oh, dear, oh, dear, that certainly was the sound of the well.

As though hypnotized, Petru advanced. He might have turned away, have slipped through the trees avoiding the place of dread, but he somehow never thought of this but advanced steadily, fascinated by the horror of the thing!

Yes, there stood the well, a dark, sinister object that he could not avoid.

In his anxiety Petru stumbled, tried to recover his footing, but fell with a little gasp at the very edge of the well!

For a moment he lay there, his face buried in the cold snow whilst great dry sobs tore his breast. But what was that? Someone else was weeping? He was not alone in his solitude, someone besides himself was in distress, and—could he be mistaken? It seemed to be a child's voice, weeping, weeping.

Petru picked himself up. He was feeling less afraid now— why should he be afraid of a little child crying in the dark?

But then came again the sound he dreaded—thump, thump. Oh! That dreadful well! His knees shook beneath him, and yet he must look over the edge—some force stronger than himself seemed to oblige him to do so.

Petru had always hated looking down into the well, even in the day-time, when his mother had held his hand; for nights afterwards he could not sleep, always imagining that he was falling down that terrible black shaft. Now he was quite alone, it was almost night, nevertheless he *must* look over the edge.

Who could be down there? What secret could be hidden in that unknown depth?

Thump—thump—was it Petru's heart beating, or did the sound really come from the well?

Then suddenly a shrill child's voice cried, "Oh, let me out, let me out, throw me down your little taper—I am all alone here in the dark, and so cold, so cold."

"My little taper!" gasped Petru, forgetting his astonishment, his fear and everything else in the one desire of guarding that most precious of possessions. "Oh, I cannot throw you down my little taper, that I really cannot, cannot do."

"But I am cold down here," cried the child's voice, "I am cold and frightened, it is Chrismas Eve, and I am all alone down here, and it is so dark."

"But my mother's ill, she is dying," answered Petru, now quite fearlessly leaning over the shaft. He did not pause to ponder about the extraordinary thing that was happening to him, instinctively his one thought was to cling to that precious taper which was to buy back his mother's health. "I cannot give you my taper"—there was anguish in his voice—"I must go to Bostea to light it in front of the Virgin's image, so that Mother may get well."

"There are many tapers lit before that image on Christmas Eve," answered the voice. "The Blessed One would not miss your poor little light, whilst down here I am cold and lost and forsaken; give me, give me your light."

"But all the other lights burning before the Queen of Heaven would not be my light," sobbed Petru, now entirely overcome by grief. "I'll never be able to get another taper, I am quite a poor little boy, and if Mother dies, I am alone upon earth, and I am too small to know how to live all alone!" and the little fellow sank to his knees, resting his forehead against the well's edge.

"In the name of the Holy Virgin's blessed Child, give me your taper," pleaded the voice. "This is the night of His Birth, can any prayer be refused if asked in His Name to-night?"

Still Petru wavered, soul torn in two—what was his duty? Both ways his religious convictions stood up to confront him; he had put all his hope in the lighting of this taper in the Bostea church.

"In the name of the Holy Child," repeated the voice which was becoming fainter. "On this night of His Birth, and in the name of His Mother—oh, I am so cold, so lonely, and I too am a child, a little child—oh, give me your light."

Petru was sobbing now, his soul seemed to be dissolving in the bitter grief. Grief for the captive child down there, grief for his mother, grief for himself, grief for the whole sad world where everything was sordid and miserable and poor—poor like their hut and like the little old wooden church with the over-large roof, and as he leaned there, all bent in two by grief, a vision of the Bostea church rose before him, that church he would now never reach. An impossible glory surrounded it, the glory of things one cannot touch, for now Petru knew that he would sacrifice his little taper—had it not been asked for in the name of the Blessed One whose birthday it was to-night?

Somehow Petru never paused to consider how his one poor little taper could save the captive down there. In the confusion of his thoughts that one small candle had taken enormous proportions, had become the one important thing upon earth.

"Here is my little taper," he sobbed; "take it. And here are the five only matches I have—be sure and catch them before the water can damp them," he added with childish anxiety, "because if they get wet they will not light." And leaning over the shaft of the hated well, little Petru made sacrifice of all he possessed.

After that he fell with his forehead against the frozen edge, his face hidden in his hands, weeping as though his heart would break.

Suddenly he raised his head. What was that? Music? Was he dreaming? A sound of harps seemed to be throbbing in the air around him, the sound of many, many harps. And whence did that light come! That wonderful golden light?

Petru stumbled to his feet, his "caciula" falling from his head as he did so. Both the light and the rapturous music were mounting out of the well, out of that dreaded dark shaft. What was it? What was happening? Why had he suddenly the feeling that his heart was filled to overflowing with joy, with infinite joy?

"Oh!" gasped Petru, and as in church, when the Holy Mystery is being fulfilled, the ragged little fellow fell to his knees.

For now a wondrous child had stepped out of the well and stood before him, a child with golden curls and a beautiful face, a child who seemed all made of light.

"Thank you," said the bright vision to Petru. "You had pity on me, delivering me from the dark, you sacrificed to me what seemed your only hope, but see what glory your one little taper can shed around," and the child held up his hand and Petru saw how his one little taper had become as a light which could light the whole world!

"Go home to your mother, she is waiting for you," said the Wondrous One; "I am going to carry your taper to the little old wooden church, for verily it is just as holy as any great church ever built."

With trembling hands Petru picked up his "caciula," but he did not put it on his head, which he could not cover in a presence so holy, and as one walking in a dream he followed the Child of Light whose radiance filled the whole forest.

Petru felt neither cold nor fear, nor fatigue, and it was as though wings had grown on his feet.

When the village was reached, the Child of Light stood still for a moment, and with his hand pointed towards poor Maria's hut.

"She is waiting for you," he repeated; "then after you've seen her, go to the old, old church."

Of course Petru obeyed the Wondrous One's bidding, and with beating heart hurried to his mother's dwelling. Tearing open the door and bursting into the room, "Mother, Mother!" he cried.

And there stood poor Maria with a smile on her face, all trace of illness wiped from her; she seemed suddenly to have become very beautiful, even the rags she wore had become lovely, so young did she look. Her arms were wide open, those arms that were the only soft place Petru had ever known upon earth. And into those arms did Petru take refuge, hiding his face upon her bosom, too overcome for speech.

Maria did not ask what had happened, she only knew that all sickness had gone from her, that it was Christmas Eve, and that Petru, her only child, was lying against her heart.

Later, Petru stole out of the hut towards the old wooden church as the Child of Light had bidden him do.

The stars were all out, but the village was fast asleep, everything was quite silent, the houses were but dark shadows on the white snow.

Generally the church was but a darker shadow amidst shadows, hardly more dignified than the peasants' dwellings, except that it possessed a small belfry. But to-night! oh! to-night, it had suddenly turned into a casket full of light!

Light streamed out through its windows, through the cracks of its beam-walls, through the chinks of the great roof; the much-despised little building had become a thing of radiance, casting long rays of light towards the heavens, and long rays of light over the frozen snow.

Hands folded, with faltering step, Petru approached God's House, like a pilgrim come from afar; with bent head he stepped over the threshold and there fell on his knees, overcome by wonder and joy. The three doors of the altar-screen stood wide open, and on the altar itself burned Petru's little taper; no other candle had been lit in all the church, and yet the light of that one little taper was strong enough to turn the lowly little sanctuary into a thing of beauty, a thing of radiance, a thing of peace and joy.

Surely even the church of Bostea could not be more beautiful than Galea's church was to-night!

Petru understood that a miracle had come to pass: his mother had been cured, the old well delivered of its curse, and although the Holy Child was nowhere to be seen, the Holy Child's hand it was which had placed Petru's humble offering upon the altar of God.

But one thing Petru had not realized: that it was his love which had brought about the miracle—his love and his faith.

And this strange thing came to pass one Christmas Eve—on the Birthday of Christ.

RUSSIA

Hail!

TRADITIONAL

Let us praise Thee, oh God in the heavens,
Let us praise Thee!
Let us worship our Lord of the earth,
Let us worship Him!
May His good servants never grow old,
Let us worship Him!
Let us sing praises for our Lord,
Let us sing praises for Him!

Where Love Is, There God Is Also

LEO TOLSTOY

(Translated by Leo Wiener)

Shoemaker Martýn Avdyéich lived in the city. He lived in a basement, in a room with one window. The window looked out on the street. Through it the people could be seen as they passed by: though only the feet were visible, Martýn Avdyéich could tell the men by their boots. He had lived for a long time in one place and had many acquaintances. It was a rare pair of boots in the neighborhood that had not gone once or twice through his hands. Some he had resoled; on others he had put patches, or fixed the seams, or even put on new uppers. Frequently he saw his own work through the window. He had much to do, for he did honest work, put in strong material, took no more than was fair, and kept his word. If he could get a piece of work done by a certain time he undertook to do it, and if not, he would not cheat, but said so in advance. Everybody knew Avdyéich, and his work never stopped.

Avdyéich had always been a good man, but in his old age he thought more of his soul and came near unto God. Even while Martýn had been living with a master, his wife had died, and he had been left with a boy three years of age. Their children did not live long. All the elder children had died before. At first Martýn had intended sending his son to his sister in a village, but then he felt sorry for the little lad, and thought: "It will be hard for my Kapitóshka to grow up in somebody else's family, and so I will keep him."

Avdyéich left his master, and took up quarters with his son. But God did not grant Avdyéich any luck with his children. No sooner had the boy grown up so as to be a help to his father and a joy to him, than a disease fell upon him and he lay down and had a fever for a week and died. Martýn buried his son, and was in despair. He despaired so much that he began to murmur against God. He was so downhearted that more than once he asked God to let him die, and rebuked God for having taken his beloved only son, and not him. He even stopped going to church.

One day an old man, a countryman of Avdyéich's, returning from Tróitsa,—he had been a pilgrim for eight years,—came to see him. Avdyéich talked with him and began to complain of his sorrow:

"I have even no desire to live any longer, godly man. If I could only die. That is all I am praying God for. I am a man without any hope."

And the old man said to him:

"You do not say well, Martýn. We cannot judge God's works. Not by our reason, but by God's judgment do we live. God has determined that your son should die, and you live. Evidently it is better so. The reason you are in despair is that you want to live for your own enjoyment."

"What else shall we live for?" asked Martýn.

And the old man said:

"We must live for God, Martýn. He gives us life, and for Him must we live. When you shall live for Him and shall not worry about anything, life will be lighter for you."

Martýn was silent, and he said:

"How shall we live for God?"

And the old man said:

"Christ has shown us how to live for God. Do you know how to read? If so, buy yourself a Gospel and read it, and you will learn from it how to live for God. It tells all about it."

These words fell deep into Avdyéich's heart. And he went that very day and bought himself a New Testament in large letters, and began to read.

Avdyéich had meant to read it on holidays only, but when he began to read it, his heart was so rejoiced that he read it every day. Many a time he buried himself so much in reading that all the kerosene would be spent in the lamp, but he could not tear himself away from the book. And Avdyéich read in it every evening, and the more he read, the clearer it became to him what God wanted of him, and how he should live for God; and his heart grew lighter and lighter. Formerly, when he lay down to sleep, he used to groan and sob and think of his Kapitóshka, but now he only muttered:

"Glory be to Thee, glory to Thee, O Lord! Thy will be done!"

Since then Avdyéich's life had been changed. Formerly, he used on a holiday to frequent the tavern, to drink tea, and would not decline a drink of vódka. He would drink a glass with an acquaintance and, though he would not be drunk, he would come out of the tavern in a happier mood, and then he would speak foolish things, and would scold, or slander a man. Now all that passed away from him. His life came to be calm and happy. In the morning he sat down to work, and when he got through, he took the lamp from the hook, put it down on the table, fetched the book from the shelf; opened it, and began to read it. And the more he read, the better he understood it, and his mind was clearer and his heart lighter.

One evening Martýn read late into the night. He had before him the Gospel of St. Luke. He read chapter six and the verses: "And unto him that smiteth thee on the one cheek offer also the other; and him that taketh away thy cloke forbid not to take thy coat also. Give to every man that asketh of thee; and of him that taketh away thy goods ask them not again. And as ye would that men should do to you, do ye also to them likewise."

And he read also the other verses, where the Lord says: "And why call ye me, Lord, Lord, and do not the things which I say? Whosoever cometh to me, and heareth my sayings, and doeth them, I will shew you to whom he is like: he is like a man which built an house, and digged deep, and laid the foundation on a rock: and when the flood arose, the stream beat vehemently upon that house, and could not shake it: for it was founded upon a rock. But he that heareth, and doeth not, is like a man that without a foundation built an house upon the earth; against which the stream did beat vehemently, and immediately it fell; and the ruin of that house was great."

When Avdyéich read these words, there was joy in his heart. He took off his glasses, put them on the book, leaned his arms on the table, and fell to musing. And he began to apply these words to his life, and he thought:

"Is my house on a rock, or on the sand? It is well if it is founded on a rock: it is so easy to sit alone,—it seems to me that I am doing everything which God has commanded; but if I dissipate, I shall sin again. I will just proceed as at present. It is so nice! Help me, God!"

This he thought, and he wanted to go to sleep, but he was loath to tear himself away from the book. And he began to read the seventh chapter. He read about the centurion, about the widow's son, about the answer to John's disciples, and he reached the passage where the rich Pharisee invited the Lord to be his guest, and where the sinning woman anointed His feet and washed them with her tears, and he justified her. And he reached the 44th verse, and read: "And he turned to the woman, and said unto Simon, Seest thou this woman? I entered into thine house, thou gavest me no water for my feet: but she hath washed my feet with tears, and wiped them with the hairs of her head. Thou gavest me no kiss: but this woman since the time I came in hath not ceased to kiss my feet. My head with oil thou didst not anoint: but this woman hath anointed my feet with ointment."

When he had read these verses, he thought:

"He gave no water for His feet; he gave no kiss; he did not anoint His head with oil."

And again Avdyéich took off his glasses and placed them on the book, and fell to musing.

"Evidently he was just such a Pharisee as I am. He, no doubt, thought only of himself: how to drink tea, and be warm, and in comfort, but he did not think of the guest. About himself he thought, but no care did he have for the guest. And who was the guest?—The Lord Himself. Would I have done so, if He had come to me?"

And Avdyéich leaned his head on both his arms and did not notice how he fell asleep.

"Martýn!" suddenly something seemed to breathe over his very ear.

Martýn shuddered in his sleep: "Who is that?"

He turned around and looked at the door, but there was nobody there. He bent down again, to go to sleep. Suddenly he heard distinctly:

"Martýn, oh, Martýn, remember, to-morrow I will come to the street."

Martýn awoke, rose from his chair, and began to rub his eyes. He did not know himself whether he had heard these words in his dream or in waking. He put out the light and went to sleep.

Avdyéich got up in the morning before daybreak, said his prayers, made a fire, put the beet soup and porridge on the stove, started the samovár, tied on his apron, and sat down at the window to work. And, as he sat there at work, he kept thinking of what had happened the night before. His thoughts were divided: now he thought that it had only seemed so to him, and now again he thought he had actually heard the voice.

"Well," he thought, "such things happen."

Martýn was sitting at the window and not so much working as looking out into the street, and if somebody passed in unfamiliar boots, he bent over to look out of the window, in order to see not merely the boots, but also the face. A janitor passed by in new felt boots; then a water-carrier went past; then an old soldier of the days of Nicholas, in patched old felt boots, holding a shovel in his hands, came in a line with the window. Avdyéich recognized him by his felt boots. The old man's name was Stepánych, and he was living with a neighboring merchant for charity's sake. It was his duty to help the janitor. Stepánych began to clear away the snow opposite Avdyéich's window. Avdyéich cast a glance at him and went back to his work.

"Evidently I am losing my senses in my old age," Avdyéich laughed to himself. "Stepánych is clearing away the snow, and I thought that Christ was coming to see me. I, old fool, am losing my senses." But before he had made a dozen stitches, something drew him again toward the window. He looked out, and there he saw Stepánych leaning his shovel against the wall and either warming or resting himself.

He was an old, broken-down man, and evidently shoveling snow was above his strength. Avdyéich thought: "I ought to give him some tea; fortunately the samovár is just boiling." He stuck the awl into the wood, got up, placed the samovár on the table, put some tea in the teapot, and tapped with his finger at the window. Stepánych turned around and walked over to the window. Avdyéich beckoned to him and went to open the door.

"Come in and get warmed up!" he said. "I suppose you are feeling cold."

"Christ save you! I have a breaking in my bones," said Stepánych.

He came in, shook off the snow and wiped his boots so as not to track the floor, but he was tottering all the time.

"Don't take the trouble to rub your boots. I will clean up,—that is my business. Come and sit down!" said Avdyéich. "Here, drink a glass of tea!"

Avdyéich filled two glasses and moved one of them up to his guest, and himself poured his glass into the saucer and began to blow at it.

Stepánych drank his glass; then he turned it upside down, put the lump of sugar on top of it, and began to express his thanks; but it was evident that he wanted another glass.

"Have some more," said Avdyéich; and he poured out a glass for his guest and one for himself. Avdyéich drank his tea, but something kept drawing his attention to the window.

"Are you waiting for anybody?" asked the guest.

"Am I waiting for anybody? It is really a shame to say for whom I am waiting: no, I am not exactly waiting, but a certain word has fallen deep into my heart: I do not know myself whether it is a vision, or what. You see, my friend, I read the Gospel yesterday about Father Christ and how He suffered and walked the earth. I suppose you have heard of it?"

"Yes, I have," replied Stepánych, "but we are ignorant people,—we do not know how to read."

"Well, so I read about how He walked the earth. I read, you know, about how He came to the Pharisee, and the Pharisee did not give Him a good reception. Well, my friend, as I was reading last night about that very thing, I wondered how he could have failed to honor Father Christ. If He should have happened to come to me, for example, I should have done everything to receive Him. But he did not receive Him well. As I was thinking of it, I fell asleep. And as I dozed off I heard some one calling me by name: I got up and it was as though somebody were whispering to me: 'Wait,' he said: 'I will come to-morrow.' This he repeated twice. Would you believe it,—it has been running through my head,—I blame myself for it,—and I am, as it were, waiting for Father Christ."

Stepánych shook his head and said nothing. He finished his glass and put it sidewise, but Avdyéich took it again and filled it with tea.

"Drink, and may it do you good! I suppose when He, the Father, walked the earth, He did not neglect anybody, and kept the company mostly of simple folk. He visited mostly simple folk, and chose His disciples mostly from people of our class, laboring men, like ourselves the sinners. He who raises himself up, He said, shall be humbled, and he who humbles himself shall be raised. You call me Lord, He said, but I will wash your feet. He who wants to be the first, He said, let him be everybody's servant; because, He said, blessed are the poor, the meek, the humble, and the merciful."

Stepánych forgot his tea. He was an old man and easily moved to tears. He sat there and listened, and tears flowed down his cheeks.

"Take another glass!" said Avdyéich.

But Stepánych made the sign of the cross, thanked him for the tea, pushed the glass away from him, and got up.

"Thank you, Martýn Avdyéich," he said. "You were hospitable to me, and have given food to my body and my soul."

"You are welcome. Come in again,—I shall be glad to see you," said Avdyéich.

Stepánych went away. Martýn poured out the last tea, finished another glass, put away the dishes, and again sat down at the window to work,—to tap a boot. And as he worked, he kept looking out of the window,—waiting for Christ and thinking of Him and His works. And all kinds of Christ's speeches ran through his head.

There passed by two soldiers, one in Crown boots, the other in boots of his own; then the proprietor of a neighboring house came by in clean galoshes, and then a baker with a basket. All of these went past the window, and then a woman in woollen stockings and peasant shoes came in line with the window. She went by the window and stopped near a wall. Avdyéich looked at her through the window, and saw that she was a strange, poorly dressed woman, with a child: she had stopped with her back to the wind and was trying to wrap the child, though she did not have anything to wrap it in. The woman's clothes were for the summer, and scanty at that. Avdyéich could hear the child cry in the street, and her vain attempt to quiet it. Avdyéich got up and went out of his room and up to the staircase, and called out:

"Clever woman! Clever woman!"

The woman heard him and turned around.

"Why are you standing there in the cold with the child? Come in here! It will be easier for you to wrap the child in a warm room. Here, this way!"

The woman was surprised. She saw an old man in an apron, with glasses over his nose, calling to her. She followed him in.

They went down the stairs and entered the room, and Martýn took the woman up to the bed.

"Sit down here, clever woman, nearer to the stove, and get warm and feed the child."

"There is no milk in my breasts,—I have not had anything to eat since morning," said the woman, but still she took the child to her breast.

Avdyéich shook his head, went to the table, fetched some bread and a bowl, opened a door in the stove, filled the bowl with beet soup, and took out the pot of porridge, but it was not done yet. He put the soup on the table, put down the bread, and took off a rag from a hook and put it down on the table.

"Sit down, clever woman, and eat, and I will sit with the babe,—I used to have children of my own, and so I know how to take care of them."

The woman made the sign of the cross, sat down at the table, and began to eat, while Avdyéich seated himself on the bed with the child. He smacked his lips at it, but could not smack well, for he had no teeth. The babe kept crying all the time. Avdyéich tried to frighten it with his finger: he quickly carried his finger down toward the babe's mouth and pulled it away again. He did not put his finger into the child's mouth, because it was black,—all smeared with pitch. But the child took a fancy for his finger and grew quiet, and then began even to smile. Avdyéich, too, was happy. The woman was eating in the meantime and telling him who she was and whither she was going.

"I am a soldier's wife," she said. "My husband was driven somewhere far away eight months ago, and I do not know where he is. I had been working as a cook when the baby was born; they would not keep me with the child. This is the third month that I have been without a place. I have spent all I had saved. I wanted to hire out as a wet-nurse, but they will not take me: they say that I am too thin. I went to a merchant woman, where our granny lives, and she promised she would take me. I thought she wanted me to come at once, but she told me she wanted me next week. She lives a distance away. I am all worn out and have worn out the dear child, too. Luckily our landlady pities us for the sake of Christ, or else I do not know how we should have lived until now."

Avdyéich heaved a sigh, and said:

"And have you no warm clothes?"

"Indeed, it is time now to have warm clothing, dear man! But yesterday I pawned my last kerchief for twenty kopeks."

The woman went up to the bed and took her child, but Avdyéich got up, went to the wall, rummaged there awhile, and brought her an old sleeveless cloak.

"Take this!" he said. "It is an old piece, but you may use it to wrap yourself in."

The woman looked at the cloak and at the old man, and took the cloak, and burst out weeping. Avdyéich turned his face away; he crawled under the bed, pulled out a box, rummaged through it, and again sat down opposite the woman.

And the woman said:

"May Christ save you, grandfather! Evidently He sent me to your window. My child would have frozen to death. When I went out it was warm, but now it has turned dreadfully cold. It was He, our Father, who taught you to look through the window and have pity on me, sorrowful woman."

Avdyéich smiled, and said:

"It is He who has instructed me: clever woman, there was good reason why I looked through the window."

Martýn told the soldier woman about his dream, and how he had heard a voice promising him that the Lord would come to see him on that day.

"Everything is possible," said the woman. She got up, threw the cloak over her, wrapped the child in it, and began to bow to Avdyéich and to thank him.

"Accept this, for the sake of Christ," said Avdyéich, giving her twenty kopeks, with which to redeem her kerchief.

The woman made the sign of the cross, and so did Avdyéich, and he saw the woman out.

She went away. Avdyéich ate some soup, put the things away, and sat down once more to work. He was working, but at the same time thinking of the window: whenever it grew dark

there, he looked up to see who was passing. There went by acquaintances and strangers, and there was nothing peculiar.

Suddenly Avdyéich saw an old woman, a huckstress, stop opposite the very window. She was carrying a basket with apples.
There were but few of them left,—evidently she had sold all,
and over her shoulder she carried a bag with chips. No doubt,
she had picked them up at some new building, and was on her
way home. The bag was evidently pulling hard on her shoulder;
she wanted to shift it to her other shoulder, so she let the bag
down on the flagstones, set the apple-basket on a post, and began to shake down the chips. While she was doing that, a boy in
a torn cap leaped out from somewhere, grasped an apple from
the basket, and wanted to skip out, but the old woman saw him
in time and turned around and grabbed the boy by the sleeve.
The boy yanked and tried to get away, but the old woman held
on to him with both her hands, knocked down his cap, and
took hold of his hair. The boy cried, and the old woman
scolded. Avdyéich did not have time to put away the awl. He
threw it on the floor, jumped out of the room, stumbled on the
staircase, and dropped his glasses. He ran out into the street.
The old woman was pulling the boy's hair and scolding him.
She wanted to take him to a policeman; the little fellow struggled and tried to deny what he had done:

"I did not take any, so why do you beat me? Let me go!"

Avdyéich tried to separate them. He took the boy's arm, and
said:

"Let him go, granny, forgive him for Christ's sake!"

"I will forgive him in such a way that he will not forget until the new bath brooms are ripe. I will take the rascal to the
police station!"

Avdyéich began to beg the old woman:

"Let him go, granny, he will not do it again. Let him go, for
Christ's sake!"

The woman let go of him. The boy wanted to run, but Avdyéich held on to him.

"Beg the grandmother's forgiveness," he said. "Don't do
that again,—I saw you take the apple."

The boy began to cry, and he asked her forgiveness.

"That's right. And now, take this apple!" Avdyéich took an apple from the basket and gave it to the boy. "I will pay for it, granny," he said to the old woman.

"You are spoiling these ragamuffins," said the old woman. "He ought to be rewarded in such a way that he should remember it for a week."

"Oh, granny, granny!" said Avdyéich. "That is according to our ways, but how is that according to God's ways? If he is to be whipped for an apple, what ought to be done with us?"

The old woman grew silent.

And Avdyéich told the old woman the parable of the lord who forgave his servant his whole large debt, after which the servant went and took his fellow servant who was his debtor by the throat. The old woman listened to him, and the boy stood and listened, too.

"God has commanded that we should forgive," said Avdyéich, "or else we, too, shall not be forgiven. All are to be forgiven, but most of all an unthinking person."

The old woman shook her head and sighed.

"That is so," said the old woman, "but they are very much spoiled nowadays."

"Then we old people ought to teach them," said Avdyéich.

"That is what I say," said the old woman. "I myself had seven of them,—but only one daughter is left now." And the old woman began to tell where and how she was living with her daughter, and how many grandchildren she had. "My strength is waning," she said, "but still I work. I am sorry for my grand-children, and they are such nice children,—nobody else meets me the way they do. Aksyútka will not go to anybody from me. 'Granny, granny dear, darling!' " And the old woman melted with tenderness.

"Of course, he is but a child,—God be with him!" the old woman said about the boy.

She wanted to lift the bag on her shoulders, when the boy jumped up to her, and said:

"Let me carry it, granny! I am going that way."

The old woman shook her head and threw the bag on the boy's shoulders. They walked together down the street. The old woman had forgotten to ask Avdyéich to pay her for the apple. Avdyéich stood awhile, looking at them and hearing them talk as they walked along.

When they disappeared from sight, he returned to his room. He found his glasses on the staircase,—they were not broken,—and he picked up his awl and again sat down to work. He worked for awhile; he could not find the holes with the bristle, when he looked up and saw the lampman lighting the lamps.

"It is evidently time to strike a light," he thought, and he got up and fixed the lamp and hung it on the hook, and sat down again to work. He finished a boot: he turned it around and looked at it, and he saw that it was well done. He put down his tool, swept up the clippings, put away the bristles and the remnants and the awls, took the lamp and put it on the table, and fetched the Gospel from the shelf. He wanted to open the book where he had marked it the day before with a morocco clipping, but he opened it in another place. And just as he went to open the Gospel, he thought of his dream of the night before. And just as he thought of it, it appeared to him as though something were moving and stepping behind him. He looked around, and, indeed, it looked as though people were standing in the dark corner, but he could not make out who they were. And a voice whispered to him:

"Martýn, oh, Martýn, have you not recognized me?"

"Whom?" asked Avdyéich.

"Me," said the voice. "It is I."

And out of the dark corner came Stepánych, and he smiled and vanished like a cloud and was no more.

"And it is I," said a voice.

And out of the dark corner came the woman with the babe, and the woman smiled and the child laughed, and they, too, disappeared.

"And it is I," said a voice.

And out came the old woman and the boy with the apple, and both smiled and vanished.

And joy fell on Avdyéich's heart, and he made the sign of the cross, put on his glasses, and began to read the Gospel, there where he had opened it. And at the top of the page he read:

"I was an hungered, and ye gave me meat: I was thirsty, and ye gave me drink: I was a stranger, and ye took me in."

And at the bottom of the page he read:

"Inasmuch as ye have done it unto one of the least of these my brethren, ye have done it unto me." (Matt. xxv.)

And Avdyéich understood that his dream had not deceived him, that the Saviour had really come to him on that day, and that he had received Him.

Vanyka

ANTON CHEKHOV
(Translated by Eric Posselt)

VANYKA SHUKOV, a nine year old boy apprenticed for the past three months to cobbler Alyochin, didn't go to sleep on Christmas Eve. He waited until master Alyochin and his journeymen had gone to early mass. Then he got a bottle of ink and a penholder with a rusty pen in it from the master's chest and, spreading a rumpled piece of paper in front of him, began to write. Before tracing out the first letter, however, he glanced furtively several times at the door and windows, squinted up at the dark icon on the wall, flanked to the right and left by the shelves holding the lasts, and sighed. The paper lay flat on the bench. He himself knelt on the floor before it.

"Dear grandfather Constantin Makarytshch," he wrote. "I want to write you a letter. I wish you a Merry Christmas and everything good from God. You know, I haven't any father or mother, only you alone in this world."

Vanyka looked over at the dark window which mirrored the flickering flame of his candle, and conjured up the picture of his grandfather Constantin Makarytshch, who was nightwatchman for landowner Shivariov, as vividly as possible. He is a small, emaciated but unusually quick and agile old man of about sixty-five, with an always gay face and somewhat bleary eyes. During the day he sleeps in the servants' room, or else teases the cooks; at night, however, he makes his rounds about the buildings, bundled in a sheep coat, and beats his gong.

Behind him walk the old dog Kashtanka and the hound Vyun who got his name because he is all black and as long and slim as a weasel. Vyun is always tremendously respectful and friendly and casts equally benevolent glances on his own people as well as on strangers; but he isn't liked just the same. Behind his respect and his friendliness lurk nothing but sham and meanness.

No one else is better at sneaking up behind someone at the proper moment to bite that someone in the calf, or letting himself get locked up in the ice cellar where the meat is kept, or pilfering a chicken from a peasant. More than once his hind legs have been broken by a club thrown at him; twice they have hung him; almost every week he is beaten half to death; but still he is alive.

Now grandfather probably stands in the main gate, squinting over at the broadly lit windows of the village church, and gabs with the servants, hopping from one leg onto the other in their heavy felt boots. He rubs his hands, shivers with the cold and, with a lusty old-man giggle, pinches first the cooks and then the maids.

"You care for some snuff?" he says, offering his snuffbox to the women. The girls take some and sneeze. Grandfather considers that uproariously funny.

Even the dogs must take a pinch. Kashtanka sneezes, snuffles, and walks away in a huff. Vyun on his part does not sneeze— out of respect, of course—and merely wags his tail. The weather is magnificent. The air is still, clear and refreshing. The night is dark, yet the entire village with its white roofs, the clouds of smoke belching from the chimneypots, and the silver frosted trees are all clearly visible.

Vanyka sighed again, stuck the pen in the inkpot, and continued.

"Yesterday the master gave me a beating. He dragged me by my hair into the yard and beat me with his belt because I was supposed to rock the cradle and fell asleep instead. And last week the mistress told me to clean a herring and I started at the tail end. So she took the herring's head and shoved it under my nose. The journeymen tease me, and I must get vodka for them and steal gherkins from the master. But then the master beats me with anything handy.

"The food is no good at all. In the morning, bread; at noon, groats; and at night bread again but with tea or broth—which they eat up all by themselves. I have to sleep on the floor. And when the baby cries I can't sleep at all because I must rock the cradle.

"Dear grandfather, for God's sake do me a favor and take me away from here, home to the village. I can't stand it here. I beg you on my knees, take me away from here. Otherwise I must die. . . ."

Vanyka pulled down the corners of his mouth, rubbed his eyes with a dirty fist, and sobbed out loud.

"I could grind your snuff," he wrote on, "and pray to dear God for you. And if something goes wrong you must beat me as hard as you can. But if you think I'd be of no use there, I'll beg the inspector to let me clean his boots. Or perhaps I could herd the sheep instead of Fedyka. Dear grandfather, I can't stand it, it is so terrible. I wanted to run back to the village before, but I have no high boots and it is very cold. But when

I am big I'll take care of you and nobody will do you any wrong, and if you die I'll pray for you just as I do for my mother Pelagaya. Moscow is a big town. Nothing but tall fine houses and many horses, but no sheep, and the dogs don't bite here. The children don't go around with the star and in church you are not permitted to join in the singing.

"Dear grandfather, when the presents are given out at the manor house, take a golden nut from the tree for me and keep it in your green chest. Ask Miss Olga Ignatievna for it and tell her it is for Vanyka."

Vanyka heaved a great sigh and looked at the window again. He thought of how grandfather each year had fetched the Christmas tree and how he had always been permitted to go along also. What a beautiful day that had always been! Grandfather croaked and the snow croaked under their feet, and when Vanyka listened to that he had to croak, too. Sometimes, before he felled the tree, grandfather would stand around for a long time, finishing his pipe, taking a thoughtful pinch of snuff, and teasing the shivering Vanyka. The young hemlocks, all covered with frost, would stand motionless and wait to see who must fall. And suddenly, like an arrow from nowhere, a hare would rush through the snowdrifts. Then grandfather would always cry:

"Catch him! Catch him! The long-eared rascal!"

Then grandfather carried the felled tree into the manor house, and there it was trimmed. Olga Ignatievna, Vanyka's special friend, always did most of the work. When Vanyka's mother Pelagaya was still alive and a housemaid for the gentlefolks, Olga Ignatievna often gave him some sweets and, out of sheer boredom, taught him to write and read, to count to one hundred, and even to dance the quadrille. But when Pelagaya later died, Vanyka was shoved into the servants' quarters with his grandfather and finally apprenticed in Moscow.

"Come here to me, dear grandfather," Vanyka wrote on. "For God's dear sake, I beg you to take me away from here! Have pity on a poor orphan boy. They beat me here, all of them, and I am always so hungry and it is so sad that I must always cry. And the other day the master hit me over the head with a last so hard that I fell down and could hardly get up again. My life here is worse than that of a dog. And I send Alyona and one-eyed Yagorka my regards, and the coachman, too, but you mustn't give my harmonica to anyone. I remain your grandson Ivan Shukov. Dear grandfather please come and get me."

Vanyka folded the letter and stuck it in the envelope which he had bought yesterday for a kopek. And after some thinking he stuck the pen once more into the inkstand and wrote the address:

"To grandfather in the village."

Then he thoughtfully scratched his head, pondered again, and added:

"Constantin Makarytshch."

Glad that nobody had disturbed him while writing, he put on his cap and ran out into the street without bothering to put his fur coat over his smock. . . .

A Christmas Story

FEODOR DOSTOEVSKY

IT was Christmas Day, the second Christmas after I had been brought to the Dead House. The convicts had been granted a holiday in honor of the occasion, and dispensed from work, which after all is not such a great favor, because it is better to work than to think, and what can one do but think when one's

hands are not busy, and what can be more dreadful than thinking, when this means the remembrance of other times and other
days, and what tormentor has ever been able to evade the agony
of thought, when it presses with all its dead weight upon a
human creature?

On that Christmas Day, the prison was very still and quiet,
while its inmates were whispering to each other in hushed
tones, as if afraid to break this silence and this calm otherwise
than by the noise of their chains which clinked whenever they
made a movement—these chains which were there to remind
the poor wretches who wore them that their misery was still
going on, and would go on . . . for how long . . . none could
tell or remember. But for some, this was certain, until death
came to release them from the burden of their doomed
existences.

The prisoners had as usual received gifts from kind people
in the town who had wanted them to share some of their own
Christmas gladness, and they had been taken to Church, and
given a better dinner than on other days. And after this meal
had been partaken of, there remained nothing more for them
to do but come together to cheer each other as well as they
could in the big hall which served them when not out of doors,
as a sleeping place and spot of reunion. Save for the flickering
of a lantern left by one of the guards next to the door leading
into the yard, darkness had fallen upon them, a weird unearthly
kind of darkness which reminded one of all the evil thoughts
kept hidden in the souls of all these men, so many among whom
were criminals but in name.

The convicts, free for a few moments from the perpetual
watch kept over their movements, were lying or sitting on the
large wooden platform on which they slept at night; and while
one of them was playing softly on a violin, half of the strings
of which were either broken or missing, another was relating
Christmas tales to his comrades whose attention was riveted
upon his words. This was Timofey, the Thief, as he was called,
who declared that he had never been so happy as in prison,
because there at least he had food, and clothes, and had a roof

over his head, luxuries which at times during the course of his adventurous and criminal life he had often been without. This Timofey was considered as something like a hero in the prison. He had not killed anybody, but he had taken a part in so many hold-ups and robberies that his reputation had preceded his arrival in the penal settlement, where he had immediately assumed a preponderant position by virtue of his past misdeeds. He was always jovial and pleasant, and ready to oblige others, and he had ever so many amusing stories to relate about his past life, before he had been arrested and sent to prison for several years, the number of which he had already forgotten, so satisfied did he feel with his present lot. The guards all liked him, because he had never been caught in an act of disobedience or insubordination; and yet there was a general feeling all around, among the convicts as well as among the turnkeys, that Timofey had better be left alone, and not be interfered with, because if aroused, he might . . . well he might turn out disagreeable, and we all know what this word means in a prison.

I was looking at all the shaved heads around me, and wondering what I could do next, when a deep sigh aroused my attention. It came from a fellow sitting a little apart from the other prisoners, all by himself, a fellow who was known by the name of Illia the Fool. He was a new-comer, and it was his first Christmas in the prison. His nickname had come to him, because of the complete indifference which he displayed in regard to everything that was going on around him, and of his dumb docility not only before the guards, but also in complying with the many requirements of the other convicts, who tyrannized over him, and used him as a kind of man of all work, saddling upon him those tasks of the prison which no one cared to perform, such as to carry out the pails, and so forth. He was about thirty years old, a short, rather stout fellow, blind in one eye, with a face deeply scarred by smallpox. He had committed murder, and was serving a life sentence, but he had never been heard to complain about it, nor to imply that his sentence had not been a just one, but seemed to have accepted it, as something that was due him, and this was what had earned for him, at least partly, his nickname of "Fool," which Timofey had been the first one to give him. As you know, nicknames are very frequent in penal settlements, liked as a rule by convicts, perhaps because their guards invariably call them by their numbers. Illia was no exception, and always grinned when he heard them call out, "Fool, where are you?"

But on this Christmas afternoon, Illia the Fool appeared to me to be different from what he was on other days. For one thing he had sighed, and this I had never heard him do before. There was such bitter sorrow in the sound of that sigh, moreover, that it struck a soft chord in my heart, and made it ache as it had not done for a long while. I drew nearer to the man and ventured to ask him of what he had been thinking, that made him so particularly sad.

"Oh, my little Pigeon, you could not understand it," he replied, "I was only thinking of my small Wassia, of my little goat. What has happened to Wassia, where is Wassia? This is the only thing I would like to know. Oh, if anybody could just tell me where is Wassia and whether Wassia is happy and well cared for, I would ask nothing further from God, or from His Saints!"

"Who is Wassia, will you not tell me?" I enquired, expecting that he would mention the name of a brother or of a sweetheart.

He looked at me, replying with an accent of surprise, "Why, I have just told you, Wassia was my little goat."

I still did not understand, but not wishing to grieve the poor fellow, who was in real misery, I asked him if he would not relate to me the history of Wassia.

"It is Christmas Day, and perhaps it would soothe your grief if you told your story to someone who could sympathize with you," I added.

He sighed again.

"Ah! Little Pigeon, how could you understand it? But you are right all the same; perhaps it will do me good to tell you!"

And as he spoke, I saw a tear drop from his one eye and roll down his cheek.

"I will tell you, Little Pigeon," he said at last, "I will tell you, although I have never yet told it to any one before; there are days when one must speak or one will die. You see, Little Pigeon, I never had a mother. I was found lying in a basket—a baby just a few days old—by the grave-digger of our village in the churchyard, when he went to dig a grave for a woman who had died that morning. The grave-digger was a good man and he took me to his home. The same afternoon, the priest baptized me and they gave me the name of Illia because it had been on the day of Illia the Prophet that I had been found. Since no one knew who were my parents, of course people thought that my mother had never been married, and had abandoned me out of shame. As I grew up, the other boys laughed at me and taunted me with my disgrace, until I used to think sometimes I hated them all. But still I was not unhappy; you must not think that I was unhappy, Little Pigeon, because it would not be true. The grave-digger was a good man, his wife, also, was a good woman who cared for me, gave me food, made me some clothes, and did not beat me too much or too often. Then when I was about ten years old, God sent them a little daughter. I loved that child so much, so much. Anisia she was called, and I used to watch over Anisia while her mother was out in the fields working. I rocked her in my arms, drove the flies away from her face, and led her by the hand when she began to walk. Then one day when a big dog wanted to bite her because she had teased it, I threw myself before her; you can see here, Little Pigeon, where that dog bit me instead of her," and as he spoke, he raised the sleeve of his shirt, and made me look at a deep scar on his arm. "Anisia was all the world to me; when I was twenty years old and she was ten, I used to take her on my knee, and to tell her that when she was grown up, I would marry her. A neighbor heard me one day, and told my foster mother, who scolded me and said that I must not say such things to Anisia because it was putting wrong ideas into her head, because she could never become my wife. But still I went on saying them to her, only I took care that no one should hear me. I really thought then that Anisia loved me and would always care for me.

"Well, Little Pigeon, one day after I had worked hard in the fields and got very wet from the rain that surprised us on our way home, I became ill, and the *feldscher* who was called to see me said that I had caught smallpox. He took me away to the hospital in the district town. After I had recovered, my face was what you see it to-day, and I had lost the sight of my right eye. I was not an object for any girl to like to look upon, and was wise enough to know it. So when I returned home, I did not say any more to Anisia that I wanted to marry her; I only tried to please her, and to make myself useful to her. After I had scraped a little money together, I bought her a present for Christmas—a little goat she had admired one morning when she had seen it in the village. It was such a pretty little white thing, we called it Wassia. I used to take care of it and to feed it, so that Anisia had no trouble whatever with it, but only played with it when she liked."

He stopped for a moment, the tears gathering in his one eye, then asked me, "Are you sure I do not bore you, Little Pigeon?"

"No, no, go on," I replied, because by that time I had become intensely interested.

"Well, time went on; at last Anisia was grown up; the boys began to hang around her, and the women to say that she would soon be married. She was the beauty of the place, and Foma, the innkeeper, who was reputed to be the richest man in the whole village, was constantly seen with her and danced with her at all the harvest festivals to which she was bidden. This did not please me, because I knew that Foma was a good-for-nothing fellow who had been in many scrapes with girls, always coming out of them by some trick or other. I tried to warn Anisia, but she refused to listen to me, and at last became very angry with me, saying that she would never speak to me again unless I stopped talking about Foma. I could see that she was quite changed. She did not care any more for Wassia and ceased to caress or play with it. So that poor Wassia, who by this time was quite an old goat, seemed to feel it, looking so sad when unable to attract her attention that I had to take it in my arms to comfort it. Then we would weep together, and I thought that at least there remained one being in the world who cared for me, to whom I could be useful.

"It is dreadful, Little Pigeon, to feel quite alone in the world. This was my case; and when one day, Anisia came to tell me that she was going to marry Foma after Lent, I felt that if Wassia had not been there, I would just have gone down to the river and thrown myself in it.

"Well, time passed, the summer was over, and the harvest had all been taken in. Then Anisia and Foma were married. Anisia came to show herself to me in all her bridal finery, with quantities of red beads around her neck, and a nice red handkerchief tied around her throat. Foma had a new pair of boots bought for the occasion, and a new pink shirt; and everybody said that they were a comely pair. Before she went away to her husband's *isba,* Anisia came to me again, and told me that she would leave me Wassia to take care of; and in saying so, seemed to imply that she was conferring a great favor upon me. Perhaps she was. Who knows!

"Well, Little Pigeon, I hardly ever saw her afterwards, and Wassia was all that was left to me. My little goat! It did not mind my one eye and scarred face. We used to sleep together on the straw in the barn; it would put its head upon my shoulder, and lick my face with its tongue. I was happy then, Little Pigeon, because I could imagine that it was Anisia who was kissing me.

"Well, this did not last long," he went on, his voice trembling a little, "there came a day when Anisia returned, and told me that she wanted to have Wassia back, to take it to her own cottage to play with as she used to do when she was a little girl. By that time I knew that she was not as happy as she had expected to be with Foma, but this was not a reason why she should want to take Wassia away from me, who had nothing else but this little animal to make me happy. I begged her to leave me the goat, I said that she would not know how to take care of it, that Wassia was an old goat requiring more attention than she would have the time or the patience to give. I said everything I could think of to induce her to leave me the animal, but she refused to listen to me. She laughed when I told her that Wassia was all I had left in the world to remind me of her. She laughed and said that her husband wanted Wassia, and that she was going to take it away with her and give it to her husband!

"Then, Little Pigeon, something went over me I had never felt before. I happened to have an ax in my hand with which I had been chopping wood and—and I killed Anisia!"

And a deep sob shook his strong frame.

"Fool, oh, you Fool, where are you?" called a voice from the other end of the room, where the convicts were all talking as loud as they could now that their attention had been diverted from the sadness of their own lot by the stories Timofey had been telling them.

"Fool, Fool, where are you?" one of the prisoners cried out again. "Come over here, you are wanted to empty the *parascha*."

"I am coming, I am coming," responded Illia as he rushed to obey, murmuring between his teeth, "Wassia—who can tell me what has become of her! Where is Wassia?"

Christmas Phantoms

MAXIM GORKI

MY CHRISTMAS story was concluded. I flung down my pen, rose from the desk; and began to pace up and down the room.

It was night, and outside the snow-storm whirled through the air. Strange sounds reached my ears as of soft whispers, or of sighs, that penetrated from the street through the walls of my little chamber, three-fourths of which were engulfed in dark shadows. It was the snow driven by the wind that came crunching against the walls and lashed the window-panes. A light, white, indefinite object scurried past my window and disappeared, leaving a cold shiver within my soul.

I approached the window, looked out upon the street, and leaned my head, heated with the strained effort of imagination, upon the cold frame. The street lay in deserted silence. Now and then the wind ripped up little transparent clouds of snow from the pavement and sent them flying through the air like shreds of a delicate white fabric. A lamp burned opposite my window. Its flame trembled and quivered in fierce struggle with the wind. The flaring streak of light projected like a broad-sword into the air, and the snow that was drifted from the roof of the house into this streak of light became aglow for a moment like a scintillating robe of sparks. My heart grew sad and chill as I watched this play of the wind. I quickly undressed myself, put out the lamp and lay down to sleep.

When the light was extinguished and darkness filled my room the sounds grew more audible and the window stared at me like a great white spot. The ceaseless ticking of the clock marked the passing of the seconds. At times their swift onward rush was drowned in the wheezing and crunching of the snow, but soon I heard again the low beat of the seconds as they dropped into eternity. Occasionally their sound was as distinct and precise as if the clock stood in my own skull.

I lay in my bed and thought of the story that I had just completed, wondering whether it had come out a success.

In this story I told of two beggars, a blind old man and his wife, who in silent, timid retirement trod the path of life that offered them nothing but fear and humiliation. They had left their village on the morning before Christmas to collect alms in the neighboring settlements that they might on the day thereafter celebrate the birth of Christ in holiday fashion.

They expected to visit the nearest villages and to be back home for the early morning service, with their bags filled with all kinds of crumbs doled out to them for the sake of Christ.

Their hopes (thus I proceeded in my narration) were naturally disappointed. The gifts they received were scanty, and it was very late when the pair, worn out with the day's tramp, finally decided to return to their cold, desolate clay hut. With light burdens on their shoulders and with heavy grief in their hearts, they slowly trudged along over the snow-covered plain, the old woman walking in front and the old man holding fast to her belt and following behind. The night was dark, clouds covered the sky, and for two old people the way to the village was still very long. Their feet sank into the snow and the wind whirled it up and drove it into their faces. Silently and trembling with cold they plodded on and on. Weary and blinded by the snow, the old woman had strayed from the path, and they were now wandering aimlessly across the valley out on the open field.

"Are we going to be home soon? Take care that we do not miss the early mass!" mumbled the blind man behind his wife's shoulders.

She said that they would soon be home, and a new shiver of cold passed through her body. She knew that she had lost the way, but she dared not tell her husband. At times it seemed to her as if the wind carried the sound of the barking dogs to her ears, and she turned in the direction whence those sounds came; but soon she heard the barking from the other side.

At length her powers gave way and she said to the old man:

"Forgive me, father, forgive me for the sake of Christ. I have strayed from the road and I cannot go further. I must sit down."

"You will freeze to death," he answered.

"Let me rest only for a little while. And even if we do freeze to death, what matters it? Surely our life on this earth is not sweet."

The old man heaved a heavy sigh and consented.

They sat down on the snow with their backs against each other and looked like two bundles of rags—the sport of the wind. It drifted clouds of snow against them, covered them up with sharp, pointed crystals, and the old woman, who was more lightly dressed than her husband, soon felt herself in the embrace of a rare, delicious warmth.

"Mother," called the blind man, who shivered with violent cold, "stand up, we must be going!"

But she had dozed off and muttered but half-intelligible words through her sleep. He endeavored to raise her but he could not for want of adequate strength.

"You will freeze!" he shouted, and then he called aloud for help into the wide open field.

But she felt so warm, so comfortable! After some vain endeavor the blind man sat down again on the snow in dumb desperation. He was now firmly convinced that all that happened to him was by the express will of God and that there was no escape for him and his aged wife. The wind whirled and danced around them in wanton frolic, playfully bestrewed them with snow and had a merry, roguish sport with the tattered garments that covered their old limbs, weary with a long life of pinching destitution. The old man also was now overcome with a feeling of delicious comfort and warmth.

Suddenly the wind wafted the sweet, solemn, melodious sounds of a bell to his ears.

"Mother!" he cried, starting back, "they are ringing for matins. Quick, let us go!"

But she had already gone whence there is no return.

"Do you hear? They are ringing, I say. Get up! Oh, we will be too late!"

He tried to rise, but he found that he could not move. Then he understood that his end was near and he began to pray silently:

"Lord, be gracious unto the souls of your servants! We were sinners, both. Forgive us, oh, Lord! Have mercy upon us!"

Then it seemed to him that from across the field, enveloped in a bright, sparkling snow cloud, a radiant temple of God was floating toward him—a rare, wondrous temple. It was all made of flaming hearts of men and itself had the likeness of a heart, and in the midst of it, upon an elevated pedestal, stood Christ in his own person. At this vision the old man arose and fell upon his knees on the threshold of the temple. He regained his sight again and he looked at the Savior and Redeemer. And from his elevated position Christ spoke in a sweet, melodious voice:

"Hearts aglow with pity are the foundation of my temple. Enter thou into my temple, thou who in thy life hast thirsted for pity, thou who hast suffered misfortune and humiliation, go to thy Eternal Peace!"

"O, Lord!" spoke the old man, restored to sight, weeping with rapturous joy, "is it Thou in truth, O Lord!"

And Christ smiled benignly upon the old man and his life companion, who was awakened to life again by the smile of the Savior.

And thus both the beggars froze to death out in the open, snow-covered field.

I brought back to my mind the various incidents of the story, and wondered whether it had come out smooth and touching enough to arouse the reader's pity. It seemed to me that I could answer the question in the affirmative, that it could not possibly fail to produce the effect at which I had aimed.

With this thought I fell asleep, well satisfied with myself. The clock continued to tick, and I heard in my sleep the chasing and roaring of the snowstorm, that grew more and more violent. The lantern was blown out. The storm outside produced ever new sounds. The window shutters clattered. The branches of the trees near the door knocked against the metal plate of the roof. There was a sighing, groaning, howling, roaring and whistling, and all this was now united into a woeful melody that filled the heart with sadness, now into a soft, low strain like a cradle song. It had the effect of a fantastic tale that held the soul as if under a spell.

But suddenly—what was this? The faint spot of the window flamed up into a bluish, phosphorescent light, and the window grew larger and larger until it finally assumed the proportions of the wall. In the blue light which filled the room there appeared of a sudden a thick, white cloud in which bright sparks glowed as with countless eyes. As if whirled about by the wind, the cloud turned and twisted, began to dissolve, became more and more transparent, broke into tiny pieces, and breathed a frosty chill into my body that filled me with anxiety. Something like a dissatisfied, angry mumble proceeded from the shreds of cloud, that gained more and more definite shape and assumed forms familiar to my eye. Yonder in the corner were a swarm of children, or rather the shades of children, and behind them emerged a gray-bearded old man by the side of several female forms.

"Whence do these shades come? What do they wish?" were the questions that passed through my mind as I gazed affrighted at this strange apparition.

"Whence come we and whence are we?" was the solemn retort of a serious, stern voice. "Do you not know us? Think a little!"

I shook my head in silence. I did not know them. They kept floating through the air in rhythmic motion as if they led a

solemn dance to the tune of the storm. Half transparent,
scarcely discernible in their outlines, they wavered lightly and
noiselessly around me, and suddenly I distinguished in their
midst the blind old man who held on fast to the belt of his old
wife. Deeply bent they limped past me, their eyes fixed upon me
with a reproachful look.

"Do you recognize them now?" asked the same solemn voice.
I did not know whether it was the voice of the storm or the
voice of my conscience, but there was in it a tone of command
that brooked no contradiction.

"Yes, this is who they are," continued the Voice, "the sad
heroes of your successful story. And all the others are also
heroes of your Christmas stories—children, men and women
whom you made to freeze to death in order to amuse the public.
See how many there are and how pitiful they look, the offspring
of your fancy!"

A movement passed through the wavering forms and two
children, a boy and a girl, appeared in the foreground. They
looked like two flowers of snow or of the sheen of the moon.

"These children," spoke the Voice, "you have caused to
freeze under the window of that rich house in which beamed
the brilliant Christmas tree. They were looking at the tree—do
you recollect?—and they froze."

Noiselessly my poor little heroes floated past me and disappeared. They seemed to dissolve in the blue, nebulous glare
of light. In their place appeared a woman with a sorrowful,
emaciated countenance.

"This is that poor woman who was hurrying to her village
home on Christmas Eve to bring her children some cheap
Christmas gifts. You have let her freeze to death also."

I gazed full of shame and fear at the shade of the woman.
She also vanished, and new forms appeared in their turn. They
were all sad, silent phantoms with an expression of unspeakable
woe in their somber gaze.

And again I heard the solemn Voice speak in sustained,
impassive accents:

"Why have you written these stories? Is there not enough

of real, tangible and visible misery in the world that you must needs invent more misery and sorrow, and strain your imagination in order to paint pictures of thrilling, realistic effects? Why do you do this? What is your object? Do you wish to deprive man of all joy in life, do you wish to take from him the last drop of faith in the good, by painting for him only the evil? Why is it that in your Christmas stories year after year you cause to freeze to death now children, now grown-up people? Why? What is your aim?"

I was staggered by this strange indictment. Everybody writes Christmas stories according to the same formula. You take a poor boy or a poor girl, or something of that sort, and let them freeze somewhere under a window, behind which there is usually a Christmas tree that throws its radiant splendor upon them. This has become the fashion, and I was following the fashion.

I answered accordingly.

"If I let these people freeze," I said, "I do it with the best object in the world. By painting their death struggle I stir up humane feelings in the public for these unfortunates. I want to move the heart of my reader, that is all."

A strange agitation passed through the throng of phantoms, as if they wished to raise a mocking protest against my words.

"Do you see how they are laughing?" said the mysterious Voice.

"Why are they laughing?" I asked in a scarcely audible tone.

"Because you speak so foolishly. You wish to arouse noble feelings in the hearts of men by your pictures of imagined misery, when real misery and suffering are nothing to them but a daily spectacle. Consider for how long a time people have endeavored to stir up noble feelings in the hearts of men, think of how many men before you have applied their genius to that end, and then cast a look into real life! Fool that you are! If the reality does not move them, and if their feelings are not offended by its cruel, ruthless misery, and by the fathomless abyss of actual wretchedness, then how can you hope that the fictions of your imagination will make them better? Do you really think that you can move the heart of a human being by telling him about a frozen child? The sea of misery breaks against the dam of heartlessness, it rages and surges against it, and you want to appease it by throwing a few peas into it!"

The phantoms accompanied these words with their silent laughter, and the storm laughed a shrill, cynical laugh; but the Voice continued to speak unceasingly. Each word that it spoke was like a nail driven into my brain. It became intolerable, and I could no longer hold out.

"It is all a lie, a lie!" I cried in a paroxysm of rage, and jumping from my bed I fell headlong into the dark, and sank more and more quickly, more and more deeply, into the gaping abyss that suddenly opened before me. The whistling, howling, roaring and laughing followed me downward and the phantoms chased me through the dark, grinned in my face and mocked at me.

I awoke in the morning with a violent headache and in a very bad humor. The first thing I did was to read over my story of the blind beggar and his wife once more, and then I tore the manuscript into pieces.

SPAIN

Shepherds of Bethlehem

TRADITIONAL

Pas - to - res a Be - len, va - mos con al - e - gri - a. A
ver a nues-tro bien, al hi - jo de Ma - ri - a; Al - li, al -
li, al - li nos es-per-a Je - sus! Al - li, al - li.

Shepherds of Bethlehem,
Come, hurry every one,
We call tonight on Him,
Who is St. Mary's son.
For we, for we, for we
Have been awaiting Jesus.

A Tragedy

ANTONIO MARÉ
(Translated by W. R. Hynes)

IT WAS a great city in the far North, a gloomy city with pointed roofs that seemed to have been carved out of the fog. The birds that hurried past it on their journey south said to themselves that it looked like a forest of steeples. Under one of these pointed roofs lived two young people whom the coldness of emigration had huddled together in a closer intimacy. They were very unconscious of the fog, and it never occurred to them that the city looked like a forest of steeples; in fact, they never thought of the city at all, and would scarcely have been surprised if they had heard it spoken of as an orange grove,—for they were lovers. The little nest they had built themselves under the pointed roof was bright with the sunshine that came from them; and the few people who entered there became intoxicated with a strange aroma of tenderness that surged to their brains like the fumes of old wine, in sweet reminiscences or disturbing suggestions.

It would not be perfectly correct to say that these young people lived entirely alone; and had they not been so absorbed in each other, living that life of double selfishness peculiar to lovers, they could scarcely have helped feeling a soft blue gaze fixed upon them, evening after evening, as they took their accustomed places before the hearth.

On the mantel-piece which overhung the hearth was a small

black marble clock, a statuette of Psyche with butterfly wings made of plaster, a little Italian shepherd of very primitively tinted clay, and a bisque vase. Now, this vase was the gem of the drawing-room. On its bosom was painted a running stream that broke into cataracts here and there over glossy brown stones. Its pitch was amazingly abrupt. It started at the brim of the vase and disappeared under it. On its banks, far away in a misty perspective of pink and violet trees, were a number of shadowy little shepherdesses, some carrying tender lambs, others dancing the minuet, but all very blithe and merry. At some distance from them, and at the very front, where the cataract roared its loudest, stood a much larger shepherdess in clear relief, thrusting herself boldly forward as though she meant to leap from the parental vase, to which she was bound only by the tip of her flowered skirt and the heel of her slippered foot. She held her crook high in the air as if to balance herself in her flight. In her other hand was a wreath of corn-flowers, with which she shaded a pair of dreamy blue eyes that gazed in perpetual wonder at the world below. Her sisters were simple little things, who were content to play with a lambkin all day long in the sun, or dance the minuet under the trees, but who had absolutely no ideas. Now, this particular little shepherdess had not only ideas, she had thoughts, and what was more, she was conscious of them. It was not to be wondered at that all things fell in love with each other in this peculiar little room; nor was it surprising that most things fell in love with the little shepherdess. The wonder was that she, on the other hand, fell in love with nothing. This superiority of thought was very isolating, and her aloneness would have been unendurable but for the gratifying nature of its cause. The clock was an unpleasant neighbor,—childless and critical, which sometimes means the same thing. Its conversation invariably took the form of a colloquy, stiff with rules, bristling with maxims; besides, having gone through life measuring out time, it had reached that stage of indiscriminate skepticism which is the greatest possible damper on the open-mindedness of others.

There was the little clay shepherd, to be sure, who was very well thought of by the community at large. The shepherdess liked him,—certainly she liked him,—and she sometimes spoke her thoughts to him, but she never could have loved him, had the drawing-room been the Desert of Sahara and he its only other inhabitant. She was always perfectly frank with him whenever he broached the subject.

"In the first place, I do not believe that you are really in love," she said to him kindly; "you only think you are, because everybody else seems to be. Reflect a little, and I am sure you will agree with me,—for my part, I have given it a great deal of serious thought. The air seems full of thrills for all of you lately, but you should be very careful; a thrill is a dangerous prism through which to look at life." And to herself she said, "Poor little fellow! he thinks he can build a bonfire out of two straws."

She could not associate love with his healthy plumpness. He was even-tempered, and had an occasional idea, but no theories; he wanted things without longing for them; his love was tender but not invariably delicate. She felt the fault to be in his head rather than in his heart; he always acquiesced, but seldom understood.

On the table in the centre of the room was a Chinese mandarin, who was also in love with the little shepherdess, but she absolutely abhorred him. To her mind he was coarse and repulsive, in spite of his wealth. His jokes never amused her. Still he was a humorist, and had a way of wobbling his head and poking out his tongue that threw the whole drawing-room into covulsions of laughter. Poor little shepherdess! Well, she did what we all do under similar circumstances. She built herself a world of her own,—a little intellectual laboratory into which she dragged bits of careful observation to be submitted to the tests of her theories. So, poised like a sparrow on a twig, she continued to peer over the edge of the mantel-piece, where she saw quite enough to set her thinking.

Her master and mistress were a source of constant study to her. Late in the evening, when he sat on a broad, low chair before the fire, and she on the floor resting her head against his knees, the little shepherdess's eyes fairly glowed with concentrated attention. "So that must be love," she thought, as she made a note of something indefinable that quivered on their lips, or trembled on their eyelids and made them droop. "I wonder how they feel! I wish I knew!" She was watching her mistress with peculiar interest one night, when she saw her slip her hand into her husband's coat-pocket, and draw out an envelope with no stamp upon it. This she held for a second or two, undecided as to whether she would read its contents. She looked up inquiringly at her husband, then with a quick movement thrust it back unopened, and laughingly threw her arms about his neck to drive away the unpleasant impression. "That is a grave mistake," thought the little shepherdess. "Why should there be anything that he should not want her to know? As a principle, it is wrong. It is because people build their love on illusions that they fear revelations. Why are they so cowardly? I do not believe the truth to be as black as it is painted. We should love, knowing,—that is the way. There must be such a thing. Oh, when I love—" and her eyes grew misty at the very thought, and the lace on her little bodice rose and fell.

The days came and went, and found her growing ever more dainty, and more thoughtful too. At last she opened her blue eyes, one Christmas Eve, upon what struck her at first as something alarming. It was midnight; and a stealthy sound of creaking boots awoke her from her first sleep and in the very midst of a wonderful dream. Her little heart was beating very fast. At first she thought it might be a burglar who had heard of her cleverness and her philosophies, and who had broken into the house to steal her away, but in a second a match was struck and she understood her mistake. Her master stood before her in the middle of the room. She saw him tiptoe to the door, close it tightly, then stand listening for a moment before lighting the gas. What could he be so mysterious about? She rubbed her eyes and watched him attentively. She soon discovered that he held a bundle under his arm, and she smiled to herself knowingly. "A Christmas present," she said; and she leaned so far forward that she almost tipped off the mantel-piece. Her master sat down, laid the package on his lap, and cut the strings with his penknife; then he removed the wrappings as noiselessly as possible. Though the little shepherdess had entirely recovered from her alarm, she began to experience a sensation entirely new to her. She felt as though there were a tight band around her waist that kept her from breathing freely. Her head grew hollow; and a sickened sense of misery—physical and mental anguishes writhing and knotting themselves in the pit of her stomach—made her feel strangely faint. What could this mean? Was it a foreboding? When the last wrapping was carefully laid aside, she opened her eyes with a great effort and looked upon the most beautiful thing she had ever seen. On the little table directly opposite her, stood a figure about eight inches high,— exquisite, dazzling! "A prince!" she thought at first; for he was richly dressed, had a noble air, and on his short dark curls he wore a crown. But no; he was not a prince.

As she looked at him again she realized that his crown was made of laurels; then she saw too that he held a violin in his hand. He was something greater than a prince; he was an artist. The master stood off and looked at him with beaming joy, and the little shepherdess felt her admiration increase with cor-roboration. Then he drew from his pocket a pink wax taper, which he fitted into the laurel crown. When it was lighted it shed a soft radiance. "What a beautiful idea!" thought the shepherdess; "that is the halo of art, glorifying, transfiguring everything." The master then blew out the light, and smiling complacently, reached up to the chandelier. Just as he was about to turn out the gas, the little artist looked up and saw the shepherdess,—one long look of surprise and eagerness; their glances met, and in that look they understood each other. Through the darkness of that whole night he played her beauti-ful strains of dreamy music that opened to her visions of blue skies and balmy orange groves; for he came from Italy, where the very air must be heavy with poetry and love, she thought. He told her wonderful tales with his violin. He alternately flooded her mind with moonlight and fairies, or peopled her fancy with vague forms of sorrow that filled her little breast with sobs. What a rapturous night that was! A bewitched moon-beam that peered in through a broken slat in the blind lay there entranced. In the pauses of the music the plaster wings of the little Psyche quivered audibly. As for the shepherdess, something had permeated her soul like a subtle essence, and opened one by one great vistas of feeling of which she had never dreamed even in the boldest flights of her imaginings. All her senses seemed suddenly to have grown exquisitely acute. "What a bursting heart there must be behind it all!" she thought. "What a fund of sentiment! What must he feel who, with a stroke of his bow, can change the aspect of the world! It is he! It is he at last!"

Christmas morning dawned upon the world. The first rays of light that penetrated into the drawing-room brought with them the muffled sound of carriages hurrying over the snow, and the occasional shout of a belated reveller mingling with the faint murmur from groups of early church-goers. But what was this to the little shepherdess? The day that had dawned for her was more momentous than Christmas. She was almost surprised to find that it was not a dream. No, there he stood; and he smiled at her with the eager smile of those who meet again after a separation.

"You look as though you were about to take flight, you beautiful, blue-eyed thing. Fly down to me. I will catch you in my arms," he said, at which the little shepherdess blushed crimson. "Perhaps you do not love me now that you see me in the light of day."

She was just about to answer something very clever about not fearing revelations because she had all her life scorned illusions, when the door suddenly opened, and her master entered on tip-toe. He walked over to the table, stood looking at his purchase with satisfaction for a few seconds; then taking it up in his hand, he discovered that the pink taper did not fit tightly enough into the little laurel crown. In moving the figure, it was apt to topple first to one side, then another. So he stood it down, and twisting the upper part carefully, he screwed it off, crown and taper, from the pretty head, and carried them both into the next room. During this incident a thought flashed through the little shepherdess's mind, and like a flash too she determined to execute it. She pulled her left foot with a jerk, and gave a little tug at her gown, and there she stood on the edge of the mantel-piece, free. She threw a hasty glance at the little shepherd, who looked on with a parched throat; it is even possible that she smiled a kindly smile upon the black clock. Then she gathered her skirts with both hands and jumped down. It was a supreme moment. The lovers stood looking into each other's eyes.

"My precious one," he said, "you are mine at last. I have waited for you through the ages, and you have come!"

And the little shepherdess, stepping up on a book. held her wreath of corn-flowers over his head.

"I have no laurels to bring you," she said, "but I will crown you with my trusting love." And she rose on her tiptoes and leaned forward to lay her corn-flowers on his brow. But what was it? Why did she start, and then lean farther forward and look again? What could she have seen to make her eyes grow suddenly dim,—those clear eyes that meant to see everything?

The fact of it was that under the laurels it was all hollow, hollow down to his belt. Where his heart should have been, she saw a little dust that exhaled a musty odor, and the wings of several dead flies. Her brain reeled. Was this all, then? And the music, where had the wonderful music come from, or was the music all? This was the shepherdess's last speculation. She felt the book sinking beneath her little feet; she grasped her crook nervously; then there was a blank in her thoughts; she tottered, and crash! she fell and broke into a thousand pieces at the feet of her lover. At first he felt that he would die too. Then he composed himself, and when he came to understand how it had all happened, he shrugged his shoulders. "Women are all alike," said he. "They fancy they are thinking when they are only brooding. They want to be analytical, and they are only cavilous." And he tuned his violin, while his eyes rested on the little plaster Psyche.

SWEDEN

O Blessed Morn

TRADITIONAL

Var häl-sad, skö-na mor-gon-stund, Som av pro-
fe-ters hel-ga mun Är oss be bå-dad vor-den!
Du sto-ra dag, du säl-la dag, På vil-ken him-lens väl-be-
hag Än-nu be-sö-ker jor-den! Un-ga Sjun-ga Med de
gam-la Sig för-sam-la jor-dens bö-ner Kring den stör-ste av dess sö-ner.

All hail to thee, o blessed morn!
To tidings long by prophets borne
Hast thou fulfillment given.
O sacred and immortal day,
When unto earth, in glorious ray,
Descends the grace of heaven
And help as could no other.
Singing, ringing,
Sounds are blending,
Praises sending
Unto heaven
For the Savior has been given.

The Legend of the Christmas Rose

SELMA LAGERLÖF

(Translated by Velma Swanston Howard)

ROBBER MOTHER, who lived in Robbers' Cave up in Göinge forest, went down to the village one day on a begging tour. Robber Father, who was an outlawed man, did not dare to leave the forest. She took with her five youngsters, and each youngster bore a sack on his back as long as himself. When Robber Mother stepped inside the door of a cabin, no one dared refuse to give her whatever she demanded; for she was not above coming back the following night and setting fire to the house if she had not been well received. Robber Mother and her brood were worse than a pack of wolves, and many a man felt like running a spear through them; but it was never done, because they all knew that the man stayed up in the forest, and he would have known how to wreak vengeance if anything had happened to the children or the old woman.

Now that Robber Mother went from house to house and begged, she came to Övid, which at that time was a cloister. She rang the bell of the cloister gate and asked for food. The watchman let down a small wicket in the gate and handed her six round bread cakes—one for herself and one for each of the five children.

While the mother was standing quietly at the gate, her

From *The Girl from the Marsh Croft* by Selma Lagerlöf. Copyright 1910 by Doubleday & Co., Inc.

youngsters were running about. And now one of them came and pulled at her skirt, as a signal that he had discovered something which she ought to come and see, and Robber Mother followed him promptly.

The entire cloister was surrounded by a high and strong wall, but the youngster had managed to find a little back gate which stood ajar. When Robber Mother got there, she pushed the gate open and walked inside without asking leave, as it was her custom to do.

Övid Cloister was managed at that time by Abbot Hans, who knew all about herbs. Just within the cloister wall he had planted a little herb garden, and it was into this that the old woman had forced her way.

At first glance Robber Mother was so astonished that she paused at the gate. It was high summertide, and Abbot Hans' garden was so full of flowers that the eyes were fairly dazzled by the blues, reds, and yellows, as one looked into it. But presently an indulgent smile spread over her features, and she started to walk up a narrow path that lay between many flower-beds.

In the garden a lay brother walked about, pulling up weeds. It was he who had left the door in the wall open, that he might throw the weeds and tares on the rubbish heap outside.

When he saw Robber Mother coming in, with all five youngsters in tow, he ran toward her at once and ordered them away. But the beggar woman walked right on as before. The lay brother knew of no other remedy than to run into the cloister and call for help.

He returned with two stalwart monks, and Robber Mother saw that now it meant business! She let out a perfect volley of shrieks, and, throwing herself upon the monks, clawed and bit at them; so did all the youngsters. The men soon learned that she could overpower them, and all they could do was to go back into the cloister for reinforcements.

As they ran through the passage-way which led to the cloister, they met Abbot Hans, who came rushing out to learn what all this noise was about.

He upbraided them for using force and forbade their calling for help. He sent both monks back to their work, and although he was an old and fragile man, he took with him only the lay brother.

He came up to the woman and asked in a mild tone if the garden pleased her.

Robber Mother turned defiantly toward Abbot Hans, for she expected only to be trapped and overpowered. But when she noticed his white hair and bent form, she answered peaceably, "First, when I saw this, I thought I had never seen a prettier garden; but now I see that it can't be compared with one I know of. If you could see the garden of which I am thinking you would uproot all the flowers planted here and cast them away like weeds."

The Abbot's assistant was hardly less proud of the flowers than the Abbot himself, and after hearing her remarks he laughed derisively.

Robber Mother grew crimson with rage to think that her word was doubted, and she cried out: "You monks, who are holy men, certainly must know that on every Christmas Eve the great Göinge forest is transformed into a beautiful garden, to commemorate the hour of our Lord's birth. We who live in the forest have seen this happen every year. And in that garden I have seen flowers so lovely that I dared not lift my hand to pluck them."

Ever since his childhood, Abbot Hans had heard it said that on every Christmas Eve the forest was dressed in holiday glory. He had often longed to see it, but he had never had the good fortune. Eagerly he begged and implored Robber Mother that he might come up to the Robbers' Cave on Christmas Eve. If she would only send one of her children to show him the way, he could ride up there alone, and he would never betray them —on the contrary, he would reward them insofar as it lay in his power.

Robber Mother said no at first, for she was thinking of Robber Father and of the peril which might befall him should she permit Abbot Hans to ride up to their cave. At the same time the desire to prove to the monk that the garden which she knew was more beautiful than his got the better of her, and she gave in.

"But more than one follower you cannot take with you," said she, "and you are not to waylay us or trap us, as sure as you are a holy man."

This Abbot Hans promised, and then Robber Mother went her way.

It happened that Archbishop Absalon from Lund came to Övid and remained through the night. The lay brother heard Abbot Hans telling the Bishop about Robber Father and asking him for a letter of ransom for the man, that he might lead an honest life among respectable folk.

But the Archbishop replied that he did not care to let the robber loose among honest folk in the villages. It would be best for all that he remain in the forest.

Then Abbot Hans grew zealous and told the Bishop all about Göinge forest, which, every year at Yuletide, clothed itself in summer bloom around the Robbers' Cave. "If these bandits are not so bad but that God's glories can be made manifest to them, surely we cannot be too wicked to experience the same blessing."

The Archbishop knew how to answer Abbot Hans. "This much I will promise you, Abbot Hans," he said, smiling, "that any day you send me a blossom from the garden in Göinge forest, I will give you letters of ransom for all the outlaws you may choose to plead for."

The following Christmas Eve Abbot Hans was on his way to the forest. One of Robber Mother's wild youngsters ran ahead of him, and close behind him was the lay brother.

It turned out to be a long and hazardous ride. They climbed steep and slippery side paths, crawled over swamp and marsh, and pushed through windfall and bramble. Just as daylight was waning, the robber boy guided them across a forest meadow, skirted by tall, naked leaf trees and green fir trees. Back of the meadow loomed a mountain wall, and in this wall they saw a door of thick boards. Now Abbot Hans understood that they had arrived, and dismounted. The child opened the heavy door for him, and he looked into a poor mountain grotto, with bare stone walls. Robber Mother was seated before a log fire that burned in the middle of the floor. Alongside the walls were beds of virgin pine and moss, and on one of these beds lay Robber Father asleep.

"Come in, you out there!" shouted Robber Mother without rising, "and fetch the horses in with you, so they won't be destroyed by the night cold."

Abbot Hans walked boldly into the cave, and the lay brother followed. Here were wretchedness and poverty! and nothing was done to celebrate Christmas.

Robber Mother spoke in a tone as haughty and dictatorial as any well-to-do peasant woman. "Sit down by the fire and warm yourself, Abbot Hans," said she; "and if you have food with you, eat, for the food which we in the forest prepare you wouldn't care to taste. And if you are tired after the long journey, you can lie down on one of these beds to sleep. You needn't be afraid of oversleeping, for I'm sitting here by the fire keeping watch. I shall awaken you in time to see that which you have come up here to see."

Abbot Hans obeyed Robber Mother and brought forth his food sack; but he was so fatigued after the journey he was hardly able to eat, and as soon as he could stretch himself on the bed, he fell asleep.

The lay brother was also assigned a bed to rest and he dropped into a doze.

When he woke up, he saw that Abbot Hans had left his bed and was sitting by the fire talking with Robber Mother. The outlawed robber sat also by the fire. He was a tall, raw-boned man with a dull, sluggish appearance. His back was turned to Abbot Hans, as though he would have it appear that he was not listening to the conversation.

Abbot Hans was telling Robber Mother all about the Christmas preparations he had seen on the journey, reminding her of Christmas feasts and games which she must have known in her youth, when she lived at peace with mankind.

At first Robber Mother answered in short, gruff sentences, but by degrees she became more subdued and listened more intently. Suddenly Robber Father turned toward Abbot Hans and shook his clenched fist in his face. "You miserable monk! did you come here to coax from me my wife and children? Don't you know that I am an outlaw and may not leave the forest?"

Abbot Hans looked him fearlessly in the eyes. "It is my purpose to get a letter of ransom for you from Archbishop Absalon," said he. He had hardly finished speaking when the robber and his wife burst out laughing. They knew well enough the kind of mercy a forest robber could expect from Bishop Absalon!

"Oh, if I get a letter of ransom from Absalon," said Robber Father, "then I'll promise you that never again will I steal so much as a goose."

Suddenly Robber Mother rose. "You sit here and talk, Abbot Hans," she said, "so that we are forgetting to look at the forest. Now I can hear, even in this cave, how the Christmas bells are ringing."

The words were barely uttered when they all sprang up and rushed out. But in the forest it was still dark night and bleak winter. The only thing they marked was a distant clang borne on a light south wind.

When the bells had been ringing a few moments, a sudden illumination penetrated the forest; the next moment it was dark again, and then light came back. It pushed its way forward between the stark trees, like a shimmering mist. The darkness merged into a faint daybreak. Then Abbot Hans saw that the snow had vanished from the ground, as if someone had removed a carpet, and the earth began to take on a green covering. The moss-tufts thickened and raised themselves, and the spring blossoms shot upward their swelling buds, which already had a touch of color.

Again it grew hazy; but almost immediately there came a new wave of light. Then the leaves of the trees burst into bloom, crossbeaks hopped from branch to branch, and the woodpeckers hammered on the limbs until the splinters fairly flew around them. A flock of starlings from up country lighted in a fir top to rest.

When the next warm wind came along, the blueberries ripened and the baby squirrels began playing on the branches of the trees.

The next light wave that came rushing in brought with it the scent of newly ploughed acres. Pine and spruce trees were so thickly clothed with red cones that they shone like crimson mantles and forest flowers covered the ground till it was all red, blue, and yellow.

Abbot Hans bent down to the earth and broke off a wild strawberry blossom, and, as he straightened up, the berry ripened in his hand.

The mother fox came out of her lair with a big litter of black-legged young. She went up to Robber Mother and scratched at her skirt, and Robber Mother bent down to her and praised her young.

Robber Mother's youngsters let out perfect shrieks of delight. They stuffed themselves with wild strawberries that hung on the bushes. One of them played with a litter of young hares; another ran a race with some young crows, which had hopped from their nest before they were really ready.

Robber Father was standing out on a marsh eating raspberries. When he glanced up, a big black bear stood beside him. Robber Father broke off a twig and struck the bear on the nose. "Keep to your own ground, you!" he said; "this is my turf." The huge bear turned around and lumbered off in another direction.

Then all the flowers whose seeds had been brought from foreign lands began to blossom. The loveliest roses climbed up the mountain wall in a race with the blackberry vines, and from the forest meadow sprang flowers as large as human faces.

Abbot Hans thought of the flower he was to pluck for Bishop Absalon; but each new flower that appeared was more beautiful than the others, and he wanted to choose the most beautiful of all.

Then Abbot Hans marked how all grew still; the birds hushed their songs, the flowers ceased growing, and the young foxes played no more. From far in the distance faint harp tones were heard, and celestial song, like a soft murmur, reached him.

He clasped his hands and dropped to his knees. His face was radiant with bliss.

But beside Abbot Hans stood the lay brother who had accompanied him. In his mind there were dark thoughts. "This cannot be a true miracle," he thought, "since it is revealed to malefactors. This does not come from God, but is sent hither by Satan. It is the Evil One's power that is tempting us and compelling us to see that which has no real existence."

The angel throng was so near now that Abbot Hans saw their bright forms through the forest branches. The lay brother saw them, too; but back of all this wondrous beauty he saw only some dread evil.

All the while the birds had been circling around the head of Abbot Hans, and they let him take them in his hands. But all the animals were afraid of the lay brother; no bird perched on his shoulder, no snake played at his feet. Then there came a little forest dove. When she marked that the angels were nearing, she plucked up courage and flew down on the lay brother's shoulder and laid her head against his cheek.

Then it appeared to him as if sorcery were come right upon him, to tempt and corrupt him. He struck with his hand at the forest dove and cried in such a loud voice that it rang throughout the forest, "Go thou back to hell, whence thou art come!"

Just then the angels were so near that Abbot Hans felt the feathery touch of their great wings, and he bowed down to earth in reverent greeting.

But when the lay brother's words sounded, their song was hushed and the holy guests turned in flight. At the same time the light and the mild warmth vanished in unspeakable terror for the darkness and cold in a human heart. Darkness sank over the earth, like a coverlet; frost came, all the growths shrivelled up; the animals and birds hastened away; the leaves dropped from the trees, rustling like rain.

Abbot Hans felt how his heart, which had but lately swelled with bliss, was now contracting with insufferable agony. "I can never outlive this," thought he, "that the angels from heaven had been so close to me and were driven away; that they wanted to sing Christmas carols for me and were driven to flight."

Then he remembered the flower he had promised Bishop Absalon, and at the last moment he fumbled among the leaves and moss to try and find a blossom. But he sensed how the ground under his fingers froze and how the white snow came gliding over the ground. Then his heart caused him even greater anguish. He could not rise, but fell prostrate on the ground and lay there.

When the robber folk and the lay brother had groped their way back to the cave, they missed Abbot Hans. They took brands with them and went out to search for him. They found him dead upon the coverlet of snow.

When Abbot Hans had been carried down to Övid, those who took charge of the dead saw that he held his right hand locked tight around something which he must have grasped at the moment of death. When they finally got his hand open, they found that the thing which he had held in such an iron grip was a pair of white root bulbs, which he had torn from among the moss and leaves.

When the lay brother who had accompanied Abbot Hans saw the bulbs, he took them and planted them in Abbot Hans' herb garden.

He guarded them the whole year to see if any flower would spring from them. But in vain he waited through the spring, the summer, and the autumn. Finally, when winter had set in and all the leaves and the flowers were dead, he ceased caring for them.

But when Christmas Eve came again, he was so strongly reminded of Abbot Hans that he wandered out into the garden to think of him. And look! as he came to the spot where he had planted the bare root bulbs, he saw that from them had sprung flourishing green stalks, which bore beautiful flowers with silver white leaves.

He called out all the monks at Övid, and when they saw that this plant bloomed on Christmas Eve, when all the other growths were as if dead, they understood that this flower had in truth been plucked by Abbot Hans from the Christmas garden in Göinge forest. Then the lay brother asked the monks if he might take a few blossoms to Bishop Absalon.

When Bishop Absalon beheld the flowers, which had sprung from the earth in darkest winter, he turned as pale as if he had met a ghost. He sat in silence a moment; thereupon he said, "Abbot Hans has faithfully kept his word and I shall also keep mine."

He handed the letter of ransom to the lay brother, who departed at once for the Robbers' Cave. When he stepped in there on Christmas Day, the robber came toward him with axe uplifted. "I'd like to hack you monks into bits, as many as you are!" said he. "It must be your fault that Göinge forest did not last night dress itself in Christmas bloom."

"The fault is mine alone," said the lay brother, "and I will gladly die for it; but first I must deliver a message from Abbot Hans." And he drew forth the Bishop's letter and told the man that he was free.

Robber Father stood there pale and speechless, but Robber Mother said in his name, "Abbot Hans has indeed kept his word, and Robber Father will keep his."

When the robber and his wife left the cave, the lay brother moved in and lived all alone in the forest, in constant meditation and prayer that his hard-heartedness might be forgiven him.

But Göinge forest never again celebrated the hour of our Savior's birth; and of all its glory, there lives today only the plant which Abbot Hans had plucked. It has been named CHRISTMAS ROSE. And each year at Christmastide she sends forth from the earth her green stalks and white blossoms, as if she never could forget that she had once grown in the great Christmas garden at Göinge forest.

SWITZERLAND

The Three Kings

TRADITIONAL

Drei Chö - ni - ge, die chö - med do, Al - le - lu-
ja! Gold, Weih - rauch, Myrr-he trä-geds no, Al - le - lu-
ja! Gold, Weih-rauch Myrr-he trä-geds no, Al - le - lu - ja!

Three kings are on their way of old,
Alleluia!
They carry incense, myrrh and gold,
Alleluia!

Each one steps softly to the stall,
The new Christ-King, they greet Him all.

Honor and praise to Thee, oh Light,
That You were born to us to-night!

The First Picture

J. C. HEER

(Translated by Eric Posselt)

FIFTY YEARS ago in the old crannied house which the river passed with a loud sing-song, we were three small boys: Jakob, Heinrich and I, Emil, the youngest of them.

Christmas stood in the distance.

Then the strange news reached us that a man in town, Peter Stephan by name, could make a true-to-life picture of any man willing to stand before his *camera obscura*. Soon we saw a product of his art. Our sixteen or seventeen year old Uncle Johannes, apprentice mechanic, had his picture taken by the photographer, and on it not even the trace of mustache which adorned his lip was missing.

Amazed at the likeness of the portrait, we boys were seized by the conceit that it would be a special joy for our parents if we placed *our* picture under the Christmas tree for them, all three of us in a group, and that father would be particularly pleased, since he frequently was away from home for long periods. Wherever he went among strangers, he could take the picture out of his pocket and say: "Here are my three boys."

Convinced as to our own importance and that of our Christmas plan, we discussed the difficult problem of where to get the money for the picture. If we wanted to keep our secret, we would have to earn it ourselves. I thought of a way.

This was the time of oil lamps as of yore when the wise and

the foolish maidens of the Bible were still walking the land.
In our neighborhood, the half-blind Mrs. Susanna Keller earned
her bread by weaving wicks for these lamps with the aid of a
spool studded with four small brass nails. We made up to the
old woman, who liked us well enough anyway, watched how she
looped the thread over the brass nails, how she pulled the
woven wick through the spool, and established ourselves as
wick-makers without betraying our plan to anyone. But since I
didn't have the skillful hands of my brothers, we divided our
work so that they manufactured while I took over the sale of
the foot-long wicks. All this with the understanding that which-
ever one should betray our secret would be beaten to a frazzle
by the other two. Our mother, who had unusually sharp eyes
and ears for the activities of her boys, learned nothing about
our new profession.

How much hide and seek we had to play toward this end!
For, to be photographed in those days was still an expensive
undertaking, and in order to raise the money we needed to
make no less than four hundred wicks. Many of them we wove
while hidden among the willow trees along the river, and others,
when the weather got colder, in the hayloft of our grandpar-
ents' house; but most of them were made at night in the little
room behind our kitchen. There we slept together in a bed so
wide that, because of its size, it was known familiarly as "The
Steamboat." Under the bedcover, which we held up with the
aid of sticks, was our workshop. If mother, after the first good
night, entered the room again, the light was out in no time,
the sticks kicked down under the coverlet, and the three boys
slept like dormice in their nests. But a minute later work
started again, work that my brothers were soon able to do in
the dark. It was my task, lying between them, to tell them
stories in a whisper so that they wouldn't fall asleep; but either
my stories weren't very good, or else I told them badly, because soon a brother to the right or a brother to the left while
sitting up would begin weaving to and fro like a pendulum.
That invariably earned him a pitiless crack in the ribs and the
admonition: "We've got to work, otherwise we can't order the

photograph." Not until midnight did the worn-out boys stop their wick-making.

I, too, had my troubles in disposing of them, even though we had set the price as low as one *rappen* per piece. To my acquaintances who had theretofore known me as a happy-go-lucky youngster it seemed odd that, all of a sudden, I was out earning money. The girls from the neighborhood began calling me "Joggeli, the wicked wick-maker." Our relatives, too, began to shake their heads over my industry and didn't display the eagerness to buy on which we had counted. Those to whom we had secretly assigned as many as fifty wicks, took only twenty, those who were supposed to buy twenty, only ten or five. And the prying questions as to the purpose of such great industry! Yes, if we had betrayed our secret, it would have been more than likely that here and there an extra twenty or so might have been sold. But that would also have meant putting an end to the charm of our secret.

Finally I had exhausted our own circle of acquaintances, and we didn't even have half of the necessary sum on hand. Then I extended my excursions to parts of the village whose inhabitants I knew less well and in my eagerness never noticed the sidelong glances; only the coppers I harvested. Then a woman who had always been referred to at home with the greatest respect told me to my face what, no doubt, all the others thought: "You've probably got too much of a sweet tooth, Joggeli. If this were for something proper, your mother would surely give you the money. Nor is it very nice of you to take the bread out of the mouth of your poor neighbor Susanna Keller, who's got to live on what she makes out of her wicks. I'm sure you snitched this wick-making from her."

The poor peddler crept away from that woman as if he had been chastised with birches. What hurt most was that we brothers were actually accused of committing a theft through learning by stealth the art which our kind hearted neighbor needed to make a living. I was so ashamed that, in my own village, I never entered another house to offer a wick for sale. Instead, I turned to a farmer's village high up in the mountains

beyond the woods. There Susanna Keller never went because
of her weak legs. Nobody knew me there, and in all likelihood
the farmers practically fell over when they saw our artistic
wicks. I had already called at a dozen houses without much
success when I came to a farmer's wife who let her eyes rest
benevolently on the little peddler. She bought twenty wicks
just like that, and I was nearly away when she said:

"Don't you belong to Mr. Stöffi, the engineer? I think I remember the mould!"

Now I was discovered again! However, she proceeded:

"Give your father my regards. He and I liked each other
once upon a time and we are not to blame, either of us, that
we didn't get married."

She was very nice to me, returned the wicks, much to my
chagrin, without taking her money back and stuffed my pockets
full of apples. I went home heartbroken. What a shame for my
father that, before he married my mother, he had liked someone else! What a shame for me if this woman now thought that
he, perhaps, needed this—this wick-peddling! And never, never
would I give my father her regards!

However, I did make another half-hearted attempt to sell
some more of my merchandise in that village, but only because
I saw the woman I intended to approach standing in her doorway. She listened to my mercantile proposition most benevolently, but suddenly her husband, a heavy-set peasant, joined
her and remarked grumpily, though no doubt merely in jest:

"Boy, I am the mayor of this village. Have you got a peddler's license? No? Well, in that case I'll have to call the policeman to put you behind bars."

Fear of the police and terror that my father might learn that
one of his sons had been jailed made me tremble in my boots.
The pair had their sport with me, and the wife finally said
with a smile:

"Quick, now, boy—run!" pointing down toward the woods.

I accepted her invitation with alacrity, ran without even
looking for a path and returned home in the dusk with my face
scratched by thorns, to tell my brothers, once we were in bed,

the story of my miraculous adventures. I wound up with the statement: "All my life, I swear, I'll never sell another wick."

"And we still have so many left!" Heinrich sighed.

We struck a trial balance and, lo and behold, only one *franken* was between us and our proposed picture.

"That's easy," I consoled my brothers. "We'll simply promise the photographer to pay the balance after New Year's. During the holidays one always gets money from someone for a Christmas present."

"And if Peter Stephan doesn't want to trust us?" Emil objected.

"Well—all we have to do is look honest and innocent."

That ended our torture, with my brothers glad that their nightly weaving had come to an end. One difficult question still remained: how could the three of us together get to town on Sunday without mother becoming suspicious?

In town we had only one relative, known to our entire family as "Grumpy Anneli." To us she always seemed like a man in disguise, big, raw-boned and loud-voiced. When, in the absence of our father, mother's patience was exhausted, she often played a threatening role: "Now I'll ask Anneli to visit us and put you to right." Anneli took care of her thankless task with complete decency and never hurt a hair on our heads; but a secret dread of her heavy, coarse hands remained with us.

But suddenly a great affection for her seized us when we wanted to get to town to be photographed. We explained to mother that, really, it wasn't nice of us at all that we never visited "Grumpy Anneli" and that, honestly, we should do so before holy Christmas. Mother laughed.

"All you rascals want to do," she said, "is look at the store windows. But since you came to me in such a sly way, you will have to pay Anneli a visit!

In order to make a good impression on our cousin she made us wear our best suits, on which green braid had been threaded in meandering playfulness; and in order to prevent our forgetting to visit Anneli, she also gave us a letter to her.

"Run along now, boys."

The road led through a long row of poplars, and the city found our young hearts filled with both joy and terror. The doors and gates were picturesque, adorned as they were with multicolored coats of arms and scenes from past wars. The less we understood them, the more they occupied our imagination. But the most marvelous sight of all for us was, as always, the "Snake Mill." On its wall was the picture of a wild man who, clad only in a laurel wreath around his forehead and a larger one around his loins, was defending himself with a tree torn out by the roots, trampling a whole pile of hissing snakes under his mighty feet. Oh—if this wild man ever came to life, perhaps at dusk, and stepped down into the street, that would be thrilling, now, wouldn't it!

"Grumpy Anneli" was so surprised and pleased to have us finally visiting her that she spread the butter particularly thick on our bread. I wondered whether it might not be a good idea to discuss the question of the missing *franken* with her, rather than go without sufficient funds to the photographer, whom we didn't even know. My brothers trembled while I told our secret to this relative whom we had always looked upon with some distrust. She, however, was so touched that she not only gave us the coin but even put on her big black silk crinoline skirt to take us to the photographer. Nor could we understand any longer why this friendly cousin had ever been called "Grumpy Anneli."

At the photographer's it went as it always does. The heavy box on its three legs, hidden under a black cloth, created some misgivings; but the jolly Peter Stephan knew how to infuse three timid country bumpkins with courage. When he lined us up before a backdrop showing a city on the sea with palms in the foreground and placed a ballustrade in front of us, Heinrich whispered, "By gosh, this is going to be elegant, all right." But Emil groaned: "Too elegant, I think. We probably won't be able to pay for all this."

Meanwhile, the photographer fumbled around excitedly with his apparatus and finally said: "Now, boys, smile!" But at this very moment it occurred to me that, no, such an important picture should be serious; and, thinking of the village mayor who had wanted to call the policeman, I forced my face to assume a most solemn expression.

"One, two, three!"

After awhile Stephan smiled and said: "Now we are all finished. It's going to be a grand picture."

In an hour we were permitted to call for the masterpiece, all framed under glass. Our enthusiasm knew no end, particularly when we found out that we had money enough to pay for it. Our fists tightened courageously as we saw our treasure safely past the wild man at the "Snake Mill," and it was agreed that each of us would be permitted to carry it alternately for a distance of three poplars. The youngest, and thus the least likely to be suspected, was assigned the honorable task of smuggling it into the house and hiding it in the attic in an apple chest under the schoolbooks of our great-grandparents. Innumerable times during the days before Christmas we got it out and studied it jubilantly even though my brothers deplored the fact that I made such a serious face. I, however, enjoyed the conceit that this was just right because in that way I looked like the cleverest of the three.

I proved once again how clever I really was the day before Christmas. As evidence of his mechanical skill, Uncle Johannes had made a small and delicately wrought branding iron for us. He proceeded to mark every broomstick and wooden handle in the entire house with this branding iron. I thought it also might look well on the back of our picture. So I sneaked up to the attic, the hot iron in my hand. I placed the picture wrong side up on the apple chest and pressed the iron on it. Then—a crash; the glass had broken to bits! Crestfallen, I removed the shreds. My brothers found me and, in their wrath, fell upon me with their fists. In my knowledge of guilt I didn't even defend myself. They were clever enough to take the picture to the glazier at the last minute. And thus it found its way under the Christmas tree in good shape.

When we told our parents that we had earned the money for the picture by honest and long toil, making wicks, they were pleased with this likeness of their three sons and praised our Christmas idea.

But even so the picture really wasn't the biggest surprise on that Christmas Eve. That was provided by father who had been installing spinning machines near Basel and returned home unexpectedly for the occasion. When the Christmas candles had burned down, he lit a big kerosene lamp which he had brought along from Basel—the first one in our village. To us it seemed as if it were turning night into day, and all through the holidays neighbors came and went, even distant acquaintances who wanted to see this new, miraculous light.

Most enthusiastic of all was Johannes, who was then attending the technical academy. "Now you can at least study at night —what a difference from all this miserable oil and candle light, and these bothersome trimming shears and snuffers! We are heading for a glorious time, boys. Why, homework will be a pleasure! Everybody will be reading at night, and a period of learning will come to all mankind. Everyone will know the laws as to what's right and what's wrong. Now they can get rid of all the judges because all accusations and crimes and trials merely stem from the stupidity of people. And not only the judges— even courts and wars will disappear from this earth. Men will be so well educated that everything will be just fine. Yes, boys, petroleum is bringing us a new epoch!"

Thus he made his speech, and we boys listened trustingly.

My good Johannes! Neither you nor my brothers lived to see mankind become much wiser or better because of the kerosene lamp or any other invention. You died too soon for that. Nor will I, the only one left of our family, live long enough, though much has changed. From the fields of our homeland the oil-giving flax, whose blooms gilded the land, has now disappeared; and no child can solve the riddle you taught us to solve: "Who am I? In my youth I wear a crown, but in my old age, with sticks and hatchets, they beat me down." Our land has become monotonous. No longer are there boys who, for the sake of a mere photograph, would make wicks under their bedcovers for weeks at a stretch.

I, too, have changed. At that time I took upon myself the obnoxious peddler's rounds in order to be photographed; to-day, a photographer frightens me. Thus, ideals change. True, I would like to look once more upon that picture showing the three of us; but to the discredit of Mr. Peter Stephan—whom this, fortunately, can no longer offend—I must confess that it didn't turn out to be particularly durable, but has long since faded out, my laughing brothers and my frowning self included.

Of all the marvels, nothing is left except the festive Christmas tree which conjures up youth even in oldsters, and the everyday kerosene lamp which smiles down upon my work.

YUGOSLAVIA

Oh, Shepherds

TRADITIONAL

Oj. Pa-sti-ri, ču-do no-vo Je - ste li-kad vi-de-li o-vo:

U ja-sli-cah pri-dih ro-di-o se Bog, ko-ji s ne-ba si-dje ra-di pu-ka svog.

Oh, ye shepherds, gaze in awe
On a sight no eyes yet saw:
Christ sleeps in a stable's gloom,
Come to save us from our doom.

Christmas Comes, After All!

BORISAV STANKOVICH
(Translated by Ernst Pawel)

WHO WOULD worry about sleeping at a time like this? It has been weeks since anybody has had a good night's sleep. First Christmas came to Skoplje; now it is at Preshevo and Bilach, and moving closer and closer. The dried sparrows strung up in chains are already beginning to crack and fall apart. The high-button shoes, the cotton blouse and the jacket made out of an old greatcoat have been ready for the longest time. There they are, on the box, neatly laid out, one next to the other, waiting for me. And somehow they give me no peace, the shoes in particular. They're yellow, are these shoes, polished to shine like a mirror, and their soles smell of cobbler's wax. Whenever mother leaves for the market, I lock the door and get all dressed up. I walk around the room trying to catch a glimpse of myself to see what I'll be looking like on Christmas Day. Only, this isn't Christmas yet. Not yet. But I can feel it in the air. The room is sweet with the scent of elecampane and dry basil above the ikon. And mother no longer dares scold me when I break something, let alone give me a threshing; that just isn't done before Christmas. She even looks at me differently, somehow. Not like a mother at all, but rather humbly like as if I were the older one.

"Will you do some shopping for me?" And she sends me to the market to buy some trifles, giving me money without even counting it.

Off I go. And when I come back, struggling with the load and trying to balance the bundles, she already awaits me at the door and rushes out to relieve me of my burden, not bothering to ask me for the change. She leaves it to me these days, so that I can grandly walk around jingling the coins in my pocket and bragging to my pals about it.

And in the meantime she slaves at her work. It's been at least a week since she last sat down at the table for a regular meal. She has the whole house to take care of. Nobody even to carry water for her. She is killing herself with work. Her blouse is torn, and her trousers keep slipping. Every other minute she stops to retie her apron strings, but the apron drops down just the same. She is hunched with age, but on she goes and works her fingers to the bone.

She has rolled up her sleeves. Her hands are grimy, and the skin around the nails is cracked and peeling from all the scrubbing and washing. She never has time to put on slippers or sandals, but runs around in some old, darned stockings, wading through the puddles and the little piles of dirt that are all over the floor. The polished pots glisten on their shelf, neatly arranged. The table and the copper baking pans have been propped up against the wall to dry out as quickly as possible. Steaming hot water still runs off them in tiny streams. Shelves, doors, thresholds and window frames have all been scrubbed to a spotless yellow. The whole house exudes an odor of moisture and scrubbing. And mother does everything herself— where does she find the strength to do it? She works as if it were no bother at all. She never is tired. From early in the morning until nightfall she goes on—slowly, it is true, but never resting, dragging herself from one task to the next, always completely engrossed in whatever she happens to be doing.

And on top of all this she also takes care of me. Some meat dish is always stewing in a pot on the fire; some cake has always just been taken out of the oven and stands there to cool off, still covered with a table cloth, spreading its seductive fragrance.

"Don't, baby," she gently restrains me, as though afraid to insult me. "Don't. It will be all yours, anyway. Whom else do

I have? Don't—wait for Christmas. It'll be here tomorrow. It's already in Tekija. . . ."

"With whom in Tekija?" I rebel. "I'm going down there to see for myself." And off I go.

"Please don't!" she stops me. "You can't see it. It'll come here, too. . . ."

And Christmas came, indeed. And what a Christmas! My poor, darling mother!

Day broke. At dawn the cannon was fired, and the shot rattled the windowpanes. From the street came the sharp click of brand-new shoes. Above my head, next to the pillow, were the suit and the underwear, all smelling very new and very clean. Under the ikon the little lamp was flickering, and the smell of incense filled the room. The room itself was warm, clean and decorated. You were already up and in the kitchen; still half asleep I heard you rummaging around, carrying in the wooden trough and a kettle of hot water. Then you came over to me, threw back the blanket, put your bony, wrinkled hands under me and lifted me the way I was, naked and still warm with sleep, out of my bed to take me into your lap, and covered me with kisses.

"Time to get up, son. Christmas has come. Time to get up, master of the house."

At the words, "master of the house," your puckered, warm lips trembled, and a tear dropped on my burning cheek.

You gave me a bath while outside the bells were ringing. No, not ringing; rather, they sounded subdued and quiet, as though trying to hum and then losing courage. The lamp was flickering. There was the smell of the clean rugs blending with the smell of straw from the mat. Voices were out in the street, and the blue of the night was entering through the window, softened and dispersed by the candlelight. Then you dressed me. The suit seemed too large for me, and so did the shoes and the blouse. I got angry and impatient.

"It isn't too big at all. Really it isn't. As a matter of fact it's a little tight for you. Goodness, how tall you are!"

Spreading your arms, still on your knees, you moved off a
little, the better to see how tall I was. And in order to make
me look still more impressive and older than my age, you put
father's dark blue silk belt around me and gave me his watch,
carefully arranging the massive chain so as to make it as conspicuous as possible. On my little fez you put a tassel, dad's old
one, of real ivory. It hung down to below my ears. You gave me
a candle, the basil and the kerchief, and saw me to the door,
giving me a last once-over, looking at me both anxiously and
with pride. Even out on the street, carried away by the crowd,
I could still see you looking after me, following me with your
eyes. . . .

On any other holiday I'd much rather have gone up to the
old Turkish cemetery to watch them load and fire the big guns.
But on Christmas that thought didn't even occur to me. I kept
my hands in my pockets. The candle I had stuck in my belt. It
was fun to listen to the click of my new shoes on the pavement
and to the rustle and crackle of my starched new blouse, even
if I did feel a little cramped in my new clothes. The collar
especially was a bit too tight.

The market square was jammed, with more people joining
the crowd every minute. There were many old men, walking
along slowly and cautiously in their long white wraps, white
stockings and stiffly starched white collars, with huge warm fur
caps on their heads. Each one of them had a few grandchildren
on either side of him over whom he was supposed to watch.

At quite a distance from the church the air was already filled
with the smell of incense, and the church itself was bathed in
a glow of candlelight. From inside came the strains of singing.
My eyes were blinded by the sudden glare, in the midst of this
sea of candles—whose flames, like so many tongues, seemed to
be licking its stone walls—the church itself stood out clearly
against the breaking day. Still at the other end of the street, I
already took off my cap, tucked it well into my shirt so no one
could pull it out, and lit my candle. I just barely made it to
the portal. People were all around me, surging forward, pushing and shoving, tightly packed; each one bareheaded, carrying

a candle, making the sign of the cross, and joining in the songs and prayers reaching us from inside the church. In the church itself nothing was visible but the light from countless candles, their smoke rising and curling and finally losing itself somewhere high under the vaulted roof. Through it all shone the altar, bright, with the holy lamps flickering on it, and the candles around the cross glistening and twinkling like so many stars from above. On the ambo, his back turned toward us, stood the deacon in an attitude of prayerful expectancy, his right hand raised, reading, no, singing out the words in his powerful, stirring voice. Daylight paled the scene, and from the depth of the choir alternately ebbed and rose the song:

"Thy day of birth, oh Christ, Our Lord."

And as the song died out, the bells started to ring and the guns thundered, and the frozen naked earth trembled and shook.

Try as I might, I just couldn't manage to get hold of a copy of the anaphora which the deacon handed out from the ambo, and had to be content with what I was given by the sexton. I went back home. The door was wide open. The yard had been cleaned, the wood under the eaves neatly stacked alongside the wall. On the shelf shone the kettles, and a long white cloth covered the pitchers. Pots were boiling on the fire, a roast was simmering in the pan. I entered the room. Mother acted as if she hadn't seen me, busying herself with the dishes and the fruit jars.

"*Kristos se rodi!*" [1]

She turned. And seeing me in my fez with my father's tassel on it, wearing father's belt, she was shaken and confused.

She drew closer.

"*Vaistinu se rodi!*" [2]

She held out her hand reluctantly as though secretly tempted to kiss mine instead. Then she kissed me on my forehead, eyes,

---

[1] "Christ is born!" Traditional Christmas greeting.
[2] "Indeed He is born!" Traditional answer.

eyebrows and cheeks. She would have continued kissing me, if
I hadn't stopped her. I offered her the anaphora and asked
whether anyone had yet come to see us—asked in a voice so
manly that it made her swell with pride and answer me quite
humbly.

"Our cousins, son. I wanted them to wait until you came
home, but they didn't have the time. Here, they left an orange
for you and send you their regards. But listen—you must be
starved! Oh my poor darling!"

Quickly she brought me a skillfully carved dried sparrow to
taste first, so that all year long I'd be light as a sparrow. And
then the rest. I ate—while all the time she was fussing over me,
watching that I wouldn't get any spots on my new clothes, and
sweeping up the crumbs as fast as they fell, just in case a visitor
came to surprise us. Outside everything was quiet and peaceful.
The fiddlers were playing 'way at the other end of the town,
at the upper market, in the rich folks' homes. The few passers-
by out in the street were in a hurry to get their obligatory visits
over with and rush home for their meals. I kept on eating,
wanting more; but mother wouldn't let me.

"Don't. You've had enough and won't have any appetite left
for dinner. And besides, someone might come, after all. . . ."

She took the food away. I wanted to get out in the street, but
she wouldn't let me. She took off my fez, combed my hair
again, unbuttoned my blouse far enough for the new shirt to
show, and told me to stay in the room.

"You sit down here. Who is going to welcome the guests?
Are you the master of the house, or aren't you? I can't do it,
after all. I have work in the kitchen and besides, I'm not even
properly dressed."

And so I stayed, pacing up and down, taking huge steps. The
room smelled sweet, warm and dry. The ikon light flickered.
Wavelike, the incense spread through the house. In the kitchen,
good food was on the fire. The guests arrived.

As they reached the kitchen door, they shouted: *"Kristos se
rodi!"* rushing in and naturally wanting to shake hands with
mother. But mother wouldn't let them. She sent them inside to

me. And they entered. Dutifully they took a seat on the couch, hands folded in their laps, ready to jump up right away and be off again. They asked me the usual questions. They looked at every single object in the room, though they had all been here countless times before and knew each piece and where it belonged. But I, bareheaded, self-possessed and perfectly at ease, stuck out my chest a little and brought them the tobacco jar. We made conversation, that is to say, I told them about their children, my pals—what we did together, where we went skating, and so forth. After a while mother came in, drying her hands in her apron.

"And how are you? How is everything?" she asked them all while arranging the shoes they had taken off upon entering in such a way that, on leaving, they would be able to step into them without even looking down. They all kissed and she withdrew again back into her kitchen to make coffee, leaving me to entertain them just as any head of a family would be doing. Soon she brought in the coffee, a separate cup for each guest and waited, hands folded, for them to finish so that she would be on hand to relieve them of their cups at once. And, of course, they were all ashamed to have her wait on them; everybody sipped his coffee as quickly as possible, put a lemon or an orange on the table as a gift, and left hurriedly.

She even took them to the door. Actually it would have been my duty as the master to see them off, but apparently she didn't quite trust me. She knew that once I set foot outside the door, I'd see the street—the ancient, crooked street with its chipped and broken walls on either side—and there surely would be some of my friends out there, bragging about how much money they had got for presents and how much cake they had eaten, and I'd be off with them, leaving her to look for me all over town.

Therefore I just didn't leave the room. It wasn't that I was afraid of her, of her scolding; but I knew how I'd feel afterwards, what that plaintive reproach in her eyes would do to me once she did find me. She would take me by the hand, silently leading me home without one angry word; on the contrary, she would even defend me before the others and would let no one say that I had deserted her on this holiest of days. But she would not look happy any more the way she did now, setting the table, bringing on the bread, the salt and all the rest, putting a lighted candle in the center, the food being brought in a pan so she would not have to get up again during the meal.

Then she washed her hands, approached the ikon and, taking off her kerchief for the one and only time during the year, began to read a prayer to bless the food. I stood behind her, making the sign of the cross. But I could not at the same time bend down and cross myself the way she did; bending down a trifle too quickly I fell on my knees and had to support myself with my hands, before touching the floor with my forehead. The strong odor of food filled the room. Above us burned the ikon lamp, throwing its feeble light upon mother's gray hair and brown neck. She whispered:

"Lord Jesus Christ! Holy St. Nicholas, my miracle-doer, my saint! Look down upon us, oh Lord, and take pity on us. Help us. Bless Thy food, bless the bread Thou hast given us." And she fell on her knees so hard that I could hear the joints cracking.

Then she put her kerchief back on again and sat down at the table, free at last to breathe after one more look around the room, still afraid lest she had forgotten something that needed doing before dinner. And I, holding out my glass filled with raki and simultaneously offering her my cheek, wished her a happy holiday:

"*Kristos se rodi,* my darling mother! A merry Christmas to you!"

"The same to you, child. This year we are alone, you and your mother. But next year, the Lord willing, you'll. . . . ." Something in her throat made her cough, and she barely managed to down her glass.

We ate. In spite of all her careful preparations she still had to get up every now and then to bring in more food from the kitchen. I had to have first choice of everything, and she merely nibbled a bit here and there, quite hurriedly. It was only after

I had had my fill and got up that she really started to eat.

Afterwards everything was quiet and peaceful. I heard the cat purring and the hen in the kitchen moving among the pots and pans looking for crumbs.

The heavy odor of overly rich food seemed to hang over the entire town. In all homes, drowsy from overeating, the men lay around the brazier or the stove, huddled in their white wraps, and the women with their aprons thrown over their heads. They have to rest for, after all, Christmas has three days, and this is only the first one. A man can't right away . . . there's plenty of time yet.

But on the stroke of midnight, as the second day began, somewhere a *zurla* [3] was blown, and soon the first song sounded through the night.

Morning came again; but this time the priests were the only ones who really stayed for the entire service; the others merely came to make a show of lighting a candle and quickly bowed out again backward, crossing themselves in double quick time as though doing penance. Everywhere the chimneys began to belch the dense black smoke that indicated meat, roast and sausages. The aroma of smoked lamb permeated the streets. Little crowds of women began to appear, plaintive and yet belligerent, walking down the streets in groups; their shoes weren't buttoned because they had to take them off every few moments; their wraps had been thrown on in a hurry, and their eyes were bloodshot and full of tears. Every servant and every child they could lay their hands on were pressed into service to help find Fatima, the gypsy girl with the fair face and the round black eyes. Later on the community had to marry off Fatima by force, since she made every man who met her completely lose his mind and his conscience, so that they drank with her till morning, night after night, spent all their money on her, beat their wives and drove them out of their homes for Fatima's sake.

Everything was changed all of a sudden, the very air bursting with exuberance and a kind of extravagant elation. Shouting,

---

[3] A native bagpipe.

singing and music everywhere! Fiddlers appeared in front of
the houses, followed by gangs of screaming children; the *zurlas*
whistled and whined, the drums were beaten till all the windowpanes shook and all the ikon lights went out.

Everywhere, that is, except in our house. We had finished
eating long ago, mostly food left over from yesterday. After
dinner I stood in front of our door listening to the revelry and
watching how Crazy Menko, drunk as a lord, rolled over into
the gutter and started to undress. And when I went inside
again, there was mother—but I hardly recognized her.

She was wearing a starched blouse, her face was scrubbed
clean, and a beautiful kerchief was tied around her head. Her
cheeks looked round and pink. She was sitting by the window,
hands folded in her lap, looking out into the street, pressing
her forehead against the pane. For all its wrinkles her face
looked soft now, fresh and almost young. The little veins were
pulsing in her thin, strong neck. The dust in the room had just
settled from the after-dinner clean-up. Neatly arranged on the
old buffet stood the glasses, and next to them a large pitcher
full of wine. The other pitcher out in the kitchen also was
filled; that's where we had poured all the wine sent us by our
rich neighbors. And the coffee was made, the cake all ready
and waiting.

Only—there was no one to whom we could offer any of these
precious gifts; no one whom we could welcome as a guest. All
those who felt obligated to come had appeared in the morning,
showing up for just a quick drink to save us expenses. They
knew we didn't have any money, and so they had come in the
morning because at that time the custom is not to sit around for
any length of time so that nobody can consume much. What
wouldn't I have given for a few guests! How I would have
waited on them, serving them food and drink! If only they
hadn't tried to spare us, if only they would let us be like everyone else. That, perhaps, was why mother smiled so sadly. Her
eyes seemed to be smarting from looking out into the street
filled with people, the crowds constantly moving past our wide
open door, and not a soul to enter. The house and the yard

were deserted, while all around us there was singing, playing and wild happiness. Even the drinking got under way.

Jovan Palamar, for example, threw brazier and stove out into the street—he was too hot!—broke all the glasses in the house and started drinking out of a pan. He didn't stand up to welcome his guests but remained seated on the floor in the middle of an empty room, leaving his guests to shift for themselves as best they could. Rista, the Troublemaker, already had had a fight and had locked himself up in his house. He was sitting on the porch, firing off his rifle whenever the spirit moved him, forcing his wife to sing for him and at the same time cursing the world at the top of his lungs. In many yards the *kolo* [4] was being danced, and the gold pieces which the girls wore in chains around their necks jingled to the beat of the music. From Stephen Dobrovanjec's house came the high-pitched screaming of his children, the desperate sobbing of his wife and his own hoarse shouting and cursing. He was, it seemed, looking for his horse and his sword, some old sword he had managed to get hold of during the wars of liberation. And sure enough, in no time at all, he appeared on his spirited charger, in full-dress uniform, red pants, cap and all, the battered sword at his hip. Riding from one door to the next he leaped off the horse right into the room, driving before him the fiddlers as well as Fatima who, in a white silken bodice and bloomers, danced around him with snake-like grace, singing:

> "I don't rue my nakedness,
> I merely rue my silver blouse,
> I merely rue my silver blouse. . . ."

"Everybody over here!" someone suddenly shouted right in front of our door.

Mother jumped. The tears rolled down her cheeks. In rushed Uncle Yovan, my late father's pal, his fur cap deep down over his eyes, and behind him, jostling one another, the fiddlers.

"Over here," he shouted, pointing at our house. "There's a song in this house, too!"

---

[4] National dance.

I don't know how mother managed to get into the kitchen, but I do know that my own heart stopped.

"Hi, Master of the House!" Uncle Yovan cried with a deep bow.

"Here we are—right here," mother answered in my stead, swallowing hard and trying to collect herself.

"*Kristos se rodi!* Lady of the House! And where be the master?"

"Here he is, right here," mother said, pointing at me and beckoning him to come in; she even let the gypsy enter. Uncle Yovan stepped inside. I kissed his hand and he, bending down, kissed my forehead, taking my whole face into his dry old paws. Then he sat down right on the floor, crossing his legs.

"Well, come on, let's have a song!" he told the gypsies who had lined up along the wall.

"What would you like, master?"

"Whatever the Master of the House wants," he said, nodding in my direction. The gypsies looked at me, and I felt the blood rushing to my head from happiness and confusion. Mother came in and in passing me whispered: "Tell them you want 'The Roses Are Blooming.'" And that's what I ordered the gypsies to play.

"Excellent, excellent," Uncle Yovan cried, surprised and happy that I had picked out his own favorite tune. "Come on, now, let's have it!" And he started to tell them all about us, about our home, and about my father with whom he had broken bread and shared his salt, and whose best friend he had been for so many years; how sometimes the celebration in our house went on for three days and three nights straight, nothing but singing and dancing all the time. And, sure enough, one of the gypsies had known my father and had played for him. My poor mother, sobbing with happiness, made the gypsies drink, too—not out of glasses but straight out of the bottle, all the raki they wanted. She waited on them, gave them meat and bread, and whatever they couldn't polish off on the spot, they stuck into their pockets.

"Sit down, dear," Uncle Yovan finally told her. "Let him take care of things for awhile." He pointed at me. "Lord, how he has grown! Here, come, sit down next to me."

He moved over to make room for her. Mother sat down and held out her glass to him, her hand trembling.

"Here, try this, Yovan. I saved it especially for you. Thank you for having thought of us." But she said nothing about her heartache, she didn't even talk about herself, just about me. "If his father were alive, things would be different. But this way. . . . Anyhow, thank you, thank you for remembering us and for coming. . . ."

"What do you take me for?" Uncle Yovan said gruffly. "Did you really think I'd forget this house?" And turning to the gypsies, he shouted: "Play!"

The gypsies played. The screech of the *zurla* must have been heard all the way over in Turkey. The drum rolled, the windows rattled, the oil kept splashing out of the lamp, and from the beams above came a fine spray of chalk dust. Outside it was getting dark and wet. In his worn-out, croaky voice Uncle Yovan sang:

"The roses are blooming. . . ."

And my mother, a tear slowly, slowly rolling down her cheek, looked at me, standing bareheaded between her and the fiddlers, as if trying to say: "Christmas has come after all, son. You see?"